"Walter and I have decided to live together."

"Live together?" Charlotte had been Windexing the mirror and stopped, blue rivulets streaking down the glass. "Just the two of you?"

"Four of us. Walter, me, and a couple of friends."

"What friends?"

"Mara and Anthony," Emily said. "I don't think you've met them. Ant's the guy who climbed Mount Kilimanjaro. He's really fascinating."

Her words bounced off the tiled walls, as if mocking Charlotte's tattered slippers, her bucket of cleaning supplies. *Fascinating.*

Emily sighed, an amused sigh. "It's fine, Mom. It'll be like one big happy family. I promise."

Charlotte felt a twinge between her eyes. *Happy family:* it sounded so incestuous, so 1960s. She wasn't sure if this casual, communal environment made the living together better or worse. "I just—it's just that you're so young, honey." She wanted to sound wise, but instead felt like she always did when trying to give Emily relationship advice: unqualified. "And living together, well . . . that's a big commitment."

"Mom." Emily's tone was matter-of-fact. "We know living together is a big commitment. We're not jumping into this blindly. Walter and I really love each other."

Charlotte was jolted into silence. How could she argue with this? It was very possible her twenty-two-year-old daughter knew more about loving a man than she did.

Also by Elise Juska

Getting Over Jack Wagner

ELISE JUSKA

the HAZARDS *of* Sleeping Alone

a novel

new york london toronto sydney

An *Original* Publication of POCKET BOOKS

DOWNTOWN PRESS, published by Pocket Books
1230 Avenue of the Americas
New York, NY 10020

This book is a work of fiction. Names, characters, places and incidents are products of the author's imagination or are used fictitiously. Any resemblance to actual events or locales or persons, living or dead, is entirely coincidental.

ISBN: 0-7434-9350-8

First Downtown Press trade paperback edition September 2004

10 9 8 7 6 5 4 3 2 1

DOWNTOWN PRESS and colophon are trademarks of Simon & Schuster, Inc.

Designed by Jaime Putorti

Manufactured in the United States of America

acknowledgments

Unlike Charlotte, I have a big and boisterous family. Never has their supportiveness, good humor, and general greatness been more apparent to me than in the past year. Much love and gratitude to: Mom, Dad, and Sally; Grammy; Aunt Kathleen, Maureen, and Billy; Aunt Margaret, David, Gina, Tommy, and George; Uncle Tom, Aunt Laura, John, and Andy; Aunt Mare, Uncle Jim, Kate, Jimmy, and Krissy; Uncle Jack, Aunt Jeanne, Ryan, Kyle, Griffin, and Declan; Nana and Poppy; Uncle Billy, Aunt Maryann, Jim and Miriam, Kristin and Kieran, Kieran, and Kenan; Aunt Paula, Uncle Tony, Will, Emmy and Shane; Uncle Paul, Aunt Leigh, Jen, Paul, and Julia.

Huge thanks to my dauntless agent, Whitney Lee, whose energy knows no bounds and whose begging for the next chapter helped keep me going. To the wonderful team at Simon and Schuster, especially my editor Lauren McKenna and my publicist Hillary Schupf, who are not only razor-sharp but lots of fun. This book could not have had a more insightful group of advance readers: my mother, Dolores Juska; my fabulous writing students, Jenn, Matt, and Brendan; and my fellow writers and dear friends Diana Kash, Clark Knowles, and Kerry Reilly, capable of whipping up profound feedback on command and always pushing me to reach further and write harder.

Book One

chapter one

A creak. A shift. The pressure of a footstep on the living-room floor. But if it were a footstep, wouldn't there be more than one? Wouldn't the creak be followed by another? Many others? Unless an intruder just happened to strike the single weak spot in the floorboards—Charlotte doesn't know yet if there is such a spot—and is, at this moment, creeping undetected toward her bedroom door.

But wait. If there's an intruder, he must have broken in. A break-in would cause more commotion than a single creak. A window shattering, a door kicked in. Charlotte would have heard him. All she heard was a creak, a shift, just the sound of a—what had her mother called it when she was a child?—"a house settling into itself."

Then again, what if the creak had been the sound of the door opening? Unlocked by a skinny MasterCard? A toothpick? Bobby pin? Charlotte can picture the sliding door in her new living room, the meager pane of glass separating her from the outside world. It wouldn't be too loud, the sound of that door sliding open. The intruder could have broken the lock, nudged the door an inch or two, and slipped inside. Which would mean he's in her living room this minute. He's easing his feet across the plush beige carpet that came with her new condo and that she doesn't like—not because it's beige, Emily's always teasing her about her wardrobe "the color of pantyhose"—but because a rug that thick could easily swallow the footsteps of a man as he made his way toward her room.

Charlotte snaps on the bedside lamp. The room is assaulted with pasty white light. She swings her legs over the side of the bed, steps into her slippers, walks down the short hall to the living room, the kitchen, throwing on lights as she goes, her white eyelet nightgown billowing behind her. She hums a little, an efficient hum. See? Nothing wrong. Everything intact. The yellow refrigerator with the "Welcome to the Neighborhood!" magnet she received in the mail from Millville County Electric. The coffee table strewn—well, not strewn exactly, but piled—with *Prevention, People,* the latest *TV Guide,* Martin Sheen's face gazing sincerely from the cover. On the mantel, Emily framed and smiling at ages four, ten, fifteen, twenty-two.

Just think, Charlotte reminds herself, in less than twenty-four hours Emily will be sprawled on this very couch. Emily will be regaling her with stories of the great book she's reading, the students she's teaching, the foods and philosophies she's discovered since the last time they talked. Emily holds passionate opinions about everything. Charlotte smiles, imagining the way her daughter will flip critically past the celebrities in *People,* tongue ring clicking between her teeth.

She realizes then that there can be no intruder tonight. It would be impossible, someone breaking in the night before Emily arrived.

In the kitchen, Charlotte retrieves a glass and slides it under the icemaker. She never had an icemaker in the house on Dunleavy Street and likes its efficiency, its dependability, the endless supply of cubes shaped like smooth half-moons. She pours herself water from her Brita (as if water had been her objective all along), then strides back toward the bedroom, nightgown swishing by her heels. She misses having two floors, misses the feeling that the space for sleeping is separate from that for being awake. But the condo is more compact, she reasons: life minimized, simplified. Condensed. Lately, Charlotte can't help but feel that she is en route to old age. That she has entered life's downward spiral, when accumulating begins to seem, well, just not practical anymore.

In the foyer, she double-checks the front door. There are three locks: the standard doorknob, the attractive (but basically useless) linked chain, and the deadbolt she had specially requested. After tugging on the door a few times, satisfied it isn't budging, she makes her final stop: the bathroom. It has an unfortunate underwater theme: fluffy toilet seat cover an algae green, tiled walls swimming with flat blue fish. At night, the fish look vaguely menacing; they don't appear to have pupils. Charlotte keeps her eyes on the floor, avoiding the fishes' blank stares. She is careful not to flush so she doesn't wake her upstairs neighbor—B. Morgan, according to the Victoria's Secret catalogs that bulge from her mailbox for days at a time. Not that B. cares about waking Charlotte. Her first few nights in the condo, Charlotte woke in a panic to the sounds of laughter and footsteps ricocheting in the stairwell. Then, the churn of bedsprings: a grating squeak that reminded her of a dentist's instrument. She imagined B. and her male friend in all sorts of contorted sexual positions. With all that noise, she'd never hear someone breaking in. Sleep was out of the question until it was over.

Marching back to her bedroom, Charlotte is annoyed with herself for letting fear get the better of her. Now it will take forever to get back to sleep. She stops and considers the gadget Emily sent sitting by the foot of her bed. The Dream Machine, it's called. It looks like a miniature white humidifier, a huge Excedrin tablet. When Charlotte moved into the condo, two months ago, she mentioned to Emily that she was having trouble sleeping. The Dream Machine had arrived in the mail two days later, addressed: SWEET DREAMS, MOM! It simulates all kinds of apparently comforting noises: ocean waves, nighttime forest, tropical rain.

Not that Charlotte hadn't had trouble sleeping before. She can't remember the last time she slept through the night. But here in the condo, her worries and fantasies have intensified. For the past twenty-four years, the house on Dunleavy Street was all she'd ever known. She moved there when she and Joe got married and stayed on when he left. It had been a simple decision, staying. She liked the neighbors, the mailman, the supermarket, the teachers at Emily's elementary school. Plus it was important for Emily to have that kind of stability, a home to come home to, especially as a child of divorce. She hadn't stayed (as her book group speculated) because she was clinging to memories of Joe. (It bothered her how the group felt it necessary to find symbolism in everything, as if to constantly prove themselves good readers.) Charlotte had missed Joe a lot, then a little, then only now and then. His absence felt natural, somehow. Even when Charlotte played house as a child, it was the make-believe sons and daughters who were well defined, while the make-believe husband was vague, absent, away at the office or cloistered in his study with the *New York Times.* In a way, being alone and raising a child, manless, was how she'd always imagined her life would be.

After the divorce, Joe had stayed in the area until Emily was thirteen, picking her up on alternate weekends and Wednesdays, splitting holidays evenly down the middle. Then the year Emily started high school, he moved to Seattle and began claiming Thanksgivings and Augusts. Even now, standing in her bedroom at 2:34 A.M. in the middle of October, the very thought of August makes Charlotte's chest constrict. She used to dread that month—the longest and emptiest of all the months. TV shows were all reruns. Neighbors were all on beach vacations. The air was thick with humidity, and her air conditioner made a nerve-racking rattle. And, worst of all, Emily's birthday was on August 27. Every year Charlotte missed it. Every year thirty-four days—thirty-one in August, plus three for Labor Day weekend—were filled with little else than waiting for her daughter to come home (and worrying every year that she wouldn't). Every Labor Day, when her daughter stepped into Newark Airport, Charlotte's lungs would relax for the first time since July.

On Emily's first night home, Charlotte always cooked the same belated birthday dinner. The presents she'd already mailed, sent overnight on August 26 to arrive in Seattle on the twenty-seventh. As much as Charlotte hated the thought of Joe and Valerie watching Emily open those presents, it was important that Emily receive them on her actual birthday. Charlotte agonized over them. She refrained from sending anything too practical, like the hairbands or rag socks she might have thrown in if Emily were at home. She knew she couldn't compete with the gifts Valerie sent at Christmastime—beaded handbags from Chile, silver bangles from Mexico, essential oils, multicolored candles made of seaweed and vegetable wax—things Charlotte would never have bought, much less *found*, in the labyrinth of the Millville Mall. The best she could do was send gifts that were, if not exotic, at least not frumpy. A T-shirt from the Gap. A book by Madeleine L'Engle. Matching melon-scented soaps and lotions from Bath and Body Works. Still, when Emily called to thank her, Charlotte couldn't help picturing Valerie in the background, picking over her gifts with an arched eyebrow and a laugh stifled behind her hand.

Of all the long and excruciating Augusts, the summer Emily turned sixteen was the hardest. Never would Charlotte have believed as a young mother—nursing her baby, changing her diapers, walking her through training bras and maxi-pads, temper tantrums and *Where Babies Come From*—that she would not be seeing that baby the day she turned sixteen. It was the day she wasn't a child anymore, the culmination of all those years of crying, pouting, bleeding girlhood. Charlotte wanted to be the one to do something special, something memorable. She had *earned* it. Instead, her daughter was three thousand miles away, turning sixteen with a woman Charlotte barely knew. She had spent the day trying to distract herself. She watched *Oprah.* She read *People.* She spoke to Emily on the phone, chewing the insides of her cheeks to keep from crying. Joe and Valerie—this is what Emily called them, she'd started calling her father "Joe" the year he moved to the West Coast—were taking her out to dinner, she said, someplace "hip." Charlotte spent the night imagining the three of them sitting on the dock of a boat, or at a sidewalk café, Joe and Valerie sneaking Emily sips of cocktails, a frothy, celebratory pink.

That Labor Day, when Emily arrived home, she seemed to have aged much more than thirty-four days. She was wearing clothes Charlotte didn't recognize, clumpy brown sandals and faded jeans patched at the knees. A silver hoop was buried in the flesh of her upper ear, and the patchwork duffel bag slung over her shoulder was crammed with bootleg CDs, sacks of flavored coffee, T-shirts for bands called Mudhoney and Mother Love Bone. (The burned coffee smell had permeated everything in her duffel and would linger in Charlotte's laundry room for weeks.) That night, Charlotte served the usual, carefully meatless belated birthday dinner: oriental salad, vegetable lasagna, and chocolate raspberry torte. Afterward, Emily usually went to her room, chaining herself to the phone to catch up with her friends, but that summer she sat at the kitchen table until midnight. Her body was "on Seattle time," she said, as she brewed cup after cup of Seattle's Best brand coffee—in flavors like hazelnut, French vanilla, chocolate almond—playing her new CDs and talking about grunge music while the curtains in the windows stirred in the thick summer breeze. Charlotte watched her, nodded exuberantly, but she was only half listening. In truth, she felt like crying. Not out of sadness, or loneliness, but sheer joy and thankfulness, that her daughter was here, real, returned, to unstick Charlotte's swollen windows and fill her empty house with sound and life. Charlotte murmured "mmm," "yes," laying slivers of cake on Emily's plate, the raspberry threads like ruby tiaras, as Emily spoke at passionate length about the death of Kurt Cobain.

Charlotte steps out of her slippers and onto the hardwood floor. Hardwood is "in," according to her realtor; people are just dying for hardwood. Charlotte thinks it's too creaky. Too cold. She thinks of her bedroom in the house on Dunleavy Street, the flat moss-green rug whose wrinkles and bald spots she had memorized. She never wanted to leave that house, but with Emily finishing Wesleyan, she could no longer justify staying. As irrational as Charlotte can be at 2:47 in the morning, she also possesses a keen sense of practicality. It didn't matter that the house was paid for, that her parents' life insurance had taken care of the mortgage years ago. The house was simply too big for her to stay in alone.

Charlotte sets her water on the nightstand, switches the Dream Machine to "ocean waves." It sounds vaguely tidal, in that the staticky sound kind of undulates. She climbs into bed, stares at the ceiling. This machine isn't helping. It's covering up the extra noise—"ambient sound," according to the side of the box—but she finds she's only more anxious because of the noise she *isn't* hearing. What if someone is breaking in and the ocean is so loud she doesn't hear it? What if the sounds of footsteps are swallowed up in the static tide? She tries to conjure up the many tips she's read for falling asleep. One suggested counting backwards from 100, which only made her progressively more anxious. Another said that simply breathing deeply would slow your heart, decelerate your pulse. In other words: *force* you to relax.

Charlotte shifts, but slightly. She's read that it is important to keep the body as still as possible when trying to fall asleep. She tries to concentrate on the ocean, on letting the waves carry her away. Instead, she's straining to hear the elusive "ambient sounds" under all that static. It occurs to her that the Dream Machine was probably manufactured by the same people who break into houses in the first place. *Perfect for concealing the sounds of lock-picking, tiptoeing, breaking glass* . . . This is what the real advertisement must say, the one that circulates privately to all the criminals. Probably on the Internet.

Charlotte turns the Dream Machine off (feeling guilty, but telling herself she'll use it once Emily gets here) and climbs back into bed. She tries to be brisk, assured, yanking the sheets to her chin, smoothing them with her palms. *You're being absurd—it's a condo! In New Jersey!* She pictures the world outside: tidy mailboxes, arc of parked cars, glowing lampposts. In the morning, she'll chastise herself. *Look at where you live. It's perfectly safe! Tonight, remember this scene. PICTURE THIS LAMPPOST.*

Charlotte pulls her knees to her chest. Was she this fearful when she was married? She's sure she wasn't. She didn't need to be. She hadn't been alone. It is the particular quality of aloneness—its detachment, its vulnerability—that sets the mind whirling and gives the imagination free reign. With Joe, she was never really frightened, just nervous. "Fussy," he called it, back when he found it endearing. She bit her cuticles. She double- and triple-checked their bank statements. She was very, very careful about cooking chicken and washing fruit.

It was when she became a mother that Charlotte's nerves intensified. Every night, before bed, she would check to make sure Emily was still breathing. It wasn't so unusual when she was a baby—awful things happened to babies in the middle of the night, she'd read it in parenting magazines, seen it on *60 Minutes*—but it continued even when Emily was four, five, six years old. It was as routine as making sure the oven was off, the coffeemaker unplugged, the front door chained and bolted, twice.

She would wait until Joe was absorbed in grading papers, then creep into Emily's room and kneel beside her bed. Emily slept on her back with lips slightly parted. Her long brown hair splayed unevenly across the pillow, holding the shape of that day's braids or plastic barrettes. Charlotte would lower her head until it was level with Emily's chest, eyeing the Holly Hobbie comforter, confirming its slight rise and fall. Sometimes, to make doubly sure, she would lean over Emily's face and turn her head, ear hovering just above her mouth, and feel her breathe.

Since graduating, Emily has been teaching in an "alternative learning environment" in Lee, New Hampshire. A middle school, essentially, except with no discipline. No attendance requirements. No report cards. No grades at all.

"But how do you assess their progress?" Charlotte had asked, after Emily got the job.

"The students assess their own progress."

"But wouldn't they all give themselves As?"

"There are no As."

"There are no As?"

"They don't use letter grades."

"What do they use then?"

"The Watt School doesn't represent a child's progress with a number or a symbol," Emily recited, as if from a promotional brochure. "There are other ways of measuring progress. Like increased self-confidence. Ability to think critically. To perform creative problem-solving tasks. To articulate one's own growth."

Charlotte had no idea what she was talking about, but didn't press the issue. Emily had always thrown herself into projects and crusades and causes, most of which Charlotte didn't agree with or even understand. When she was five, Emily came home from kindergarten and announced she was no longer eating hamburgers. She'd learned about the food groups that day and realized her dinners bore a direct relationship to the cows she saw grazing off Route 9. (She would soon make the connections between lamb/veal, pig/pork chop, and the suddenly obvious chicken/chicken fingers.) From then on, whenever Joe grilled hot dogs, Emily would heap her plate with macaroni salad and let out dying oinks.

Charlotte found the strength of her daughter's convictions enviable. Even admirable. They were also, she secretly believed, a product of her youth. As Emily got older, Charlotte suspected the reality of day-to-day living would dampen her enthusiasm a little, make her more practical, less volatile. More realistic. But until then, Charlotte certainly wasn't going to be the one to do it.

Besides, she was sure Joe had no objections to the alternative learning environment. He was probably okay with it. In favor. Having an ex-husband so "with it" only accentuated how very much Charlotte was "without it." Toward the end of their marriage, when Emily was five and six, Joe managed to absorb all the latest fads and trends in a seemingly unconscious way. Emily would mention a cartoon, or sneaker, or video game, and Joe would know exactly what she meant. Charlotte was clueless. (She once pronounced M. C. Hammer "McHammer," thinking it was an Irish rock band.) Now, in such situations, rather than draw attention to how unhip she was, Charlotte had learned to keep her doubts to herself.

Which is why she hadn't pressed the issue of the school with no report cards. Just like she hadn't let on her true feelings about Emily's tongue ring, or belly ring, or women's studies major, or aimless cross-country road trip between her junior and senior years of college. But in June, when Emily called about her new living plans—what Charlotte has since termed the "alternative living arrangement"—she found it impossible to remain her quietly supportive self.

"Walter and I have decided to live together."

It was like a scene from a bad made-for-TV movie: the pivotal moment where the rebellious daughter, chin held high, announces to her conservative parents a decision she knows they won't agree with. Usually the declaration is followed by the parents threatening, the daughter shrieking, possibly the lines,

"Not while you're living under my roof!" or "I'm eighteen! You don't own me anymore!" and some slamming doors, stone-faced sidekick boyfriends, Harleys gunning ominously in the distance.

In her version, however, Charlotte was cleaning the bathroom. Her forehead was sweaty, the portable phone clutched between her chin and shoulder. Emily was speaking to her from Hartford, where she was living temporarily, subletting an apartment and working at a day camp for inner-city youth. Charlotte hadn't been crazy about the camp plan (Emily was a Wesleyan graduate, after all) and felt a little hurt that Emily hadn't come home to spend her last few months on Dunleavy Street. But as soon as she lamented any detail of Emily's summer plans, she reminded herself of the only one that truly mattered: She wasn't spending August in Seattle.

"Living together?" Charlotte had been Windexing the mirror and stopped, blue rivulets running down the glass. "Just the two of you?"

"Four of us. Walter, me, and a couple of friends."

"What friends?"

"Just some Wesleyan people."

"What Wesleyan people?" It was all Charlotte could do to echo her daughter, even though these other people were not, at all, the point.

"Mara and Anthony," Emily says. "I don't think you've met them. . . . Ant's the guy who climbed Mt. Kilimanjaro. He's really fascinating."

Her words bounced off the tiled walls, as if mocking Charlotte's practical rubber-soled slippers, her bucket of cleaning supplies. *Fascinating.* She watched as the streams of Windex snagged and merged, like a map of blue veins on the inside of a wrist. Behind them, Charlotte's blurred reflection stared back at her: faded blue eyes, cheeks flushed and freckled from the summer heat, cropped brown hair she colored dutifully every six weeks. At first glance, she looked younger than she felt. But upon closer inspection, worry lines were rising around her mouth. Crow's feet were nibbling at the corners of her eyes. Every sleepless night etched her wrinkles deeper, though the change was invisible to the naked eye, like a patch of rust forming imperceptibly under a drip in the sink.

"Mara's cool," Emily went on. "She lived in my dorm."

"Oh?"

"She's Anthony's girlfriend. Well, sort of."

"Oh."

Emily sighed, an amused sigh. "It's fine, Mom."

"Is it?" Charlotte leapt. "It is?"

"It'll be like one big happy family. I promise."

Charlotte felt a twinge between her eyes. *Happy family:* it sounded so incestuous, so 1960s. She wasn't sure if this casual, communal environment made the living together better or worse. She thought about calling Joe to discuss it, to have one of their rare parental checkpoints. These had occurred a few times over the years: when Emily had mono, when she was applying to colleges, after she pierced her tongue. (Charlotte had regretted that one, after Joe found her concern so amusing.)

But she suspected Joe had no problem with the alternative living arrangement, just as he'd had no objection to the alternative learning environment. After all, he'd set a precedent for it, living with Valerie before they were married. God only knows what kind of example they set during those endless Augusts. Charlotte hated that her ex-husband had the power to make life-altering decisions, set important examples that she could do nothing about. Of all the emotional aftershocks of divorce—

loneliness, jealousy, resentment—the worst was this lack of control.

"I just—it's just that you're so young, honey." She wanted to sound wise and knowing, but instead felt like she always did when trying to give Emily relationship advice: unqualified. What experience did she have to back her up? A strained marriage, a cold divorce, and fifteen years without a man in her life? "And living together, well . . . that's a big commitment."

"Mom." Emily's tone was matter-of-fact. "We know living together is a big commitment. We're not jumping into this blindly. Walter and I really love each other."

Charlotte was jolted into silence. How could she argue with this? She believed Emily probably *was* in love with Walter. In fact, it was very possible her twenty-two-year-old daughter knew more about loving a man than she did.

Charlotte had met Walter just once. It was last spring, at the Wesleyan graduation, the event that had been the final impetus for Charlotte's decision to move. That way, she told herself, when Joe asked, "What's new, Char?" she would have something to tell him. She'd imagined the moment many times over: her new sundress, her grayless haircut, and her unwavering tone of voice as she said, "Well, Joe, I've decided to sell the house," without a flicker of self-doubt. Without a flinch.

But the actual graduation was nothing like she'd envisioned. It was oppressively hot. Her new haircut wilted. Her makeup blurred. The new dress hung limp on her shoulders (despite the pert shoulder pads) as if it, too, were defeated by the heat. Her announcement to Joe went successfully enough—in that she said all the words she'd planned on saying—but her satisfaction was dulled by the fact that Valerie was there listening, all sweatless five-feet-ten of her, topped with a stylish, wide-brimmed hat. When the conversation was over, Charlotte snuck away to a Port-a-Potty, a place she avoided except for extreme emergencies, and fished a wad of fuzzy pink tissue from the bottom of her purse to blot her underarms dry.

Charlotte had envisioned many things wrong about that afternoon. But of all of them, the most wrong was Walter. She blames it on his name. Who in this young generation was named Walter? She had pictured someone old-fashioned, traditional, a character from *Our Town.* Plus, Emily had mentioned Walter played rugby. To Charlotte, this conjured images of *boys:* real, rough-and-tumble boys. Boys who wore scuffed baseball caps. Boys who never cleaned their rooms. Boys who acted cool around their friends but at home were lovably helpless, who needed their mothers to pick up after them and keep track of their practice schedules and cook them meaty dinners they would inhale before giving Mom a peck on the cheek and clattering out the back door toward a carful of friends honking in the driveway. Charlotte loved having a daughter—she couldn't imagine being nearly as close to a son—and yet she'd always been able to imagine herself mothering a boy like that.

Perhaps, then, it was only natural that when she pictured Walter, it was *that* boy she imagined. An ally: someone like-minded, someone of her world.

After the ceremony, they stood on the lawn under a yellow pinstriped tent. There were four of them: Joe, Valerie, Emily, and Charlotte. The untidy, untraditional modern family. Getting divorced, Charlotte often thought, was the hippest thing she'd ever done. Joe, Valerie, and Emily were talking about the honorary graduates and keynote speakers whose names Charlotte had already forgotten. She was nodding now and then, but not really paying attention, feeling the self-consciousness that always set in on Wesleyan's campus. As if she had snuck in the side door and was going to trigger an alarm any second: a woman who never finished college mingling with the academics, a woman with a wardrobe the color of pantyhose lost in a sea of stylish hats.

Her eyes drifted to the dessert table, a delicate pyramid of tiny cakes, a colorful cascade of fruit. At the center was an ice sculpture in some sort of angular, abstract design. It seemed to mirror the women strolling past it, all glittery jewelry and chiseled bones. New Yorkers mostly, Charlotte thought. She could make out the sharp lines of their ankles, hips, jaws. Hands and ears were freighted with diamonds, faces sliced with expensive sunglasses, manicured fingers spearing pieces of cake.

She was contemplating how she might eat cake without being seen eating cake when from out of nowhere a large, muscular black boy grabbed Emily from behind. She shrieked as his dark forearms wrapped around her waist, lifting her flailing feet off the ground. Charlotte's heart seized, raced. She glanced wildly around her. Only when she saw the small smiles flirting on Valerie's and Joe's faces did she register the boy's silky blue robe and gold-tassled hat. He was a Wesleyan student, she realized—well, of course. A fellow graduate. Still, it never occurred to her he could be Walter until Emily wrapped her arms around his neck and they started kissing.

Out of habit, Charlotte looked away. This Walter looked nothing like the one she'd spent the last few weeks mentally cooking for and cleaning up after. First of all, she'd had no idea he was black. Not that she cared, not that it mattered, it was just that in all the times Emily had sung the praises of Walter this, Walter that, she'd never mentioned it. Not once. As Charlotte studied the boy, she felt her Walter being erased line by line, detail by detail. This Walter wore his hair in an Afro, peeking out from under his hat, glistening wetly in the sun. Beneath his robe he wore a loose white shirt and faded blue jeans. He had a diamond in his left ear, a patch of scruff on his chin. The last trace of Charlotte's Walter disappeared as she noted, with something like resignation, his eyebrow ring.

Emily and Walter stepped apart. Walter kissed her forehead. Emily slid an arm around his waist. As if observing someone else's family, Charlotte watched an exchange of hands and smiles.

"Good to meet you, Walter," Joe said.

"You too, Mr. Warren. Ms. Warren."

"Please, call me Joe."

"And me Valerie."

"You can call me Mr. Nelson," said Walter.

Joe and Valerie laughed appreciatively. Emily cupped Walter's cheek, like a proud mom. They were affectionate with each other, but it didn't seem overly deliberate. Not like the teenagers Charlotte saw at the Millville Mall who clung to one another with such determination, hands clutching hands, fingers hooked in belts. Charlotte was amazed that Emily had inherited such ease with her body.

"Congratulations to you both," Valerie was saying. "It's a real accomplishment, graduating from a school like this one. You should be proud."

"Thanks."

"You're celebrating tonight, I hope," Joe said.

"You know it," said Walter. Laughs all around.

Now that he was facing forward, Charlotte saw that Walter had not just one diamond earring, but two: one in each lobe. Around his neck hung a wooden cross on a fuzzy cord made of something that looked like, well, "hemp" sprang to mind. Charlotte felt her vision blur. Could this necklace be some kind of universal symbol of marijuana? The secret handshake of the drug underworld?

"Walter," Emily interjected. Charlotte blinked. She saw her daughter beaming at her and realized she was about to become a part of this scene. "This," Emily announced, with what sounded like pride, "is my mom."

The boy took a big step forward and thrust a hand out from the silky folds of his sleeve. "Really glad to meet you, Ms. Warren," he said, and Charlotte flinched at the public acknowledgment that she still used Joe's name. "I've heard a lot about you," he said. "Em seriously talks about you all the time."

Charlotte took the hand he held out, felt its firm grasp. He was big (he was a rugby player, after all), with broad shoulders and a wide chest. She sensed she should say something witty—"All good things, I hope" or "Don't hold it against me"—or at the very least return the compliment, but she found she couldn't speak. It was as if, upon physical contact, her brain shut down.

"Please," she heard herself say, a weak echo of her ex-husband and his new wife. "Call me Charlotte."

Emily laughed, the affectionate *Oh, Mom!* laugh she had honed to perfection. But Walter just smiled, warm and genuine. "Okay, Charlotte," he said, then reached out and lightly touched her shoulder. It was as if he sensed her discomfort and wanted to put *her* at ease. Before Charlotte could respond, he was wrapped in a bear hug by another graduate, a boy with a nest of unruly blond dreadlocks and bare feet.

Charlotte was staring at the locks when she heard a whisper: "So?"

It was Emily, materialized by her shoulder. She hooked Charlotte's elbow and steered her away from the group.

"What do you think?" Emily's voice was hushed, conspiratorial. "Isn't Walter amazing?"

Charlotte glanced at her daughter. Her cheeks were flushed, teeth nibbling on her lower lip, as if to restrain herself from squealing. She looked again at Walter, who had Valerie, Joe, and the dreadlocks engaged in one big conversation, their hearty laughter rising and falling as if they'd all been friends for life.

"Well, I'm sure he is, honey," Charlotte said. "But I hardly know him."

Emily stopped by the tower of fruit. "First impression."

"First impression? Well—I'm just not sure." She watched as Emily plucked a fat strawberry off the top. "He's not exactly what I pictured, I guess."

"What had you pictured?"

Was it wrong to say she hadn't pictured Walter black? Charlotte didn't know the politically correct way to handle these situations. But why would that be wrong? It was true. She hadn't. Would she be hesitating if he were Asian? Indian? What if Walter was French? *Well, I hadn't pictured him French.* She wouldn't have thought twice!

"I hadn't pictured him black, I guess."

"Right." Emily was smiling slightly, as if she had anticipated this, was even amused by it. She bit into the strawberry and kept walking, arm still hooked in Charlotte's.

"And also, I just thought," Charlotte hurried on, "well, I think it was the name. *Walter.* I don't know. I pictured someone . . ." She glanced again at the boy. He was gesturing animatedly about something, Joe and Valerie nodding in recognition. Probably a grunge band from Seattle.

"Wait." Emily stopped walking and released Charlotte's arm. Charlotte turned, sure she'd offended her somehow, but instead found Emily nodding, the amusement gone, the forgotten strawberry held aloft in midair. "Mom, yes."

"Yes what?"

"You're exactly right."

"I am?"

"It's like, he *defies* his name. The name Walter—it's so *un*cool he actually manages to *make* it cool. Right?"

Charlotte hadn't thought the name Walter was uncool, just old-fashioned. As far as she was concerned, Walter's name was his most winning trait. But as she opened her mouth to explain, she was stopped by the expression on her daughter's face. Emily looked so excited, so expectant, her eyes bright, shining, as if lit from behind. She's in love, Charlotte thought. She's in *love.*

"Yes," Charlotte answered, and forced a smile. "That's exactly what I meant."

The next morning, driving to the Super Fresh, Charlotte is humming. The sun is shining. She is right on schedule. Emily is on her way. She reviews her mental Emily checklist: lettuce, tomatoes, bell peppers (red, green), grapes, Boca Burgers, soy milk. She assumes Emily won't be here for lunch; New Hampshire is a good six hours away. Still, it's possible she could arrive by midafternoon. It would mean leaving New Hampshire by dawn, probably—but who knows. Maybe they're early risers. They're nature types, after all. A happy vegetarian family living in the wilds of New Hampshire.

Charlotte gives her head a shake, airing out the cynicism. She wants to be home by noon regardless, in case Emily calls from the road. She might be running late, or lost. The condo is only about fifteen minutes from the house on Dunleavy Street, but still, Emily's never been there. Charlotte doesn't have an answering machine (a point Emily argued with her about regularly) but maintains she doesn't need one. "Anyone who really needs to reach me will call me back," is her defense. She won't admit the real reason: she doesn't want to record an outgoing message because she hates the sound of her voice on tape.

She is humming the *Today Show* theme—pitch perfect, she thinks—when, two blocks from the Super Fresh, traffic stops. Charlotte cranes to see around the massive back of an SUV and glimpses a long line of taillights. ROADWORK AHEAD, says the sign propped tiredly in the breakdown lane. The car behind her lets out a long honk. Charlotte's fingers tighten on the wheel. She feels her temples start to pound, her careful itinerary unspool. She can hear the phone ringing inside her empty condo as she sits here, hour upon hour, in a clot of giant, overheating SUVs. She imagines herself standing on the hood of her Toyota, shouting: "My daughter is coming! I must be let through!" at which point the traffic will part and a squad car will arrive, siren wailing, to escort her to the Super Fresh like a pregnant woman in labor.

The car behind her honks again. Charlotte glances into the rearview mirror. It's a woman in a tailored blouse, talking agitatedly on her cell phone. A businesswoman, Charlotte thinks, and feels a pinch of guilt for what Emily calls her "life of leisure." Charlotte has never worked full-time. When she was married, Joe worked, and she stayed home with Emily. Then when Emily was starting third grade, a year after Joe left, Charlotte's mother died—two years after her father, neatly bracketing Joe's departure—leaving behind not only life insurance but a surprisingly large savings account. She'd never known her parents had that kind of money; they'd always scrimped and saved like they were on the brink of ruin. At the time it had seemed like a sign: work wasn't financially necessary, so she should stay at home and be with Emily. But deep down, as Charlotte grieved for her parents, sifted through their house, packed up her father's books she'd never read but couldn't bear to give away, guilt gnawed at her insides. Because she knew it was her parents' deaths, and their lifetime of frugality, that freed her to do what she really wanted: stay home, take care of her child, and avoid the world.

She stares hard at the bumper sticker in front of her: PROUD PARENT OF AN HONORS STUDENT AT MHS! Mentally, she recites all the things she still has to do before Emily's arrival: make egg salad, make fruit salad, vacuum, clean the bathtub. Last time Emily came to visit, she was fanatical about her bath taking. She talked at length about the bath's "healing properties," the various salts and soaps, oils and beads, how necessary they were to one's "spiritual well-being." (Charlotte herself never takes baths, too preoccupied by how easy it would be for someone to break in while she was in there.) Last week, she went to the Millville Mall and picked up some lavender bubbles and a "bath glove." She'd never heard of one, but the saleswoman told her it was very popular. She called it "restorative" and "revitalizing." The very ambiguity was its selling point; if it was unfamiliar to Charlotte, chances were Emily owned five.

Now, Charlotte digs her nails into her palms. No point in getting upset, she reasons. Nothing she can do about her checklist from in here. She decides to try being mindful—in part because mindfulness is supposed to be particularly effective in traffic, in part because she knows Emily will be quizzing her on it later. In August, Emily sent her a book called *The Miracle of Mindfulness.* It was her personal copy and had her excited reactions spilling into the margins, asterisks and exclamation points and comments like YES! or WALTER. Charlotte had picked loyally through a chapter or two, more interested in Emily's notes than the book itself. She tried to grasp the concept of meditation, but just didn't get it. To sit alone with her thoughts? *Her* thoughts? She could think of nothing less relaxing.

"It isn't really about *thinking,* Mom," Emily had explained over the phone. It was the week Emily moved into the alternative living arrangement, and she was talking to Charlotte while she unpacked. "It's kind of the opposite. Like being really inside your body, not your mind."

She paused, and Charlotte heard a zipping sound.

"It's being engaged in what you're doing while you're doing it," Emily said. "Like, if you're stuck in traffic, instead of spazzing, just stop and *be* in the traffic. When you're doing laundry, really *experience* the moment of doing laundry. Do the best laundry you've ever done."

How in the world Emily came across these things Charlotte had no idea. It wasn't just her youth. Charlotte had been young once and hadn't found herself exposed to radical approaches to grading report cards and doing laundry. She had lived as she lived, known what she knew. But with Emily, new ideas seemed to just land in her lap. Charlotte might have chalked it up to a liberal arts education if her daughter hadn't always been this way. When she was nine, and Charlotte took her on a day trip to Philadelphia, Emily grabbed at every crumpled piece of paper strangers thrust at her on the street. Greenpeace literature. Concert flyers. Psychic hotlines. Anti-Bush propaganda. "Thank you," she smiled, stuffing all of it in her Hello Kitty backpack. Once, when Emily was in eighth grade, Charlotte had come home to find her sitting on the back porch after school, snacking on trail mix with two ambassadors from the Church of Latter-day Saints.

It was wonderful that Emily was so engaged in things—so *interested.* But most of the time, Charlotte found her daughter's ideas exhausting. She preferred the concrete world. Coupons to snip. Bathtubs to scrub. *Jeopardy!* every night at seven. Lean Cuisines to microwave for three to five minutes. She couldn't admit this to Emily, but she had no interest in adopting a new philosophy, a new religion. She didn't want to make her life more complicated, not at this stage. Besides, having opinions invited differences of opinion, which invited conflict. Charlotte believed more strongly in avoiding conflict than she did in any stance or slogan. It might sound lame, or weak, or passive, but she didn't feel a need to be a highly opinionated person. Some people just weren't cut out for it.

On the phone, explaining mindfulness, Emily's voice had alternated between loud and muffled. Charlotte had pictured the portable pinned under her daughter's chin, resting in the bony hollow of her collarbone. She hadn't seen Emily's new home and naturally was imagining the worst. Brown tap water. Moldy tub tiles. Weeds growing through the floorboards. Roommates in bare feet or bath towels or worse.

"Hang on a sec," Emily said, and Charlotte wondered what she was doing. Talking to one of her new family members? Talking to Walter? Kissing Walter? Unzipping Walter's— She blinked away the thought.

"Sorry. Back."

Charlotte heard the clicking sound that she recognized as Emily's tongue ring swatting against her teeth. It was a habit that usually signaled something was making her agitated. Charlotte wondered if it was their conversation, or something else.

"What was I saying?"

"I was doing the best laundry I'd ever done."

"Right." Emily paused, exhaled a long breath. For a second, Charlotte was convinced she detected Walter's breath on the line too. Maybe he was on a different extension, listening to their conversation. Worse, maybe his face was huddled next to Emily's, nibbling her ear above the phone.

"Basically," Emily said, "mindfulness comes down to living in the moment."

"Right."

"No matter what you're doing. Even if it's the most boring, mindless thing in the world. Don't you think that makes so much sense?"

"Oh, yes," Charlotte answered automatically. At the moment, her main concern was not sounding foolish, especially not with Walter possibly listening. Maybe, if she acted as though she had a firm handle on this mindfulness business, they could move on to something else.

"The whole practice really boils down to *awareness,*" Emily went on.

Charlotte felt the beginnings of a headache, each temple a pulsing dot of pain.

"Being aware of your breath. Being aware of your body."

"I *am* aware of my body," Charlotte snapped, a touch more defensive than she meant to be. Emily's tongue ring clicked, twice.

Well, it was true: she *was* aware of her body. She was meticulous about her doctor's appointments. She had regular mammograms and dentist's cleanings. She knew all there was to know about what had killed her parents: her father's cancer (stomach, liver, and finally brain, phases of hope and hopelessness strung out over seven years like some kind of extravagantly awful tease) and her mother's sudden heart attack two years later. She was aware of the risk factors, vigilant about the symptoms. She'd memorized the cycle of her seasonal allergies, her stubborn patches of dry skin, the right eyelid that twitched when she was tired. "I'm in perfect health," she said. "Just ask Dr. Weiss."

Emily laughed the *Oh, Mom!* laugh. "Not that kind of aware," she said.

Charlotte felt tired. She wondered if it was possible that the human body existed on a sensory plane that other people experienced but of which she was biologically deprived, and therefore couldn't understand—like a blind person who couldn't begin to conceive of sight.

Focusing on the bumper sticker in front of her, Charlotte tries hard to be mindful. She listens to her breath: yes, there it is. She hears it. She tries to be *aware* of her breathing—is that the same thing as listening to it?—and notes it going in and out, in and out. She knows this can't be what Emily was talking about, that "being aware of your breath" implies something much deeper, more internal, involving the whole body. But when Charlotte tries to be aware of her whole body, she succeeds only in being aware of her whole belly. It seems to be getting softer lately, rounder, the kind of belly women trap under jeans with elastic waistbands, gardeners and grandmothers, proof that they have paid their maternal dues.

That night at 8:00 P.M., precisely the hour Charlotte had decided she would call someone—the Jersey police or the highway patrol or, least appealingly, the roommates in New Hampshire—she hears Emily's car. Charlotte knows the rattle of it by heart, an old barn-red station wagon Emily inherited from Joe when she first got her license. Charlotte rushes to the foyer and presses her face to the cloudy glass blocks framing the doorway, like a child in a toy store window. She watches Emily's thin silhouette open up the trunk, hoist out a bag. Hears the dull bang of the trunk as she shuts it. Sees her pause, chin lifted, surveying the row of condos for the right address.

Charlotte yanks open the front door and starts waving. "Em! Here!" She pushes open the screen door, and cold air wraps around her, snaking under her sweater sleeves and up the legs of her tan capri pants. "Over here, honey!"

Emily lifts a hand and starts walking across the lawn. Charlotte feels a rush of love just looking at her daughter's familiar shape: the thin shoulders, bowed head, pointy chin. Emily has always been tiny, but what might otherwise come across as fragile is challenged by the utter confidence of her stride. Emily has walked with this same assurance—a near defiance—ever since she was two years old and took her first fearless lunges toward a neighbor's kiddie pool.

Emily arrives at the porch step with an emphatic clomp. "Hi, Mommy."

"Hi, sweetheart."

Emily gives her a kiss on the cheek. As she steps inside, Charlotte takes a quick inventory of her daughter: hair, clothes, accessories. It wouldn't be unusual to discover something new, something that's been pierced or altered since the last time she saw her. But today, nothing radical. Nothing permanent, anyway. Emily is wearing rust-colored corduroys, a white T-shirt, brown hiking boots. A wide pink silk bandanna, like something women wore in the 1920s, is swathed around her head and knotted at the nape of her neck, the tail of the scarf tangled in her long, messy brown hair. Her eyes look tired. Sunken. Well, naturally. She must be exhausted from the drive.

"How was your drive?" Charlotte asks. "Any problems? Any traffic? Did you get lost? I was expecting you a while ago—"

"I got a late start."

There is a pause, a silence that feels tentative, unfamiliar. For a long minute Emily gazes around the house, and Charlotte just watches her, a nervous smile pasted to her face. Then Emily shrugs off her duffel and starts rooting around inside it. "Here," she says, and holds out a plastic bag full of what look like green flower petals.

"What's this?"

"Arugula. From our garden."

"Your garden?" Charlotte takes the bag. "You grew these yourself?"

"Me and Walter."

"Oh! Well, they're just—that's just great. Grew them in your garden!"

Her enthusiasm is too much, she can feel it, but it's better than the awkward quiet a moment before. Charlotte isn't used to awkwardness around Emily. When Emily used to arrive for visits on Dunleavy Street, there would be an immediate flurry of activity, familiarity, dropping bags on the floor, flopping on the couch, digging through mail, rifling through the kitchen cabinets.

"Well, here, here, come in, come in," Charlotte blusters, shutting the door. "Let me give you a tour of the place. This is the foyer."

"God, Mom. You have a foyer?"

"I didn't specifically *ask* for one, but you know. It comes with the place."

Emily nods. She probably considers living in a condo community "selling out." A house with a style and layout exactly like all its neighbors, no personality of its own. Charlotte is comforted by the predictability of the complex; Emily probably finds it stifling. Dehumanizing. Depending on her mood, she might start comparing it to some kind of Communist state.

"I don't spend much time in here," Charlotte prattles, "but, you know. Nice for greeting guests." She heads quickly toward the living room before Emily can ask her to elaborate on who these guests might be. "And this is the living room."

The clop of Emily's boots disappears as they step onto the plush carpet.

"Are these my digs?"

"If it's not comfortable, you could sleep in my—"

"It's great," Emily says, dropping her duffel on the neat stack of pink bedding. Charlotte readies herself for some comment about the room's neutral tones, "the color of pantyhose." Instead, Emily wanders toward the built-in shelves lined with their framed photos, tiny tea sets, careful rows of books (one for the book group, one health/nutrition, one loans from Emily). She kneels down to peer at the fireplace that, despite the bundle of cedar logs in the cast-iron basket, hasn't yet been touched.

"I was thinking we could use it while you're here," Charlotte volunteers. "It just hasn't been quite cold enough yet."

Not to mention she's too paranoid to build a fire on her own. The flames might leap out of the grate, a burning ember might fly onto the carpet, she would have to stay awake until every last bit of ash was cold, oh—she feels tired just thinking about it.

"But this weekend it's supposed to go down to the thirties," she says, "so we could definitely build one. Would you want to? That would be cozy, wouldn't it? A fire? I always wanted a fireplace on Dunleavy Street."

Emily says nothing. Which isn't like her. Maybe she's concentrating on absorbing the place, taking it all in before unleashing her assessment. She pauses in front of the thick, tweedy curtains that conceal the sliding glass door.

"What's out here?" Emily reaches into the curtains and taps glass.

"That's the garden patio," Charlotte says, quoting from the brochure. "Isn't it nice? Let me open it up so you can see."

As a rule, Charlotte keeps these curtains closed. As far as she's concerned, the "garden patio" is the condo's biggest drawback. She doesn't like to be reminded of the half inch of glass separating her from potential robbers, murderers, rapists, wild animals. Every night at 7:00 P.M., the porch light automatically snaps on; from inside, the curtains emit a faint yellow glow.

Charlotte tugs the cord, and the heavy curtains shrug apart, creaking on their metal hinges to unveil a perfect square of smooth fake stones. The patio's only furnishings are two metal lounge chairs and a glass-topped table with an umbrella poking through the middle, bound tight as a swizzle stick. Under the glare of the lightbulb, the glass tabletop is marred with stray leaves, sticky pine needles, bird droppings. The puffy, flowered chair cushions are still folded and stacked in the corner, exactly where Charlotte found them.

Emily leans into the glass and cups her hands around her eyes. Charlotte watches a moth attack the porch light as she waits for Emily to speak. It's amazing how much her daughter's opinion matters. The opinion of a person whose diapers she changed, whose temperature she took, whose milk she made—a person she herself created.

After what seems like several minutes, Emily turns. "This room must get great natural light."

Charlotte thinks she can literally feel her heart swell. "Well, yes," she says. "I guess it does, now that you mention it." She gives the cord a few tugs, smothering the window in tweed again. As she heads for the hallway, her steps feel more confident. "The bathroom," she says, snapping on the light.

Emily points to the fish on the walls. "Yikes."

"Oh, I know. Aren't they awful? I try not to look them in the eye." Charlotte laughs, swinging open the lacquered bedroom door. "And last but not least."

The moment Emily steps into the bedroom, Charlotte is struck by what a comfort it is to have her in it. These four walls have already contained so much anxiety, so much fear, so many exaggerated dreams and overblown nightmares, that the mere fact of Emily's presence punctures some of that unreality somehow, connects the room to the real world. Next time she's scared at night, Charlotte thinks, she'll remember Emily being here.

Gratefully, she watches as her daughter moves around the room. She is as thorough as a prospective buyer: peeking in the closet, peering through the plastic slats of the blinds. Charlotte tries to see the room as her daughter would, but has spent so many countless hours staring at every crack and crevice that it's impossible to view it now through fresh eyes.

"Cool fan," Emily says, swatting at the gold chain dangling from one of the ceiling fan's wooden fins.

"It is nice, isn't it? Not too much of a breeze, but enough. Enough to keep me cool if I need it."

In truth, Charlotte rarely uses it. The whirring noise is too distracting. Like the Dream Machine, it's capable of concealing other, more important, sounds.

"Do you like the hardwood floor?" Charlotte asks, as Emily wanders toward the dresser. "The realtor said hardwood is popular these days. At first I wasn't sure, but it looks nice, don't you think?"

"Yeah. It's nice."

Emily hasn't commented on the Dream Machine sitting by the foot of the bed or *The Miracle of Mindfulness* on the bedside table. Instead, she pokes listlessly in Charlotte's jewelry box. Charlotte is sure her daughter has no interest in her bland clip-on earrings and unassuming gold chains. In the mirror above the dresser, she has a perfect view of Emily's blank expression. Something is clearly bothering her, something more than a long ride. She's lacking her usual spunk, her spirit—her engagement with the world.

"Honey," Charlotte ventures. The chain from the ceiling fan swings slightly. "Is everything all right?"

Emily doesn't look up, doesn't change expression, as if she's been expecting this. She fingers a knotted clump of necklace chains. "I'm fine."

"Are you sure? Are you tired from your drive? I could make you some tea. Or coffee? I could make you coffee."

"That's okay."

"How about a nice hot bath? I bought some lavender bubbles. And something called a bath glove."

Emily looks up. "You use a bath glove?"

"Well, no. I bought it for you."

"Oh."

In the mirror, Charlotte sees a smile.

"Remember last time you were here, you were taking lots of baths? Do you—are you still?"

Emily shrugs. Without her usual volume and energy, she looks smaller. A wisp of a thing, really. Her corduroys hang loose on her hips, boots are weighing down her feet. Under the bandanna, her naturally big eyes look enormous, like the starving children on those infomercials.

"It's just that"—Charlotte inhales—"you don't seem like yourself."

Emily clicks her tongue ring slowly, once, twice, like a metronome, as if measuring her response. Then she gives the tongue a decisive click and claps the lid shut on the jewelry box. "It's all good," she says, turning and smiling broadly. "I'm good. Just starving. Got anything to eat?"

Charlotte stashes the arugula in the produce bin—she'll have to use it during Emily's visit, but what on earth will she make?—while Emily starts opening cabinet doors. It feels good to be in the kitchen: a place of briskness, efficiency.

"What do you feel like eating?" Charlotte claps her hands. "I have egg salad, I have fruit salad—"

"You have Suddenly Salad." Emily yanks the box off the shelf and frowns at it. "Is this for real?"

Charlotte laughs, always the good sport. "It's not as bad as it sounds," she says, then opens the freezer to reveal a box of Boca Burgers propped against a bank of diet dinners-for-one. "I have Boca Burgers, honey. Want a Boca? It'll take ten minutes."

But Emily is surveying a shelf of boxes: pasta, rice, instant mashed potatoes. "Mom," she says, "do you realize almost everything you eat is off-white?"

Charlotte laughs again. She knows her food and clothes are easy bait and accepts this as part of her role as "the dowdy mom," especially if it will make Emily feel more like herself. She can't stand knowing her daughter is in pain and wants to find the origin immediately: trace it, name it, like a sound in the night. Watching Emily poke in these unfamiliar cabinets, it occurs to Charlotte she might feel unsettled by the new house. She hadn't anticipated this, but it would make sense. It would be strange if Emily *didn't* feel a little displaced. The house on Dunleavy Street was the only consistent home she'd ever known—the place where she'd had her own room, her closet, her bulletin board full of concert tickets and photos and dried corsages. It was the den where she studied for every test, the living room where she curled in front of the TV under a pile of fuzzy afghans, the pantry she shut herself inside to talk on their single phone—a rotary attached to the kitchen wall—before convincing Charlotte to get a cordless.

Charlotte can still remember that beige phone cord, how it strained under the door to the pantry—or "Emily's Office," as they later called it—and the serious tones of her daughter's voice leaking from within. On any given night, Emily would be dispensing advice to one of her many girlfriends or arguing heatedly with one of the boys in her class. Charlotte would try not to interrupt, but sometimes, if she was cooking, she couldn't help it. She would rap on the door, sing "Ex-cuse me!" and reach in quickly to grab whatever ingredient she needed. Emily would be sitting on the floor, knees bunched under her chin, head resting against a shelf of canned peaches or Cheerios. "Hold on," she would tell her caller, then press the phone to her chest until Charlotte closed the door. One afternoon, when Emily was a freshman, Charlotte found her at the kitchen table decorating a square of poster board with bubble letters: EMILY'S OFFICE. She wrote IN SESSION on one side, OPEN FOR BUSINESS on the other. They laughed about it and hung the sign on the doorknob from a piece of red yarn. Even after the pantry became a pantry again, and Emily and the cordless began disappearing to her bedroom, that sign remained on the pantry doorknob until Charlotte packed it, last summer, in a box labeled MISC.

That's what the kitchen on Dunleavy Street felt like. A hodgepodge, a treasure chest, a room packed to bursting. The refrigerator door was crowded with scribbled notes, photos, coupons, postcards. In the "junk drawer" was a sludge of matchbooks, takeout menus, rubber bands, recipes ripped from magazines, extra packets of ketchup and sugar three inches deep. The kitchen—the whole house—had a sense of accumulation. History. Here at the condo, the refrigerator door was blank except for a Bed, Bath and Beyond coupon attached with the magnet Charlotte received in the mail from Millville County Electric.

"I was thinking," Charlotte says, voice lurching as it always did when she broached an uncomfortable subject. "That it must be hard for you, honey, being here. At the condo."

Emily faces an open cabinet, back turned.

"I know it's different from the house on Dunleavy Street. It's smaller, and the stove's electric, the closets aren't as deep . . ." Charlotte sucks in a breath. "I felt strange too, at first. But you get used to it. Believe me." She pauses and asks, hopefully, "Is that what's upsetting you? Do you miss Dunleavy Street?"

Emily turns. She smiles, but it is a sad smile, the kind of smile an adult gives to a child who has said something so naive it is endearing. "It's fine, Mom," she says. "I'm fine. Don't worry."

Charlotte waits, wanting something more. A "but" or an "except for." A sag of the shoulders, even a tear or two. Instead, Emily hops up on the counter with a burst of new energy. "If you really want to know what's upsetting me," she says, "it's that my mother's taste buds are dying a slow death." With a flourish, she grabs a wire whisk and stands up, head inches from the overhead light. "Charlotte Warren?" she announces into the whisk.

"Yes?"

"You are today's lucky winner."

"I am?"

"You and your daughter and your deprived taste buds have won an exciting trip for three to"—she drums the whisk on a cabinet door—"a fabulous restaurant in southern Jersey. There you will try something new. Something exotic."

"Oh, but I can just make something here—"

"We're going out." Emily points the whisk at her. "No excuses."

"But you must be tired from the—"

"I'm fine."

"But," Charlotte protests, voice rising, "it's almost nine o'clock!"

Emily's arms flop to her sides. "Fine. We don't have to *eat* out. We'll go get takeout and bring it back. How's that?"

Charlotte looks up at her daughter. She has lived this moment, felt this feeling, countless times before. Does she want to go out? No. She really doesn't. But she knows that once Emily has a plan, there's no stopping her, especially when it comes to exposing Charlotte to new things. Joe was the same way, always trying to cajole her into trying sushi, or mussels, or dousing her food in garlic or pesto or curry, then seeming disappointed—no, more than disappointed, truly *let down* in some larger spiritual way, as if Charlotte's basic moral fiber were in question—when she declined. Why, Charlotte wonders, is her taste in food a character flaw that needs correcting? She hates when people felt the need to *make* her adventurous: to sing in the car or dance at a wedding reception or try the bite of raw, pink, glistening fish dangling from the end of their fork. Why should it matter if she doesn't want to? If it doesn't bother *her,* why should it bother *them?*

She doesn't want to leave the house. Doesn't want to go out in the chilly night air, drive in the dark, eat something unfamiliar. But, more important than all the things she *doesn't* want to do, is the one thing she wants most in this world: to see her daughter happy. And, like every moment before this, Charlotte will choose her daughter's happiness over her own. Maybe that's what being a mother is all about.

Thai Heaven is in the same strip as Bed, Bath and Beyond, though Charlotte has never noticed it before. From the outside it's easy to miss, the front window obscured by a forbidding film of steam. But inside, the dining room is an explosion of the senses—deep reds and golds, tassels and sconces, brass emblems of elephants and gods. The place is nearly empty, it being 9:00 P.M. on a Thursday in Millville. The only customers are couples. There is an intimacy about the place—its steaminess and smallness and spiciness—that makes Charlotte uncomfortable.

A pretty Asian woman appears at the front desk. Charlotte gives her the encouraging smile she reserves for people who don't speak English, and is embarrassed when the woman says, "Are you ready to order?" with a perfect American accent.

Emily looks at Charlotte.

"Nothing too hot," she manages, before Emily begins rattling off questions and selections, fingers flying around the Vegetarian section. Charlotte doesn't mind eating vegetarian when she's with Emily. She's not hiding the fact that she eats meat, just doesn't see the point in forcing Emily to be around it. She watches her gesture to dishes with several intimidating little red spice leaves lined up next to them. One involves something ambiguously described as "brown sauce."

Maybe she's better off not knowing. She takes a seat by the

door and occupies herself by dropping mints into her palm with a tiny silver spoon until Emily is done.

By the time they return to the condo, the bottom of the brown bag is damp with some unknown seeping sauce. Charlotte agrees to try a little of everything—what choice does she have?—and cringes as Emily piles her plate high, all of it drenched in sauces and spices, colors and flavors running together in an indefinable wet mess.

Charlotte holds her tongue and says, "It all looks delicious!" When she tries what looks like a relatively safe piece of celery, all she can taste is heat.

"So?"

"Good," she manages, taking a gulp of water. "Very interesting."

Emily laughs. "If you don't like it, you can say so."

"It's not that—it's just hotter than I'm used to."

Her water is gone before she's made it through the first three bites.

"So," she says, grabbing the Brita pitcher and getting up to refill it. "Tell me all about your house. Is it all decorated?"

"Pretty much."

"Pretty much? What do you need?" Charlotte turns on the tap water, sticks a finger in it, lets it run until it's cold. "I know there's always those odds and ends you don't think of before you're actually in the place . . . shower curtains, can openers, kitchen towels. Tomorrow we can take a ride to Bed, Bath and Beyond, and I'll buy you whatever you need."

"But we don't need anything."

"You must need *something.* And I just got a coupon in the mail. Twenty percent off any purchase over—fifteen dollars, I think." She plucks a clean bowl from the dish rack and holds it under the icemaker. At the churning sound, Emily looks up.

"Icemaker," Charlotte explains. She was hoping to sound nonchalant, but even she can hear the note of excitement in her voice.

Charlotte carries the pitcher and bowl to the table. "It's just that sometimes the things you need for a new house don't occur to you until you see them in the store." She drops two ice cubes in her glass. "Just the other week, I was out shopping when I saw this soap dish and realized I needed one. Remember how on Dunleavy Street, the soap dishes were built into the walls? Here, I had my soap just sitting on the sink, which was fine, but the soap dish looks so much nicer." She takes a sip of water. How mundane her life must sound. "Besides, I want to buy you something. Something fun. You need a housewarming gift. It's your first house!"

"But there's really nothing we need." Emily shrugs. "We just deal, you know? Walter built some shelves. Anthony has this great old trunk we're using as a coffee table. Mara made some tapestries and rugs. We're pretty self-sufficient."

Charlotte looks down at her plate. She often feels, when talking to Emily, as if she's dodging tiny, invisible barbs. She doubts they are intentional; most likely, they are the product of her own insecurities. She and her daughter just live so differently, think so differently, that she could take virtually any comment Emily makes and twist it into a subtle criticism even if it wasn't meant that way.

"Yes, well, I guess you are." Charlotte forces her fork into a spongy broccoli head. "I'm still so impressed by you, growing that arugula." She pops the broccoli in her mouth, and her tongue goes up in flames.

Emily, she notices, has barely touched her dinner. She feels a flicker of panic as she adds up tonight's strange behavior: her moodiness, her thinness, and now, her untouched plate. Could she have some kind of eating disorder? Charlotte doubts it—Emily has never worried about food, except to make sure it's organic—but then again, these eating problems are so rampant these days. Linda Hill's daughter, Rachel, was just diagnosed (was that the right word, diagnosed?) with anorexia. She'd gone to live at a clinic in Philadelphia. Linda told the book group that Rachel had been hiding rocks in her pockets, trying to trick her doctors into thinking she weighed more than she did.

"You know," Charlotte ventures, careful to keep her eyes away from Emily's food, "Rachel Hill has anorexia."

"No kidding," Emily says. "Rachel Hill hasn't eaten a meal since fifth grade."

Charlotte looks up. "Fifth grade?"

"She always threw her lunches away in the cafeteria."

"Fifth grade?" Charlotte repeats. "How in the world would a fifth-grader even know to *do* a thing like that?"

"Easy." Emily twines her legs onto her chair lotus style. "Girls in this generation grow up much faster. It's a biological fact: puberty now starts earlier than it used to. So being in fifth grade is the same as being, I don't know, thirteen."

Charlotte puts down her fork.

"If you ask me," Emily continues, picking up a chopstick, "schools need to stop showing filmstrips in health class. Do they really think kids watch them and worry about overdosing on drugs or starving themselves to death? Wrong." She jabs the chopstick in the air for emphasis. "They watch them and get ideas. They leave class psyched to try out bulimia or take some Ex."

Charlotte stares at her daughter. Her daughter, who is so startlingly, endearingly, terrifyingly honest. Charlotte reminds herself, as she has many times before: I'd rather have an honest child than an evasive one.

"Well," Charlotte says, picking up her fork, "Rachel's at a clinic in Philadelphia." She struggles to keep her voice even. "Inpatient."

"That's great. Good for her."

"Apparently she's been putting rocks in her pockets." She can't help but feel a hint of pride, relaying this tidbit of inside information. "To trick the doctors into thinking she's heavier than she is."

"Yeah, I've heard that."

Naturally. Nothing she could reveal would surprise Emily. She reaches for her water. At this rate, she'll be up all night.

"One of my students was in a clinic last year," Emily says, absently poking the chopstick at the palm of her hand. "Her parents forced her to go when she started growing fur."

Charlotte almost chokes. "Fur!"

"It's the primal survival instinct kicking in. If the body gets too thin, it gets cold because there's not enough fat to keep it warm. It starts growing fur to protect itself."

Charlotte is speechless. Emily sounds more animated than she has all night.

"It's amazing, isn't it? At the end of the day, humans are all just animals, you know?" She shakes her head in fascination. Not a morbid fascination, but a genuine awe for the natural workings of the world. "It's really incredible, if you think about it."

Well, Charlotte thinks, at least she's not being so listless. She'd rather Emily be acting animated and fascinated, fur and all.

With renewed energy Emily turns to the shelf under the window, where Charlotte keeps miscellaneous piles. Two packs of moving announcements she bought six weeks ago and hasn't been able to bring herself to open. The Book Group snack schedule. A pink soap shaped like a hippo that she saw in the mall, thought was cute, then never used, realizing she didn't want to watch it disintegrate bit by bit each day. On the bottom is her dust-filmed laptop. It's Emily's old computer, the one she used in high school and gave to Charlotte when she left for college and Joe bought her one that was "cutting-edge." Emily had encouraged Charlotte to use it as a journal, but she was so confounded by the technology that the few times she tried to use it, she only got frustrated. It froze on her two years ago, and she hadn't opened it since.

Charlotte braces herself for a comment on the unused computer, the unsent moving announcements, but Emily reaches instead for a book with a bright logo stamped on its cover. "What's this?"

"I didn't choose it," Charlotte says quickly. She knows Emily's opinions on corporate book clubs. "It's for my group."

"You still do the group?"

"The second Saturday of every month."

Emily looks up. "Isn't that this Saturday?"

"Well, yes, but I'm not going, obviously. Not with you here. I'm still reading the book, though, for, you know. Pleasure."

Emily scans the inside flap.

"So," Charlotte says. She knows she has to ask sooner or later, and the brink of a book discussion seems as good a time as any. "How are things with Walter?"

Emily lets the book fall shut. "Fine."

Charlotte pauses, a forkful of brown rice halfway to her

mouth. It's the first time she's ever heard Emily mention Walter with anything short of unbridled enthusiasm. "Honey?" She puts the fork down. "Did something happen?"

"No."

"Then what is it?"

"It's nothing." Emily tosses the book back on the shelf. "I don't want to talk about it."

"So it's something."

"Mom," Emily warns. "I'm serious."

Charlotte watches as Emily pokes at her food with a chopstick. She knows if her daughter doesn't want to talk, there will be no convincing her otherwise.

"Okay." Charlotte nods. "Fair enough."

Emily doesn't look up. Watching her, Charlotte realizes that this entire evening—Emily's moodiness, her quietness, her lack of appetite—now makes sense. Emily doesn't have an eating disorder. She isn't upset about the condo. She's having problems with Walter. Charlotte doesn't know why she didn't suspect this in the first place. In retrospect, it's obvious—inevitable. Living together was such a big step, an *adult* step, they were bound to have trouble. They couldn't have known how hard it would be, no matter how in love they were. Besides, it only makes sense that Emily's fascination with Walter would fade eventually. She's always lived from cause to cause, passion to passion, phase to phase. When one hobby loses its novelty, she throws herself into the next, and the next, and there's nothing like utility bills and dirty socks and caking toothpaste tubes to speed up the process.

As sorry as she is, Charlotte can't help but feel relieved. She doesn't know what she would have done if Emily didn't like to come visit. And although she'd never admit it, she feels the tiniest bit validated. She's known all along Walter and Emily weren't right for each other. In fact, she's always known exactly what kind of man Emily will settle down with. He'll be her opposite: proper, reserved, conservative. The man who provides the sense and steadiness to counter her impulsiveness, contest her radical ideas, soften her stubborn will.

Emily, of course, would hate that Charlotte presumed to know this, so she's never told her. She doesn't need to. She is secure in her prediction. She knows that one day—maybe at Emily's wedding reception, as Charlotte raises a glass of wine, wearing a pale blue dress with mother-of-pearl trim—she will say: *Even back when my daughter was young and impulsive, even when she got that pierce in her tongue* (laughs), *I always knew she would settle down with a man like . . .*

"So what about you?"

Charlotte blinks, refocuses. "What about me what?"

"Do you have a man in your life? A *beau?*" She leans on the word just enough to undermine it.

"Emily." Charlotte reddens. "Don't be ridiculous. Have you seen a parade of men lining up at my door in the past fifteen years?"

"And? That doesn't mean it can't happen. Maybe now's the perfect time. You have a new place. You have time on your hands. You're only forty-seven. There have to be some eligible bachelors in The Heights."

On the surface, her words sound supportive, but Charlotte can hear the hint of a challenge underneath. Emily is prying into her mother's personal life in exchange for Charlotte prying into hers.

"Don't be silly."

"Why is that silly? It's the exact *opposite* of silly. It's what people do."

Charlotte stabs at her plate. "I have plenty of things to do."

Emily pauses. Charlotte knows well what her daughter thinks about the "things she does." She's never watered down her opinions on Charlotte's lack of career ("It's not about *needing* to have one, Mom, it's about *wanting* to") or the eight college credits Charlotte needs to graduate ("But wouldn't it feel satisfying?") or the fact that she's never had a "real" job. Which isn't exactly true. Before she was married, Charlotte did part-time clerical work at LaSalle University, where her father taught philosophy. And for two years after Joe moved out, she was an office aide at Emily's school. The pay was low, but with alimony and child support it was enough; plus, it allowed her to be home after school with Emily.

"Fine," Emily concedes. She's peeled apart a spring roll and is now dissecting its insides like a lab experiment. "You're busy. I respect that."

Charlotte pops an unknown vegetable in her mouth: white, seemingly innocuous, shaped like a poker chip. Her throat burns.

"But dating doesn't have to mean a total lifestyle change, you know?" Emily says. "It might just add some spice to your life."

Maybe I don't want more spice in my life, Charlotte snaps, but only on the inside. She stares at the forbidding orange-red sauce that has now pooled in front of her, invaded her sinuses, tinged everything on her plate a warning shade of red. Her throat is burning, nose starting to run. Suddenly she feels intensely resentful of everything: the Thai food she was made to eat, the worry she's continually made to feel, the footsteps she treads in tiny, careful circles around her daughter, only to get ridiculous inquiries about her love life in return.

Beau. What a silly phrase. It's so old-fashioned. Embarrassing.

Charlotte plucks a napkin from the plastic holder and looks directly at her daughter. "Why aren't you eating?"

Emily pauses for a second, then says evenly, "I am eating." She picks up a wrinkled pepper, leans her head back, opens her mouth, and drops it in.

Charlotte looks away. She presses the napkin to each eye. She hopes Emily knows it's the spices that are making her cry.

"Mom." Emily sighs. "I don't have an eating disorder, if that's what you're worried about."

"That's not what I'm worried about." Charlotte blows her nose.

"Right."

"I mean, well, fine. Yes. It did cross my mind. Because you've barely touched your dinner." She folds the used napkin into a tiny, damp square and places it in her lap. "But I didn't really think you had one."

"Good. Because I'm not that trendy."

"I know."

"Good."

Charlotte picks up a teabag and fingers the paper tassel. "Good Taste Tea Bag," it says, in sticklike orange letters.

"Want me to put on some water?" she asks, knowing the answer.

"No, thanks," Emily says. "You should try some, though. It's good."

"Oh, I could never drink tea before bed." Charlotte laughs. It's an unattractive laugh, bitter and self-deprecating. "I'd lose more sleep than I do already." Then she scrapes back her chair and starts packing up the leftovers, pinching the plastic lids to the sides of the sagging foil containers.

Emily uncrosses her legs and stands to help. "You know what you need, Mom?" she says, her voice more gentle.

"Hmm?"

"Sleepytime tea. It'll put you right out."

"Wouldn't that be nice." Charlotte picks up the bowl of half-melted ice and dumps it in the sink. The truth is, she's considered taking something to help her sleep, but the thought of being alone in the middle of the night, drugged, semiconscious, makes her feel more vulnerable than she does already.

"Just don't take No-Doz." Emily starts stacking dishes. "Janie took it cramming for our Chem 101 final and didn't sleep for the next four years."

Charlotte pauses, dripping foil pan in hand. "Janie Grobel?"

"She got addicted to it."

"She did?"

"She started taking it to help her study and got completely hooked." Emily is carrying a stack of dishes to the sink, where Charlotte stands frozen to the spot. "Senior year we had this whole intervention thing where we flushed all her pills and Janie started freaking out." She starts scraping plates into the garbage disposal. "It was all very *90210.*"

"Why didn't you ever tell me?"

Emily turns the disposal on and raises her voice. "I don't know. I mean, over-the-counter caffeine pills? It's kind of lame as far as addictions go." She flicks the disposal off and looks at Charlotte's face. "Oh, come on, Mom. Please don't get all freaked out."

But it's too late. Charlotte *is* all freaked out. She can't help but *be* all freaked out. She pictures little Janie Grobel, Emily's roommate freshman year at Wesleyan, a sweet blond girl from Minnesota. She was on the swim team and always had a pair of pink goggles dangling around her neck. Her mother used to send the girls packages of home-baked banana bread.

Watching her daughter, Charlotte feels fear. The same fear that creeps over her when she sees drunk driving commercials. The same fear she feels watching *20/20* and *Dateline* about raves and date-rape drugs and AIDS. The fear she felt reading *Reviving Ophelia* (a book group favorite) and absorbing story after story of happy, well-adjusted adolescent girls who suddenly, and with no warning, turned addictive, delinquent, rebellious. Now, like then, Charlotte senses the presence of an ambiguous, dangerous world—a world of girls addicted to over-the-counter pills and girls staging interventions and girls growing fur because they've starved all their body fat away—a world from which she can't begin to protect her daughter. She can't protect her from these dangers because she doesn't understand them. Because she isn't even aware of them. When she hears about such things, and thinks of her own sleepless nights, she sees her fears for what they really are: imaginary.

chapter two

Charlotte waits in the kitchen. Emily is still asleep, a pink tangle of blankets on the living room couch. It's good for her, Charlotte thinks, sleeping late. She must need it. Charlotte herself has been awake since 7:04 A.M., trying to be as quiet as possible. She bypassed the coffeemaker, knowing it would hiss and gurgle. The teapot would whistle, the toaster pop, the microwave drone and beep. The *Today Show* was out of the question. She settled for a glass of lemonade, skipping the ice.

Now it's 11:33 A.M. Charlotte tugs at the belt of her old bathrobe, orange stitched with yellow butterflies. Carefully, she peels over a page of the *Better Homes & Gardens Cookbook,* the third cookbook she's scanned for recipes with arugula. As it turns out, these are not easy to come by. She wonders if it could be used as a substitute for something else. Mixed greens in the Twelve-Hour Vegetable Salad? Radicchio tossed with toasted walnuts and gorgonzola?

When the phone rings, Charlotte stumbles over the chair trying to get to it. "Hello," she whispers, glancing at the couch.

"Hello?" The background is loud with the sound of machinery. "Charlotte?"

It's Walter's voice. "Yes?"

"Hey, how you doing? It's Walter."

"Walter." From the living room, she hears a stir. "I'm fine."

"Listen, I'm at work, so I've only got a minute. Think I could speak to Em?"

"Well, just a—let me check." Charlotte carries the cordless to the couch, where Emily's head has emerged from the nest of blankets, watching her with a sleepy squint.

"Honey?" Charlotte cups the receiver and speaks softly. "It's Walter."

Emily extends one thin arm to take the phone, then burrows back down in the covers. "Hi," she says, pulling the blanket to her chin.

Charlotte returns to the kitchen. She feels oddly purposeless. If she strained, she knows she could make out Emily's conversation, and this makes her feel intrusive. She wishes she had a bigger house, more places to retreat. She heads for the bathroom, where she dabs a spot of concealer under each eye. She runs a brush through her hair, colored an even brown, and checks the roots. Just a hint of gray. In the bedroom, she changes out of her bathrobe and into a blue cable-knit sweater and a pair of jeans. She sucks in as she zips, then yanks the sweater down, concealing the slight bulge in her belly. She gained twenty-five pounds when she was pregnant with Emily, and lost just ten of them; the other fifteen she has carried ever since.

By the time she emerges, Emily has moved onto the patio. Charlotte can see just half of her through the stripe of glass unobscured by curtain. She's still wrapped in a pink blanket, huddled in a cushionless aluminum chair, cradling the phone to her ear.

It can't hurt to make coffee now. Charlotte gets the pot brewing, sponges off the counters, rinses a bunch of grapes and sets them in a bowl. She hears the suck of the patio door being pulled open. Emily shuffles into the kitchen, blanket clutched around her head.

"Good morning!" Charlotte chirps.

"Morning." Emily curls up in a kitchen chair, depositing the cordless on the table. Remembering her warning of the night before, Charlotte doesn't ask questions. She concentrates instead on topping off the sugar bowl.

Then: "Walter's coming."

Charlotte's head snaps up. "Coming?"

"I know, I know, it's totally short notice—"

"Coming *here?*"

"It's not a big thing. Really. He doesn't require much." Emily looks up. "Is it okay?"

Charlotte stares down into the white slopes of the sugar, feeling something twist in her chest. She forces her gaze to the coffeemaker, the slow, methodic drip of it, trying to keep her pulse from racing. She reminds herself of her daughter's sadness the night before. The exhaustion on her face this morning. The sleepy, squinty eyes. The left side of her face still creased with pillow marks.

"Of course," Charlotte says, trying not to sound devastated. She caps the sugar bowl with what she hoped would be a brisk clap, but instead is a barely audible clink. "Of course it's okay."

She waits for Emily to offer something more, some urgent reason, some couldn't-be-helped explanation for Walter's visit, but she doesn't. In fact, she doesn't seem that surprised. Is it possible she knew about it? That they planned it together before she left? The mere possibility that Emily could have known Walter was coming—*wanted* Walter coming—is even more awful than the prospect of his being here. Maybe her funk last night wasn't because she was mad at him, but because she missed him. Because she was miserable here without him. Maybe the reality is simply this: Emily would rather spend the weekend with Walter, whom she sees every day, than with Charlotte.

"So!" Charlotte's voice is unnaturally loud. She opens the cabinet, plunks two mugs on the counter: WESLEYAN UNIVERSITY and YOU CAN'T BE COOL WEARING FUR. "What time will Walter be getting here?"

"Not until late. Around two, probably."

"Two—"

"A.M."

Of course. There would be no way Walter could arrive from New Hampshire by two in the afternoon, yet this entire visit seemed so surreal Charlotte was leaving nothing to chance.

Emily reaches one hand from the folds of the blanket, plucks absently at the bunch of grapes. Something about the lackluster way she pops them in her mouth, letting the spiny stems fall to the table, angers Charlotte. She yanks open the refrigerator and reaches for one carton of regular milk, one of soy.

"So," she says again. She must remain focused on the details. "He'll leave New Hampshire tonight, then?"

"After he gets out of work."

"Does he have a car?"

"No." Emily sighs, as if reminded of the burden of being the sole auto owner. "Train."

"And how will he get from the train to the house?"

"Cab."

"Cab?" This was a foreign concept in Millville, New Jersey. Had Charlotte ever even *seen* a cab since moving here?

"That's what he tells me."

"Shouldn't you pick him up at the station?"

Emily simultaneously raises her hands, shoulders, and eyebrows in an exaggerated *don't-ask-me.* "He says he doesn't want me waiting in the dark. Apparently, an empty train station at two in the morning is no place for me to be." The resentment in her tone is not surprising. Emily has never liked being seen as vulnerable, as needing protection. Though Charlotte, much as she dislikes Walter at the moment, is glad he's insisted on this.

"Plus," Emily says, "he doesn't want to inconvenience anyone."

A little late for that, Charlotte thinks.

"You won't even have to get up when he gets here. I'll listen for him. You'll sleep right through it. I promise."

Charlotte slams the gaping refrigerator door. "And he'll be staying until—"

Emily gives her a quizzical look. "Sunday?" She phrases it like a question, to reinforce the obvious. It is the twenty-two-year-old tonal equivalent of the schoolyard phrase Charlotte hated most when Emily was a child: *No duh.* It was always delivered with such condescension. "No duh, Mom," Emily would say, if Charlotte told her the school bus was late, or to take an umbrella because it was raining. "Yeah, Mom," Joe would chime in. "No duh."

"He'll just ride back with me, you know?"

"Right." In other words, Walter would be here to suck up every last moment they had together. It would be too kind of him, too humane, to leave them with a few hours, minutes, to say good-bye. She feels her face beginning to get hot. "Of course."

Charlotte faces the counter, takes hold of the smooth Formica edge. She can feel herself beginning to lose control, the pressure of tears building behind her face, stiffening in her jaws. It isn't just that Walter is coming, but that it's all happening so casually. So nonchalantly. A quick phone call, a few details, and voilà: the plan is in motion, the weekend ruined. And there is nothing Charlotte can do about it without looking like the bad guy.

The more she thinks about Walter, the angrier she gets. It's galling, really: intruding on their weekend, imposing on the hospitality of a woman he barely knows. Even if Emily and he had come up with this plan together—even *if*—Walter should have had the sense to refuse. He should know by now that Emily can be reckless, spontaneous, irrational sometimes. He should know he needs to be the one with the head on his shoulders. She wonders about Walter's sense of manners, his upbringing. What must his parents be like?

"I just didn't know if Walter might have to work on the weekends," Charlotte goes on, voice wobbling as she tries to override the tears thickening in her throat. She yanks open the utensil drawer and fishes for two spoons. "If he might have to be at the—where is it?"

"Woodworking shop."

"Right."

"He's an apprentice."

Apprentice. It might be worse than "alternative learning environment."

"He doesn't have to work weekends. His master is cool about his hours."

His *master.* God Almighty.

"Well, that's good, isn't it?" She rattles the drawer shut with the palm of her hand. "Isn't that lucky? To have a master who's cool about his hours?"

And just as she feels her head might burst, she grabs the coffeepot and aims it over YOU CAN'T BE COOL WEARING FUR. As she starts to pour, her hand is shaking so badly the coffee splashes over the lip of the pot. Charlotte just stands there, pot in hand, as spilled coffee leaks across the counter. She watches as it hovers for a moment at the curved lip of the Formica, then begins drizzling steadily onto the floor.

"Mom!"

It's the sound of her daughter's voice, like some kind of Pavlovian trigger, that brings Charlotte back to life. She sets the pot down, rips a paper towel from the roll above the sink, soaks up the puddle on the counter, then crouches on the floor to blot the tiles dry. When she lifts her head, she notices a thin stain running down the front of the cabinet doors.

"I'm sorry," Emily says, grabbing another paper towel. She's on her feet now, having abandoned her blanket in a pink heap by her chair. "Really, Mom. I didn't know it would get to you like this."

Still crouching, Charlotte catches a glimpse of herself in the glass of the oven door. Her reflection is dark and mottled, but her eyes have the wide, panicked look she's seen staring back at her from countless mirrors on countless sleepless nights. In that moment, she realizes how ridiculous she's being. How much she's overreacting. What's important here is not what she wants. It's what Emily wants: whatever makes her happy.

Charlotte closes her eyes. She feels the anger that has been hardening behind her face begin to break up, soften into flesh again. When she opens her eyes, she finds Emily kneeling beside her, scrubbing at the cabinet doors.

For a moment, Charlotte lays her hand against her daughter's cheek, then lets it fall away. "So," she says. "What does Walter like to eat?"

The upside of guests, even unwanted guests, is the busywork. While going to the Super Fresh to stock up on Walter's favorite foods is not exactly how Charlotte pictured her first—and now, only—full day with Emily, it's better than staying home feeling resentful. It's an activity, a job to do, a way of spending time together. Still, as Charlotte drives by the shiny Bed, Bath and Beyond presiding over the Millville Mall, she can't help but feel a pang of regret, picturing the soap dishes and can openers she wanted to buy Emily as housewarming gifts.

In the supermarket, Emily steers. Charlotte walks beside her. It's the same way they used to navigate grocery stores when Emily was a little girl. Emily always liked to control the cart, which left Charlotte free to squeeze produce and compare prices. Today, threading through the aisles, Charlotte maintains an orderly running dialogue about Walter's food and drink preferences: soda (root beer), breakfast cereal (Apple Jacks), snack food (cheese popcorn), juice (apple), bread (rye).

"You talk like he's staying for a month." Emily laughs.

Despite the purpose of their trip, it's fun shopping with Emily. Charlotte can't remember the last time they roamed a supermarket together, especially since Emily's diet became too complicated for mainstream stores. In high school, Charlotte used to give her money and send her off to Parkway Health Food, from which Emily would return home to stuff the refrigerator with soy, tofu, tabouli, tempeh.

"I'm assuming Walter's a vegetarian," Charlotte says, as they pull to a stop in front of Meats & Seafood. Above the glass cases, the wall is swimming with a mural of blue fish that bears a disconcerting resemblance to Charlotte's bathroom tile.

"Nope."

"Nope?" She is shocked. She can't imagine Emily could eat with, much less fall in love with, a meat eater. "Really?"

"I've tried to talk him out of it, believe me."

This part doesn't surprise Charlotte, having been on the receiving end of a countless number of Emily's boycott campaigns. Plastic. Leather. Cleaning products tested on rats. She knows how relentless Emily can be and can't help but feel a hint of warmth toward Carnivore Walter, simply for his refusal to bend.

Back at The Heights—this is what Emily has taken to calling it, like a prime-time TV drama—they are heading toward L1, grocery bags clutched to their hips, when Charlotte hears: "Well, hello there!"

It is her neighbor, Ruth O'Keefe, a widow who lives alone with her cat and never stops talking. The day Charlotte moved in, she stopped by to "say a quick hello," and an hour later Charlotte had said less than ten words and was holding a bundt cake topped with a nonpareil smile.

"Hello, Ruth," Charlotte says, not breaking stride.

"Gross," Emily mutters. "What is that thing?"

She is referring to Ernie, a fat golden cat resembling a butterball turkey, straining awkwardly from a leash as Ruth hurries toward them.

"Seriously," Emily says. "Is that a—"

"Hello!" Ruth descends, yanking Ernie to a stop. She looks expectantly at Emily. "I'm Ruth!"

"Ruth," Charlotte says, "this is my—"

"Emily," Emily says. "Nice to meet you."

"She's my daughter," Charlotte adds.

"Oh! How fun! A mother-daughter visit! Emily, this is Ernie. Ernie, say hi to our new friend."

Emily raises her eyebrows at Charlotte.

"Come on, Ern, don't be shy," Ruth says. When the cat still doesn't speak, she shakes her head in genuine confusion. "I don't know what's wrong with him. Usually he'll meow for new people. Come to think of it, he's seemed a little under the weather all day."

Charlotte shifts her bag to the other hip.

"I sense these things, you know," Ruth goes on. "It's like with a child, you can just tell when something's off even if they don't say it." She appeals to Emily. "The vet says it's amazing, the way I read this cat."

"I wouldn't worry," Emily says. "He looks fine to me. But hey, if you don't mind my asking—what's up with the leash?"

This is more than all the incentive Ruth needs to launch into the numerous rationales behind leash-walking Ernie: quotes from magazines, assessments by veterinarians, a catalog of Ernie's strikingly doglike qualities. "He can heel and roll over," she says. "Sometimes he even fetches my slippers. The vet says he's never seen anything like it."

Emily nods, the expression on her face carefully engaged, but Charlotte can see the laughter simmering beneath it. And in that moment, she realizes what makes having Emily here so wonderful: it reinforces the difference between Charlotte and the kind of people who live at these kinds of places. Sad people, single people, people who live alone in condos with cats on leashes, wishing their children would visit more often. With Emily here, Charlotte has a partner. Someone to echo her reactions, confirm her opinions. To set her apart.

"We really better get inside," Charlotte says, nodding her chin at the bags.

"Oh, sure," Ruth says. "Well, it was fun to meet you, Emily. Hopefully we'll run into you again, won't we, Ern?" She bends over the cat's thick golden head, cups her hands around her mouth, and whispers: "Say bye-bye, Ernie! Say bye-bye!"

Thankfully, Ruth draws the line at actually voicing Ernie. Charlotte and Emily rush for the door before laughter overtakes them.

"What *was* that thing?" Emily says, giggling.

"Ssshh!" Charlotte splutters. "Not until we're inside."

"But what was it?"

"A cat."

"That was no cat."

"Of course it was."

"Mom, that woman was insane."

"Be nice. She's a widow."

"An insane widow."

They huddle in the doorway while Charlotte wrestles with her locks. She can't remember the last time she felt this giddy. She grabs her mail and pushes open the door. Emily is behind her, peering into B. Morgan's mailbox. She plucks out the pink Victoria's Secret catalog poking from the top.

"Emily!" Charlotte hisses. "Put that back!"

"Why? Whose is it?"

"Well, hers, obviously." Charlotte steps into the foyer and beckons Emily inside. "B. Morgan's."

"B? Is that her real name or does it stand for something?"

"I have no idea what it stands for."

"You don't?"

"I've never met her. I've never even seen her."

"That's weird."

"Is it?" It hadn't struck Charlotte as weird. She heads for the kitchen, Emily trailing behind her, resuming her normal volume.

"You don't think it's weird you've never seen the person who lives directly upstairs?"

"Not really. She seems to go out most nights. Weekends she must sleep late, I guess."

"Maybe she's a hooker."

Charlotte feels a tug at her lungs. "What?"

"I mean, long shot, but it would explain her schedule. And her, you know, nightlife." Emily heaves her bags onto the counter. Without looking at Charlotte's stricken face, she says, "Mom, please don't freak out. I'm sure she's not. I'm just saying." She dips a hand into her bag and pulls out the Victoria's Secret.

After a dinner of arugula salad (Charlotte's own improvisation), pasta alfredo, and pistachio ice cream, Charlotte hums while cleaning up. Emily is on the couch in the living room, paging through *People.* With her daughter here, even simple, everyday actions—loading the dishwasher, wiping down the counters—feel steadier. Slower, somehow. Maybe this is what it feels like to be mindful.

"No *way,*" Emily moans from the living room.

"What?" Charlotte turns off the sink. "What is it?"

"J. Lo broke up with her husband? And she's dating Ben Affleck? Already? How long was she married to the other guy, like two weeks?"

Charlotte's read the article already (it was more like ten months) but plays along. "Was that all?"

"I thought I did quick relationships," Emily clicks her tongue ring. "But that's nuts."

By the time the dishes are finished, it's nearly 11:00 P.M. Charlotte's eyelids are heavy, but she doesn't want to go to bed yet. Because after tonight—what? Walter will be here until Emily leaves on Sunday. Charlotte's mind flips ahead to Thanksgiving: Emily will be in Seattle. And now that she's unbound by divorce agreements and visiting schedules and academic calendars with their reliable winter and spring breaks, her vacations will be even less predictable. Take next summer—the open-endedness is enough to make Charlotte feel faint.

She strides into the living room, stops at the foot of the couch, and announces: "Let's stay up all night."

Emily lowers the magazine. "Excuse me?"

"We can make tea. Or—there's beer in the fridge." This being the six-pack of Sam Adams Summer Ale they had picked up for Walter. "I can heat up last night's leftovers if you want."

"You mean the Thai food you pretended to like?"

"I didn't pretend to like it. At least I was eating it."

She feels a ripple of tension as soon as she says it, a palpable movement in the room. The last thing she wants is to drag up last night's would-be eating disorder. She ignores it, hoping Emily will do the same.

"Come on," Charlotte says, perching on the sofa arm. "Let's do it. Let's stay up all night."

Emily raises an eyebrow.

"It'll be fun! We can talk, I'll make tea. We can eat the Thai food straight out of the boxes," she adds, because this seems a very sleepoverish thing to do.

"Okay," Emily says, with an amused smile. "But can I ask why?"

"Because it'll be fun! Remember that night you came home from Seattle?"

Emily's face furrows. "Which night that I came home from Seattle?"

Charlotte pauses. The night she's referring to, the summer of Emily's sixteenth birthday, the night she stayed up late playing music and brewing coffee, was so special to Charlotte, she's not sure she can handle knowing Emily has forgotten.

"Which night?" Emily prods. "There are tons of nights I came home from Seattle."

Tons? Charlotte is jarred, tongue-tied. It's a sensation she's grown used to whenever Emily mentions Seattle. Even after all these years, she's incapable of having a conversation about Joe or Valerie or the month of August without analyzing every word of it, every nuance, so the conversation moves in fits and starts, tapping one insecure nerve and then another, like the hammer the doctor uses to search your knee for reflexes. Now, Emily's saying that she's been to Seattle *tons* of times feels like an assertion of her closeness with Joe. When really, if you think about it, there haven't even been that many return trips. Certainly not *tons.* If she wanted to get literal, it would be return trips from Thanksgiving and return trips from August vacations each year from the time Emily was thirteen to twenty-one. That's eight years, two return trips a year. Sixteen total. Plus Joe's wedding. Seventeen.

"It was the year you turned sixteen," Charlotte ventures, carefully. "The year you brought home all that coffee."

Emily frowns.

"You had all that music with you—those new CDs. You talked about Kurt Cobain?"

"Mom, oh my God." Emily laughs. "I can't believe you remember that." Then she picks up the *People,* as if the mere mention of Nirvana reminded her of the wealth of pop culture sitting dormant on her lap.

But Charlotte is rattled. How could moments—whole phases—of Emily's childhood be completely forgotten? Moments that were still etched in such perfect detail in her own mind? It lent every moment in the present a thin, fleeting feeling. This visit, for instance. Emily would probably remember the first time she came to Mom's new condo. But would she remember the bag of arugula? The trip to Thai Heaven? The talking cat? Charlotte would remember all of these things.

Maybe this is just how memories work: the brain has only a finite capacity for them, so you hold on to the ones that make the deepest impression. If that's true, Charlotte guesses, the majority of the memories she carries are of her life with Emily on Dunleavy Street. She honestly can't imagine she's forgotten a single day of it. But her daughter's memories, she suspects, will be largely of other people, other places, things Charlotte can't even begin to know.

"Well, it doesn't matter," Charlotte decides. She isn't going to force the issue. With a little prodding, Emily might have remembered, but she doesn't need to know for sure. "But tonight we should stay up. At least until Walter gets here. It'll be like a little slumber party."

"Okay," Emily says, amused. "But you do realize I am going to be here for two more days, right?"

"Yes, but—"

But the difference between tonight and tomorrow is so obvious, Charlotte doesn't know how to explain it. She's hurt that she would even need to. How can Emily not recognize how completely different it will be once Walter gets here? That her visit, in essence, ends tonight?

"But those two days don't really count."

Emily looks up from her magazine. "Why not?"

"Well, no, they *count.* Of course they count. But you know what I mean. They won't be the same. We won't get this opportunity again."

"Which opportunity?"

"To be *alone,* Emily," Charlotte says, exasperated. "Just the two of us. Just you and me."

Emily tosses the *People* on the coffee table. All the images Charlotte had of staying up confiding over tea and Thai food go swirling down the drain.

"Mom."

"Yes, honey?"

"You don't want Walter to come here, do you."

"It isn't that," Charlotte lies.

"What is it, then? Do you not like him?"

"No."

"No, that's not it? Or no, you don't like him?"

"Honey, I hardly know him." Though at the moment, truth be told, she's fairly sure she doesn't like Walter. In fact, she might hate Walter. She certainly blames him for ruining her weekend.

"So maybe his visit will be good for you," Emily says, scratching her elbow. "Help you get to know him better. He's a fascinating person."

Charlotte clenches her teeth. She is so tired of all these *fascinating* people, these *fascinating* ideas and *fascinating* theories. "I'm sure he is."

Emily nods, as if Charlotte has just proven her point. Though what point that is, Charlotte has no idea. She's irritated by her daughter's air of knowingness, her presumption that she has her mother all figured out, when in reality Emily is missing the most obvious of truths: that Charlotte misses her daughter.

That she wants to spend time with her. She is lonely without her. Why should she have to spell out such a need?

All at once the anger Charlotte has been barely restraining since Walter's phone call comes rushing out. "If you want the truth, Emily, no, I don't want Walter coming here. And it isn't because I don't like Walter, it's just—we never get to spend time together. I never get to see you. *Just* you. You see Walter every day!"

She stops, blinking quickly. Emily's expression remains calm. Charlotte wonders if this was part of her teacher training: how to respond to unexpected outbursts in the alternative learning environment.

"Is there anything else you want to say?" Emily asks.

"Well, yes, as a matter of fact." Charlotte hoists herself higher on the sofa arm. Her voice is shaking, but she will not fall apart. "I want to know if you two planned this."

"Planned what?"

"This trip. Walter's trip. I want to know if you planned the trip before you left."

Emily doesn't reply, so she keeps on explaining.

"If you planned for Walter to come here tonight, planned for him to stay the two whole days you're—"

"Stop calling it a *plan.* There was no plan, Mom. It's not like this was some big plot Walter and I cooked up in our basement dungeon to trick you." Emily lets her head flop back against the pillows. "It's not one of your paranoid—" She stops, clicks her tongue.

"One of my what?" Charlotte says.

Emily speaks to the ceiling. "I had no idea Walter was coming. This morning was the first I heard of it. I swear."

"What did you mean before?"

"Nothing." Emily sits up and pulls her knees to her chest. "You can just get overly worried sometimes. And I'm saying, don't think this was some plot we made up to fool you, because it wasn't." She stares at her kneecaps, a soft pink slope under the fuzzy blankets. "If you want to know the truth—" She opens her mouth, then closes it. "If you want to know the truth, I *wasn't* completely surprised to hear Walter was coming. But not because we planned it. Because of reasons you know nothing about."

This revelation is delivered with a fair amount of drama. But it comes as no surprise to Charlotte. She's all too aware of these "reasons she knows nothing about"—the whispered phone calls, vague problems Emily will allude to but not explain. In fact, she's tired of them. When Emily and Walter's problems were confined to New Hampshire, to ask about them was prying. But now, Charlotte is involved. It's *her* house that will be the site of their fighting, or reconciling, or whatever happens when Walter pulls up in the middle of the night, and Charlotte wants to know what's going on. She's entitled to it.

"I want you to tell me what's going on with you and Walter." Charlotte pauses, squares her shoulders. "Now that he's coming, I think I deserve to know."

In the silence, Charlotte's gaze bounces around the room, skipping from the crowded bookshelves to the wood-paneled TV stand to the heavy curtains with their dull gold glow. When she alights on her daughter's face, Emily's expression is unchanged. If anything, it looks harder. More defiant. And the defiance is enough to firm Charlotte's own resolve. She's spent years being so careful, so respectful of Emily's privacy, never prying, never asking too much, trying to read her for signs of trouble, tiptoeing around the beige phone cord that strained so urgently from under the kitchen closet door. She is tired of being oblivious, out of it, "without it." Most of her life as a mother has been spent in the dark. Now, after all these years spent imagining dangers, she deserves to be told this one small thing.

But just as Charlotte is gearing up to say so, Emily's face softens. Her lips quiver. Two bright spots of pink appear on her cheeks. It's the same transformation Charlotte used to watch when she was a baby, right before she started to cry. She feels a familiar panic rising, like watching a wound open, wanting to heal it, make it stop. Emily wraps her arms across her knees and draws them under her chin. She drops her head down on her thin, freckled forearms. "I just don't want to get into it," she says, voice muffled by tears, or blankets, or both.

And just like that, Charlotte feels her anger melt. Her heart relent. Emily has always been capable of this—her fierce, tiny body brimming with so much feeling, so much drama, that she can evoke anger or tenderness within the same breath. Just being in her close proximity is, for Charlotte, something like being pregnant all over again: the hormonal shifts, the unpredictable mood swings, the emotional crescendos. The dynamic began with Emily's conception—kicking and squirming in Charlotte's gut, dictating her sleep patterns, pulling her strings—and has gone on ever since.

"Honey," Charlotte says. No longer is she the naive, out-of-it old lady. She is the mother again, the one whose job it is to comfort and listen. She lays a hand on the blanket covering Emily's feet. "Why don't you tell me what's going on?"

Emily's head is still bent, only the top exposed, the part in her hair endearingly crooked. "I don't know."

"Maybe I can help."

"I doubt it."

Charlotte rubs her feet; part in comfort, part encouragement. Finally Emily looks up and exhales a shuddery breath. "We're going through some kind of big stuff."

"What stuff?" Charlotte pounces. Too eager, she thinks.

"Just . . . some differences of opinion." Emily wipes a sleeve across her nose. "We're not seeing eye to eye on some things."

This time Charlotte waits a measured beat. "Like what?"

"Nothing tangible really." Emily hesitates. Charlotte can see her face working, looking for the right words. "It's more like differences in ideologies. Belief systems. I mean, I have strong opinions, Walter has strong opinions . . ."

Probably the kinds of opinions they didn't stop to consider before moving in together, Charlotte thinks. They jumped in, and now they're in over their heads.

"It's just hard to, I don't know, compromise sometimes. Or even know if you *should* compromise," Emily says. "I mean, if you really believe strongly in something, you shouldn't bend for someone. No matter who it is." She looks up at Charlotte, her cheeks flushed.

Charlotte gives her what she hopes is a reassuring smile. "You know," she says gently, "you don't have to keep living together."

Emily sighs. "That's not the point."

"But—it's just good to know you have options," she says quickly. "You can always move out. You can always move back here."

Emily looks at her incredulously. "This is so not about that." She flops backward. "Just forget it."

"What?"

"You're not *hearing* me. I'm not moving anywhere. I'm trying to do the opposite. I'm trying to—" She stops, then yanks the blanket up around her shoulders. "I know you have some weird thing against Walter, but we're a couple. We're together. You need to accept that."

Startled, Charlotte retracts her hand and tucks it between her knees. "But I thought you were having problems?"

Emily draws a deep breath. For a moment Charlotte thinks she might start confiding in her again, but she just looks down at her chewed fingernails and says, "It's complicated."

The insinuation is unmistakable. "Complicated" is something Charlotte can't understand. Because she's never had a "real" relationship. One that is passionate and turbulent, romantic and dramatic. She's had only Joe: ten years of politeness that receded into resentment and, finally, distance.

And Joe *has* managed to achieve a "real" relationship—at least in Emily's eyes. Over the years, Charlotte has listened to her recount fights between Joe and Valerie in which voices were raised and insults hurled and objects thrown—mirrors, phone books, bowls of Caesar salad—things Charlotte, when she was married, would have never dared do. It was strange imagining her ex-husband in this relationship, such a far cry from the tense calm of their marriage. And yet, though Charlotte had never seen that side of Joe outright, she wasn't surprised it was there. There had always been an undercurrent to him, something willful, temperamental. It was the quality he channeled into his trademark clipped humor, into jokes that were never really jokes, into running laps at the gym and playing video games. The quality that prevented Charlotte, for ten years, from ever feeling truly relaxed around him.

Emily, on the other hand, never seemed unnerved by these marital dramas. There was fascination—even admiration—in her tone as she described scenes of Joe yelling and Valerie storming out and how, afterward, they sat on their deck overlooking the crashing Pacific, holding hands, breathing in the salt air. Maybe, Charlotte thought bitterly, you can afford to have fights with your husband if your house has a deck with an ocean view. Fighting in South Jersey, well, that's more of a risk. Because afterward, where do you go? The bathroom? The basement? The garage, with its broken toy bikes and sagging lawn chairs? A wife could feel much more secure fighting with her husband if she knew they'd be stepping into a postcard after, that the tide would be there to carry their words away, the ocean air to dilute any anger they'd let loose.

She wonders in spite of herself how Valerie would handle this conversation. From her limited exposure to the woman, she knows Joe's new wife exudes no maternal quality. She's too fashionable, too angular, without hips or belly—it's obvious she devotes too much time to herself to be truly devoted to a child. She seems less like a mother than a remote, revered older cousin, one who moves in a mysterious world of college boys and Virginia Slims. Charlotte feels sure Emily would never let herself cry in front of her stepmother. (Charlotte hates that word, just the presence of "mother" inside it.) Yet she guesses Emily would be more forthcoming with Valerie, more likely to ask for advice. Valerie would probably offer inappropriate stories from her sordid dating past, then treat Emily to an impromptu shopping spree or rock concert.

It is as Charlotte is imagining Valerie and Emily with arms linked, wearing jeweled sunglasses and ripped jeans, elbowing their way through a crowd of sweaty teenagers, that she hears the noises from outside. The jangle of keys and the sounds of two voices: one female, one male.

She glances at Emily, who has lifted her head. Together, they listen to the sounds of feet stumbling up the stairwell. One a tinny, unsteady pair of high heels, the other a heavy, clomping set of work boots.

Charlotte looks at her daughter. To her relief, she finds a smile on her face.

"B. Morgan?" Emily whispers.

Charlotte nods, chewing on her bottom lip.

They listen, watching each other, as the floorboards begin to creak. A loud thud—a shoe kicked across the room?—is followed by the sounds of bodies tripping, stumbling lustily across B. Morgan's bedroom floor. Charlotte remembers what Emily said earlier and is flooded with unwanted images of handcuffs, whips, ropes. Within seconds, the crunching of bedsprings echoes through the ceiling. Charlotte feels her face turn red.

"My God." Emily flops backward on the couch and picks up the Victoria's Secret catalog. "That is the most boring prostitute I've ever heard."

When Charlotte hears the knock, her beside clock glows 2:37 A.M. Fear follows its usual progression: moment of alarm, surge, sweat. Racing heart. Bedside light. Quick survey of room to recall herself to where she is, the borders crystallizing between being asleep and awake. It takes a moment to realize that, while usually these knocks are only in her head, this one is real. She hears it again, then remembers Walter. The knock is tentative, probably not loud enough for Emily to hear.

Charlotte gets out of bed and pulls on her old orange robe. The butterflies, she notes, are beginning to fray around the wings. She waits a moment longer, ear to door, making sure Emily isn't getting up. But there's the knock again: a notch louder, but nothing capable of waking Emily.

Charlotte knots her belt around her middle. She thinks despairingly of her bare face and worn robe and pillow-matted hair before stepping out of her bedroom and into the hall. She unbolts the front door and opens it just a crack. Sure enough, Walter is squinting in the fluorescent glow of the porch light. Behind him, a taxi is winding down the driveway toward the street.

"Charlotte?" Walter whispers.

"Yes?"

"I thought Em was going to let me in."

"She's asleep."

"Oh." He pauses. "Oh, man. I'm sorry."

A moth finds the porch light and flings itself, buzzing, against the glass. In the square of orangey light, Walter looks different than he did at graduation. What he wore that day—the short Afro, the blue jeans, the scruffy hint of beard—is the way Charlotte has been picturing him ever since. Tonight, he has on sneakers and running pants with white stripes down the sides. He's clean-shaven, his hair coiled in braids, or cornrows—are they still called cornrows?—tight against his head. The earrings and eyebrow ring are missing. The wooden cross around his neck remains.

"I'm sorry," he says again, shifting his feet. "Em was supposed to let me in. You were supposed to sleep right through it. I'm really sorry."

Charlotte can't help but feel a little sorry for the boy. She feels the chill creeping in from outside and knots her robe tighter, folds her arms across her chest.

"It's fine." She whispers too, though she's not sure why. After all, the idea is to wake Emily. "I was awake anyway."

Walter half nods, clearly not believing her. Behind him, the cab's taillights disappear, the rumble of the engine melting away.

Charlotte clears her throat and speaks louder. "Well, come on in." She widens the door a bit. "It's too cold to stand out there."

She takes a step backward and is so preoccupied with her blank face and ratty robe that she's caught completely off guard when Walter, stepping over the threshold, says, "Good to see you again, Charlotte," and enfolds her in a tight hug.

It happens so quickly, she doesn't have time to react. Her chin is pressed against Walter's collarbone. Her arms, still folded, are lodged awkwardly between her chest and his. She has no free hand to return the hug, or even pat his shoulder in a maternal sort of way, and before she knows it, he's standing in the middle of the foyer a good three feet away.

Charlotte shuts the door, feeling herself redden. She hopes she hasn't offended him by not returning the hug, hopes he can't see her face. In the weak light spilling from the hallway, she can barely make out his. She can see, however, that he's still holding his duffel bag.

"Can I take your bag, Walter?"

"Nah, I got it."

"How about a drink? Some water? Or—root beer?"

"No, thanks."

"I have beer, too. Sam Adams Summer Ale. How about a Sam Adams Summer Ale and something to eat? I have some pasta alfredo I can heat up. Take me two minutes. You must be starving."

"I'm good." He laughs a little, shifts the bag to his other hand. "I've been enough trouble already, waking you up."

"I was awake anyway." For some reason, she wants him to believe this. "I was."

"All right." He nods. "Okay. Well, I appreciate it."

A sleepy voice calls out from the living room. "Wal?"

"Hey in there," Walter says. His voice instantly loses its formality, growing tender. "Wake up, sleepyhead."

"What are you doing?" Emily murmurs.

"Talking to your mom."

Charlotte looks at her feet.

"She had to get up to let me in."

"Oh," Emily says, the word riding on a long yawn. "Sorry, Mom."

Walter adds, "Sorry again, Charlotte," before moving in the direction of Emily's voice. The dark in the living room is fuzzy, gray-black, tinged with the faint light from the patio. Charlotte can just make out Emily's silhouette sitting up, Walter's form easing toward her. When she lifts her face toward his, Charlotte hurries back to her room.

chapter three

Charlotte watches the clock. She's perched on the edge of her bed, hands folded in her lap. She's quarantined herself to her bedroom until 9:30 A.M., not wanting to emerge too early and risk waking Emily and Walter or, worse, interrupt something—changing, fighting, cuddling, God knows what else—by coming out too late. Best to catch them somewhere between deeply asleep and fully conscious. Nine-thirty seems right.

She focuses on the objects on her dresser, trying to keep her mind a blank. Framed photo from her parents' wedding. Bottle of Jergens extra-moisturizing lotion. Domed gold clock, its elegant hands like the stems of typewriter keys. The purple perfume bottle Emily once bought her at a yard sale, its ornate pump and tassel so unlike Charlotte they struck Emily as hilarious.

Charlotte tries to fill her mind with these things, their angles and colors and shapes. Unfortunately, she can't keep her mind from sneaking out the door, down the hall, and to the living room, where she imagines Walter and Emily entwined in the tangle of sheets. What were they wearing? How were they sleeping? Was Emily sleeping on her back, like she always used to? Or did she fit inside him, curled on her side, his breath on her neck?

She stares at the limp chain dangling from the ceiling fan. Its tarnished beads look like a string of black-eyed peas. She realizes she'd forgotten to remind Emily how the sofa bed worked—well, not forgotten. To have acknowledged that the sofa turned into a bed would have been acknowledging that Walter and Emily were sleeping in a bed, a reality Charlotte was trying her best to avoid. If they didn't have a conversation about it, she wasn't condoning it. Nor was she objecting to it. She'd left out an extra set of bedding without comment, stacked under the extra set of towels. For all she knew, Walter slept on the floor.

Of course, if the sleeping arrangements had really been bothering her, she should have spoken up. But really, when? This plan had been dropped on her so abruptly. Maybe if they'd stayed up gossiping and eating Thai food out of cartons like she'd wanted to, she could have brought it up when the moment felt right. But now a sleeping precedent had been set. To object tonight would be silly. *We live together!* Emily would argue. *We sleep in the same bed every night!* Charlotte doesn't want to make any more waves, especially now that Walter's here. And even if they did sleep separately, where would they go? Emily would sleep with her, she supposed, Walter would take the couch . . . oh, it was simpler to just not ask.

When the filigreed tip of the minute hand grazes the six, Charlotte stands. She gives herself one more quick survey in the mirror. Unlike last night, today she is fully showered, concealed, arranged. She even took special care with her makeup, applying a light foundation all over her face to make up for the sight she must have been at 2:37 A.M. She opens the door. No sound from the living room, but the world outside is awake. She hears the slam of a car door, the rustling of leaves, bark of a dog. She can even smell a neighbor's coffee brewing. Yes, she thinks: her timing is right. Not too early, not too late. She'll make pancakes. No—too sizzly. Muffins. Quiet dollops of batter and a silent thirty-minute bake.

Charlotte steps lightly toward the kitchen, calculating how much flour she has, whether the blueberries she bought Monday will still be fresh, and is startled to find Walter sitting at the table. He's paging through the well-worn *People* and sipping coffee from WESLEYAN UNIVERSITY.

"Hey." He smiles and raises his cup. "Morning, Charlotte."

He's wearing the same running pants he arrived in, dark blue with stripes down the sides. A ribbed gray tank top bares his muscled arms. And the jewelry is back: ring in his brow, diamond in each ear.

"Walter, I—I didn't expect to see you up so early."

"I've been up a while." He shrugs. "Em's the sleeper. I like to get the day going, you know?"

She does know, more than he knows. She looks at the full coffeemaker, usually her first stop, and is at a loss for what to do.

"Hope you don't mind I made the coffee."

"No, no, not at all."

"It's one of my talents."

"Oh?"

"Seriously, I make a good cup of coffee." He grins. "Woodworking and coffeemaking. Not a bad package, huh?"

Charlotte can manage nothing but a nervous smile. It sounds as if Walter is kidding, or flirting—is he flirting? Whatever his tone, she doesn't understand it. Maybe his humor is young for her, too hip, or too, well, urban. Urban? Does she mean black?

"Nice day out, huh?"

"Oh, yes." She glances toward the window. "Lovely."

In truth, the sunlight is so bright she finds herself squinting. Walter opened the blinds all the way; usually she leaves them half open, slanted upward, giving her just enough light to see by yet total privacy from her neighbors.

"Bright," she adds. The light makes the braids glisten in Walter's hair. The silver ring glints in his eyebrow. When she turns to the cabinet, white spots swarm before her eyes.

"Good day for a jog," Walter says.

Maybe he'll take a jog right now. "It is."

She opens the refrigerator, extracts a carton of milk from the door. It occurs to her that Walter must have been in here—for the coffee grounds, if nothing else—and this makes her feel acutely embarrassed. She scans the contents: Slim-Fast shakes, fat-free margarine, low-cal whipped cream. She pictures the Weight Watchers Smart Ones stacked in the freezer, their fancy menus—piccatas, marsalas—packaged into lonely, frozen portions for one. Her mind races to the bathroom cabinets: wrinkle concealer, wart remover, antacids in assorted tropical fruits.

Charlotte shuts the refrigerator, not caring if the noise wakes Emily. She *should* be woken. She invited Walter and should be out here keeping him entertained.

"Hey, this any good?"

She turns to see Walter flipping through the book still sitting on the windowsill where Emily left it. She can hear Emily ranting about corporate book clubs: *The books are all the same, Mom! Mediocre writing with an unrealistically hopeful ending!*

"I'm enjoying it," Charlotte says carefully. She likes the hopeful endings, even if they do sometimes feel a bit forced. "But—I didn't choose it."

"One of Em's?"

"It's for my book group."

"Yeah?" Walter says, scanning the back cover. "What's your book group?"

Charlotte wishes he would just leave her and her things alone. Put down the book, stay out of the fridge, stay away from the coffeemaker, do not open the bathroom cabinet, do not touch the blinds, do not feel obligated to make comments or ask questions. She feels like a charity case: the girlfriend's mother the boyfriend must treat politely until the girlfriend shows up.

"It's just a group of women," Charlotte says, pouring carefully. "Friends from my old neighborhood. Not even friends, exactly—our children went to school together."

"Okay," Walter nods. "Friends by default. So how does the group work?"

Charlotte stirs a half teaspoon of sugar into her cup. "It's not too exciting, really. We just read a book each month, then get together to talk about it." She puts her spoon down. Then, because she feels too awkward drinking standing up, she pulls out a chair and perches stiffly on the edge.

"I'd love to get into something like that." Walter cracks the book open and now appears to be reading the inside flap. "How does it work? Who picks them?"

"Well—" Discreetly, Charlotte scoots a few inches back on her chair until her whole rear is safely on it. "First we tried rotating—you know, one person choosing the book each month. But that didn't work very well."

"How come?"

She takes a sip of coffee. It is good, she has to admit, less watery than when she makes it. "Some people have very different tastes, for one. Some were just petty about it, refusing to read what others picked because they hadn't liked the book *they* picked, or they didn't like them personally, that sort of thing. People can be difficult for the sake of being difficult."

"I hear you," Walter says, shaking his head. He picks up his coffee mug, watching her over the rim. "What book did you pick?"

Charlotte crosses her feet at the ankle. She can't imagine any of this is actually interesting to Walter, knows he is just being polite. Still, she has to admit it is nice to be asked. "Anne Tyler?"

He nods.

She takes another sip. "*Dinner at the—*"

"Hold up." Walter tilts his chair forward and reaches across the table, taking Charlotte by the wrist. "The coffee."

She looks at him blankly, pulse fluttering in her throat.

"It's good, right?"

She swallows, laughs a little. "It *is* good."

"Told you," he says, taking his hand away. He tilts his chair back again and picks up his mug, grinning triumphantly. "You were saying. Dinner."

"Right." Charlotte looks at the table for a moment, trying to resume her train of thought. She can still feel the pressure of Walter's hand on her wrist. "It's a book called *Dinner at the Homesick Restaurant.*"

"Cool title." He takes a deep swallow of coffee and leans his chair back, balancing on the back legs. "So what happened? Did they go for it?"

"They did, eventually. To be honest, I don't think most of them really care, they just like the debating. Some weeks picking the books takes just as long as talking about them."

Walter rolls his eyes and expels a deep sigh. "Women."

There's such sincere commiseration in the word, such world-weariness, that Charlotte can't help but laugh. "Yes. Well." She looks down at her mug, touches the handle. "There are some strong personalities in the group, that's for sure."

"Like who?" He leans forward again, bringing the chair legs clattering to the tile, and hunches over the table as if poring over a battle plan. "Give me names."

She pauses. "Well, there's Rita, I guess."

"Last name?"

"Curran."

"Damn that Rita Curran. What's her problem?"

"There's no *problem,* exactly. She's a nice woman—"

"Charlotte?" Walter raises an eyebrow. "Don't hold out on me."

Charlotte smiles in spite of herself. "In that case, I guess she can be very know-it-all sometimes—one of those people who thinks she sees symbolism in everything, you know? I mean, I know most books have symbolism in them, but sometimes Rita takes it a little far."

Walter is nodding, listening intently. It appears as if Fascinating Walter actually finds *her* fascinating. Fascinating Charlotte.

"Like last month, we were discussing a dinner scene, and the woman in the scene was holding a fork. Rita thought the fork represented a pitchfork, which meant that the character was Satan."

"Was she?"

"Was she what?"

"Satan?"

"I don't think so. I think she was just cutting her filet mignon."

Charlotte laughs then, a real laugh, and Walter laughs too.

From the living room, Emily calls, "Hey, what's so funny in there?"

Charlotte stops laughing, but Walter bellows back: "Why don't you get up and find out!"

"It's so *ear*ly . . ."

Charlotte glances at her watch.

"Hey, kid," Walter says. "I'm wide awake and I was in a cab six hours ago. Get your tired butt in here."

Charlotte looks into her coffee. She's never heard anyone speak to Emily this way: challenging her, teasing her, refusing to indulge her. Emily's has always been such a strong, stormy personality that, historically, people have simply stepped aside to make room for it. This was true of Joe, of Valerie, of an endless string of friends and roommates and boyfriends. And most of all, of Charlotte.

She hears Emily sigh dramatically, then pad across the living room rug. In the kitchen doorway she appears with bare feet, wearing a men's white V-neck undershirt and baggy plaid pants. "You guys are nuts."

"Hey, lazy," Walter replies.

"Hi."

Emily sits down next to him. He kisses her cheek.

Charlotte stands. "Coffee, honey?"

"Yes, please."

"Walter made it."

"Of course he did." Emily yawns, stretching her arms toward the ceiling, T-shirt rising to expose her belly ring. She deepens her voice and says, "Woodworking and coffeemaking. Not a bad package, huh?"

Walter tickles her armpit. Emily yelps, clutching her arms to her sides. "No, Wal, get off me! Get off!"

"Come on," he teases her. "You want a piece of this?"

"It's too early!"

"Fine." He raises his hands in surrender, then whispers loudly near her ear. "Punk."

She narrows her eyes at him, a smile squirming on her lips. "Goody-goody."

Walter lifts her shirt and tickles her. Emily lets out another squeal. Charlotte turns to the counter just as she hears the squelch of a kiss.

"I was going to make muffins," she says, fixing her attention on pouring coffee into YOU CAN'T BE COOL. "Or pancakes. Would you two like pancakes?"

"Don't go to any trouble, Charlotte."

"She doesn't mind," Emily says, slightly out of breath.

Charlotte turns and sets the coffee on the table. She can see the dark outline of Emily's nipples through her shirt.

"She loves doing for others," Emily says, sliding Walter's silver ring up and down his knuckle. "It's the thing that makes her happiest in the world. Aren't I right, Mom?"

It's one of those moments, like so many moments, that treads the line between harmless conversation and subtle criticism. Before Charlotte can shrug and laugh and respond that it's not a big deal, it's no bother—it's just a few *pancakes*—Walter hops out of his chair, saying, "Wait! I almost forgot."

He lopes from the kitchen, his running pants making a quick, swishing sound. From the living room, Charlotte can hear the sound of a duffel bag being unzipped. When she glances at Emily, she appears preoccupied, blowing ripples across the surface of her coffee.

"Here." Walter reappears, presenting Charlotte with what looks like a box of candy, slightly smushed. "Brought you something."

"Oh." *Needhams,* says the curling script on top. "Walter, you shouldn't have."

"They're Needhams."

"I see."

"It's a candy. Not exactly breakfast food, but—"

"Oh no, it's perfect. It's very thoughtful of you."

As Walter resumes his seat, Charlotte skims the ingredients: mashed potatoes, coconut, chocolate. Mashed potatoes and chocolate? How strange. Maybe it's a black food. Oh, what an awful thing to think. But—is it? An awful thing? Had it been an Irish boy bringing soda bread, or a German boy bringing sauerkraut, it would have been perfectly fine to think that—

"They're a local thing," Walter explains, as if in answer to her thoughts. "New England tradition."

"Oh. Well, they look very interesting." She turns to retrieve a dish. "Thank you very much."

From behind her, Charlotte hears Emily whisper, "Kiss-ass." Charlotte stiffens, wishing she hadn't said it. It denigrates the gesture somehow, makes it something less genuine than it seemed.

"I bet it's better than what you brought," Walter teases back.

Charlotte opens the box and arranges eight dark square chocolates, equidistant from one another, around the perimeter of the plate.

"I bet you didn't bring anything for your mom."

"I did too!"

"Yeah? What?"

Charlotte turns and places the dish on the table. Walter gives her a knowing wink. "Some kind of vegetable, right, Charlotte?"

"It was arugula!" Emily interjects. "From our garden! Don't you go knocking the arugula, Wal! You like it!"

"I know I like it. Hell, I planted it. I also like giving you a hard time."

He grins and puts his hand on her knee. Emily knocks it away, but a smile twitches on her lips. Charlotte finds it hard to believe this trip all started because these two were having problems. If they are, she can't detect a trace. Maybe they're just hiding it well. No, that can't be it—Emily is no good at hiding anything, even when a situation calls for it. Hiding things offends her basic moral code.

Maybe it's just that affection is more casual, less meaningful, for them than it is for Charlotte. Clearly, Walter is a naturally affectionate person. Maybe he was simply raised in that kind of environment. Charlotte pictures gospel churches, potluck suppers, affectionate aunts and mothers and grandmothers. Could it be a cultural difference, his ease with older women?

"You know what we should do?" Emily says.

She looks up. Emily is fully awake now, her face flushed, eyes sparkling.

"Take the train up to New York and see a play."

Charlotte feels a lump rise in her throat. She smiles faintly and lifts her mug, hoping this plan, like many of Emily's plans, is forgotten quickly in the interest of something else.

"We are *so* culture-starved up in New Hampshire," Emily laments, appealing to Walter. "And I haven't been to the city for-*ever.*"

"Fine with me," he says.

Charlotte feels herself grow warm. The mere thought of New York City calls up images of speeding taxis, dark alleys, shootings, crushing crowds.

"Sound good to you, Charlotte?" he says. "You catch a lot of plays?"

"I really don't," she admits. "I should, I know—"

"Mom doesn't get out much."

"Emily," she says quickly. "That's not true."

"Fine. You go out. But you don't go into the city to see theater." She turns to Walter. "Last night she tried Thai food for the first time."

Charlotte looks at the table. Trying Thai food now seems like a walk in the park compared to the prospect of venturing into "the city" to see "theater." Much as it pains her to give up any of her time with Emily, she lifts her mug and says: "You two should go without me."

"No way." Emily's voice is firm. "We're all going. We'll catch a train, grab some Vietnamese, and see *The Vagina Monologues.* I've been absolutely *dying* to see that. It's supposed to be amazing."

Before Charlotte can launch several more protests, involving Vietnamese food and vaginas, Walter interjects: "Here's an idea, Em. How about you don't speak for all three of us?"

Charlotte freezes, mug held in midair. She stares at Walter, part in gratitude, part in awe, part in fear for what Emily will do next.

Emily flops backward in her chair and crosses her arms over her chest. Her tongue ring clicks once, twice. "Fine."

"Oh, come on." Walter extracts one of her limp hands. She pulls it away. "It's a good idea, let's just make sure we're all on the same page. How about after breakfast I jump online and see what tickets are still out there, what's playing where—"

"My mom doesn't have Internet."

Charlotte apologizes. "I'm a little behind the times."

"No big deal," Walter says. "My parents don't have it either. I'll make a few calls and check it out. Okay?"

"Okay," Charlotte answers, feeling helpless.

"Okay, you?" He pushes Emily's hair behind her ear and kisses her cheek. She frowns. Then, in one motion, Walter reaches across the table, grabs a Needham and pops it in his mouth.

"Oh, I can't believe you just ate that!" Emily says, springing forward. "That will stick in your intestines for, literally, the rest of your life, Walter."

"Yeah?" He picks one up and holds it to her lips. "Open up."

"No!" Emily squeals.

"Open!"

Emily presses her lips together, tossing her head from side to side, kicking her bare feet as if paddling with a kickboard. When one foot knocks against the table, coffee sloshes over the lip of Emily's mug. Neither of them notices. Walter is busy pinching Emily's nose to force open her mouth, and she is giggling and gasping.

Charlotte watches the spilled coffee inch toward the edge of the table. She's beginning to feel uncomfortable, as if Walter and Emily are in the midst of some kind of foreplay that she's not only intruding on but encouraging somehow, her presence making it more taboo. Only when the coffee starts drizzling onto the floor do they jump apart.

"Damn!" Walter says, grabbing a handful of napkins. Emily pulls her feet out of the way. He leans over her lap to wipe the floor, then sops up the coffee on the table.

"What a good guest," Emily says, patting his head.

"Got some chocolate on your face," he replies.

Emily smiles to herself as she watches Walter cross the room to throw away the napkins. Distractedly, she runs the tip of her studded tongue along the corners of her mouth, missing the smudge of chocolate just under her nose.

"So, Mommy," she says, but her eyes are on Walter. "What are you doing today?"

To Charlotte, the subtext could not be more obvious: *When are you leaving the house so we can have sex?*

"Well," Charlotte says, as Walter picks up his mug to refill it, "I have the book group this afternoon."

Emily pauses, retracts her tongue, looks at Charlotte. "I thought you weren't going to that?"

"I changed my mind."

"Why?"

Charlotte doesn't answer. She is through clarifying things. Through explaining, through apologizing, through spelling things out. She looks at her daughter for a long moment, and when she does, a look of real sadness and, finally, understanding, crosses Emily's face.

"Mom, no," Emily says, sitting up straight. "Stay. Hang out with us."

"I don't think so."

"Come on. Please."

"You never know, Emily." Charlotte brushes an invisible crumb from the table. "The book group may need me."

If her tone is horribly self-deprecating, Walter doesn't seem to notice. He plunks his mug on the table and drops back in his chair, saying, "It's true, Em. She might need to decode some forks. Isn't that right, Charlotte?"

Charlotte smiles at him weakly.

Walter grins back, then reaches out to erase the smudge of chocolate from Emily's face.

When Charlotte leaves for the book group, Walter and Emily are on the couch, reading. He's sitting on one end, face bent over a magazine. She's lying down, head resting on his lap. Her feet are crossed at the ankle, smothered in thick rag socks, and she's holding a paperback book over her face. They've refilled their mugs, which sit steaming on coasters on the coffee table beside them. They look more at home here than Charlotte has felt in two months.

"I'm off!" she calls from the foyer.

Emily sits up quickly, swiveling her head around. "Okay, Mom, bye," she says. "Have a good time. See you when you get back."

Walter calls over his shoulder, "Put Rita in her place, Charlotte!"

When she goes to open the front door, Charlotte realizes the chain is unhinged. Not only that, the deadbolt is open. The knob is unlocked. She must have been so disoriented last night that she never relocked the door. She stares at the locks for a long minute, the carelessly loose links of the gold chain, the gap between door and sill where the solid brass of the bolt should be. It's the first time she's forgotten to lock her house in twenty-four years.

"Charlotte! What are you doing here?"

This is the reason she had contemplated doing some shopping instead of actually showing up to the book group: having to explain to the others why she's there.

"I thought Emily was in town?" says Rita. The group is meeting at her house this week and is clustered in the living room, a highly coordinated palette of stain-free creams and pale pinks. The perfect color scheme is dotted here and there with bright spinach puffs, lemon squares, cherry pinwheels, each with Saran Wrap coverings tucked like petticoats under the sides of their plates.

"She is," Charlotte says, as casually as possible.

"Is she still here?"

"Did she leave early?"

"Is she sleeping late?"

"Is something wrong, Charlotte?"

This last question is from Linda Hill, and is the only one that stems from genuine concern. Charlotte looks at Linda, at the deep triangle of wrinkles between her eyes. She thinks of Rachel in the eating disorders clinic in Philadelphia. She knows that, for Linda, "something wrong" can never again be a casual question, but carries the possibilities of serious, once unimaginable, things.

"Nothing's wrong," she says, for Linda's sake. "Emily's boyfriend showed up last night."

"I didn't know Emily had a boyfriend!" Rita settles onto a suede ottoman and assumes her "do-tell" pose: bent forward, legs entwined, chin cupped in hand. "How long has it been going on? Is it serious?"

Charlotte has never mentioned Walter to the group, and until now she hasn't stopped to examine why. Swapping news about their children was half the purpose of their meetings, and she'd never hesitated to mention Emily's boyfriends before. Was she embarrassed to admit Emily and Walter lived together? She'd like to believe that was the whole story, but the worse—and perhaps truer—reason was Walter's race. Was it possible she didn't want to admit he was black? To avoid the group's raised eyebrows and skittery responses? Could she be that afraid?

She recalls again the way Walter handled Emily this morning. He was so unfazed by her, challenging her assertions, laughing off her wayward moods. For Charlotte, Emily's dramatics had always provoked an immediate need to appease. But watching Walter, it occurred to her that Emily's angry flashes were not insurmountable. If anything, they were little burrs, tangles, nothing with real staying power. Walter would entertain them, toy with them, contest them, and Emily's anger would simply be shucked off and set free.

"Where did she meet him?" the group wants to know.

"How old is he?"

"Where does he live?"

"Do you like him?"

"I do," Charlotte says and realizes, as she says it, that it's true. "His name is Walter. They met at Wesleyan. They graduated in the same class."

Charlotte pauses and surveys the crowd, their faces hungry for more, and decides to deliver. "Now they live together, in New Hampshire, and he's black."

It is a rare day that Rita Curran is speechless, and in the silence that befalls the cream-and-pale-pink living room Charlotte feels a surprising sense of satisfaction, followed by a prickle of guilt. For which is worse: not mentioning Walter at all, or trotting him out for his shock value? To mention him and *not* mention his race would have felt deceitful somehow—as if she were embarrassed by it and deliberately concealing information. Then again, if she were being truly honest, she could tell them so much more. How Walter makes her nervous. How she doesn't know how to read him. How simply being near him has her in a constant state of self-beratement, doubt, worry, fear that she's offended him, said or done the wrong thing.

Charlotte looks at her lap. Her brain is tired. All this debating, analyzing, second-guessing—her life has never involved issues like these before. Not that she hasn't lived in a state of constant worry, God knows she has, but those worries revolved around what to make for dinner, how to dress for weather, how to structure her evening so she finished loading the dishwasher at the exact moment *Jeopardy!* began. Issues of political correctness—"PC," as Emily calls it—are so complex. There are so many rules. She wonders if there's a manual she can buy for this sort of thing.

Kit Hapley breaks the silence. "Well, I think it's *wonderful.*" Her tone is overly, annoyingly sincere, designed to convey her evolved liberal-mindedness.

"Yes," the others murmur. "Wonderful."

Charlotte bites into a spinach puff.

"So," says Rita, going for the dirt, "where are the lovebirds now?"

"I don't know," Charlotte admits, swallowing. "I thought I'd give them some privacy. He just arrived last night, after all."

This time there's no question she's acting cooler than she is. But she's not about to admit her real reason for leaving: that she felt she was in the way, an intrusion in her own home. That she feels her daughter and her boyfriend have more of a right to be in her new condo than she does.

Suddenly, from the front porch, there is a stampede of footsteps. The door bursts open to admit a flood of teenage boys.

"Shoes!" Rita yells, on autopilot. "Shoes by the door, please!"

A mound of shoes materializes next to the umbrella stand: sneakers with shiny swollen casings, sandals with Velcro black straps flapping like loose tongues. The swarm of bodies migrates from the doorway to the plate of M&M brownies, their hands smothering it like a Betty Crocker commercial.

"Just one!" Rita commands. "One only!"

The crowd heads for the basement in a mass of jostling bodies, low laughter, socked feet, brownies devoured whole. They thunder down the carpeted stairs, gone as quickly as they appeared, leaving behind a stir of warmth and energy, crumbs and shoes in an endearing disarray. From the basement, the bass line of the stereo starts thumping through the floor.

Rita marches to the basement door, opens it, flicks the lights on and off. "Volume!"

A beat later, the music goes down.

"Thank you!" she calls, and shuts the door.

This, Charlotte thinks, is raising boys. It is avoiding stains, controlling portions, turning music down. Raising girls is about the intangibles, the moods and feelings and secret thoughts that swim beneath the skin, just out of reach. Even the tangible things happen on the inside: getting periods, counting calories, having sex. Boys are nicked, scratched, punched, wrapped in a condom, put in a sling. With a girl, there is so much more a mother doesn't see. Charlotte glances at Linda Hill, who flashes her a smile of what looks like empathy.

"Well!" Rita resumes her chair and smiles brightly, opening her book. "Shall we begin?"

Back at the condo, Charlotte tries to sense the presence of sex. She's not sure what she's searching for exactly: a stray sock, a shirt tossed carelessly over a chair back, or something less definable. A smell, maybe. A stir of passion in the air. But the couch is folded up neatly (this must have been Walter's doing). Coffee mugs are rinsed and set upside down in the dishwasher. Everything is tidied, replaced, repackaged, as it was before.

And yet, there is a tremor of something. Charlotte can feel it. Not necessarily sexual, but the feeling of something made vulnerable, exposed. The blinds in the living room and kitchen are open, light filling the rooms in unfamiliar patterns—short white stripes brightening the floors, long pale bands yawning down the bookshelves. The patio door has been cracked open, letting the autumn air leak inside, air that carries with it the smells of distant fires, the sharpness of coming cold. Charlotte peeks through the opening in the sliding door, expecting to see Emily or Walter or both, but the patio is deserted. They've assembled the chairs, though; each aluminum frame is now softened with a cushion of twining vines and purple flowers.

From the bathroom, Charlotte hears a squeak and the rush of water hitting the tub floor. She tenses. Is that where they are? Maybe the reason the house felt so undisrupted is that they've contained their disruption to the bathtub, slipping under the new lavender bubbles, letting the room fill with thick steam. But would they really risk it? Maybe they expected Charlotte home much later. Or maybe, for them, sharing a bath doesn't seem out of line. Maybe they will emerge any minute now, Walter with chest bared, towel slung around his waist, wooden cross resting on his breastbone. Emily will be drowning in a towel, hair piled messily on top of her head, bare legs covered with the downy hairs she refuses to shave.

Charlotte steps onto the garden patio. She sits down carefully in one of the chairs, hears a faint hiss as the puffy cushion deflates beneath her. It is pleasant out here, she has to admit. She should use it more often.

"Hey."

Charlotte jumps and looks over her shoulder. There's Walter, filling the doorframe, arms over his head and hands gripping the sill. To her relief, he's fully dressed and dry. Emily must be in the tub alone.

"Sorry." He steps outside. "Did I scare you? Again?"

Was that an edge to his voice? Did he think it was suspicious, her tendency to jump at his presence? That her alarm was something personal? Something racial? With every word out of her mouth, every move she makes, Charlotte feels like she is trapped in another quandary of political correctness.

"Oh, no," she says. "Just lost in thought, I guess."

"I was checking out your laptop." Walter moves to the other side of the table and drops into the empty chair. "Hope you don't mind."

"Oh." Her mind flits nervously to the few journal entries she'd attempted to "open new" and "save as"—what was in them? Could he have read them?

"Em said it'd be okay," he adds.

"Oh, it is," she assures him, trying to appear unfazed. The truth was, she would rather Walter be scouring her journal entries, even snooping in her medicine cabinet, than in the tub with her daughter, a bath glove, and an assortment of products from Bed, Bath and Beyond. "No problem at all."

"How was the book group?"

"Oh, you know." What would he say if she told him that he was a highlight of the afternoon? "The usual."

"Rita acting up?"

"Rita was being Rita. Finding symbolism everywhere, of course. Today she was particularly interested in the toaster as a metaphor for giving birth."

Walter smiles, but it is a tight smile, without his earlier exuberance. In fact, his smile looks a little sad. Charlotte wonders if he and Emily had a fight while she was gone. He's staring into the yard, a tidy square of clipped grass with a few balled bushes, identical to the clipped grass and balled bushes of the condos on either side. He's probably comparing it to their garden in New Hampshire, Charlotte thinks. A real garden, one with vegetables and flowers and roots and, well, purpose.

Walter leans forward, elbows on his knees. "Listen, Charlotte."

She looks at him in surprise. "Yes?"

He opens his mouth as if to say more, then licks his lips and looks down at his hands. The long fingers are knotted loosely, cradled between his knees, a casual approximation of prayer. It's the same way Joe used to hold his hands on the rare occasions he found himself in churches: weddings, christenings, Charlotte's parents' funerals. At her father's, he'd been sitting beside her; at her mother's, a year after the divorce, he'd slumped like a distant cousin in the back of the church.

"Man, this isn't easy," Walter says, laughing a little. When he sits back and licks his lips again, Charlotte realizes he is nervous. His nervousness makes her nervous.

"Walter? What is it?"

He inhales deeply through his nose, then leans forward again. "Okay. Here it is. There's something I want to talk to you about."

Suddenly she can hear her heart.

"It's actually the reason I wanted to come down here this weekend." His hands are flat now, palm to palm, fingers pressed tightly together. "To talk to you."

So overwhelming is Charlotte's fear that she senses herself beginning to detach as he speaks, her body shutting down automatically, like an iron left on by mistake. She surveys the yard, recording it, memorizing it, storing it away for future use. Because at the same time she is living this moment, she is suddenly, acutely aware that this lawn, this afternoon, these flowered chair cushions, are about to become the trappings of a significant memory for the rest of her life. From inside, she hears the faint trickle of the tub: warm water to keep the bath from going cool, dribbling down Emily's feet.

"I wanted to talk to you this morning," Walter is saying, "but I was afraid Em might hear."

She realizes what's happening: he wants to marry her. That's what this is about. He's asking her permission to propose. The first thing she feels is relief, that it isn't something worse. The second, unreasonably maybe, is anger at Joe. This should be *his* question. This is the father's responsibility. Unless Walter has already talked to him. Maybe they've already had some back-slapping, congratulatory conversation, and Walter just doesn't want Charlotte feeling left out. Because Joe would condone the marriage, of course. Bless it. No, "bless" is the wrong word. Nothing about Joe has ever been religious, not even superficially.

Charlotte blinks. Her mind is sprawling nervously, illogically. An image of a pale blue mother-of-the-bride dress with pearl brocade floats through her brain, quickly replaced by an image of Valerie in burgundy lipstick, sipping a glass of champagne and leaving a deep red stain.

"She doesn't know I'm talking to you about this."

Charlotte nods, tries to focus on his words.

"She's going to kill me when she finds out."

Of course. Emily would find the idea of asking permission for anything—much less her own marriage—unacceptable.

"Go ahead, Walter," Charlotte says. To her own ears, her voice sounds impossibly calm. Her thumping pulse has quieted now, ready for his question. "You can ask me."

Walter gives her a funny look. "There's nothing to *ask,* really. But it's something I think you should know."

At that, the heartsound Charlotte had tamped down a moment ago rises again full force. Blood crashes in her ears, her head, at the surface of her chest. So strong is the sheer force of it that she can't imagine her body isn't physically jolting with each beat. *Something I think you should know. Something I think you should know.* Her heart beats in the palms of her hands. This isn't a marriage proposal. This is something awful. Unimaginable. An eating disorder, an illness, the reason Emily seemed so listless and out of sorts. It's something threatening to harm her daughter, consume her, eat her alive.

"Walter." Charlotte's voice is surprising in its force. "Tell me."

His eyes flicker to her face, then drop to the ground. "Em's pregnant."

It is as if all of her senses stop working at once. Instead of being one loud pulse, she is a silence. An absence. Curiously, she wonders if her heart has in fact stopped beating. Numbness spreads inside her, a literal numbness, pins and needles shutting her down limb by limb. The prickly sensation crawls up her legs, down her arms, into her fingertips. She is reminded of her mother, of how she taught Charlotte to fall asleep as a child: *Say good night to each body part, one by one, and let them drift off to sleep . . .*

Good night, toes, Charlotte would think in the darkness. *Good night, foot. Good night, heel. Good night, ankle.* The numbness is spreading up her neck, into the tops of her ears. Her cheeks begin to tingle. If Walter held her wrist now, she would feel nothing.

"Em didn't want you to know."

She can hear him speaking, but faintly.

"I know it's not fair to get you involved, but here's the thing. I want to keep it, and she doesn't."

"What?" She looks at Walter's face, trying to extract meaning from the sounds of his words. "She wants to what?"

"Get an abortion," he says. "You know, terminate the pregnancy. I was scared she was going to do it when she came down here. I seriously think she would have, but I made her promise not to, said I wanted to be there with her, but the truth is—" He pauses and his face looks firm. Determined. As determined as Emily's has ever looked. "I'm not letting her do it. I won't."

Hearing the conviction in his voice, seeing his hard jaw, Charlotte feels afraid. Not a fear born of a creak, or hum, or a voice startling her from behind. This fear is bigger, unspecific; it has no bounds. She has no idea whose life she is living, whose patio she is sitting on, whose condo is propped behind her, who this boy next to her might be.

"I was hoping you could help me talk her out of it," Walter is saying. "I know it's kind of shady, going behind her back, but she won't listen to me. I thought maybe she would listen to you." He pauses. "I mean, I assume you don't want her to get rid of it, right?"

In some instinctive part of herself, Charlotte hears the words "get rid of it" and feels relief. To get rid of it, get rid of all of it—the drama, the decision, this conversation. "It" represents the new world Charlotte has found herself living in. "It" is her new and unrecognizable life. To excise "it" means a return to normalcy, to familiarity, to life as she knew it.

But this is only abstract thinking. These thoughts don't have eyes, ears, toes, a face. As soon as she stops to imagine the reality of "it"—an actual baby—the phrase "get rid of it" is like a blow to her chest.

"Charlotte?" Walter is saying. "You okay?"

She blinks, looks at him, feels herself returning to her skin. "Yes," she says, tentatively waggling her fingers. "Fine."

"You want her to keep it, right?"

"Of course," she says. "Of course I do."

Walter leans his head back and covers his face with his long hands. Charlotte wonders if he is going to cry. Instead he sighs, a deep-down sigh, a sigh of immense relief. He drops his hands to his lap and lets them dangle between his knees. "I can't watch her every minute, you know? Em does what she wants."

Yes, Charlotte thinks. That she does.

"And usually, you know, that's her thing. That's cool with me. But—" He presses his fists to his eyes, then exhales slowly and lowers them. He looks at Charlotte. "But this is my kid we're talking about. This is my life too."

Charlotte hears the bathroom door open behind her. She hadn't noticed the water stop trickling, hadn't heard the guttural sounds of the bathtub draining. Now, at the sound of Emily's approach, she feels nothing short of terrified.

"Wal?" Emily's voice floats toward them from inside. Walter looks straight ahead. Charlotte keeps her eyes on his face. She hears Emily at the door behind them. "Hey, what's this? Are you two bonding without me?"

She hops onto the patio, wrapped in Charlotte's orange robe, her wet hair hanging loose and uncombed. The smell of lavender trails behind her. Barefoot, she hops lightly on the smooth concrete stones, and perches on Walter's lap. She hooks her legs in the crooks of his knees, then looks at Charlotte's face. There is just a moment more, just a beat, and then it's over.

"Oh my God." Emily jumps to her feet. She looks at Walter, and whatever panic she must have seen on Charlotte's face is confirmed by the seriousness on his. "You didn't."

"Em—"

"I can't believe you would go behind my back like that. I told you not to tell!"

"Em." Walter stands. "I love you."

"You don't! If you loved me, you wouldn't have told!"

"But I am not letting you do this. I'm going to do whatever it takes. And if it means telling your mom—"

"Let me? It's not about *letting* me. It's my body!"

"But it's my kid." Walter's voice is trembling. "And you don't get to make this decision on your own."

"Wrong." With her eyes sparking, her hair flying, Emily seems much bigger than her body. The bit of silver flashes on the tip of her tongue, igniting her every word. "I *do* get to make this decision, Walter. It's my fuckup, my baby, my body, my decision. Mine. Read the fucking literature. It's a woman's choice, and there's nothing you"—she turns to Charlotte—"or you can do about it."

She turns and runs inside. Walter runs after her. Charlotte hears fast footsteps on the rug, bare feet slapping the tiled floor, Emily yelling, "Get out!" and the front door slamming. And then, nothing.

Charlotte stares into the yard. Silence rings in her ears. She is beginning to distinguish her own pins and prickles. Feeling the absence of feeling: it must be like being in a coma and knowing it. Faintly, she detects the sweet scent of lavender in the air. How innocent, she thinks. How naive. Buying bubble bath, stocking up on root beer. Worrying about getting up too early. Worrying about traveling to New York. Worrying about offending Walter, the blinds, the sunlight, the unlocked door. Everything that an hour ago seemed so threatening is now just a tiny, laughable problem from a distant life.

She hears a stir behind her, and Emily appears. She curls into the empty chair, tiny again. Her eyes are red, her body lost in the folds of the robe, hands swallowed by the sleeves. There is a child in her, Charlotte thinks. There is a child inside my child.

"What's ironic," Emily says. Her voice is soft, tenuous, as if testing this new reality, stepping onto new ground that may break beneath her feet. "What's ironic is that I was taking a bath, and I didn't even want to. I was only doing it because you bought all that stuff for me. I did it because I felt *bad.*"

She tucks her feet beneath her, swallows, shuts her eyes. Charlotte focuses on the tips of her toes peeking out from under the robe, raw and pink from the bath, like a row of freshwater pearls.

"I felt *bad,*" Emily says again, irony giving her voice a notch of strength, "so I'm in there trying to be a good daughter. Meanwhile, Walter's out here stabbing me in the back."

"Where is Walter?" Charlotte asks. Her mouth is dry. "Did he leave?"

Emily continues as if she hasn't heard. "It's like you two planned this or something. You set me up with the bath stuff, make me feel guilty, he catches you alone—" She hiccups, part laugh and part cry. "God, I sound as paranoid as you."

Charlotte knows she shouldn't ask again, but can't stop herself. "Did he leave for good? Did he—go back to New Hampshire?"

"God, Mom." Emily turns to her. "Yesterday you hated the guy, now you don't want him to leave. What, are you afraid to be alone with me or something?"

Charlotte says nothing.

"Are you afraid you'll have to take a stand?"

"No," she whispers, stung.

"Well, you don't have to bother." Emily burrows deeper in her chair. "Because I'm not having this baby."

At the words "this baby," Charlotte is recalled to reality again. She remembers watching Emily sleep as a child, the peaceful look on her face, the rise and fall of her chest. She remembers how she would tuck her tiny, balled fists under her chin. When she was nursing, her dimpled fingers splayed so wide they looked translucent.

"Having a baby is a choice a woman makes," Emily is saying, "and I'm choosing not to have one."

"But why?"

Emily looks at her.

Charlotte swallows, feeling the thick presence of her voice in her throat. "I just don't understand why you don't want it."

"I just told you."

"But you love Walter, don't you?"

"Not at the moment," Emily quips.

Charlotte recoils. Her tongue feels heavy, unwieldy. "If you need help—or, or if it's because of money—I can—"

"I don't want help. I don't want money, I don't want advice. I just want everyone to leave me alone." She squeezes a palm against her forehead, then rakes it through her damp hair. "This just wasn't my plan right now."

"But that doesn't mean—"

"It's my decision. It's a woman's decision."

She's quoting from a brochure, Charlotte thinks. She's reciting a stance, the way she's recited them for years—alternative learning and veganism and mindfulness—wafting in and out of them with more and less conviction. Charlotte has always indulged Emily's whims, nodding along, happy just to hear her happy. But now, her instinct to protect her daughter's feelings is outweighed by another instinct: to protect her daughter's baby.

"You're not going to talk me out of it," Emily is saying, "so you can just go back to pretending like you never knew."

"I can't do that," Charlotte says.

Emily's eyes narrow, then drop to her thumbnail, inspecting it with seeming indifference.

"This is a life, Emily, a human life—"

She drops her hand. "You sound like a fucking bumper sticker, Mom."

She's right, Charlotte thinks. She does. Her words sound as recycled as Emily's. It isn't the concept of "human life" she's worried about. Her opinion has nothing to do with ethics in general, but this situation in specific: this baby, this life. *This* life.

"You're right," Charlotte says.

Emily looks at her.

"I don't care about saving a human life. I care about saving my grandchild." Just saying the word makes her eyes fill.

"Mom." Emily's voice is tight. "This isn't about you. It isn't about Walter. It's about me."

And under normal circumstances, Charlotte would have been too intimidated to go forward. Too threatened by Emily's anger, too afraid of estranging her. But now, she feels no fear. There's no room for fear; too much is at stake.

"Emily," she says, "I've always tried to do whatever made you happy."

Emily's face furrows.

"I've tried to let you make your own decisions."

"Mom," Emily says, sounding uneasy. "Why are you saying this?"

"Because you're wrong," Charlotte says, as gently as she can. "You're wrong this time, sweetheart."

Pink blotches are beginning to rise on Emily's cheeks. "Why are you trying to ruin my life?" she says in a fierce, tear-filled whisper. "It's *my life.*"

"It always was," Charlotte says, like an apology. "But this time, it's not."

chapter four

Rarely in the fifteen years since Joe left her has Charlotte felt compelled to consult him in matters of parenting. She's never wanted his input on raising Emily; in fact, she preferred to avoid it. Joe's loose approach to raising children, to being a father—to life in general—unsettled her.

"You can't plan anything," Joe used to say. "Not a goddamn thing."

Charlotte would nod, at least in the beginning, because this sounded carefree and laid-back and all the things she wished she could be. But inside, she disagreed. You *could* plan things. And, through planning, safeguard against unwanted consequences. Sun damage, flu, dry rot, ring-around-the-tub. You could anticipate these things and avoid them.

But Joe was different. Joe lived in the moment. Even his marriage proposal, delivered in a moment of impulse—a diner, two half-drunk vanilla milkshakes, a dab of ice cream on Charlotte's upper lip, a sweet-tongued kiss across the table, Formica digging into their ribs, and a charming, makeshift ring made out of a piece of knotted plastic straw—had a haphazard quality that was, by all objective standards, romantic. No matter they'd known each other less than a year. The women Charlotte worked with in the LaSalle admissions office melted when they heard the story, the corners of their eyes and mouths drooping downward. "It's so *spontaneous,*" they said, longingly, so Charlotte reasoned spontaneity was a good thing. She liked it, in theory. But in practice, it alarmed her. She imagined it made her feel the way her father felt but wouldn't say: his face tightening, eyes narrowing, glancing at the plastic ring and then quickly away, as if the gesture were so inadequate he felt ashamed to even be looking.

When they began planning the wedding, Charlotte made lists. She spent many hours calculating and recalculating prices. She arranged various combinations of guests at various combinations of tables. She labeled these configurations Plan A and B and C, and kept them in a red spiral notebook in a locked drawer in her bedroom. She was still living at home, naturally, and it was rare that Joe was ever even upstairs; still, she didn't want to risk him accidentally finding the notebook and seeing her neuroses laid out in such painstaking detail. She planned on keeping those lesser qualities to herself.

Because Charlotte had realized, early on, Joe liked her for the things she kept hidden. She was shy. Contained. The reserved, bookish only child of two reserved, bookish parents. Her father was a philosophy professor, her mother a homemaker. They'd had Charlotte later in life; her father was nearly sixty when she graduated high school. Nights in their house growing up had been virtually silent: the only sounds the click of knitting needles, slip of a book's pages, shudder of the minute hand as it slid past the seven on the grandfather clock. Falling asleep, Charlotte had grown used to the sound of her own voice. *Good night, ankle. Good night, heel. Good night, toes.*

Charlotte met Joe when she was twenty-two, at a New Year's party she was dragged to by a classmate at LaSalle. She was taking night classes (she got free tuition as a "faculty daughter") and working part-time in the admissions office. She had little experience with men, except for awkward high school dances and a smattering of setups. She'd never thought of herself as especially pretty, though the women in the admissions office disagreed: *You have perfect eyebrows, Charlotte. Look at her bone structure! You're probably one of those people who can eat anything and not gain an ounce.* But these were women—didn't they always compliment each other like that?

The night of the party, Charlotte wore a red dress she'd bought for Christmas. It was unlike her to wear such a bold color, but in the store it had looked festive. Holiday red, she'd thought, in the dressing room. But that night, the dress turned a different shade. Suddenly it was fiery red. Attention-getting red. At the party, when Joe approached her, Charlotte was nowhere near so bold as her dress. She was so nervous she couldn't speak. She could barely even smile. But to her shock, Joe Warren seemed smitten. All night he gazed at her from across the room, eyes wide as saucers. He appeared at her side with glasses of wine and watched a blush swim into her cheeks. When the clock struck midnight and the crowd toasted the arrival of 1977, he kissed her dry knuckles, one by one. And when they said goodbye, Charlotte agreeing to let him call her, Joe gazed at her wonderingly, shook his head, and called her "hard to read." It was that night Charlotte concluded that, in the adult world, if you were thin and looked aloof, you were no longer considered shy; you were mysterious.

For a while, Charlotte was able to sustain her aura of mystery. While inside she felt constantly nervous—in peril! in love! in fear! in danger!—her nerves were so intense as to be paralyzing. They had the ironic, opposite effect of making her appear calm. Joe, with his long, loose limbs and garrulous nature, saw Charlotte's unrevealing exterior as a challenge. He was fascinated by this little person, determined to unlock her. Squeezing her shoulder, pinching her hip, resting his hand on her knee—he was always trying to get as close to her, as close to inside her, as he could.

Joe was equally fascinated by Charlotte's father, a professor of philosophy for the past nearly-thirty-five years. For Joe, finishing his master's in sociology and preparing to teach at Temple in the fall, George Rainer was a windfall. Joe would coax him onto the Rainers' front porch, where they would drink brandy and talk Hegel and Freud and chaos theory while the sun sank below the trees. Charlotte would sit in the living room, trying anxiously to listen, her own homework abandoned on her lap. When they returned, Joe would slap her father on the back or squeeze his sloped shoulder, as if emerging from some good-natured game of cards. Joe's face would be bright, energized, while her father's seemed a careful map of tweaks and tucks—upturned corner of the mouth here, skeptical squint of the eye there. Charlotte had the feeling that if one feature loosened, the entire face would fall apart.

In this, his near-reverence for her father, Joe was much like his daughter would one day be: easily seduced by ideas. Overwhelmed by passions that were flighty, fleeting. Charlotte often wondered if her entire marriage—Joe's nine-year stint as a suburban husband—was a symptom of this innate curiosity, this desire to experiment with life.

Once Charlotte and Joe were married (a simple summer ceremony that, in retrospect, captured them perfectly: his insistence on a nondenominational justice of the peace, her conservative dresses and discount tulips), Charlotte began to realize it was impossible to keep select parts of herself to herself. Maybe in a different marriage, this would have been possible. Maybe in a marriage like her parents', so private it occupied different rooms at different times of day, so deeply routine that perhaps it was inevitable her mother would die not two years after her father. But not in Charlotte's. Not with a husband who strolled into the bathroom when she was clipping her toenails. A husband who stepped into the shower with her in the morning and massaged her back. A husband who, lying in bed, whispered, "What's going on in there?" and tapped her on the temples. A man who wanted to share everything.

Within a year of being Mrs. Joe Warren, Charlotte's nerves began bubbling to the surface. First in small ways: a spotless kitchen, a double-locked front door. "Fluttery," Joe called her, holding her hands so she wouldn't nibble them when they watched TV. He would smile and kiss her knuckles, one by one. Then, gradually, she noticed him pausing over her hands. She noticed him notice her jagged cuticles, the flecks of loose skin. While before they were married he'd looked at her with eyes that were wide—so wide, she worried, he might be seeing more of her than was really there—his eyes had been gradually shrinking, narrowing to a squint, like a physical manifestation of his dimmed expectations.

She knew what was happening: her husband was becoming unfascinated. He'd been deadset on "unlocking" her, and—like any mystery, she supposed—had convinced himself that once he did, what he discovered would be worth it. But the truth, once the mystery of Charlotte was revealed, was this: there was no mystery. Charlotte was not intriguing; she was ordinary. She felt guilty for having let Joe believe she was anything other than this, a woman capable of being called "Char"—so breezy and blasé, it begged to be yelled after a speeding taxi or into a whipping wind. She even slunk away from academia, reducing her course-load to just one class each term. Her father would have argued harder had he not been diagnosed with cancer soon after their wedding. Suddenly he was no longer a wellspring of abstract thought, but a man rooted firmly in the world of the flesh: chemotherapy treatments and hair loss and bedpans.

Something had begun shifting between Joe and Charlotte, something they both recognized but wouldn't admit. The more Charlotte felt herself exposed, the more nervous she became. The more control of herself she felt slipping, the more she needed to reclaim. Her fearfulness translated into terse formality. There was no fighting about it, no articulating of it, just a mutual accommodation. Joe no longer tried to probe her mind, to know her thoughts. He stopped coming into the shower to soap her shoulders. Instead of kissing her ragged fingernails, he began buying her manicures. He joined a gym, burning off his aggression by swimming laps and lifting weights. For their first anniversary, he gave her a certificate for a massage. "So you can relax," he quipped, and smiled, but his smile held something else inside it. "You deserve it." Charlotte thanked him, but never went. The mere thought of undressing for a stranger made her anxious.

Now, as she stares at the cold fireplace, Charlotte sees only more evidence of her neuroses. The brass grate is polished to glinting, the insides of the hearth swept clean. Like a womb that's been vacuumed out, scoured spotless. She squeezes her eyes shut. Everything has an extra weightiness about it; it's a fitting payback for making fun of Rita Curran's symbolism. Charlotte's own world is now composed of nothing but symbols: babies and wombs, life and death.

She forces her eyes open. Funny how plans to build a fire had seemed so daunting just twenty-four hours ago. Now she would light the flames without a flinch. She would stir the embers, fling in old newspapers and *TV Guides.* She could become one of those people who run their fingers through candles, snuff them out with a pinch of their finger and thumb. Emily used to torture her with stunts like these: lighting a tapered candle at the dinner table on Dunleavy Street and running a finger lazily through the flame.

She wonders where Emily is now. After Walter finally knocked on the door, just after 4:30 P.M., the two of them had driven off in Emily's car. When they returned, at 6:15, they weren't flirting. They weren't fighting. They just seemed tired.

"Where did you go?" Charlotte asked.

"For a drive," Emily answered.

Charlotte looked at Walter, thinking he might be more forthcoming, but he only fingered his eyebrow ring and looked at the ground.

"Anyplace in particular?"

"No."

"Not even to eat?"

"Mom," Emily snapped, "I didn't get an abortion, if that's what you're getting at."

"We just drove," Walter added, then looked back at the floor. There was a current of guilt between them now, that of two co-conspirators who had been caught in an act.

Emily and Walter had retreated to the couch, Emily curled on one side and Walter upright on the other. They turned on the TV, a rerun of *Seinfeld,* and watched in silence. There were so many things Charlotte wanted to ask, but neither seemed like they were in the mood to talk. She got up, once, to ask if they were hungry. Emily said no, they weren't. So Charlotte returned to the kitchen table, listening to the sounds of canned laughter, staring at the six uneaten Needhams until, finally, getting up to stretch a film of plastic wrap over the plate.

"We're going out," Emily announced, when the show was over.

"Where?" Charlotte hurried into the foyer, where Walter was pulling their coats from the closet.

"Out," Emily repeated.

"Out to eat? But I could just put something on here—"

"That's okay."

"I have Boca Burgers, I have pasta, I have plenty of—"

"We're not hungry," Emily said, shrugging into her coat. It was a heavy olive thing, capelike, and looked like it weighed more than she did. Walter was easing into a black leather jacket Charlotte had never seen him wear, much less hang in her closet.

"Where are you going then?"

"We'll probably just look for a bar or something," Emily said. "God knows what we'll find."

Charlotte pressed her lips together, telling herself to stay out of it, but she couldn't. "Just don't drink," she blurted, as Emily unhooked the chain.

Emily paused.

"Because of the baby," Charlotte said, keeping her voice down. She felt irrationally afraid that the baby might hear her and start to worry.

"Perfect." Emily let the chain tumble against the wall. She shot Walter an accusing look, then swung the door open and strode off, boots crunching heavily on the lawn.

Charlotte looked at Walter, and a flicker of guilt crossed his face. "See you later, Charlotte," he said.

Charlotte watched from the doorway as the car pulled away. She noticed the slight movement of a curtain in the front window of Ruth O'Keefe's and shut the door. She didn't regret what she'd said. And she didn't feel hurt by Emily's reaction. She couldn't afford to. Even if it meant making Emily angry, ensuring that she wasn't drinking, finding out where she was going, she would do it. For the baby's sake.

Now, three hours later, staring at the fireplace, Charlotte thinks of calling someone. But who? There's no one she can bring herself to admit this to. Especially if, God forbid, Emily doesn't keep it. The closest thing she has to friends is the book group, where telling one of them is as good as telling all. She couldn't bear their reaction anyway: the intake of breath, the thick concern, and yet, the unmistakable twinge of excitement. It was how she herself had felt telling Emily about Rachel Hill hiding rocks in her pockets. Remembering that now, Charlotte feels awful, so awful that she can't call Linda, the one person in whom she might have been able to confide.

She wonders where Walter and Emily are right this minute. What if they're at some kind of clinic? It's late, but who knows what kinds of hours these places keep. Then she reminds herself of Walter's conviction just a few hours ago; she can't imagine he would bend so completely, so fast. Of course, even if he could prevent an abortion tonight, he's ultimately powerless. *I can't watch her every minute.*

Charlotte is engulfed by a wave of helplessness. Maybe Joe was right after all: you *can't* plan anything. She certainly couldn't have prevented this. Though Joe, she can't help but think, contributed to it somehow. His laissez-faire, live-in-the-moment attitude. His *spontaneity.* Even when Emily was little, he set such a childish example—playing games, slapping fives, taking impromptu drives to the playground, the Dairy Queen, while Charlotte was left to deal with the important things: baths, meals, lights out. When Charlotte called them to dinner and reminded Emily to wash her hands, Joe would roll his eyes at her as if they were both children who'd been reprimanded.

Charlotte walks into the kitchen. She checks the oven clock: 9:16 P.M. If it's 9:16 on the East Coast, it's 6:16 in Seattle. This seems a safe time, if ever there is one. Not so early that Joe is still lolling in bed (as he was known to do on Saturdays) but not so late that he and Valerie have already started yelling or throwing salads or reconciling on their deck with the red wine and the picture-perfect view.

She removes the cordless from its cradle, pages through her phone book to the gold tab marked "J." Her fingers are trembling as she dials. It rings five times before Joe answers.

"Hello?" He sounds slightly out of breath, as if he's been jogging.

"Joe. It's Charlotte."

"Char?"

Something about his breathiness, his aura of preoccupation, makes Charlotte's anger swell.

"Please don't call me that," she says. "I don't like it when you call me that."

"Whoa," Joe says, laughing, his breathiness abruptly disappearing. "Whoa, whoa, whoa." This is his signature tactic: slowing down the world to match his own pace. "Slow down there."

Usually she and Joe exchange words with a well-worn politeness, but tonight she can't rein herself in. "I won't slow down," she says, words tumbling out of her mouth before she can stop them. "I can't."

He laughs again. He probably thinks this is like the last phone call, the one about the tongue ring. Her distress then was a little disproportionate, but still—she hates it when Joe laughs at her. She hates it so much that she rushes past their usual pleasantries, so much that a very small part of her relishes the moment when she says: "Your daughter is pregnant."

She hears a faint crackle on the other end. It could be static, or the phone shifting, or Joe's joints cracking as he sinks into a chair.

"Joe?" she says, feeling a pinch of remorse. "Are you still there?"

"I'm here."

"Did you hear what I said?"

His voice has lost its usual jocularity; it sounds dull, shell-shocked. "I heard." He is silent for a beat. "What's she going to do?"

Charlotte feels her heat rise. "She wants to get an abortion."

Joe falls silent again.

"Well, are you surprised?" Charlotte says, unable to contain her bitterness. "There's no way she'd ever do anything but the *cool* thing, the cool *left-wing* thing, whatever the cool word for being cool is these days." She is tripping over her tongue, words tumbling out haphazardly. "Thanks to you."

"Wait." Joe's voice is firm. "Hold on. Don't go throwing this in my face. I never told Em what to believe in, she did that on her own. And being pro-choice, there's nothing wrong with that. I know you probably don't agree—"

On the other end of the line, Charlotte hears the slow whine of a door opening. "Hold on," Joe says. She can make out the muffled rhythms of conversation: the rumble of Joe's voice under the receiver, probably pressed to his chest. A pause, another rumble, then the sound of a door closing—not quite a slam, but close.

Joe returns. "Sorry."

Charlotte is dying to know if he told Valerie about the pregnancy—and what she said in return—but won't ask. "That's okay."

"What was I saying?" He pauses, then adds, "I'm pretty sure I was just about to make a brilliant point." It's as if seeing his wife has pulled him a few steps away from the situation, recalling him to his signature charm.

"You were about to say you're in favor of abortion."

Joe sighs then, the playfulness gone as quickly as it surfaced. "No, actually, I wasn't about to say that. What I was about to say is that it's fine for Em to be pro-choice. And, yeah. Yes. I'm pro-choice. But that doesn't mean I'm glad she's decided to do this."

"It doesn't?"

"No." She hears a sound she knows to be Joe running one palm down the length of his face, as if washing it off. She can see him pinching the bridge of his nose, then letting go. "Not exactly."

"You mean you want her to keep it?"

"Yeah, of course I want her to keep it. I don't know. I want to have a grand—" He pauses. "Jesus. Give me a minute. I'm kind of blindsided here, you know?"

Charlotte feels her heartbeat speed up. "Well, she isn't doing it," she says quickly. "I mean, she hasn't done it yet. Maybe if you talk to her—"

Joe says nothing; thinking, she supposes. Charlotte begins pacing the kitchen while she waits, a tidy four-cornered square:

coffeemaker to refrigerator to toaster to table. Coffeemaker to refrigerator to toaster to table.

"It's Walter's, I assume?"

She stops, staring at the coffeemaker. "Well, of course it's Walter's." She's furious that Joe would even suggest otherwise. "Who else's would it be?"

"I don't know. It could be anyone's."

"Like who?"

"Like any guy in the state of New Hampshire! Who the hell knows?"

"Are you saying Emily's—? Why would you say a thing like that?"

"I'm not saying she's sleeping around. I'm just saying, we don't know a goddamn thing about her life. Christ, Char. Why are you making this even harder? I'm just being realistic! You should try it sometime!"

Charlotte stops. Blinks. Surprisingly, though, she doesn't feel hurt by his words, or even anxious; she feels something like electrified.

"Sorry," he says.

She begins pacing again, coffeemaker to refrigerator to toaster to table.

"So it's Walter's. Does Walter have an opinion on all this?"

"Of course Walter has an opinion." Charlotte feels emboldened, remembering her ally. "He has a very definite opinion. He wants her to keep it. The reason he followed her down here in the middle of the night was because he was so afraid she was going to get rid of it behind his back."

"Jesus," Joe says again.

Charlotte stops, facing the window. The plastic blinds have been returned to their original position, revealing only thin stripes of night sky. She wants more from Joe than this. More than this passive reacting, this joke-cracking and cursing and sighing. Historically, he's the one with all the convictions. The one who's not afraid to take a stand.

"So that's it?" she says, feeling glib, careless. "You have no opinion?"

"No, Charlotte." Joe sounds weary. "I don't have no opinion. I'm just not about to force my opinion on my adult daughter. She's very capable of making her own decisions. She's been doing it for twenty-two years."

Charlotte's eyes fall to the table and the six chocolates swathed under plastic. She feels a tightness building inside her, words that have been lodged for years in her jaws, her temples, her throat. "She hasn't been doing it for twenty-two years," she hears herself saying. Her voice is shaking. "She's never once made her own decision. She believed in whatever looked right, whatever the trend was, whatever her teachers at college were doing, or her friends in the commune or—or you."

"That's not true."

"It is."

"You're not giving her enough credit."

"Maybe you just don't know her as well as I do." Charlotte bites down on the inside of her cheek, tasting blood. She feels the buried tension on the line: layers and layers of unslung insults, unfought fights. She senses she is on the brink of venturing into a different realm entirely, about parenting and priorities and shirking responsibilities and moving to the West Coast and being seen as a hero regardless—but, she tells herself, that's not what this is about.

"Fine," she concedes, still chewing on her cheek, trying to keep her anger in check. "Let's say she has been making her own decisions. Let's say she's always thought them through. She's still never once had to take another person into account, or another person's feelings—she doesn't even know how!"

"Are you talking about Walter?"

"Of course I'm talking about Walter. Who else would I be talking about? Some strange man in New Hampshire? This is Walter's baby, Walter wants this baby, and—and it's like his opinion carries no weight at all!"

"Charlotte," Joe says. His tone has softened into one of affection, even amusement. It feels demeaning: *Look, isn't it cute? Charlotte's getting angry!* "Are you listening to yourself?"

"Of course I'm listening to myself!"

"Do you think this is really about Walter?"

"What do you mean?"

"I mean, is this about Walter or is it about you?"

His words are overmeasured, overenunicated. He sounds so much like Emily, he may as well have been trained at the alternative learning environment.

"Is this about not wanting her to have the abortion or about wanting her to listen to you? To take your side?"

"What is this," Charlotte sputters, "some kind of pop psychology? Do they teach you that on the West Coast? Did *Valerie* tell you to say that?" She feels her control slipping even further out of reach, words falling from her mouth before she can edit them, organize them. Joe is twisting this into *her* problem. It's so selfish! So unfair! Yet she feels like a novice trying to argue with him, a toddler trying to walk and leaving a trail of damage in her wake. "I don't know how you can accuse me of this being about me, when you—you're where she learned irresponsibility. You do whatever you want, whenever you want, you leave me, leave us, take up with a—"

"Charlotte," Joe warns. "Watch it."

Charlotte stops. Tries to breathe. She listens to the sound of the silence that stretches between them. She lets herself drift inside the quiet, be suspended in the nothing, like an air-filled sail. She doesn't want this pause to end. She can almost pretend it never will, that none of this is even happening, because look, look at the slanted blinds! The laptop! The magnet from Millville County Electric! All of it so ordinary, so oblivious—how could these things still exist if all of this were really happening? The kitchen where she heats her Lean Cuisines cannot be the same kitchen in which she and her ex-husband are fighting about their daughter being pregnant! Her daughter being pregnant cannot exist in the same world as the icemaker and the coupon from Bed, Bath and Beyond!

"Listen," Joe is saying. His tone has relaxed. "I know you want me to tell Emily what I think she should do, but I'm not going to. It just doesn't sit right. But maybe I should come out there so we can all talk about it."

Charlotte pauses. "Fly out here?"

"No. Swim." She can hear him smile.

"You would do that? Fly out?"

And just that quickly, the calm is shattered. "What do you mean, I would do that? I am her *father,* for Christ's sake. I do care about what happens to her. God, just because I'm not as controlling as you are doesn't mean I love her any less."

Charlotte leans against the counter, holding the phone to her warm cheek. She looks at the thin slivers of night sky peeking through the blinds, the few faint stars visible through the slats of plastic. She looks for the moon, but it must be blocked; she can't find it. The window grows blurred with her tears. "Just tell me what to do."

"Run my trip by Em," Joe says. "Tell her I want to come out and talk all this through. Tell her we're not disappointed, there's no pressure—this is her decision to make. But it's a big decision, it's complicated, so we want to be there to help her make it. Because we support her and we love her."

Listening to Joe speak, Charlotte feels tiny hairs prickle on the back of her neck. She thinks she might be glimpsing a side of Joe she's never seen. Not the fun dad, the hip dad, the fluent-in-pop-culture dad, but a father who is sensible and loving. There's a quality about his words and tone that is *paternal*—there's no other way to describe it. And Charlotte is amazed. Not so much by the sentiments themselves, but the way he can articulate them, the words just easing off his tongue, feelings into flesh. Even when they were arguing, he seemed composed while Charlotte was rattled to the core. Where did he learn to be this way? Was he always, and she'd just never known?

Charlotte feels like she's been punched in the gut. For the first time since Emily's birth, she considers the possibility that Joe might be the better parent. That he was aware of the important things all along. And that she, as a mother—her purpose in life, her identity, her primary role in this world—falls short.

"Charlotte?" Joe says. "You there?"

"I'm here." Her voice sounds small, detached, floating beside her.

"Sound like a plan?"

"Sounds fine."

"You'll call and let me know what Em says?"

"Okay."

Joe pauses, then says, "Don't worry. This will all be okay." His words sound awkward, even tender, and Charlotte just manages to hang up the phone before she starts to cry.

When she hears the noise, Charlotte goes through all the usual motions: panic, sweat, racing heart, bedside light, eyes adjusting, reality sinking in. Clock check: 1:47 A.M. She gets up and turns the Dream Machine off, then stands still, listening. Faintly, she hears it again: voices. Under her bedroom door, she sees a bar of light. Charlotte pulls on her robe, steps into the hallway, and blinks into the brightness. Lights are on in the living room, kitchen, even the bathroom. But the sounds are coming from outside, on the patio. She can make out Emily and Walter, but there are other voices, ones she recognizes but cannot place.

Charlotte starts toward the sliding door, then hears a burst of loud laughter and picks up her pace. It's much too late for them to be making this kind of commotion; the neighbors are going to get angry.

When Charlotte yanks back the sliding door, four heads turn in her direction. She processes the scene quickly: Emily and Walter occupying one of the chairs, Emily in his lap, Walter resting one hand on top of her head. Cross-legged in the other chair is a woman Charlotte doesn't know, and sitting on the ground, propped against the house, is a man. The woman holds the glowing stub of a cigarette. The man is smoking too, legs bent, an unfinished carton of Thai food resting on his knees. On the table are the remnants of the six-pack of Sam Adams Summer Ale: the cardboard box, scattering of twisted caps, empty amber-colored bottles glowing orange in the porch light.

"Hey!" Walter shouts. "Charlotte!" He is seemingly oblivious to the time, to his voice. Charlotte looks quickly at Emily, who flinches for just a second. Then the flash of guilt is gone; she is still angry.

"Is this your mom?" the woman says eagerly.

"Yeah." Emily looks at Charlotte. Even in the darkness, Charlotte can see the clenched knot of jaw below her ear. "Mom, meet your mystery neighbor."

The woman untangles her legs and stands, transferring her cigarette to the opposite hand. Charlotte watches her wobbly approach across the fake stones. This is B. Morgan? The woman she's been hearing upstairs for the past two months? It can't be. B. should be in her early thirties, thirty-five at most. This woman must be pushing forty, despite her best efforts to appear younger. Her hair is dyed an unnatural black, tapering to sharp points by her ears. She's wearing a jean jacket over a tight pink shirt and a pair of jeans, the jacket and jeans two slightly different shades of blue. The whole outfit is unflatteringly tight, serving only to accentuate the slight bulge of her belly, the plumping of middle age. Her face is soft, vaguely self-conscious.

"I'm Bea." The woman extends her right hand. "I live upstairs."

Charlotte pauses, disoriented. Could her name actually be "B"?

"It's Beatrice," Emily supplies, reading her thoughts. "Bea, this is my mother. Her name is Charlotte."

"Yes," Charlotte says, taking Bea's limp hand. "Charlotte Warren."

"Nice to meet you." Bea smiles a warm, crooked smile.

Charlotte withdraws her hand, gives her terry-cloth belt a tug.

"And this is Bill." Bea gestures to the man on the ground. "My boyfriend."

"Pleasure," Bill says, forking up some pad thai.

"We met them in O'Grady's," Emily says. "It's a pretty good bar, right around the corner. Ever been there, Mom?"

Charlotte glances at her daughter. Walter raps his knuckles on top of her head, as if in reprimand.

"Have you, Charlotte?" Bea says, her face furrowing in genuine confusion. "I don't think I've ever seen you there—wait, have I?"

"Oh, no," Charlotte assures her.

"Mom keeps to herself," Emily says.

Charlotte looks again at her daughter. Is she just angry about earlier, or has she been drinking? She turns to Walter as if for a signal: a firm shake of the head, a thumbs-up, an assurance that he would not have let that happen. But Walter is taking a swig from his bottle. Charlotte feels deserted. It's the same way she felt as a child when her parents had a few glasses of wine. They would grow giddy, distant, distracted, becoming other people, people who existed in a world apart from hers. She looks at the empty bottle on the table; it could belong to any of them.

"Still," Bea says, "isn't that funny that we've never run into each other? Being neighbors and all?" She laughs, and Charlotte recognizes it as the laugh from the stairwell, though it sounds different coming from these slightly overlapping front teeth. Bea's red lipstick clings to her mouth unevenly, darker on the edges and faded in the center from beer bottles and cigarettes.

"It is strange, I guess."

"It's fucked up," Emily snorts. Walter reaches a hand around her face to cover her mouth.

Bea takes a final drag, then leans down toward Bill. She grinds the stub of her cigarette into what Charlotte realizes is serving as an ashtray: a Thai carton, presumably empty, propped precariously on the lopsided stones. Charlotte feels herself beginning to sweat. She wants nothing more than to just get off the porch and back into bed. She wishes she'd never known this was happening, that she'd slept right through it. Still, she can't leave without saying something about the neighbors. Not only are these people on Charlotte's porch, making too much noise, but Bea Morgan is one of them. God knows what kind of reputation she has at Sunset Heights.

Bea goes to sit back down, then stops. "Oh, did you want to sit here, Charlotte?"

"No, no, I'm fine."

"Seriously, I'll take the floor."

"I'm going back to bed," Charlotte says firmly, with a look at Emily.

But it is Walter who responds, albeit sluggishly, the rules of conduct triggered somewhere in his brain. "Aw, did we wake you up? *Again?*" A broad smile stretches across his face. "You'd think I could make it through one night here without waking you up, huh, Charlotte?"

His words are slurred slightly. Charlotte doesn't like talking to him like this. He is not the same boy he was this afternoon. All the pieces are there—his politeness, his light, teasing affection—but they are blurred by alcohol, and devalued.

"Oh my God," Bea says, clapping a hand to her mouth. "We woke you up?"

"Oh, no no," she says, though she has no idea why this should be surprising. It's two in the morning. Then again, Bea's night has probably just begun. "I was already awake." It has become her mantra this weekend. "In fact, I should go back to bed."

"Us too," Bea says quickly. "Come on, Bill. Get up."

"Guys, you don't have to—" Emily says.

"It's late. Bill's half asleep already."

Bill hoists himself from the ground as Bea hugs Emily and Walter. "Next time you're in town, we're all going out."

"Definitely," Emily says.

"Take care, guys," from Walter.

"See you soon." Bea smiles at Charlotte. "Neighbor."

She gives a flustered wave to the patio at large and then, to Charlotte's chagrin, steps through her sliding door. She watches as Bea and Bill cross her living room, exiting by her foyer. Granted, it's a quicker route than walking all the way around the house, but she's still shocked they would walk through without asking. Then it occurs to her they've probably been traipsing in and out of her house all night. Using her bathroom, picking through her refrigerator. Bill was probably peeing just yards from where Charlotte lay asleep. She vows never again to use the Dream Machine.

Standing on her patio in the middle of the night, clutching her bathrobe around her, Charlotte feels what is becoming a familiar sense of disbelief. Walter and Emily are cuddled in a chair as if their earlier conversation never happened, as if there is not a baby growing between them. The smell of Thai is overbearing, mingling with the beer's sour afterhaze. Charlotte wants to pry open Emily's mouth and check her breath.

Instead, she begins to tidy up. She picks up the now-empty Thai cartons, the makeshift ashtray, the empty cardboard shell of the six-pack.

"Just leave it, Mom," Emily says, but Charlotte ignores her. Walter has leaned his head back and closed his eyes—is he asleep? disinterested? unconscious?—as Charlotte picks up as much as her arms can hold and walks inside.

In the kitchen, she is detached. Efficient. Scraping the insides of cartons into the garbage disposal. Throwing empty boxes in the trashcan. Compressing the six-pack into a tidy cardboard square. But in the bottom of the final carton, oily droplets clinging to its inner walls, she sees a nest of cigarette butts in a puddle of "brown sauce," and it is this that finally brings tears to her eyes. She puts the carton down, sags against the refrigerator door. Then, afraid Emily or Walter might find her, she bolts for the bathroom and locks herself inside.

Pressing her forehead against the mirror, she smells smoke, probably bar smoke that clung to Bea and Bill as they washed their hands in her sink. When she goes to sit, she sees that the toilet seat's been left up. She slams the lid down, only to be taunted by the ridiculously fluffy cover. She considers sinking to the tub ledge, but it seems so melodramatic. She's seen people in movies sinking to tub ledges, clutching at shower curtains, and it's always struck her as over-the-top. But maybe it isn't. Maybe the tub ledge is actually the last refuge of the truly devastated, the locked-in-bathrooms, foreheads-pressed-to-mirrors, and she's just never felt quite that desperate before.

It's the flat fish swarming the walls that keep Charlotte at eye level. Leaning against the sink, she examines herself in the mirror glass. She studies her naked face, her matted hair, her worn orange robe; she cannot believe two strangers just saw her looking this way. She is furious at Emily for bringing them here without asking, for letting her look so old and unkempt and foolish, for taking such liberties with her home, breaking its seal, disrupting its routine, forcing all these introductions, these interconnections, these stimuli—smoke and neighbors and Thai food and beer bottles and laughter splitting apart the quiet night—forcing the circles of her life to widen and widen when all she wants to do is stay inside and untouched and alone.

From upstairs, Charlotte hears the bedsprings. She doesn't know which is worse, imagining attractive, exotic strangers or knowing who is really up there: soft, drunk, insecure Bea and Bill. She squeezes her eyes shut, wanting to plug her ears, take a pill to make her fall asleep and wake when it's light and quiet and everyone is gone and all of this is over. To think she was worried about Emily not feeling comfortable here, not feeling like she could treat the condo like home. To think that she, Charlotte, was craving company. She wants nothing more than to have her house back to herself.

Heading back to the sliding doors Charlotte feels unsteady on her feet. From the doorway, she sees Walter and Emily haven't moved, except now they are kissing. Emily is curled up in his lap, his face tilted back and obscured by her long tangle of brown hair. But instead of retreating, Charlotte steps outside and begins collecting the empty bottles to drop into the recycling bin.

"Mom," Emily says, her voice flat. "What are you doing."

"Cleaning up."

"Do you have to do it now?"

"Well, someone has to sometime." She places three bottles into the bin, careful not to let them clank.

"We'll take care of it. Just leave it."

"I'll help," Walter says, starting to slide her off his lap.

"No, Wal." Emily puts her hands on his shoulders.

Charlotte stares at her daughter. "Emily, have you been drinking?"

"Just because we were kissing doesn't mean we're drunk, Mom."

"Have you?"

"Maybe I have. Maybe I haven't. It doesn't matter anyway."

Charlotte crosses the patio and picks up the half-empty bottle left beside Bea's chair.

"It doesn't matter if I'm poisoning the baby," Emily says, louder. "Because *I'm not having it.*"

Charlotte pours what's left in the bottle onto the lawn.

"You're killing your grass," Emily mutters.

Charlotte spins to face her. "Well you're killing your baby!"

Only after she yells does she realize how late it is, and how loud she was. Gently, she places the bottle in the bin. Out of the corner of her eye, she sees Walter is standing. For a moment she thinks he might be rising with her, in an act of solidarity. Instead he walks off into the backyard without a word. Maybe he's so drunk he doesn't realize where he's going. Maybe he's lost and thinks he's back in New Hampshire.

"Where is he going?" Charlotte demands. She can barely contain her whisper.

"He's getting wood."

"What on earth for?"

"To build a fire."

"No." Charlotte shakes her head. "Absolutely not."

"Why not?"

"Because it's two in the morning. You're going to bed."

"Why are you suddenly treating me like I'm fifteen?"

"Because you're acting like you're fifteen!" she hisses.

"You're the one who said you wanted to use your fireplace tonight."

"Don't pretend you're doing this for my sake." Charlotte's voice is trembling. "I'm going to bed. And you are too." She presses her lips together. "Remember, you are a guest in this house."

Emily stares at her for a long minute. Neither looks away.

Then Emily shakes her head. "Whatever," she says, and tilts her chin back to look at the sky.

She's been drinking, Charlotte decides. She's been drinking and compromising this baby.

"Stars here suck." Emily wraps her arms around her knees. "In New Hampshire there are tons of them. They're everywhere. They look so close you could touch them."

She's compromising this baby, Charlotte thinks, compromising it knowingly. Maybe even doing it out of spite. She's never cared what I think, never listened to what I say.

"Here you can hardly see the stars because of all the shit in the air. But in New Hampshire there's no smog, no buildings, no factories on the side of the highway pumping pollution into the atmosphere . . . up there it's totally pure." Emily stretches her arms toward the sky.

"I spoke to your father."

Her head snaps up. "What?"

"I called your father."

"When?"

"Tonight."

"You called Joe?"

Charlotte nods.

"You told him?"

She nods again. Then steels herself for the attack, the kind of rebuke Walter got for betraying her this afternoon. Instead, her daughter seems to shrink inward, arms lowering, face crumpling. Her voice drops to a whisper. "What did he say?"

And in that moment, as clearly as she perceived her own ineffectualness just moments before, Charlotte realizes there *is* one person with influence over Emily: Joe. Emily adores him, idolizes him like children do whose parents are distant, and therefore romanticized. The parents they see once or twice a year, who aren't involved in the menial things, the day-to-day things, the rainy nights in February when the homework's unfinished and the oil burner's acting up and there's nothing for dinner but hot dogs (which your daughter won't eat, but which you boil for yourself, wrapped in a heel of wheat bread) and a single can of lentil soup that your daughter slurps while sitting cross-legged at the kitchen table complaining of cramps and scowling at her algebra, which she finds not only technically confusing but morally unfair. Time spent with Joe was fun time, vacation time; it was the not-real life. As much as Charlotte knows her daughter loves her—sees her as a lovable, endearingly uncool mom to whom she can tell anything—she loves her father in a different way. She wants to please him. To make him proud. She is afraid of letting him down. Her mother's pride is never in question; her mother compliments her, agrees with her always, acts like an echo of herself. But her father is a separate person, with a separate coast, wife, beach, and arsenal of opinions. Her father is the one who holds sway.

"He said to tell you"—Charlotte picks her words carefully, trying to remember exactly what Joe said—"that he wants to come out and talk to you about it."

"He wants to fly out here?" Emily sounds alarmed.

"That's what he said."

"Who? Just him?"

At first Charlotte isn't sure what she's asking, then it hits her: Valerie. She hadn't even thought to ask. "I'm not sure," she says, the very thought of it making her nauseous. "I think just him. I'm pretty sure he meant just the four of us—you, Walter, Dad, and me."

Emily looks at her knees. Charlotte wonders if she's disappointed.

Quietly, Emily asks, "Was he mad?"

"Oh, no," Charlotte says quickly. "He's not mad." Though she knows it's not her reassurance Emily is looking for. "He just—" What were Joe's exact words? His perfect blend of reason and affection? "He just wants to talk things through. Because it's a big decision. A hard decision."

"What did he think I should do? Did he say?"

"He was—well, he was divided."

Emily lets her head fall back, eyes to the sky, but only for a moment. When she lifts her head again, her eyes are full of tears. "Did he sound disappointed?"

"Oh, honey." Charlotte takes a fervent step toward her. "He isn't disappointed. In fact, I remember him saying those exact words. He said to tell you he's not disappointed. He isn't. I promise."

From behind her, Charlotte hears the sounds of Walter approaching, wet grass shushing, twigs snapping under his feet. When he steps onto the patio holding a log in each hand, Emily reaches her arms up like a child. Without a word, Walter drops the logs, sending them rolling around the patio. He kneels in front of her. Emily falls forward, pressing her face into his neck.

Book Two

chapter five

Charlotte's house feels different now. Though it's sealed up as before, it no longer feels contained. Certain rooms, objects, have new memories attached. The coffeemaker. The patio. The flowered seat cushions. Voices in the stairwell have faces and names. Charlotte is not alone in her house. There's a stir of memory, a sense of history. Her house has been opened up and the world is seeping in.

Since Sunday, when Emily and Walter left, Charlotte has been clinging fiercely to her routines. This new life feels so fragile, so unpredictable, she must maneuver carefully to preserve what little order she has left. Grocery shopping on Monday. Bills on Tuesday. Laundry on Wednesday. Ten pages of reading each night for the book group. And on Friday afternoon, at 2:00 P.M., her appointment at Pretty Nails.

She consults her watch: 1:18 P.M. Grabbing coat and gloves from the hall closet, her eyes graze the calendar hanging on the back of the door. On the twenty-sixth, she's drawn a tiny asterisk. She was going to write something, but when she faced the calendar, pen poised, she didn't know what to put down. This impending visit is something she could not have begun to picture, even in her most irrational middle-of-the-night imaginings. Yet now, she finds it hard *not* to think about: a speck in her peripheral vision, voice in the back of her head.

Joe couldn't fly out next weekend, a lecture he's giving at a conference in Oakland, so they decided they would meet the following Saturday. Just one night: Saturday night. Emily had been clear on this. Charlotte had worried she might try to bring the group to New Hampshire, but she hadn't mentioned it. Maybe she wanted to remain in control of her own leaving. Seattle was too far, obviously. By default, they were coming to Charlotte's.

Charlotte had talked to Joe twice since Sunday. Once (she called him) to say Emily was open to his visit. Once (he called her) to solidify the details. Their conversations had been cordial, friendly; she was surprised to find none of the tension from their last call seemed to reverberate. If anything, there was less tension between them. This was a curious thing about conflict, and one she didn't think she'd ever understand: that differences of opinion could remain just that. That sometimes there was no resolve, no closure. Here were Emily and Walter experiencing this enormous difference of opinion, and yet they carried on, kissing and teasing, wrapped in each other's arms.

Much as Charlotte doesn't understand it, this must be how relationships survive. For how can two people agree on everything? How can they reach consensus on every point? Of course, her marriage ended for *lack* of conflict—having hardly any disagreements at all. She considers her parents' marriage; they never disagreed, not that she observed. If it's true what they say (or what Emily says they say) about your parents' relationship serving as a model for all your future relationships, it's no wonder Joe's undercurrent of anger always made Charlotte nervous. It's no wonder she not only found the prospect of fighting with her husband alarming, but viewed it as a flaw.

She gazes at the October picture, a little girl in dress-up clothes: floppy hat, pearls, high heels. She'd bought the calendar because the photos reminded her of Emily as a child, always acting older than she was. She was always remarkably assured about relationships, matter-of-fact about what she called the "essential qualities in a man" (a phrase she'd coined at age thirteen and used from that point forward). Though the qualities fluctuated—from "musical ability" to "awareness of his spiritual side"—the matter-of-factness never did. Charlotte remembers once, when Emily was a sophomore in high school (with "ambition" and "desire to travel" ranking at the top of her list), listening to her explain her breakup with Peter McCann.

"We're just really different," Emily had said. She was stirring brown sugar into a bowl of oatmeal while Charlotte rinsed dishes at the sink.

"Yes," Charlotte agreed. Over the past few months, she'd observed poor Peter with a twinge of sympathy, knowing he wouldn't last. When he laughed hard, it sounded like a whimper. "I can see that."

"And not different in a good way."

Charlotte stopped, dish in hand, faucet running. "How can you tell if you're different in a good way?"

"You just can." Emily shrugged, raising a heaping spoonful of oatmeal to her mouth. "You can feel it. In your gut."

The gut: that elusive place located somewhere around her middle, the place she'd carried Emily for nine months and that she was now, twenty-two years later, trying in vain to disguise under control-top pantyhose. The gut eluded Charlotte. Listening to it, living by it, literally *feeling* something in it—she had no idea what this was like. Maybe her gut didn't work. Maybe when Emily was growing in there, her presence had become so strong that it lingered even now, so that it was she—instead of the all-knowing gut—that dictated what Charlotte felt.

"I mean, there will always be differences," Emily had said, spreading the A section of the Sunday paper across the kitchen table. "It's just about striking the right balance. Not too different, not too the same. You want to make sure you agree on the big things. It's all about priorities."

Oh, the assurance of it. *You want to. It's all about.* Charlotte knew this was Joe's influence—and, most likely, his new wife's. Charlotte used to torture herself imagining Joe and Valerie sitting on their deck, candidly discussing marriage and relationships and things like "striking the right balance." At the time, she was critical of this kind of openness. But now she wonders if she should be grateful. For if not them helping Emily navigate relationships, then who?

This is the precise fear that's been lodged in the back of Charlotte's mind ever since she spoke to Joe: that she, as a mother, is inadequate. She remembers how Joe sounded on the phone, the practiced way he delivered advice about their daughter, and doesn't think she could ever speak like that. She knows she is a loving mother, that her daughter means the world to her, but as far as advising Emily on complex decisions, preparing her for difficult situations—Charlotte has been so busy trying to prevent them she never stopped to equip Emily for dealing with them if they arrived.

And now, she's estranged her. They've spoken twice this week; both times blunt, perfunctory. On Sunday, Emily called to let Charlotte know they arrived safely. On Tuesday, Charlotte called to tell her the details of Joe's visit. As the week wore on, she's started to wish she'd never said anything about the baby. After a lifetime of shirking strong opinions, she went out on a limb, and now look what happened. Much as she feels convinced of her rightness, Charlotte knows full well that there are equally strong—maybe even equally valid—opinions besides her own.

The first time she discovered this, she was ten and had just gone to see the movie *Double Trouble* with her friend Becky Freeman. Charlotte was very sure, watching this movie, that it was a terrible movie. But as the lights came up and they gathered their coats, Becky exclaimed: "Wasn't that great?"

Charlotte smiled, thinking she was joking, then realized, seeing her bright, flushed face, that she meant it.

"What's so funny?" Becky asked. "I loved it. Didn't you?"

Charlotte said nothing—which wasn't the same thing as lying—but she was reeling inside. As surely as she knew *Double Trouble* was a terrible movie, Charlotte realized that Becky knew just as surely it was a great one. It struck her then, crossing the gummy lobby carpet, that for every thing she knew to be true in the world, there were hundreds—maybe millions—of people who felt otherwise, and felt it with the same certainty she did. And what was worse, these people would think Charlotte just as wrong, just as utterly misguided, as she thought them.

By the time she climbed into the backseat of Mr. Freeman's car, Charlotte felt lightheaded. She touched her forehead, as her mother would have; it was clammy. She didn't say a word the entire ride, but Becky didn't seem to notice. It wasn't unusual for Charlotte not to say much. While her friend chattered away, Charlotte stared out the window at the world and felt how insignificant she was.

It might have been that same afternoon that Charlotte began

to feel the first leanings toward what would appear, in the eyes of the world, noncommittal. Wishy-washy. On the surface it seemed like passivity, like softness of character, but in reality there was nothing soft about it. The puzzle was this: how could Charlotte believe in anything for sure if there were other people who believed just as surely in its opposite?

Shortly after *Double Trouble,* Charlotte began punctuating almost every statement with "I think."

"My mother? She's at the supermarket (I think)."

"I have a math test tomorrow (I think)."

She spoke these endings at a whisper, to be heard only by herself and God (if there was one). They were disclaimers: safeguards against lying by mistake. Although her mother *should* have been at the store at that moment, there was always the possibility that she wasn't. Maybe she got a flat tire. Maybe she realized, passing the liquor store on Route 30, that her husband had drunk the last of the brandy and so stopped there first. And though she had every reason to *think* her math test would take place the next day, a tornado could strike the school. Mr. Bakersfield, her math teacher, could die in his sleep.

The world began to feel like a very fragile place, a fearful place, one where nothing was under anyone's control. Charlotte's "I think"s became more urgent, more frequent. Now and then she realized she'd spoken one too loudly when she elicited a curious look from someone: a librarian, the mailman, a cashier. Then one June evening her father, sitting in his reading chair, folded down the top right corner of his *New York Times.* "Charlotte, my dear," he said. He spoke with the top half of his face only. "It's time you put an end to that whispering." Then he shook the paper upright and disappeared behind it.

Now, staring at the tiny asterisk, Charlotte shoves the closet shut. She checks her watch: 1:30. Right on time. As she's unlocking the front door, she hears the phone ring and pauses. If she picks it up, she might be late, but—what if it's Emily?

"Hello?"

"Hey! Charlotte!"

"Walter?" Charlotte feels her breath catch. "What happened? Is something wrong?"

"No, no, nothing's wrong."

"Where are you?"

"I'm at work." As if to confirm it, she hears a metallic screech in the background. "Listen, I only have a minute. I just wanted to tell you something."

Charlotte feels her heart flail against her rib cage as she prepares for the worst.

"I hooked you up to the Internet."

She blinks. "You what?"

"When I was messing with your computer last weekend, that's what I was doing, seeing if you had a modem, and you do, so I plugged you into the phone jack—"

Charlotte lets her purse sag by her feet.

"—then I called and got you hooked up. You could get on right now. Check the play listings in New York." She can hear the smile in his voice. "Just joking."

"Oh."

"But seriously, you can get e-mail. Buy books, look up recipes. Whatever."

"Well, thank you—that was thoughtful." She glances at the laptop sitting innocently on the shelf by the window, newly possessed of these hidden capabilities. Sure enough, a thin silver cord is coiled on the floor, plugged into a jack concealed somewhere beneath the table. There's something almost sinister about it, technology slithering into her house without permission.

"Charlotte?" Walter says. "You all right?"

For some reason, the question makes her eyes fill. "Oh, I'm fine, fine. I'm just heading out the—"

"Oh, sorry—"

"No, no, I didn't mean—I'm just distracted." She swipes quickly at her eyes.

"Well, listen, it's really easy to get online. Do you have ten seconds? I can tell you fast. First, just turn on the computer like usual."

Charlotte grabs for the stubby pencil and multicolored block of Post-it notes squatting by the phone. Running along the top border, the Post-its say: "Home Sweet Home!" She starts scribbling.

"You'll see a little picture on the side of the screen. Internet, Internet Explorer, something like that. Click on it, then it dials up the—" His voice is drowned out by a high metal whine, like a buzzsaw. Charlotte holds the pencil still, waiting. "—and just type in what you want to know."

"All right," she says dubiously.

"Did you get all that?"

"I think so."

"Listen, call me if you can't figure it out. Or else I'll show you next weekend. Once you get the hang of it, you'll use it all the time."

"I'm sure I will."

"All right, take it easy—" His last few words are smothered by a burst of noise.

Carefully, Charlotte replaces the receiver. She looks down at her scattering of notes. Edging the bottom border of the Post-it block are little pictures meant to evoke home: a latticed pie crust, a doormat, a kitten. She rereads what she wrote: *little picture, Internet, click it,* and, in larger, sprawling letters, *WHAT YOU WANT TO KNOW.*

She looks up from her notes then, glances down at herself: buttoned coat, muffler tucked around her neck, purse sitting at her feet like a pet waiting to be fed. Where was she going? It's a Friday. One-thirty. She was on her way to her appointment.

And now it's 1:38. She's late.

The weekly manicures began some twenty years ago. An effort, on Joe's part, to get Charlotte to stop picking at her fingernails. "If they look pretty to begin with," he said, with a pinched smile, "maybe you'll keep them that way."

Not surprisingly, Joe's strategy backfired; Charlotte was soon picking and nibbling more than ever. The surprising part was, she loved getting her nails done. She began actually looking forward to her weekly appointments. There was something comforting about the process: the dependable cause-and-effect, the transformation from ragged squares to shapely, shiny pink ovals.

The manicurists never mentioned Charlotte's abused cuticles, and this, too, was part of why she liked going. They were petite Asian women who smiled mildly and worked diligently. They rarely spoke to her at all. It was the opposite of being at the hairdresser, where Charlotte felt a constant pressure to make small talk or—depending on the quality of conversation around her—share intimacies and forge some kind of womanly bond. She spent most of her six-week trim and dye jobs feeling awkward, trying to avoid eye contact with the hairdresser in the mirror.

But at Pretty Nails, Charlotte felt no pressure. What she felt was an absence of herself. She didn't have to say or do or think. She could be docile, merely an extension of her hands, which were treated like objects, moved, soaked, scraped, buffed, picked up, put down. She didn't even mind the brief hand massage, so impersonal was the kneading of skin and prodding of bone.

Today, though, she doesn't feel her usual calmness. She is ten minutes late, a result of Walter's call, and is now winded from half-jogging to the salon from her car. As she perches at one of the tiny tables, her breaths are wheezy, and the sound makes her uncomfortable. It prevents her from being invisible. She tries to focus on the manicurist—Shirley, according to her nameplate—who has her head bent over Charlotte's hands, exposing a shiny black scalp and arrow-straight part. The pose reminds Charlotte of Emily's brief stint as a palm reader. In fifth grade, Emily and her friend Gretchen Myers would sit in the kitchen every day after school, practicing their palm-reading while Charlotte made dinner.

"One . . . two . . . ," Emily would count, excruciatingly slowly, hunched over Gretchen's palm. "Three . . . four." She would look up then and, in her *abracadabra* voice, intone: "You . . . shall . . . have . . . four . . . babies."

The girls delivered all their predictions in what they called their *abracadabra* voices: deep, spooky, some variation on the disembodied man on Nickelodeon who counseled Mork from Ork. The voice had a dash of the biblical too, probably modeled after Gretchen's exposure to Sunday school. The *abracadabra* voice always rang with authority, despite the fact that the predictions changed daily and the palms never did.

"One . . . two . . ." Emily ducked down again, scrutinizing some intersection of tiny lines. "Three. You shall have three husbands," she pronounced; then her voice returned to normal. "That's not bad."

Then one night, when Charlotte was tucking her in, Emily asked if she could read her palm. Charlotte had obliged, of course; truth be told, she was tickled to be asked. She perched on the side of the bed while Emily grasped her palm in her sturdy little fingers. In the trapezoid of light from her Mickey Mouse lamp, Emily bent her head, loose hair tumbling over her pajamas, while Charlotte waited patiently for her tally of future pets and babies and husbands. After several minutes, Emily spoke in a low, ghostly *abracadabra*: "You . . . shall . . . not . . . be . . . sad."

It caught Charlotte off guard; she'd never heard their kitchen-table predictions go beyond the countable.

"You shall smile every day," Emily went on. "You shall go on dates and fall in love."

Charlotte was touched, saddened, stunned. Were these the things her daughter secretly wished for her? Things she truly felt, in her gut, but probably thought she was inventing?

"You shall sit on a nice beach. You shall do good on *Jeopardy.* And before bed . . . you shall let Emily have a Chipwich." Then she snuck a glance upward, and they both laughed.

"Water?"

Charlotte looks up. Shirley is gesturing to a cooler in the corner.

"Oh, no," Charlotte says. "I'm fine."

The wheezing must be distracting, Charlotte thinks, and smiles apologetically. As she crosses one leg over the other, an effort to make herself less conspicuous, she jostles the dish of nail-polish remover and spills it onto the table.

"Oh!"

A few customers look over.

"I'm sorry," Charlotte says. From out of nowhere, another

manicurist flutters over with a handful of paper towels. "I'm so sorry."

Now Charlotte's leg hurts, but she doesn't dare move again. She feels too pronounced: all breath and body. Her eyes roam to a sign that says WE DO PEDICURE. A drawing of a lotus flower in a brass frame. She alights on a little boy sitting on the floor, a row of toys lined up on the rug beside him: action figures, baseball cards, a shiny truck with oversized wheels. Charlotte watches as he picks up a wedge of cards and crunches them in his chubby fists. He grabs an action figure, picks up the truck, and bangs the two together like cymbals.

"Ssshhh," one of the manicurists says every so often, without looking up. It's not clear which one is the boy's mother; it seems they all are.

This little boy is typical of Charlotte's new world. In the same way, after Joe left, she noticed married couples constantly, this week she's been inundated with babies and mothers. They're everywhere: book covers, TV shows, crossing in front of her car in the street. On Wednesday, Oprah did a show on new techniques in breast-feeding. *People*'s cover story was "Hollywood Moms!" In the supermarket, Charlotte found herself in line behind a woman with two young children. She watched, riveted, the seemingly unconscious way this mother tended to them—touching their cheeks, wiping their noses, giving them Honey Grahams to gnaw on—all while unloading her cart and paying her bill. She never once appeared to look at them directly.

It wasn't the first time she'd witnessed this kind of maternal sixth sense. The first time she met Joe's family, more than thirty people were gathered at his mother's house for dinner. To Charlotte, the scene was chaos: children running wild, screaming, giggling, brandishing foods and toys as weapons. Sometimes they tumbled to the floor, indulged in the requisite cry, then righted themselves and barreled on.

Charlotte perched on the edge of a love seat. She felt Joe's hand moving at the small of her back—his hands were always on her, always moving—but she couldn't focus on him, or the adult conversation around her. She was too busy fearing for these children's lives. She was terrified one might run into the corner of the coffee table or smack into a doorjamb or go flying down the basement stairs. But to her amazement, their mothers barely seemed to be paying attention. The longer she watched, though, the more she realized these mothers were actually aware of the children's every move. When one ran by needing attention, the mother would simply extend an arm—still nodding along in conversation, slathering a cracker with cheese, never skipping a beat—and gather the child in her lap, wipe its nose, dry its tears, and set it free.

Now, seeing this little boy and listening to his chorus of mothers, Charlotte doubts she ever cultivated this instinct. Did she ever, as a young mother, sense Emily's irritation and slip a pacifier in her mouth, part of a fluid choreography of chopping vegetables for dinner? What she remembers is just the opposite: hovering over Emily's crib, watching as she crossed the street, never taking her eyes off her child for a minute.

"Miss?"

Charlotte looks up.

"Done." Shirley emphasizes the word in a way that indicates she's said it before.

"Done? Already?" Charlotte looks down at her hands and, sure enough, there are pearly pink islands marooned amid the clutter of her bitten skin. It happened so quickly. She feels sad to have missed it. "I guess I wasn't paying attention."

Shirley stands and moves toward the hand dryers, a signal Charlotte should follow. Charlotte uncrosses her legs with difficulty. The left one has fallen asleep. As she struggles from her chair, the little boy looks up at her. Charlotte pauses. She smiles at the boy, a smile that feels too eager, too bright, too much; she can feel it twisting oddly on her face. But the boy smiles back just the same, a grand smile, toothless and drooling and exuberant. Charlotte feels her eyes water again.

"Miss?"

Charlotte hobbles toward Shirley, murmuring apologies. Obediently, she offers up her limp hands, lets Shirley lay them inside the dryer like fish on a grill. Charlotte smiles, grateful and embarrassed. With her wet nails baking, leg tingling, eyes brimming, she is unable to do a thing about it when a tear escapes and races down her cheek.

"Mom? Is that you?"

Charlotte can't blame Emily for sounding confused. She knows how out of character it is to be calling on a Saturday night. In fact, Charlotte doesn't think she's ever called Emily on a Saturday night. Certainly not since she moved into the alternative living arrangement. There's something about a Saturday that feels more forbidden than a Friday, couched in the middle of the ambiguous stretch of weekend hours. But tonight she couldn't help herself.

"Is something wrong?" Emily says, her confusion edged with concern.

"Not at all!" The words feel so forced, Charlotte thinks her voice might break. She pauses, takes a breath. "I just wanted to call and say hello."

On the other end of the line, Emily is waiting. She knows the call was motivated by more than this, and Charlotte agrees, it was. The need was something physical, primal, not a need for words but for sound: the sound of her daughter's voice. But this she couldn't bring herself to say.

"I just wanted to thank Walter," Charlotte says, opting out. "For the Internet."

"The what?"

She's surprised Walter hasn't told her, and hopes it's okay that she just did. "Well," she hesitates. "Walter called yesterday."

"Oh God," Emily moans. Charlotte can practically hear her eyes rolling. "What did he do now?"

"He, well, he set me up on the Internet. On your old laptop. Last weekend." Charlotte pauses. "I thought he would have said something."

"Are you kidding?" Emily laughs. "Walter? Mr. Do-good-deeds-and-take-no-credit? God, he's so perfect. Isn't he so ridiculously perfect?" She laughs again, then adds, "It's almost annoying." Which sounds like a joke, but isn't quite.

"Oh," Charlotte says.

"Did you want to talk to him?"

"That's all right. You can just tell him for me. Tell him thanks."

"Uh-huh."

Charlotte takes a breath. "So how are you doing?"

"How am I doing?"

Her tone is instantly suspicious. She probably assumes Charlotte is calling to probe for information, when she actually wants to hear nothing serious at all. Her "how are you doing" was delivered not with emphasis on the *are,* or even the *you,* but the *doing.* Emily's students. Lessons. Snack times. Weekend plans. She wants Emily to speak to her the way she always has: like a verbal journal, relaying the daily litany of her life.

But tonight she isn't forthcoming. She uses colorless phrases like "the usual" and "nothing much." Listening to her, Charlotte desperately wishes she'd never been so adamant about this baby. She feels tears prying at her eyes, bites down hard on her lip.

"Mom?" Emily says. Her voice is wary. "You okay?"

"Oh, sure," Charlotte says, furiously blinking. "Don't worry about me."

It's not exactly a lie—she doesn't actually say she's okay, because she's not okay—yet she isn't being honest. If she were, she might tell Emily how hard this week has been. She might tell her how, though she's been clinging to familiar routines, they aren't working like they used to. How she no longer gets the same satisfaction from a good deal at the Super Fresh: two-for-one soup, plastic wrap for 99 cents. How in the evenings, when she settles on the couch at the exact moment *Jeopardy!* is starting and the dishwasher is churning and the patio light is snapping to life, she doesn't feel her usual sense of accomplishment. What she feels is empty.

If she were being honest, she could tell her about the self-doubt that's been plaguing her night and day. How even the most innocent exchange can arouse it. How when the bag boy at the Super Fresh numbly recited, "Paper or plastic?" she worried about the implications, weighing the question for a full minute. She could tell her how she's been inundated with babies and mothers and even—black people. African Americans. African-Americans. How she isn't even sure what word to use, or what punctuation, but in the five days since Emily and Walter's visit she thinks she's seen more black people than she has in her entire life. She would admit that today, all day, Saturday, she stayed inside on purpose. That although she drummed up reasons for it—it was drizzling outside, she felt a tickle in her throat—the truth was, she just didn't dare leave.

And yet she feels no calmer in here. There's a restlessness

inside her, like a moth batting at a lightbulb. A feeling not unlike being unable to sleep that persists in every waking hour.

"Mom?"

She missed what Emily was saying. Something about a sleeping bag? A camping trip, maybe?

"Are you there?"

"I'm here," Charlotte says quickly. "I'm listening."

Emily pauses. "Is there something you want to say?"

She could tell her all of it, Charlotte thinks. Tell her everything, this minute. Her eyes comb the living room, grasping at solid objects. She wants just this: the concrete world. She doesn't want it disrupted. She knows that to speak her feelings out loud is to confirm them—once said, they have always been said. Still, she might feel better to have shared them.

"I—" She falters. "I just wanted to make sure we're—"

"Hold on a sec, Mom," Emily says, and Charlotte hears a voice in the background. It's not Walter; one of the roommates, probably. Charlotte hears a muffled laugh and wonders irrationally if they are laughing about her. A picture of Emily's surroundings rises in her mind. Lumps of multicolored candle wax. Burning incense sticks. Full-bellied wine glasses, the bottoms stained deep red. She hears Emily say, "Be there in a minute," followed by a thump.

"Sorry," she says, returning.

Charlotte stares at her lap.

"What were you saying?"

"Nothing." Her nerve is gone.

"No, what was it?"

"It was—I just wanted to see how you were."

Emily pauses. Then Charlotte hears a click she knows all too well: tongue ring on teeth.

"I shouldn't have called so late in the first place."

"I don't care if you call me late," Emily says. "It's *not* late."

"Still," Charlotte says, trying to keep her voice from trembling. "I should let you go."

The closed laptop stares blankly up at her from the kitchen table. The red numbers on the oven clock glow 10:48. Slowly, Charlotte peels the Post-it from the laptop cover and sticks it on the windowsill. Through the slats of the blinds, she can see a sliver of parking lot. The matching porch lights of her neighbors' houses. The belly of the moon, just over half full. She opens up the laptop and, with one fingertip, wipes off the dusty screen.

She consults the series of aging notes and signs affixed to the machine. Years ago, when Emily passed on the computer, she'd known that even the slightest confusion about turning it on would be enough to make Charlotte give up. So she'd taped arrows to the sides, directing Charlotte to the back left corner. Next to the button itself, she stuck the words: TURN ME ON!

Charlotte finds the button and presses it. The machine emits a tone both sharp and shaky, as if snapping to extreme alertness from a deep, deep sleep. The screen awakens to a recurring pattern of geometric gray shapes. Then the machine begins to hum, hesitantly at first, surging and faltering like a car engine in the cold.

Charlotte watches as a dribbling of words and objects emerge on the screen. She consults her Post-it. *Little picture,* it says. *Internet. Click it.* She focuses on the blue lowercase "e" that says "Internet Explorer" and prods the plastic ball, inching the arrow across the screen. With the arrow centered in the "e," she pushes down. At once, the computer emits a startling series of noises—

"Dialing," it says—the strenuous zapping and pinging like something out of a video game.

The refrigerator starts humming, as if sensing a companion. New ice churns somewhere in its belly. Then, without warning, she finds herself looking at an entirely new screen, smothered with pictures and photos and headlines: *Entertainment Shopping Money Get A Job Find An Apartment.* The sheer amount of stimuli is enough to make her shut it off and crawl to bed. But there, along the top, she sees an island of empty space, a long blank column bracketed by the words *Search* and *Find.*

She refers to her notes again, even though she knows just what they say: *WHAT YOU WANT TO KNOW.*

Tentatively, she moves her cursor into the empty box. She thinks for a moment, then types: *I want to know how to have a better relationship with my daughter.* She pushes her cursor to the end of the box and taps *Find.* A long list appears in response. Her eyes scan the wealth of options, articles, authors, information—she can't begin to take it all in.

She bites down on the inside of her cheek, repositions her cursor. Types: *I want to know the correct spelling: African American or African-American?* Clicks: *Find.* Again, a list of answers unscrolls on her screen. The concept is so simple: type a question, send it off, and be told the answer. To be *told,* she thinks, savoring the word. To be *told.* To empty all her ambiguities and worries and uncertainties into an anonymous box on a computer screen—fling them into space.

Charlotte begins typing faster, one question on top of another. *I want to know the latest a pregnant woman can safely get an abortion.* Click: *Find.*

I want to know what a feeling in the gut means.

I want to know about interracial dating.

Alternative learning environments.

Mindfulness.

Political correctness.

Arugula.

Bulimia.

Fur.

God.

It will be hours before she lifts her head, feeling surprised at how late it's gotten, how many hours have slipped by without her notice. The computer screen will stare back at her, glowing benignly in the dark. When she turns it off and makes her way to bed, she will fall asleep instantly. Because while she used to fear the imaginary, now it's the real she's afraid of. And the danger is much, much greater. Maybe true danger has simply never touched her life before, and now that it has, it's cracked her imaginary world wide open.

chapter six

Charlotte holds her breath as the taxi pulls up. Even though she feels certain that Valerie isn't coming, she braces herself as Joe steps out, waiting for a long, thin calf to emerge behind him. She waits as Joe walks around to the trunk, waits as he slings his bag over his shoulder, peels bills from his wallet, pays the driver, slams the door. Only then does she let out a sigh of relief. Joe is alone.

Quickly, Charlotte turns to the hall mirror for a final once-over: straight denim skirt, pale blue rollneck sweater. She feels silly to have bought a new outfit, but tells herself she needed one anyway; the timing was just convenient. The trickier rationalization was the rescheduling of her hair appointment. ("A family reunion," she explained to the colorist, Cynthia, who regarded her skeptically as she swathed her head in foil. "An unexpected one.") Regardless, her hair is now freshly de-grayed. Her fingernails are buffed and Shell Pink.

Joe raps at the front door, his old confident *rat-a-tat-tat.*

Charlotte waits a measured beat—about as long as it would have taken her to walk in from another room where, presumably, she had been doing something other than watching him arrive—and opens the door.

"Hello, Joe."

"Hi, Char." Joe grins, then corrects himself. "I mean, Charlotte."

He looks about the same as the last time she saw him, at Wesleyan. Stylishly unkempt clothes, slightly cocky smile, brown hair swept back as if he's just raked his fingers through it. But then, Joe has never seemed to change much physically. His appearance seems to originate in his personality, in a liquid charm and easy talkativeness that necessitates lanky legs, loose arms, that requires room to roam.

Charlotte steels herself for a hug, having been caught off guard with Walter. But, as suspected, she needn't have worried. Despite the many years that have passed since they were married, Joe and Charlotte have never hugged or kissed hello. This can't be unusual, Charlotte reasons, with couples who are divorced ("couples" seeming the wrong word, somehow, for what they used to be). The difference with them is that the distance doesn't stem from old resentment or hostility, from anger that's taken the place of passion. It's the opposite: a chaste kiss or platonic hug would be too blatant a reminder of what was always missing in their marriage, of the passion that was really never there to begin with.

Joe steps inside. Charlotte closes the door and, for the second time in two weeks, watches the receding bumper of a Millville Taxicab. Maybe it is, in fact, *the* Millville Taxicab. And she is its sole customer lately. She wonders if her neighbors have noticed, if they are wondering who this strange man is who just stepped out of the taxi, is clearly not from the East Coast, and has disappeared inside Charlotte's—

"I'm the first one here, I take it?"

Charlotte turns. It takes a moment to accept the fact that Joe is actually standing in her foyer. His hair seems a bit thinner, a bit blonder. (Does he get it colored? Does Valerie insist on it?) He's wearing tan pants, a loose white shirt, a thin cotton blazer the color of sand. On his feet, brown loafers that look like they are made of thatched leather. He's very tan, his teeth very white. (Does she make him bleach his teeth too?)

"You're the first," Charlotte says. "But they should be here soon." She has no way of knowing this for sure, but maybe saying it will make it true. "Emily said they would leave about ten, which would get them here about five, if they don't hit any major problems. But you know how she likes to sleep in. Walter, though, Walter's a different story. He gets up early and he's just, you know, very responsible."

Charlotte stops talking. She'd made a promise to herself about this weekend: she was staying out of it. Emily could voice her opinions—and Joe, and Walter—but Charlotte was just here to facilitate and listen. She'd been opinionated the first time around, and now she deeply regrets it. Charlotte wants her daughter to keep this baby. Desperately. But, more than that, she wants to preserve her relationship with her daughter.

Joe is looking at her with a small smile. Not the old pinched smile, but a smile of amusement, even affection. "You're a trip, Char," he says. "Really and truly." Then, with what seems like unnecessary flourish, he hoists his bag off his shoulder and drops it on the floor. It is made of dark leather, riddled with furled travel tags: Athens, Paris, Aspen. "So," he says, smile widening to a grin, "aren't you going to offer me something? I know you have a thousand appetizers hidden around here somewhere."

"Not a thousand," Charlotte says, mentally calculating the puckered shrimp and vegetable dips and other nonmeat snacks she has packed away in the refrigerator. "Are you hungry?"

"Nah. Still recovering from the plane cuisine. But a drink would do me good."

Charlotte nods and starts toward the kitchen. Instead of following, Joe ducks around the partition and into the living room. "These are the new digs, huh?"

"Yes," Charlotte says, to the empty kitchen. "I guess."

She hears the hinges creaking on the curtains and sneaks a peek into the living room. Joe is peering out at the patio, hands cupped around his eyes, much like Emily her first time through. Charlotte glances around nervously. The place is spotless; she couldn't have been more thorough cleaning. But suddenly she wishes she had done a better job, well, editing. Confiscated the *People* with its montage of pregnant celebrities on the cover. The Bed, Bath and Beyond coupon on the refrigerator door. She spots the two packs of moving announcements on the windowsill, still wrapped in plastic, and quickly shoves them into the utensil drawer.

"You've been here since, what, September?" Joe calls out, accompanied by the creak of retreating hinges.

"August, actually."

"And you're liking it?"

"Oh, yes," Charlotte says. Of all people, she can't tell Joe how she pines for the house on Dunleavy Street. "I am. Very much."

Joe appears in the kitchen doorway. "How are the neighbors?"

"They're fine."

"You know them?"

"Some." It isn't a complete lie. How many people does

"some" entail? "One woman, Ruth. She lives over there." Charlotte gestures pointlessly at the hidden kitchen window. "And the woman upstairs. Bea."

"Bea, huh?"

His tone prickles Charlotte. It sounds belittling somehow. Was he implying "Bea" was a condo person's name? An old-lady name? A single-lady name? That nobody was named "Bea" in the entire city of Seattle?

"Emily and Walter know her too," she adds. "And her boyfriend. Bill. They all went out to a bar together. When they were here, two weeks ago. Visiting."

She winces, listening to herself, knowing all too well what she's doing. Creating a false sense of closeness with her upstairs neighbor, leading Joe to believe they're better friends than they are. Mentioning "bar" and "Bill" with such nonchalance it's almost laughable. Reminding him that Emily and Walter came to visit. It's the same need Joe aroused in her so many years ago: a pressure to sound laid-back, to act easygoing, to be something she's not.

"Fantastic," Joe says. He knocks on the top of the doorjamb, as if to verify it's real wood, then takes an exaggerated step to where Charlotte is standing. From the middle of the kitchen, they face the spotless counter with its single bottle of wine. It couldn't look more conspicuous, standing tall beside the flower-patterned paper towels and row of chubby ceramic canisters (sugar, flour, coffee) like a worldly impostor trying unsuccessfully to blend in.

Joe reaches for the bottle. Charlotte watches him spin it in his hand and scan the label. She had no idea what brand to buy, had asked the cashier at the liquor store to recommend something. If it's a bad choice, Joe doesn't let on.

"Got an opener?"

Charlotte opens the utensil drawer, blocking it with her hip so he doesn't see the stashed moving announcements.

"Thank you, ma'am."

Joe whistles as he spears the cork. Charlotte removes two wineglasses from the cabinet. She gives them a quick once-over to make sure they aren't dusty. She can't imagine the last time they were used; they were probably last touched when she was moving. If she were being truly sanitary—if this weren't, say, the first time she'd been alone with her ex-husband in fifteen years—she would wash them for any traces of the inky *Jersey Tribunes* they'd been wrapped in. But now, she reasons, is not the time.

Charlotte places the glasses on the counter. As he twists the cork, Joe is alternately whistling and grunting, punctuated by a pop that makes Charlotte flinch.

"There we go," he says, sniffing the smoking lip of the bottle. He fills each glass just over halfway. If Emily were here, she'd make a comment about the shock of seeing her mother drinking. Charlotte is glad, for the moment, that she isn't.

"Cheers," Joe says, handing Charlotte a glass.

"Cheers," she repeats.

"To parenting," he says. They clink.

"Yes." She takes a sip, managing not to wince at the bitterness.

Joe swallows, smacks his lips, and lets out an exaggerated "Ahhh." Then he moves toward the table, his loose strides looking comfortable here already. He's whistling again; Charlotte had forgotten about the whistling. Joe had whistled his way through their entire ten years together. In the beginning it was light, endearing; then it increased in volume and frequency, until by the end of their marriage the whistling had become almost constant, unconscious, even aggressive. Even light tunes—"Take Me Out to the Ball Game," a Coke commercial jingle—contained a hint of anger. A few times, Charlotte had found Emily trying to whistle in her crib, her wet lips pursed and heaving soundless puffs of air, like blowing out candles on a birthday cake.

They sit, facing each other. Joe crosses his legs at the knee. This must be a West Coast thing, Charlotte thinks; he never used to sit like that. In fact, he probably scoffed at men who did. His top leg is so long that the end of it—the thatched-looking leather loafer—reaches halfway across the kitchen, its length intensified by the shoe swinging casually from his toe.

Charlotte takes another sip of wine, feeling her cheeks grow warm. She drinks so infrequently it's embarrassing. Joe studies his glass, turning it in his hand. "I remember these."

"You do?"

"They were your mom's, weren't they?"

They'd been her grandmother's, but like the unwashed glasses, this seems too minor a point to dwell on. "I think so," she says, then amends her lie. "They might have been."

Joe takes a swallow. "They're great," he says. "I always liked these glasses. Real antiques. Authentic."

Charlotte is suddenly aware of the weight of history between them, the presence of a shared past, uncomfortable in its intimacy. It's almost impossible to believe that these two people were once married. That they once shared a bed, that once upon a time this man stepped naked into the shower behind this woman and spread his long fingers over her wet shoulders, that his body was once inside hers. How is this possible? How could those same two people sit here now, on an autumn day more than two decades later, talking about wineglasses that did or didn't belong to her mother?

"Great lady," Joe says.

Charlotte looks up. "Who?"

"Your mom."

"Oh."

"George too. Good guy."

Joe had always made the assumption of calling her father by his first name. Her father, Charlotte recalls, never seemed to like it.

"How's old Polly doing?" he asks. "Still kicking?"

Polly: Charlotte's great-aunt, her father's sister. She lived in Texas, near her grown children, was ninety-three and seemingly immortal.

"She's starting to slow down a little," Charlotte replies. "Linda says her hip is mending, which is good, but her mind isn't what it used to be. And her sciatica's been worse." She looks at Joe's face, his expression of fixed politeness, and stops herself from saying more. "She's hanging in there," she concludes. It was one of her mother's favorite catchphrases. "And your family? How are they?"

"Let's see." Joe frowns into his glass, as if the family news might be written inside it. "Mike just got into Notre Dame."

Mike, Michael: Joe's sister Martie's son. The last time Charlotte saw Michael, he was in diapers.

"That's wonderful news."

"Baseball scholarship. The kid can really hit."

"Wonderful," Charlotte says again.

Joe shifts legs, flopping the right one over the left knee. He presses the heel of his hand against his forehead, then sits forward abruptly, jostling the table. "Char," he says. Wine sloshes in his glass. "We can do this, can't we?"

Charlotte is alarmed. "Do what?"

"Sit here? Drink a glass of wine? Act like two people who used to be married?"

He grins, but there is none of the usual ease about it; this grin looks like something spread on deliberately, for appearance's sake, like Brie.

"What do you mean?"

"I mean, it seems ridiculous to not talk about what's really going on here. What we're really doing—*here.*" He waves his arms in an aimless sort of way, as if to say: Look at where I am, for God's sake! In a condo! In New Jersey! "I mean, I don't really feel like talking about sciatica and my nephew Mike, do you?"

Charlotte's face burns, a combination of wine and embarrassment. She assumes that Joe is implying the fault lies with her. For this conversation feeling stilted, for the subjects being bland and boring, for—why not!—the marriage ending in the first place. She wishes she hadn't told him about the sciatica. That was a mistake. His throwing in "my nephew Mike" was, she knew, a mercy mention.

"Of course," Charlotte says, a note of false confidence in her voice.

"Okay," Joe says, leaning back. He smiles a genuine smile. "Real conversation."

Charlotte glances toward the window. She would give anything for Emily and Walter to pull up right now. Or, better yet: for her house to be empty. To be purely alone. She could cry, she wants to be alone so badly.

"I'll start." Joe picks up his glass and twines the stem between two long fingers, eyebrows gathered in what resembles deep thought. Charlotte wonders if this is his "professor" persona:

legs crossed, brow pinched, hungry for a debate. She can just imagine him presiding over a seminar table of eager college students, reeling them in with playful questions, pouncing on their answers. They must love him, Charlotte thinks. Love him, or be in love with him.

"Tell me about Walter," Joe says finally, setting his wineglass down. "You sound like you really like the guy."

This Charlotte hadn't expected. "I do?"

"Don't you?"

"Well, I guess. Why wouldn't I?"

"So this is an easy one." Joe smiles. "Why do you?"

He lifts the glass again, confident now that the ball is rolling, and studies Charlotte over the rim. His expression—this entire scene, in fact—reminds Charlotte of a dinner party when they were first married, thrown by Joe's new colleagues from Temple and their wives. After dinner, among the dirty dishes and baguette crumbs and mangled wedge of cheese, they had played a game of ethics. In it you were asked how you would handle certain delicate situations, and the others could challenge you if they believed you weren't telling the truth. Charlotte can still remember the other wives sitting around the table: one wore a black turtleneck so thick it engulfed her chin, two were clearly not wearing bras. They struck her as the kind of women who might swap husbands, not that she had any direct experience with that kind of thing. They all delivered their questions in the same wary tones, peering over the rims of their Chiantis. Charlotte felt as if those narrowed eyes were boring right through her, seeing her very core, all her conflicted emotions and formless opinions and fearful, partial truths.

But, as it turned out, they couldn't read her at all. Charlotte won the game. "Isn't she amazing?" Joe marveled, over and over.

He squeezed her knee so hard it hurt. "Sweetheart," he said, kissing her cheek. "You have a perfect poker face."

Now, Charlotte pauses, flustered. "Tell you why I like Walter?"

"Yeah." Joe sits forward, elbows resting on his knees. "Tell me why you like Walter."

There's the slightest hint of anticipation in his pose, in his half smile, remnants of a time when he hung on Charlotte's every word. He was always waiting—maybe he couldn't help but be waiting, still—for the moment she would finally surprise him, when her inner self would be revealed.

"Well—" She swallows, and attempts being glib. "Why did *you* say it sounded like I liked him?"

It doesn't work. The glibness sounds like what it is: cowardice.

Joe leans back. He lifts his glass and shrugs. "Because he wakes up so damned early. Because he's so damned responsible. He sounds like a man after your own heart, Char."

Charlotte feels herself redden. She looks down at the table. She can't just sit here. She has to say something. She picks up her own glass, stares at it for a moment, then says, "He's just different from Emily," and takes a sip.

"You mean he's pro-baby." Joe sits forward again, a touch eagerly, the professor sensing a gray area in a student's thesis.

"No." Charlotte shakes her head, swallowing. "That's not what I meant."

"But he is."

"Well, that's what he says, so yes, I guess he is."

"That must make you happy, since you're pro-life."

Charlotte balks at the label. She doesn't like the depth of commitment, the sense of identity, it implies. Politically, she is registered an Independent, but the word has always struck her as misleading. It should be Undecided.

"I suppose," she says.

"Okay." Joe's voice is more animated. "So he's pro-life. Why else is he different? Because he's black?"

Charlotte's eyes fly to Joe's face, wondering what he's implying, but sees immediately that it was just a joke.

"He's more traditional," she amends.

"Again, pro-baby."

"It's not just that. He—" She gropes for a safe example. "He eats meat."

Joe laughs loudly. "Does he?"

"He wears a cross around his neck."

"Fashion or religion?"

"Religion," Charlotte says quickly. She's never asked Walter, but feels absolutely sure that this is true. "He set me up on the Internet, and he brought me candy—he, he asked about my book group. He actually seemed to want to hear." She stops herself. She hadn't meant to say all that, never would have if it weren't for the wine. When she dares to look at Joe's face, anticipating his amusement, what she finds there is worse: sympathy.

To his credit, Joe leaves it alone. "So," he says. He uncrosses, recrosses his legs again. "A conservative, God-fearing meat-eater. They do sound pretty different."

Charlotte can't help but wonder if, in his mind, "different" means incompatible. She remembers Emily's assessment of poor Peter McCann in tenth grade: *We're just really different, and not in a good way.* But if there's a *not*-good kind of different, there must be a good kind. Maybe that's the kind of different Emily and Walter are. For the first time, she realizes she really wants this to be true.

"How are they doing, anyway?" Joe says. He is tracing one finger around the rim of his glass. "Em and Walter. Are they cool? Are they fighting?"

"I'm not sure," she answers truthfully.

He looks toward the window. Charlotte wonders what he's thinking.

"Have you talked to Em any more? About all this?"

"No," she admits, knowing how irresponsible this must sound. She might explain: *I was terrified.* Or: *I was plagued with doubt.* Instead she says, "Have you?"

"Not really. Not seriously, anyway." Joe picks up his glass and looks inside it, swirling the last of the wine around in the bottom. "But I do know Val had a pretty long talk with her the other night."

Charlotte feels a sudden crushing weight, like a lead blanket falling on her shoulders, muffling her senses. "She did?" she says, voice flattened to a whisper.

"I don't know what they talked about." Joe swallows the last of his wine in a matter-of-fact gulp, then raises both palms as if to plead innocence. "I don't pry."

Don't *pry?* Charlotte feels her body's unconscious reaction: heat rising, head aching, heart hammering. To pry—the concept is so misplaced, so irrelevant. This isn't about eavesdropping on two teenagers gossiping about their homeroom teacher or the cute boy in math class. This is about a *baby.* This is about his *daughter.* Charlotte closes her eyes, wine swimming behind her lids. She reminds herself of the promise she made to stay out of it. She reminds herself what the past two weeks have felt like, of her new respect for Joe as a parent and, most importantly, her doubts about herself.

Joe scrapes his chair back, making Charlotte's eyelids flutter open. "You all set there?" he says, raising his eyebrows at her glass.

She manages a nod.

He heads to the counter, whistles while pouring, as Charlotte is assaulted by thoughts of what Valerie might have said. She knows Emily idolizes her stepmother; the woman can probably convince her of anything. Maybe she recounted an abortion of her own, dismissing it as casually as the facelift Emily once mentioned Valerie had—so breezily, so nonchalantly. Emily, who had always scoffed at plastic surgery. Who rolled her eyes when she heard Marion from the book group had her stomach stapled. And that wasn't even cosmetic! That was for medical reasons!

"Char," Joe is saying. "Charlotte."

"What?" She blinks.

Joe laughs and starts heading toward the door, glass in hand. "They're here."

For what seems like minutes, Emily clings tightly around Joe's neck. Her face is buried in the hollow of his collarbone, his lips pressed to the top of her head. When he pulls back, he pushes her tangled hair behind her ears to look in her face. "Hi, princess."

"Hi, Joe," Emily says.

Charlotte feels her heart swell at the sight of her daughter. She's wearing a zippered, hooded sweater over a pair of corduroy overalls. The sweater is a thick, woolly brown that's starting to pill at the cuffs and collar, the overalls a burgundy color that looks like it was dipped in rust. Charlotte's eyes move instinctively to her belly, even though she knows she couldn't be showing yet. She remembers the single pair of overalls she herself ever owned, a gift from Joe's sister when she was pregnant. She can still remember the pressure of her stomach pushing against the denim, the snug space it created, like a papoose.

Charlotte hears the slam of a trunk. Seconds later, Walter appears.

"Wal!" Joe says. His exuberance is irritating. He extends a hand, keeping the other arm around Emily, wineglass hovering by her left ear. "Good to see you, buddy."

"Same here, Joe." Walter drops two battered backpacks on the floor and shakes Joe's hand, then turns to Charlotte. "Charlotte, how you doing."

This time, when he gives her a hug, she doesn't flinch. In fact, for a moment she loves him for it.

"Hi, Mom," Emily says. She disentangles herself from Joe and gives Charlotte a kiss on the cheek.

They all step back then, resuming their respective spaces. There's an awkwardness about them, an uncertainty about where to go next, what to do. As host, Charlotte feels it's her responsibility to fix it; and yet there's no precedent to work from here. The purpose for their being together feels so palpable, so obvious, it would be silly to go into normal hosting mode—taking drink orders, ushering guests to chairs, setting out trays of water crackers and cheeses.

She notices something tucked under Walter's elbow: a sleeping bag. Army green, sleeved in plastic, drawn tight with a frayed cord. Why has he brought it? So he and Emily won't have to sleep together? Maybe it's a sign that something's wrong, that they've been fighting. Or maybe it's a gesture of courtesy, to put Charlotte at ease.

"Walter?" Charlotte says. "Can I take that for you?"

"It's not for me." Walter smiles and tosses the bag in Joe's direction. Joe catches it with a laugh.

"Why—" Charlotte starts to ask, then stops. They are all smiling; she's the only one confused.

Emily gives her an emphatic look. "It's for *Joe,* Mom." When Charlotte's blank expression doesn't change, she gets impatient. "Remember, we talked about this? Last weekend? On the phone?"

Charlotte has a flash of their conversation last Saturday, the one to which she'd been only half paying attention. Had she unknowingly agreed to Joe's staying here? In a sleeping bag on her floor? Which floor? Which room? She begins to sweat.

"Mom. We talked about this."

"Right, I know, I—"

"Hey," Joe shrugs. "If it's a problem, I grab a hotel. No big deal. I could use some new shampoo anyway."

A good-natured laugh from Walter.

"It's not a problem," Emily says quickly, eyes on Charlotte. "We already talked about this, Mom. Right?"

Charlotte recognizes the need in her daughter's eyes, the near-pleading. "Right," she says, forcing a smile. "We talked about it. It's fine."

Emily looks expectantly at Joe. Charlotte's smile remains pasted to her face.

"Well, damn," Joe says. "I was starting to look forward to that free cable."

Walter laughs again, the perennial good sport. Joe raises his glass in his direction. "Thirsty, Wal?"

"Sure." Walter nods at the glass, now near-empty. "What's that about? You crack open the good stuff without us?"

"No worries." Joe claps him on the back. "I'm only getting started."

Charlotte watches as the two of them head toward the

kitchen, Joe's hand on Walter's shoulder. For a moment she has a flash of Joe and her father emerging in similar fashion from her parents' front porch, twenty-five years ago.

"So everything's cool?"

Emily is still standing in front of her, hands sunk deep in her pockets.

"What?"

"Everything's cool?"

"Oh, you mean about—" Charlotte pauses, nods. "It's fine. I just must have forgotten what we talked about, that's all," she says, though she senses Emily is asking about more than this.

Emily pushes her fists against the insides of her pockets, making the front of her overalls go flat. "You seemed sort of out of it, or something, last weekend. On the phone."

"I guess. Yes."

"You're doing better now, though, right?"

Charlotte pauses to soak in her lovely daughter: brown hair falling messily over her thin shoulders, catching in the hood of her sweater, the sprinkling of freckles across the bridge of her nose. "Yes," she says.

Emily peers up at her, offers a faint smile. Up close, Charlotte can see the dark thumbprints under her eyes. Another mother might chalk them up to blurred eyeliner, makeup that smudged in the car, but Charlotte has no such luxury. She sees those smudges for what they are: marks of weariness, of worry. And she knows that Emily is seeing her with equal clarity. She feels closer to her daughter than she has in two weeks, and the relief is enormous. From the kitchen, she can hear the clinks of dishes, thumps of cabinet doors. Two men are picking through her home, possibly stumbling upon her vitamin supplements and frozen diet dinners, but right now, she doesn't care.

"So your drive down? It was fine?"

"Yeah."

"It must be good to see your dad."

Emily pauses. "Yeah." She looks at her feet. Something about being near Joe makes her seem younger, more sheepish. Like a schoolgirl with a crush. She nudges the toe of her boot against Joe's satchel, making the travel tags rustle like leaves. She says, "I didn't know they went to Aspen," almost too softly for Charlotte to hear.

In the kitchen, they find Joe and Walter engaged in energetic conversation. Joe has found a fresh bottle of wine and is pouring while he talks, something about the Supersonics—a sports team? a rock band? Charlotte doesn't know. She's preoccupied with whether or not Emily will drink too. To her relief, she opens the refrigerator and extracts a bottled water.

"They have momentum, Wal," Joe is saying, handing him an overfull glass. "The team's hungry."

"No way." Walter shakes his head. "Takes more than hunger to put the ball in the hoop."

"Mark my words. Everyone's so busy watching L.A., they're not going to see it coming."

"Sorry." Walter laughs. "You wait. Sixers all the way."

It feels like they're on a weekend retreat, Charlotte thinks, or at a dinner party. She recalls what Joe said earlier about not ignoring "what we're doing here" and feels aggravated that he's doing just that. Talking about Supersonics, filling up on wine, calling Walter "Wal" (he barely knows him!). And yet she's not surprised. It's so like Joe: to maintain his "coolness" at all costs. Amazing how, twenty years later, he can annoy her in exactly the same way.

Without discussion, the four of them gravitate to the kitchen table. Their personalities are in their feet: Charlotte's ankles folded neatly under her chair; Emily sitting in the lotus position, boots sloughed off to reveal gray rag socks; Walter with his chair turned backward, straddling it, one high-top sneaker planted on each side. Joe's loafer has resumed its lofty perch, dangling halfway across the room.

"Hey," Walter says, noticing the laptop. He taps the cover affectionately with one finger. "You get this up and running, Charlotte? No problems?"

"Nope." Her scrawled Post-it is still stuck to the front, though she no longer needs it. "None at all."

"And you actually use it?" from Emily.

"I do." Wouldn't they be surprised to know how much. "It's been wonderful, actually."

"What has?" Joe tunes in. He's holding a salt shaker in front of his eyes, squinting into the tiny holes. "What did I miss? What's your mother using?"

"Wally set Mom up on the Internet."

"Did he!" Joe bangs the salt shaker on the table. "What's your secret, Wal? I couldn't get this woman near technology for seven years. Electricity either, for that matter." He grins, picking up his glass. "Isn't that right, Char?"

Charlotte offers a mild smile. She's familiar with being this person: the one they can all focus on, joke about, agree upon.

"Remember the time with the Christmas lights?" Joe addresses the table at large, as if a rapt gathering of students. "One year Emily's mother, God love her, brought Christmas lights to hang around our living room, get us in the holiday spirit. They were the white ones at least, not those tacky multicolored things. Tasteful. Char couldn't figure out how a toaster worked, but she had good taste." He takes a swallow, gives Charlotte a wink.

"Problem was, she didn't know how to get the damn things on. She plugged them into an extension cord, attached it to the TV, and next thing you know we lost power on the whole first floor." He reaches over to poke Emily in the side. "Somebody cried her eyes out because she couldn't watch *Electric Company.*"

"Hey," Emily protests, smiling. "*Electric Company* was a cool show."

"You remember that, don't you, Em? With the lights?"

"I think so."

Charlotte bristles. Of course Emily would recall Joe's memory, or at least claim she did.

Joe studies Charlotte over the rim of his glass. His face is getting redder. "Poor Charlotte." The smile is rubbery, the emotion in it hard to pin down. "She was trying to turn me into an upstanding Christian from the day we met." He takes another swallow, jostling his glass. Three fat red droplets spill onto the table. "Never worked."

Charlotte looks into Joe's face. His features, wine-warmed, are becoming vague, soft. Then she dares to look at Walter, expecting some combination of amusement and sympathy, but his face has gone hard. His jaw is set. She looks at the wooden cross around his neck; it occurs to her these stories are reflecting worse on Joe than on her.

"Anyway," Joe concludes. "Sounds like you worked some kind of techno-magic, Wal."

"Happy to help."

"Wally and Mom are like, best buds," Emily adds.

"So I've heard."

Charlotte drops her eyes, embarrassed, but Walter speaks up. "We're just the only people around here who got their heads on straight."

Charlotte feels a movement in her chest, a tiny, tentative fluttering. Never in this triangle of father-daughter-mother has she had an ally; it's always been some version of her against them. But now, she feels the weight in the room shifting. The energy bending. She's not alone this time. And her ex-husband, instead of his usual cool, is looking kind of, well, silly.

Walter picks up his glass. He leans his head back against the wall. "Sorry," he says. "Didn't mean to start something. Just feels like we're getting a little off topic here."

"Fair enough." Joe nods. His tone is instantly formal, professorial.

Charlotte watches Emily watch Walter. Her face is arranged in something like a reprimand, but Charlotte detects a tremor of worry running through it. It must make her nervous to see Walter challenge her father. Or maybe, for Emily, being around Joe always carries some degree of worry—that her father, if made unhappy, will simply up and leave.

But accused of delaying the proceedings, Joe rises to the occasion. He sets his glass down, lets his face deepen into a frown of concern. Amazing how easily he can switch tempers. Like Emily, his personality contains such extremes—adult one moment, child the next—and careens from one to the other without a hitch. Charlotte expects him to step up now and steer the conversation, to recite all the perfect, parental things he said on the phone last week, but it is Emily who speaks first.

"So here's the deal," she says. She picks up her water bottle and takes a swig, then plunks it bluntly on the table. "I know this is kind of abrupt, but I don't really feel like screwing around making small talk."

Charlotte glances quickly at Walter. His eyes are closed.

"I've done a lot of thinking over the past two weeks. Wal and

I have done a lot of talking." Her gaze sweeps the table and comes to rest on Walter, who opens his eyes and looks back at her. "And bottom line is, I've changed my mind. We're keeping it."

Charlotte doesn't trust her own ears. Her eyes flit around the table like nervous moths, hunting for confirmation that she just heard what she thinks she heard.

"Honey," Joe says. As if from a distance, Charlotte registers him stretching one arm across the table, taking Emily's hand. "That isn't why I came out here." Joe's voice is soft. "You know that, don't you? I'm not here to convince you to keep it."

"I don't think that."

"Because this is your decision. I'm not here to influence you in any way. I'm just here to support you, not to judge—"

"I know, Joe. Really."

"It's not like that, Joe," adds Walter.

Joe sits back, keeping his eyes on Emily. He's still wearing that unreadable smile, more a slackening of muscle than an expression of any specific feeling. If she had to, Charlotte would call it *bemused.* It's probably the same look he gives the rare student to offer a comment that throws him off guard.

"Well, I'll be goddamned," he says, retracting his hand.

Emily squares her shoulders. She seems to grow taller in her chair. With one hand, she tucks her hair behind her ears, carefully, one ear and then the other. Her hand is so tiny, Charlotte thinks. The cuff of her sweater comes almost to her middle knuckle.

"At first," she explains, "I wasn't even thinking of all this in terms of a real baby. It just wasn't ever how I saw my life going, and I didn't really consider it beyond that." She runs one finger across the wrinkled label on her bottle. "It was all about the choice—the right to *make* the choice. But then I realized, that's not a good enough reason to do it."

"It's also not enough of a reason *not* to," Joe interjects.

All three look over at him. He shrugs, feigning innocence, and picks up his glass. It's the professor persona again: the temptation to play devil's advocate, find gaps, poke holes. Charlotte wants to clamp a hand over his mouth and tell him, Watch what you say, she *listens* to you—but she can't. She promised herself she wouldn't bear any responsibility for this decision. She only wishes he'd be more careful. One misplaced word, one too many sips of wine, and Emily might change her mind.

"Emmy?" Joe says.

It's their old pet name.

"Yes?"

"One question?"

She is still toying with her water bottle, picking at the edges of the label like a scab. "Okay."

"Why do you *want* to have the baby?" Joe says. He puts his glass down, folds his hands leisurely behind his head. Charlotte wants to knock his elbows down.

"The decision's made, Joe," says Walter.

But Joe is looking at Emily. "Honey?" he says. "What made you change your mind?"

Emily stops fiddling with the bottle. She meets Joe's eye, holding it for a long moment. "Actually," she says, then pauses. She looks nervous, Charlotte thinks, her eyes searching Joe's face. "It was Val."

Charlotte feels a lump rise in her chest: a confused feeling, grateful and resentful and distrustful all at once.

Emily continues slowly, spooning each word from her mouth. "She told me about the abortion."

Charlotte glances quickly at Joe, just in time to see a look of pain cross his face, like a shadow on a wall.

Emily waits a beat more, watching her father. Charlotte realizes now that her hesitation isn't for her own sake, but for his. "She told me how she did it when she was my age. And how much she regrets it now. And, how, you know"—she pauses again, waiting for a cue to stop, and getting none, says—"how she can't have children."

For a moment Joe seems frozen. His eyes are glazed, legs crossed, arms still folded behind his head. Then, with a loopy, boneless flourish, he lets the arms drop to the table. He grabs for his glass, tilts it back to take a drink before realizing it's empty. Then he stares inside it, looking forlorn, as if this glass, like life, has deprived him of something.

Emily reaches out and takes his hand. "I'm sorry, Daddy."

Charlotte looks away. She focuses on the spilled drops of wine on the table. She imagines how the three spots of color are, right now, seeping deeper into the wood, growing roots. She thinks about how, years from now, every time she looks at those three spots, every time she tries to scrub them off with a sponge or conceal them under a place mat or a bowl of fruit, she will remember this conversation.

"I'm so sorry," Emily says.

"Yeah, Joe," Walter says. "I'm sorry too."

Charlotte doesn't speak. She knows no one expects her to. They are turned to Joe, leaned toward him, listening. She sees the three of them as if through a pane of glass. Emily picks up Joe's hand and lays her cheek against it. Joe's arms are limp, his eyes full. And Charlotte thinks: These are the mechanics of consolation. This is what a body does with sorrow. And these two young people, they respond to it without hesitation. They sense pain and move toward it. For Charlotte, the emotion on her ex-husband's face gets only smaller, more contained, reduced to something tangible, quantifiable: a quiver of the lip, glistening in the eye.

"I just want to be clear about something," Emily says.

They've relocated to the patio. No one wanted a real dinner, so Charlotte laid out her carefully planned appetizer trays: hummus with triangles of pita, cheese and crackers, baby carrots, celery stalks, jumbo shrimp. It's twilight, the sun burnishing the tops of the trees, separating the sky into bands of blue and violet. It's beautiful, Charlotte thinks. Its obliviousness makes it even more beautiful.

Emily and Walter have resumed their patio position, Emily snuggled in Walter's lap. The other chair belongs to Charlotte. Joe dragged the beige wing chair out from the living room, its wooden legs scraping boisterously across the patio stones. He's slouched low in it now, the engraved back rising high above his head like a throne. He's holding his sixth glass of wine. Charlotte is counting.

"I just want everyone to understand," Emily is saying, "when I said Valerie changed my mind about the baby, I didn't mean I think now if I get an abortion I won't be able to ever have kids. She told me all about what happened and that pseudo-doctor who fucked it up."

Charlotte's eyes flicker to Joe, but his face has become impassive. The wineglass tilts precariously in his hand.

"And this isn't some sort of freaky Freudian thing either, like I want to have my father's baby because he couldn't have his own or something. It just made me see the whole thing in a different way. It made me think seriously about what having a baby would be like." She draws a breath. "I mean, six years from right now I'll have a five-year-old."

Walter puts his hand on her shoulder.

"There'll be this whole new incredible little person to get to know. And we'll have *made* her. How amazing is that?"

Walter starts to rub her arm. Emily leans forward. She has a shine about her: a glow in her face, eagerness in her voice. As ever, Charlotte notes this with a combination of gladness and worry.

"And I'm thinking, if I *did* have the abortion, would I always walk around wondering who this kid would have been? What she would have been like?"

"That one's easy," Walter says. "She'll be fucking cool, that's what."

Joe laughs, a kind of snort.

"Just look at her mom." Walter ignores him, kissing Emily's shoulder. "We have an obligation to bring her into the world. Be a crime not to."

Charlotte feels disappointed in Walter. For being so casual, so cavalier. Maybe she's been relying too much on his maturity. He's only twenty-two, after all.

"When I'm twenty-eight," Emily says, "she'll be five. I think that's the perfect age difference. I'll still be young enough to play with her and really get involved with her life, but not so young so that we're too close in age and turn into some kind of weird friends instead of mother and daughter, you know?"

Where is she getting this? Charlotte marvels. Has she read some kind of holistic parenting manual already?

"She, huh?"

They turn to look at Joe. It's the first time he's spoken since they came outside.

"What's that, Joe?" from Walter.

"*She.* It's a *she.* You keep saying *she.*" The *sh*s sound like hisses. Joe's chemically white teeth, Charlotte notices, are now stained light red.

"It's a girl," Emily says. "I'm sure of it."

Joe smiles a tiny, twisted smile. It looks knowing, the smile of experience bestowed upon innocence. "I hope you're right," he says. "I hope that she is full of sugar and spice and everything—"

"Hello?" A voice floats toward them, invisible, accompanied by the sound of uneven footsteps, high heels pricking stones. "Hello? Anybody home?"

From the side of the house, Bea Morgan appears. She's standing in the yard, backed by the sunset, wearing what looks like a uniform: black pants, blue collared shirt. Her appearance is so incongruous, no one can speak.

"Oh—" she balks. "I'm interrupting something. I saw your car in the parking lot, so I just thought I'd—I'm sorry. I'm leaving. Bye."

"No, hey." Walter recovers as she's turning away. "No. Hell no, Bea. You didn't interrupt anything."

She turns. "You sure?"

"Sure I'm sure. Get on over here."

Bea steps tentatively onto the patio, glancing at the ornate living room chair containing Joe's slumped form.

"Actually," Emily says. She swivels to look at Walter, then turns back to Bea, smiling. "Your timing is perfect. We have big news."

Bea raises her eyebrows uncertainly.

"Walter and I are pregnant."

As if a switch were flipped, Bea's eyes bulge and eyebrows fly up, cartoonlike. She claps one hand over her mouth, and her eyes fill with tears. Charlotte is amazed at this ability to react in the moment, by instinct, as the situation calls for. Bea simply hears the word "pregnant," and her eyes water, her hands move.

"Oh my God!" she says, rushing across the patio to wrap Emily and Walter in an awkward hug. "Oh my God! Congratulations! I'm so happy for you guys!"

When Bea steps back, her lipstick is smeared, her eyelashes wet. Charlotte wonders if Emily will take offense at the word "guys"—one of her biggest pet peeves in college—but she is beaming.

Bea wipes a finger under each eye, smearing her mascara. "You too, Charlotte," she says. She steps forward as if to hug her too, then stops. "Congratulations. Really. That's such exciting news."

"Well, it's not *my* news—"

"Sure it is." Bea's arms flap about her ears. "You're going to be a Granny!"

Charlotte reels a bit. "I guess I am."

"I'm not sure she's a Granny," Emily muses.

Bea says quickly, "Oh you might be right."

"A Nanny?" guesses Walter.

"Grandma?" from Bea.

"I was thinking Nana," Charlotte says.

"Well I was thinking Grandmamamamamama," Joe offers, tongue flapping. Then he shuts his mouth and grins like the cat that swallowed the mouse. "Personally, I'd like to be called Supergranddad."

Bea laughs, but nervously.

"Joe," Emily says. "This is Bea. She lives upstairs. Bea, this is my dad, Joe Warren."

"Oh," Bea says, stepping forward and extending a limp hand. "Pleasure." Charlotte imagines it's the same word—and hand—Bea uses anytime she's introduced to new men. She highly doubts Bea uses the word "pleasure" when meeting women.

Joe takes the hand, still wearing that unreadable smile. "Pleasure's all mine," he says, then adds, "Bea." But he doesn't say it the way he said it earlier. This time he sounds almost flirtatious. "Why don't you sit down? Take a load off?"

"Oh, I don't know, I—"

"Sit," Joe says. "And take this." He hands her a napkin. "You're getting all choked up over there."

"I'll get you a chair," Walter offers.

"Don't bother." Bea waves him off and lowers herself ungracefully to the ground. Up closer, Charlotte can see the red cursive *Friendly's* stitched on Bea's shirt. Her arms are strung with gold bangles. Bea shifts her knees awkwardly to one side, tugging her shirt down over the glimpse of bare belly. "I won't stay long," she says, blowing her nose in the napkin. "I just wanted to say hi. I need to get out of this uniform and get a shower."

Charlotte sees something cross Joe's face, and wonders if Bea's shower reference could have been deliberate. But Bea doesn't seem that calculating. Still, Charlotte knows what her nightlife sounds like. And knows that Joe, even Joe on six glasses of wine, doesn't let an opportunity for innuendo to pass him by.

"Bea, have some hummus," he says, gesturing to the food. "It's good for you."

"I'm fine, thanks."

"Don't like hummus? Can't say I blame you. But we're in the minority here." He winks vaguely in Emily's direction. "Surrounded by a bunch of health nuts."

"No, I like it," Bea says, with a quick look at Charlotte. She pokes the used napkin into the top of her purse, made of banana-shaped red leather. "It's just, I ate at work."

"And where is work?"

"Friendly's." She gestures to her shirt, where an Izod alligator might be.

Joe repeats the word with a broad, loose smile. "Friendly's."

"The one in Newfield?" she adds helpfully. "Cherry and Devon?"

"Don't know it, I'm afraid."

"Joe lives in Seattle," Emily explains.

"Oh!" Bea sounds as impressed as if she'd said "Bangkok." She seems to relax then, runs one hand through her hair. "I've always wanted to go to Seattle."

"Not worth the hype," Joe shrugs. "Rains every day. Organic this, tofu that. Not a Friendly's in sight, I'll tell you that." He picks up a shrimp, the first thing he's eaten all night, and dunks it in cocktail sauce. It glistens when he lifts it to his mouth and wraps his lips around it, smiling. "If you're not going to eat, Bea," he says, tossing the tail on the table, "at least have a drink."

"Yes," Charlotte manages. She feels like she's swimming in subtext. "What would you like? I have wine, I have beer—"

"A beer would be great."

"One beer coming up," from Joe.

Charlotte stands, and is about to ask if anyone else needs anything, but stops herself. She doesn't want to refill Joe's glass. Instead, she heads to the kitchen just as Joe is saying, "Bea, what's your cocktail of choice? Wait, let me guess."

Inside, Charlotte leans against the refrigerator. She closes her eyes, listening to its comforting hum, feeling it thrum against her back. She feels the hard, raised script of the General Electric logo pressing into her shoulder. From outside, she can hear Bea's laughter as Joe pries into her, asking questions. Charlotte's head is beginning to pound. She opens her eyes and watches the red numbers on the oven clock roll slowly forward; 6:51 to 6:52 P.M.; 6:52 to 6:53. Soon, she thinks, it will be tomorrow. It will have to be.

She looks toward the window. Her eyes fall on the laptop, the book, the pink hippo soap. She misses her things. She misses her life alone among them. From the corner of her eye, she sees those three red drops of spilled wine on the table and lunges for the sink, wets a sponge, douses it with cleanser. She scrubs at the red spots until her wrist begins to burn. But when she pulls back and wipes away the suds, it's as she suspected: the spots are there for good. And to make matters worse, she's chipped one of her Shell Pink nails.

Charlotte hears a tinkle of laughter from outside. Reluctantly, she grabs a beer from the crisper and heads for the living room. She hears Bea's voice, and Emily's. Maybe Joe has stopped talking. Maybe the effort at socializing—or interrogating, or flirting, or whatever he was doing—has left him depleted.

"I've never been to New Hampshire either," she hears Bea saying. "I bet it's beautiful, though. Are you going to have the baby up there?"

Charlotte stops, halfway across the room.

"Yeah," Emily says. "That's our home. At least for now."

"Are you going to get married?"

Charlotte sucks in her breath. Outside, it is silent. From her vantage point, steps from the doorway, she can see Bea's eyes widen again, hand moving to her mouth.

"Oh my God," she breathes. "I'm sorry—I'll stop talking now. I should just stop talking. Bill's right. He's always telling me to think before I speak."

"It's okay—" Walter starts to say, when Joe cuts him off.

"It's more than okay!"

His voice is almost a shout. Charlotte steps tentatively to the doorsill.

"In fact, Beatrice—may I call you Beatrice?—it's much more than okay, Beatrice. It's encouraged. Let's *talk* about the real stuff. Go straight for the dirt! Rile them up! It's good for them."

"It's fine, Bea," Emily says tightly. "Really. And no, we're not." She pauses. "Getting married, I mean."

Charlotte stares out at the darkening sky. She isn't sure what she's feeling, exactly. Relieved that Emily isn't rushing into a big decision. Surprised, actually, since she's always rushed before. Sad that this baby will be born out of wedlock.

But Bea is shaking her head in admiration. "That's so modern of you guys."

It's Charlotte's cue to move. She steps outside and hands Bea the beer.

"I mean—oh, thanks Charlotte—I wish I could be so calm about the future. With Bill and me, I mean. But I need the security. I can't help it, you know? I keep telling Bill, if he thinks I'm going to hang around forever with no ring, no kids, he's got another think coming."

Emily gives her a sympathetic nod. Charlotte resumes her seat.

Bea twists the cap off, bracelets jangling. "But you two, you're still so young. You don't need to worry. You're smart, not rushing into it too fast." She tilts the bottle back at the same moment the patio light snaps on, dousing the porch in pale yellow. She laughs and glances upward, choking on her swallow. "Looks like somebody upstairs agrees with me!"

Walter laughs with her.

"That's charming," Joe says.

They stop laughing and look over at him. His red face is tinged with something soft, like nostalgia.

"That's lovely," he says. "You never hear people say *somebody upstairs* anymore."

Bea laughs again, but less confidently, as if unsure whether he's complimenting her or not. Charlotte knows the feeling.

Joe picks up a shrimp and starts bobbing it aimlessly in and out of cocktail sauce. "So who's this Bill guy anyway?" he says, eyes on the shrimp. "The one with the commitment issues."

"Daddy," Emily warns, lightly. "Easy."

But Bea pipes up, "Bill's my boyfriend."

Joe smiles again, that ambiguous nostalgic semi-smile. "*Boyfriend.* That's charming too. And how long have we been with Bill the boyfriend?"

"Three years. A little over three, actually." Charlotte can't tell if Bea isn't picking up on Joe's condescension, or just doesn't care. If it's the latter, she might just be Charlotte's new hero. "Thirty-eight months, to be exact. We just had our anniversary."

"Congratulations," says Walter, loyal as a clock.

"Your thirty-eight-month anniversary?" Joe says. "Do they make cards for that?"

"Our three-year anniversary." Bea shakes her head wonderingly. "Three years! Doesn't that sound like such a long time?"

Emily nods.

"And you're in love, I assume?" Joe says.

Charlotte cringes, even though the question wasn't directed at her. But Bea looks him squarely in the eye. "Yes." There's a note of defiance in her reply. "We are."

Walter raises his beer.

"And he lives with you?" Joe moves on, unfazed. "Upstairs?"

"No. I mean, more or less, but he still has his own place.

Technically. I told him, no moving in unless we're married. I don't want to be splitting bills and signing leases with someone who's not in it for the long haul, you know?"

"Smart girl," Joe nods. He looks toward his glass, sitting empty on the table, but leaves it there. "And where is Bill the boyfriend this evening?"

"He'll be here soon. He gets off work at seven."

"And what is Bill the boyfriend's line of work?"

"He runs a gas station. On Humphrey."

Joe's smile cracks. He turns to Bea, and his gaze is wistful, sentimental, as if she is a relic preserved from a forgotten world. "A waitress and a gas station attendant," he says. "It warms the heart. It does. Someone should write a goddamn country-western song about the two of you."

"Back off, Joe," Walter says.

"Daddy." Emily's voice is kinder. "Be nice."

"I am being nice!"

Bea drops her eyes, unzips her purse, and starts fishing for her cigarettes.

"Wait!" Joe sits forward, lurching toward her. "Bea! Wait. Don't take me the wrong way, Bea. If you think I'm making fun of you, you're wrong. I am one hundred percent serious. *One hundred percent.*"

She pushes a cigarette in her mouth, snaps her lighter.

"Bea," Joe says, speaking intently. "Bea. Look at me."

She hesitates, then looks up.

"You warm my heart, Bea. You and your Friendly's and your boyfriend and your 'somebody upstairs.' I love you. I am fucking *in love* with you. Both of you. I want to take you home and put you in a fucking test tube."

"Jesus, Joe," Walter says.

Bea gets the cigarette lit and quickly inhales.

"You're the real thing," Joe pushes on, sloppily, passionately. "You are the *real* people. Living in America, smoking butts—what are those, Marlboro Reds? Please tell me you smoke Marlboro Reds."

"Lights."

"Fine. Yes. Same thing. You live in America and smoke Marlboro Lights. You make minimum wage and collect tips and live in a small town waiting for a gas station attendant to propose to you. It's fucking beautiful."

"You know," Bea says, zipping her purse. "I should probably get going."

"Are you sure?" Emily says, but weakly.

"Yeah." Bea flashes them an apologetic smile. "Bill's going to be here soon."

She starts to stand, but Joe is no longer paying attention. His head is bowed, muttering to his lap. "I'd trade it all in a minute," he says. "I'd trade it all for the life you've got. All of it. A fucking minute."

Bea hugs Emily and Walter. "Congratulations again, you guys."

"Don't let him get to you, Bea," Walter replies, kissing her cheek. "He's drunk. He doesn't know what he's saying."

"I am *not* drunk!" Joe shouts, rearing his head. He overenunciates to prove his point. "And I *do* know what I'm saying. I'm *complimenting* this woman." He looks at Bea, and his voice goes soft. "I'm sorry if I scared you, honey. I just get passionate about things. Especially people. I'm a sociologist."

"Oh," Bea says. There's a note of relief in her voice, as if this information makes his behavior more legitimate somehow. "A sociologist?"

"This is what I *do,*" Joe continues. "I examine people's *lives.* Try to figure out what makes them tick. How the hell they do it. How they avoid getting jaded. Like you did. You don't have a jaded bone in your body, do you, Bea?" He squints at her, as if through a thick fog. "In fact, I think you might actually *like life.*"

Bea turns. "Thanks for the hospitality, Charlotte."

"Wait!"

She pauses, looks at Joe reluctantly.

"Just one more question before you go. Just one."

Bea raises her cigarette to her lips, then plants one hand on a hip.

Joe sits forward, leaning his elbows on his knees. "Do you?"

"Do I what?" she says, inhaling.

"Like life." His voice is quiet, urgent. "Do you like life?"

Bea looks at him for a long moment, then says, "Yeah." She exhales. "I do."

Joe shakes his head and flops backward in his throne. "She does," he says flatly. "She really fucking does."

In that moment, Joe transforms completely from subject to object. Instead of condescending, he seems pitiful. A man who hates his life. This side of him, Charlotte thinks, this hardness, it never used to be there. He was always curious, always probing the world, challenging it, but it was never so negative. So bitter. Charlotte looks at Emily, so like her father in so many ways. She thinks of the unborn baby inside her, like those painted wooden dolls with the innocent faces, one inside the other, and wants nothing but to keep them all safe.

chapter seven

Charlotte dreamed of becoming a grandmother. In her dream, the scene was always the same: the news was delivered over an elaborate Christmas dinner, at a long, glossy table set with silver bowls, white tapered candles, tasteful poinsettias. Though the table seemed to stretch forever, there were only ever three of them: Charlotte, Emily, and Emily's husband. The husband's face was never clear, but he had strong hands. A gold wedding band. A wool sweater. They'd been married a year and a half, trying to get pregnant for a month or two.

It was the husband who made the announcement. Emily leaned into his arm, her face glowing in the candlelight. He gazed at her as she spoke. She was pregnant, he told Charlotte. The baby was due in August. Which would mean Charlotte could help out in the hot summer months. Which would mean she could bring Emily peach sorbet and ice packs and hold cool washcloths to her face. And the husband would come home from work each night, wearily loosening his tie, saying, "Mom, I don't know how we would do it without you." And when the baby was born, her middle name would be Charlotte.

Now, staring out her kitchen window, Charlotte feels her dream dismantled. Reduced to a slurring ex-husband with red-stained teeth. A daughter who lives in an alternative living arrangement five states away. And a son-in-law who is not a son-in-law at all, but a twenty-two-year-old boyfriend with an earring in his eyebrow.

But at least they're having the baby, Charlotte reminds herself. There would be a baby. A grandchild. The rest of it she would just have to accept. Lately, her life had begun to feel like a continual process of revision; this was just one more story she would have to rewrite.

Suddenly Joe appears at the far side of the parking lot, a speck in gray T-shirt and black running shorts. As he gets closer, she can make out the bib of sweat on his shirt, the white-lettered BERKELEY stained darker in the middle. She watches as he jogs through the empty spot where the red station wagon was parked not two hours ago. Charlotte can't believe their visit is already over. Emily and Walter left for New Hampshire just before 11:00 A.M.; Joe's flight doesn't leave until 2:30.

Joe slows to a walk as he nears L1. Charlotte notices he's carrying a brown paper bag. Did he pick up breakfast? Pastries, maybe? The top half of him disappears from view as he stretches, leaning his palms against the side of the house. Charlotte can see the backs of his legs only: calves flexing, heels digging into the lawn. He's wearing modern sneakers, shiny, puffy, laceless, like the ones piled by the door at Rita Curran's. They look like sausage casings, Charlotte thinks. Ridiculous, really. Really ridiculous on a man almost fifty years old.

The legs disappear, and seconds later, Charlotte hears the front door open. "Honey, I'm home!"

It isn't funny.

Joe strolls into the kitchen. "Hi," he says, wiping the back of his hand across his upper lip. He props one sneaker on a chair, revealing a bare leg furred with damp blond hair. At least he isn't sitting *in* the chair, sweat dribbling onto the seat, joining the other permanent damage he's done since he's been here: spilled drops of wine on the table, nicks he caused dragging the wooden feet of the wing chair outside.

"Here." He holds out the paper bag, sweat-darkened around what suddenly clearly resembles the neck of a bottle. "Peace offering."

Charlotte extracts a bottle of champagne. Bad champagne. Even she can tell.

"Best the drugstore carried," Joe says, and shrugs. "It'll have to do." He drops his foot to the floor and starts humming as he pops the top cabinet open.

"What are you doing?" Charlotte says.

"Mimosas."

"Oh, no. None for me."

"Come on, Char, indulge me. All your required daily vitamins and nutrients in one glass."

"I don't think so."

"It'll help relax me on the plane."

"I really don't drink in the mornings." She takes a breath. "Besides, you don't need help relaxing."

"Charlotte." Joe shuts the cabinet, turns, and lets his arms droop at his sides. "I know I was an asshole last night. I just want the weekend to end on a good note."

At least she agrees with him there. On both counts.

"Fine," she sighs. "A small one."

He yanks open the refrigerator door.

"Juice is on the—"

"I got it," he says, waving her off. "You go. Meet me on the patio before all the good seats are taken."

With his hair damp, Charlotte thinks, the thinning is much more obvious. She walks out of the kitchen, past the sofa bed and bedding that has been perfectly remade and refolded. She pulls the patio door open, blinking into the chilly sunlight. Funny how two weeks ago she'd never used the garden patio, didn't even like looking at it. Now, as a porch chair deflates beneath her, she feels relieved to be there.

Charlotte absorbs her backyard. Dry russet leaves cling tenuously to the trees. Cool sunlight filters through the branches. She spots a bottle cap on the ground and a forgotten hairband on the table. It's one of Emily's, a thin pink elastic tangled with a single strand of brown hair. Suddenly Charlotte misses her daughter with a sharpness that almost takes her breath away. It feels like Emily and Walter's visit was a dream—something she blinked and missed. This morning, they'd said they needed to leave early, that Walter had to get back to "apprenticing," but Charlotte suspected they just wanted to get away. Away from the divorced parents, the drunk father, the awkward conversation. Their decision was made, their job done. They hadn't needed adult guidance after all; they acted more adult than Joe did.

She couldn't talk them into breakfast, not even coffee. Emily, now decisively pregnant, thought she was feeling a little morning sickness. Walter ate a piece of toast standing up. Their goodbye, by the car, was less dramatic than their arrival. Joe hauled himself up from the sleeping bag, mussed but coherent. He padded outside in bare feet, chewing noisily on gum. Walter offered him a stiff handshake. Emily hugged him tightly as ever; maybe to her, his behavior was normal, and she'd just never mentioned it before.

As Charlotte said her good-byes, she wanted to say something about the baby, tell them they'd made a good decision, the right decision, but she couldn't find the words. It was all too flurried, too fast. They hugged her, kissed her, thanked her, a series of doors opening and slamming, then they were driving away, Emily flashing a peace sign out the window. Charlotte had wondered, watching their receding bumper—a virtual collage of stickers for bands and beliefs and causes amassed over the past seven years—if they were frustrated there hadn't been more discussion of the baby. That the enormity of their decision—the reason for their coming—had been diluted by Joe's behavior. If Walter was saying right then, as he honked and pulled out of the driveway, "Well, that was a waste."

Charlotte hears a noise behind her. Joe, still in jogging gear, is carrying two of her grandmother's wineglasses. Each is nearly full of a frothy orange concoction. "For you," he says, as Charlotte extracts one from his fingers.

"Thank you," she says, then wishes she hadn't. What was she thanking him for? Making her drink bad champagne before noon?

Still standing, he lifts his glass. "To grandparenting."

"Yes. To grandparenting."

They clink. Charlotte takes a sip; it's surprisingly good.

Joe sinks into the other chair and stretches his legs out long before him, gazing at his feet. "Grandparents."

"Yes."

"Can you believe it?"

"No." She smiles. "Not really."

She glances at Joe, and he's smiling too, but his gaze looks distant, vaguely unsettled. Charlotte wonders if he's thinking about Valerie and the abortion. She realizes his initial reaction, his wanting Emily to have the baby, makes more sense now. Maybe he sees it as another shot—his only shot—at having another child in his life.

Joe lifts his head abruptly and looks out into the yard, as if returning to the present, then sighs through his nose.

"It's no ocean view," Charlotte commiserates.

He looks at her, then bursts into a laugh. "What makes you say that?"

"Because." She feels herself blush. "I heard about your house in Seattle."

"Yes?"

"With the deck. And the ocean view."

"Ah."

"It sounds lovely."

"Well, my dear," he says, crossing his feet at the ankle, "things are not always as they sound." He holds the stem of his glass between two fingers and twirls it slowly, methodically, staring inside it like a kaleidoscope. "I don't know what the hell got into me last night, Charlotte."

It catches her off guard. Suddenly she wishes someone else were there.

"I think I scared your friend."

"She's not my friend," she says quickly, as if in consolation.

"Even better."

"She's just my neighbor. I hardly know her," she rambles, then shuts her mouth. She hopes Bea didn't hear.

"Well," Joe says. "Apologize to her. Whoever she is. I don't remember details, but I'm sure I was out of line."

He's still staring into his glass, but it's stopped turning. The smile is gone. "Valerie thinks I drink too much."

Charlotte pauses. "Do you?"

"I don't think so." He sets the glass down carefully on the table. "Honest. I don't. It's not a problem—just a, I don't know, a hobby." He smiles, sadly. "I drink, she does yoga. She sees a psychic, I see a shrink. We all have our coping mechanisms, right?"

Charlotte wants to ask more about the shrink—why he goes, what he says—but Joe is looking at her with a familiar expression. She senses an interrogation coming on.

"What are yours?"

"My what?" she asks, playing dumb.

"Coping mechanisms." Like a reflex, he crosses one leg over the other, a pose that looks even more ridiculous in running shorts. He leans forward just slightly, assuming all the affectations of "professor," but it seems halfhearted. It lacks conviction. As if he's only asking the questions to confirm his own answers.

"I don't know," Charlotte says. "I don't think I have any."

"You?" Joe says. "You, Charlotte, have coping mechanisms. You of all people."

"What does that mean, me of all people?"

"It means you're good at coping mechanisms. You're the *queen* of coping mechanisms."

His tone, after less than five minutes, has taken on a kind of easy familiarity, as if recycling a conversation they've had a hundred times before. They could be an old married couple sitting on their back porch swing, poking fun at each other tiredly, affectionately, having used up all the heated dramas years ago. It's as if they've managed to compress the entire arc of a marriage into just under two weeks.

"So?" he says, raising his eyebrows.

Charlotte sighs. She has no choice but to play along. "Well, organizing is one, I guess."

He ticks off one finger.

"And cleaning."

"Yes."

"Cooking. Grocery shopping."

"Yes. Yes." He adds, "Checking things off lists."

He's right, she thinks. She's surprised he knows this, and surprised it should surprise her.

"What else?"

"I don't know. I think that's it."

"Come on. One more."

"One?" Charlotte tilts her head back, considering the sky. "Getting my nails done."

Joe looks at her in amazement. "You still do that?"

She drops her chin, picks up her glass.

"Oh, don't be like that. Please. At least your coping mechanisms are practical. They get the tub clean and the nails filed. Mine just get me incapacitating headaches and piss off my wife."

It's the first time Joe has acknowledged any real trouble in his marriage, and Charlotte can feel the shift between them, teasing yielding to something more real. She swallows, feeling her pulse thump, wondering what to say next—should she ask what's happening with Valerie? is that the reason he mentioned her?—but any potential awkwardness between them is drowned out by Joe's loud, sudden groan.

"Ah, Charlotte." He sinks down in the chair until he's practically sitting on his tailbone, like Emily used to in junior high. (Charlotte, having flashes of scoliosis, would beg her to sit up straight.) Joe spreads his hands dramatically across his face, then peers at her through splayed fingers. "Tell me. How the hell is it we were ever married?"

Instantly she hears it as a criticism, as a comparison to Valerie: *How could* I *ever have been married to* you?

"You're so organized," he continues, dropping his hands in his lap. "You're so together. And I'm like this big, sloppy kid. How and why did you put up with me for so long?"

She was wrong. Joe isn't criticizing her, he's criticizing himself. And it isn't like him; he never used to put himself down like that. Then again, her frame of reference is fifteen years old. God knows what's really gone on in Joe's life those fifteen years. Still she finds it almost impossible to reconcile this bitter man with the easygoing, fun-loving guy Joe used to be. He's still easygoing, she supposes, but it used to be so genuine. Now it seems more by design than by instinct.

"Charlotte," Joe says, breaking her reverie. "Did you hate my whistling?"

"What?"

"I ask because Valerie"—his tone has an air of drifty nonchalance, though Charlotte is quite sure there's nothing nonchalant about it—"she hates my whistling. I'm wondering if it bothered you too."

"Not really," Charlotte lies.

"Are you lying?"

"No." She amends, "Kind of."

"So it bothered you."

"Only sometimes."

"But you never said anything."

"That's because I was shy."

"No." Joe shakes his head. "It's because you were nice."

He's looking at her closely. Too closely. It's an odd look, one she hasn't seen in many years—his eyes squinting, face soft—as if seeing her, literally, in a different light.

Then he smiles. "Want to fight about it?"

"Not really."

"Oh, come on," he teases. "We're just starting to get good at the fighting thing."

"What do you mean?" She knows what he means.

"The other week, on the phone. Our first real fight. Only took us nine years of marriage and fifteen years of divorce."

Their eyes meet, and the equation is so absurd, they both start laughing.

"I'm not good at fighting," Charlotte apologizes. It occurs to her she's often apologizing around him. "I get too flustered."

"It's an acquired skill," Joe says. "I've just had a lot of practice."

Smiles fade. Silence enters. Not a cautious silence, but the opposite: Charlotte feels like she could ask or say anything. This conversation, this whole scene, feels oddly removed from the parameters of real life. Joe is so honest, and so unfazed by being honest. Nothing she says could possibly compare to the kind of soul-baring, dish-throwing West Coast drama that he's used to. He could be her real-life Internet, telling her WHAT YOU WANT TO KNOW.

She looks at the ground, at her feet folded neatly at the ankle. Joe's teenage-style sneakers stretch presumptuously across the stone floor. "We're very different," she says, looking up. "Aren't we."

To her the line felt brave, but Joe shrugs it off. "Everybody's different."

Charlotte looks again at the ground. "Do you think there's such a thing as good different and bad different?"

"Nah. Doesn't work like that." Joe hoists himself higher in his chair. "Too easy. It's not about good or bad, just being able to appreciate the differences. No matter what they are."

"What about you and Valerie? Are you different?"

He barks a laugh. "That's an understatement."

Different how? she wants to ask. Different in a good way? Instead she says, "Oh," and they continue sitting, letting the untold story seep into the silences between them. Joe picks up his glass and looks inside it. Charlotte realizes he hasn't taken a sip since they first came outside.

Then he says, "It's not an ocean."

"What?" She looks at him.

"The view, at my house. It's not an ocean." He meets her eye, lips quirked in a meek smile. "It's a lake."

"A lake?" Charlotte pauses. "Emily always said it was an ocean."

He raises his eyebrows and shrugs. "Then Emily said wrong."

Charlotte stares into the backyard, her own version of a "view," and tries to reconstruct the mental panorama she's carried with her all these years. Joe would have no idea how often she's imagined this mythical deck of his, the place he and Valerie retreat after fighting, where they are magically cured by the pounding ocean and the tangy sea air. So, she thinks: there's no drama after all. No crashing waves to suck up their angry words and pull them away from shore. Instead the water is flat, placid, unresisting, words simply falling and sinking to the bottom like pennies in a fountain. She wonders how else Emily may have stretched the truth.

"What do your students call you?" Charlotte asks suddenly.

Joe looks up, as surprised by the question as she is. "My students?" He seems to think for a minute. "Some call me Professor Warren. But most call me Professor Joe."

It's so perfect she can't help but smile. "Do they have crushes on you?"

"Some." He puts his glass down and folds his arms across his chest, amused. "Next?"

She only pauses for a second. "Do you know what mindfulness is?"

"Mindfulness?" His eyebrows fly up, but he doesn't break stride. "Let's see. Mindfulness. I believe I do."

"Do you believe in it?"

"Sure. If by believing in it, you mean believing it's a crock of shit."

She laughs out loud.

"Anything else?" Joe is studying her face again, but the amusement is gone. He's watching her with a curiosity so intense she feels a tingling up and down her spine. From beyond the yard a wind lifts up, making a far-off porch chime rattle. The dry leaves rustle in response: *shhhh, shhhh.*

"I don't think so."

"You sure?"

"Well," she says, "there might be one thing." The breeze feels cool on her warm cheeks. She fixes her eyes on the forgotten pink hair band. "Do you think that I'm maternal?"

She expects a laugh, but Joe doesn't laugh. Nor does he ask why she's asking. "You, Charlotte," he says, "are maternal. You of all people."

She feels her heart leap and, as if a switch were flipped, her eyes fill.

"You are mother," he says, watching her closely. "That's your thing. The love of your life. Mothering and coping mechanisms. Mothering *as* a coping mechanism. It could be your business card."

"But," she says, licking her lips, vision blurring, needing to be sure. "I know I care about being a mother. But *am* I motherly? Am I—comforting?"

"You are comforting," he says. "Yes. You are."

Through her tears, Charlotte catches that expression on his face again. For a moment she wonders, wildly, if he might kiss her. Maybe it's the champagne, or her overactive imagination. Is it merely kindness on his face? Is it sympathy? She blinks back her tears, and when her vision clears, she can see: after all these years, all his waiting, Charlotte has revealed something unexpected. Finally, she's surprised him.

Alone that night, Charlotte feels the pressure of the past. Joe's presence lingers in the empty house, scenes from this weekend blurring with moments from fifteen, twenty, twenty-five years ago. Joe staring at her with wide eyes. Tapping a finger against her temple. Reaching across the kitchen table to grip Emily's hand. His white teeth stained red. The gentle, curious expression on his face that afternoon. The three drops of red wine sunk permanently into the kitchen table.

Charlotte stares at those drops now, willing them to sink into the wood and disappear. But like her memories, they are stubborn. She marvels at how much Joe has changed; at least, how much she thinks he has. Maybe she's not remembering him honestly. Have Seattle and Valerie made him that much harder? Or are her memories just inaccurate? Maybe he was never so lighthearted. Maybe there was always a sad complexity she didn't see, or didn't choose to see.

Because she knows the story of their marriage, and in it, Joe never acted this way. Then again, the details she leans on—the hidden wedding lists, soapy backrubs, her bitten fingers, his narrowing eyes—have been so carefully honed over fifteen years, polished into so smooth a plotline, that she can't be sure anymore they really happened that way. Maybe, if asked to tell the story of their marriage, Joe would remember different details entirely. Hers are shallow memories, really, never venturing too far beneath the skin. As harmless as her old, stock answer when people asked her what happened: "It just wasn't meant to be," she'd say, then smile to let them know she was still functioning. If they looked particularly concerned, she'd roll her eyes, as if relieved.

She tightens her sash, as if tucking in her body might rein in her thoughts. It's useless. Despite Joe's drunkenness, his presumptuousness, there's something about him that still, even after all these long years, gets under her skin. Something she finds compelling, even a little frightening. Yes, he's a careless man. Reckless, dramatic, messy. But so earnest in his messiness. So sincere in his shortcomings. There's so much *sprawl* to him—blurted thoughts and unfiltered feelings and crossed lines—that his personality invites mistakes. And yet, that messiness allows for the possibility of surprise, for moments of unexpected loveliness.

Now the house is empty, just how she wanted it, but the emptiness feels like absence. It seems impossible that just twenty-four hours ago Emily and Walter were tangled on her couch, Joe snoring on the hard foyer tile. He was barely conscious when Walter steered him toward the sleeping bag. He didn't even get inside it, but splayed on top, fully dressed, legs askew—he always slept that way, Charlotte recalls, taking up most of the bed.

She folds her arms across her belly, gathering herself to herself. But the memories crowd her, insisting on themselves. Joe's sporadic snoring, his curly mat of chest hair, skin that was always warm to touch. The first time they slept together (in either sense of the word) was on their honeymoon in Virginia Beach. They were on a tight budget, so options had been limited. What Joe had really wanted was to drive to southern Florida, rambling aimlessly down Route 1 to just "see what we see." Charlotte had imagined this was the kind of thing the women at work would have thought "spontaneous," but she cringed at the planlessness. She pictured run-ins with bikini-clad collegiates and aging surfer bums who would keep Joe up all night, drinking rum and swapping stories. In private, she dreamed of Maine: a little B & B with a quiet porch and sweet, kindly, snowy-haired owners. But when she dared mention this to Joe—offhandedly, as if the idea had just occurred to her—he kissed her nose and said, "You just described your parents' house." Charlotte never mentioned it again.

So Virginia Beach it was: a compromise both financial and emotional. Joe joked about the appropriateness of the "virgin" in Virginia. Charlotte booked a room at the Drift Inn and Sea, which was on a traffic circle but promised to be just a short walk to the beach. On their first day, he bought her a black T-shirt that said "Virginia Is for Lovers!" in glittery aqua blue. Somewhere there exists a picture of her wearing it, sitting in their hotel room with Drift Inn and Sea stationery and paper-capped drinking glasses lined up beside her on the fake wood desk.

Charlotte had always envisioned honeymooning couples as lingering over romantic dinners, while the other diners flashed them smiles and waiters knowingly looked on. But Joe had planned to spend the better part of five days in their hotel room. Instead of being a source of public envy, Charlotte felt illicit: squirreled away in a bed that wasn't her own, under a comforter made of slippery peach-colored polyester. She felt apologetic around the maid, self-conscious while she slept. And Joe had hung the DO NOT DISTURB sign on their doorknob, which seemed so blatantly sexual it was embarrassing.

"Relax," he whispered, his face hovering above her, colliding with the cheap seascapes hanging on the wall.

Charlotte closed her eyes and tried, despite the dull pain. *Good night, ankles,* she thought. *Good night, toes.*

"Just give in to it," he said. "Just let go."

Give in to what? she worried silently. What was she letting go of?

Afterward, he asked, "Were you close?"

"I think so," she told him, and because he looked so sad, added, "Yes." She knew it was what he needed to hear. Then, because she felt so guilty and confused, she hid her face in his hot, damp shoulder.

"We'll get there," he told her, pressing his lips to the top of her head. "It just takes a little time."

At first, Joe liked that she'd never had an orgasm. It added to his sense of challenge, his mission to "unlock" her. But soon, like other parts of her biology, Charlotte began to wonder if the orgasm was another basic malfunction. Maybe she simply wasn't capable of having one. Six months passed, then a year, and Joe wasn't so reassuring anymore.

"What's the point," he would say when they climbed into bed.

"What do you mean?" Charlotte asked him, anxious. She wanted them to have sex, not because she especially enjoyed it, but because she worried what it might mean if they didn't.

He rolled away from her and focused on the alarm clock, jabbing at the "time set" button: 6:31. 32. 33. 34. 35. "I feel like I'm in this alone," he spoke to the clock, red numbers skittering by. "I don't know what else to do, Char. Maybe you're never going to get there. Maybe you're never going to get there with *me.*"

"It's not you," Charlotte said quickly, and this she wholeheartedly believed. "And besides, I don't care, it doesn't matter—"

"Of course it matters."

"But why?" she said, feeling desperate.

"If you'd ever had one," he said, switching off the bedside lamp, "you wouldn't have to ask."

Charlotte believed this was probably true. Still, she had no problem missing out on orgasms. She planned on missing out on lots of potentially pleasurable things: Godiva chocolates, gondolas in Venice, tropical islands. Plus, orgasms weren't proving to be pleasurable; they were causing her nothing but trouble. She didn't need them. She didn't even want them. And if this didn't bother her, why should it bother him?

But it did, she thinks now, staring at the ceiling. She squeezes her eyes shut, trying to stop the memories from coming, but even more than twenty years later the night Joe finally snapped is all too vivid. It was a Saturday, early December, and they'd spent the day Christmas tree shopping. They'd splurged on a full-sized tree, an upgrade from the foot-high shrub that had perched on their radiator the year before, bowing under the weight of the few cheap, flaking ornaments Charlotte bought at the drugstore. Although Charlotte was by far the more money-conscious of the two of them, it was she who had pushed for the big tree. She wanted the house to feel fuller, to contain something besides her husband and herself.

As it turned out, the tree trip rewarded both of their most old-fashioned instincts. Joe was pleased with himself for shoving it through the front door in a manly heave, sawing off just enough trunk so that the top grazed the ceiling. Charlotte felt a wifely satisfaction vacuuming up after him—the swoosh of needles up the vacuum bag giving her a slight rush—and retrieving the box carefully labeled "Our Ornaments" from the basement. Joe boasted pine sap under his nails, stray needles in his hair. Charlotte gingerly threaded cranberries and strung them in the branches. From the outside, everything appeared as it should.

That night in bed, Joe was feeling confident. He didn't grumble, didn't punch the alarm clock. Instead of unbuttoning Charlotte's nightgown, he lifted it up over her head in one swift motion. He slid her underwear down to her heels. He left the bedside lamp blazing, the covers bunched at the foot of the bed. Charlotte saw her thighs glowing white in the harsh lamplight, the faded pink cotton underwear caught around her left ankle like some kind of sad, stretched garter. She tried to subtly shake it off as she watched Joe move on top of her—lips parted, eyes closed, two pine needles stuck in his hair—when suddenly, he opened his eyes and looked into her face. Abruptly, he stopped moving. He leaped up, wrenching himself out from inside her, jumped off the bed, and stood naked in the dull moonlight, furiously grabbing at his clothes.

"I can't do it," he muttered, throwing on boxer shorts, sweatpants, a Temple T-shirt inside out. "I can't do this anymore."

Charlotte grabbed for the covers and pulled them to her chin. Her heart was racing. She hadn't seen this side of Joe before. What could her face have looked like to make him so angry? But he didn't explode, didn't say another word, just stormed out of the room and down the stairs.

For what seemed like hours she sat there, staring out the window at the stars. She replayed over and over the physical shock of what had just happened: his being inside her one moment, leaping out of her the next. His words echoed in her head—*I can't do this anymore.* She couldn't bring herself to speculate about what they might mean. It was the middle of the night that she moved, tentatively. She felt like she'd been ripped open. When she tiptoed to the landing, she saw Joe slumped in front of the TV downstairs, next to the dark silhouette of the Christmas tree. The next morning, he was back in bed beside her. They never spoke of it again.

But after that night, Charlotte knew she had to take action. She felt like a failure, responsible for ruining their sex life with nothing more than a look on her face. Though the things they talked about were pleasant, ordinary—how his classes went, what they should buy his sisters' kids for Christmas—Charlotte was aware of what was going unsaid. For once, she wished she could play his bedtime game, tapping her finger to his temple and saying, "What's going on in there?" Was he deciding whether or not to leave her? And what would she tell people if he did?

Next time, Charlotte decided, she would fix it. Whatever it took.

It was almost two weeks later, a Sunday, and Charlotte had been awake for hours. Joe was sleeping late, sprawled across the bed with the ropy sheets tangled in his legs. When she crept into the room with a basket of laundry, he rolled over and squinted. "Hey," he said sleepily. "Whatcha doing over there?"

Charlotte paused. She knew this tone, the hint of playfulness. And yet, there was something more than playful this time. Something distinctly unplayful, in fact, like hard enamel behind a soft smile. Joe was taking this as seriously as she was.

Charlotte put the laundry basket down. She took a step toward the bed. She couldn't have been feeling less sexual—she had the washing machine going, Christmas cookies baking, the oven timer would go off in five minutes, the kitchen would smell, the cookies burn—but she put all that aside. Joe touched her knee lightly, traced a finger up her thigh.

She sat on the edge of the bed, which smelled warm and salty, like oversleeping. Joe cupped her face in both hands. The kiss wasn't pleasant—his breath was sour, his whiskers hurt—but it was important. She could feel it. His tongue roamed her mouth, lips were hard on her face. He was kissing her with determination, as if he too had something to prove.

Closing her eyes, Charlotte summoned her courage and started to make soft, moaning noises. She felt Joe draw back in surprise, then move more quickly. As he undressed her, climbed on top of her, weight bearing down on her, Charlotte kept her eyes closed and moaned louder. When she sensed he was close, she opened her eyes and took in the look on his face—it was hopeful, even happy—and so, she pretended. She'd seen it enough times on soap operas and TV movies to know what to do. She let her voice get higher, culminating in a squeal, then let out a long, breathy sigh.

Joe held her so tightly she thought she might break. He was sticky with sweat, but so happy with her she didn't care. "What changed?" he said, his eyes like plates, drinking her in. "What was different this time?"

"I don't know," she whispered, though she did, of course. What was different was there was too much at stake. What was different was she couldn't bear feeling broken anymore.

Joe held her closer, chin pressed into her neck. "How did it feel?"

"Good," she said. "Really good."

She wasn't lying, exactly. It hadn't felt *bad.* And he hadn't specified the word "orgasm." It was much like everything in their marriage: they made assumptions about each other. They never verified them, but never asked.

Over the next few weeks, Charlotte's act became a pattern.

They were having sex almost daily, sometimes more than daily. Once Joe came home in between his classes and laid her down on the living room floor, right beside the Christmas tree. He called her things he never had before, "sensual" and "sexy." For Christmas, he gave her lingerie—her first ever—short red satin with lace around the hem. Charlotte tried to push the guilt into the back rooms of her mind. Because here was the thing, she reasoned to herself, as she kept busy wrapping gifts and baking cookies: the only way she would ever relax was if Joe relaxed, and the only way he would relax was to let him *think* she'd relaxed. So really, she was improving her chances of legitimately having an orgasm by pretending to have one. Or a few.

But as the days passed, Charlotte realized she'd blown any chance at ever having a real one. She'd so perfected her own version of the orgasm that it *became* her orgasm; it wasn't a lie anymore, just her own definition. She actually started to wonder if maybe she wasn't faking after all. Maybe she was having them? Maybe this is what they felt like? And if she was unsure, then she wasn't lying, just confused. Misinformed. But deep down, Charlotte knew that if she wasn't sure she'd had an orgasm, she hadn't.

So this is how it happened that Charlotte Warren, for a few brief weeks in her forty-seven years, had a wild, passionate sex life. Passion that was half pretend, but passion nonetheless. It lasted just under a month; never happened before, never happened again. In early January, unbeknownst to Joe, she sat in a thin paper gown in a doctor's office with snow floating lightly past the tiny window, while a nurse squeezed her hand and said, "Congratulations!" And it was the one thing she regretted most about that month: that Emily was conceived under false pretenses.

Now, alone in her kitchen more than two decades later, Charlotte stares at the blank computer screen. The silence is deafening. She begins tapping at the space bar. When she hears the click of Bea's heels approaching L2, it is in the spirit of denial that she goes leaping from her seat.

She peeks behind the kitchen curtain, confirming that Bill's not there, then hurries to the front door, which yields only an inch before jerking to a stop. She forgot to unhook the chain. "Bea?"

"Yes?" Bea looks alarmed. Charlotte doesn't blame her; she must look maniacal, peering through the crack in the door.

"I'm sorry. Sorry to scare you. Hold on. Just a sec." Charlotte pushes the door shut, cursing herself, and unhooks the chain. She starts to open it, then stops. "Oh." In the pale light, she can see that Bea's been crying. "I'm sorry, I just heard you coming in, I thought I'd—"

"It's okay," Bea says quickly, as Charlotte starts to close the door. "You just took me by surprise, that's all."

Charlotte pauses. As her eyes adjust, she can see Bea's eyes are very red. Her face is shiny and swollen. Charlotte is seized with worry. Could Bea still be upset about Joe last night? Or—worse—could she have overheard Charlotte this morning, denying their friendship on the patio? Her words come back now, pounding firmly in her ears: *She's not my friend. She's just my neighbor. I hardly know her.* Why did she say those things? And right under Bea's window!

Although, Charlotte thinks, it's true: they're really *not* friends. But her tone didn't imply she wished they were; it said she was glad they weren't. Either way, there was no reason for her to emphasize the point. What if Bea now thought Charlotte didn't want to be associated with her? That she looked down on her short skirts? Her loud sex? Her Victoria's Secret catalogs? That she was reacting to some sort of difference in class? Or economic background? And what if she was? What if she's the kind of person who *thinks* such things?

"I didn't know you stayed up this late," Bea says.

Charlotte manages to locate her tongue and move it. "I don't." She swallows. It's difficult making small talk through the clamor in her head. "Not usually, anyway."

"I thought I was the night owl in the L block," Bea says, then smiles her kind, lopsided smile. It is then Charlotte realizes Bea didn't overhear anything. She feels her head relax, the heap of nervous questions dissipate instantly, wasted energy, exhaled and sent swirling down the drain.

"Couldn't sleep?" Bea guesses.

"Actually, no," Charlotte says, pulling herself together. "I mean, no, I couldn't *not* sleep. I haven't even tried. I was just on the computer." She thinks of her idle tapping on the space bar and adds, "Typing."

"Really? Are you a writer?"

Charlotte hesitates. "I keep a journal," she says. It's shameless. She thinks of the two old journal entries she couldn't retrieve now if she wanted to. "I mean, I used to."

"Figures," Bea says. "All the Warrens are so artistic."

The reference makes Charlotte skip a beat. The last time she used the phrase "the Warrens" was on her humble attempt at Baby's First Christmas cards in 1980.

"Makes sense too," Bea is saying. "I always thought you seemed really quiet down there. I'd always think, what does she do that's so quiet? But you were probably writing."

Guilt tugs at the back of Charlotte's brain. "I really don't write that often—"

"You're still doing better than me. I wish I kept a journal."

Charlotte nods sympathetically, hoping that she drops the subject.

"A few of the girls from work do it," Bea goes on. "I just don't have the discipline. I get really easily distracted. But I wish I did. They say it helps them get things off their chest."

Charlotte tugs her bathrobe closer. Now not only has her writing turned into a profession, it's beginning to suggest some sort of emotional health. "I've heard that's true," she says. "I saw something on it once. On *20/20.*"

Bea smiles politely. She probably has no idea what's on television on Friday nights. Charlotte realizes Bea is still wearing her Friendly's uniform, clutching her keys in one hand, mail in the other. "Well, that's really all I wanted," Charlotte says. "I should let you get on with your night—"

"There's no night to get on with," Bea interjects, then offers a trying-to-be-indifferent shrug. Her voice trembles slightly as she says, "Bill's sleeping at his place."

Charlotte looks at Bea. Bea looks at Charlotte. For a moment, it feels as if they are all alone in the world, caught under the faint, unflattering porchlight of Unit L in a shared kinship of manlessness and loneliness and condo living.

"Well. In that case." Charlotte speaks briskly. "Would you want to sit out on the patio? Just for a minute?"

"I don't want to intrude, especially if you're writing—"

"You're not intruding. And," Charlotte says firmly, "I'm not writing." She takes a breath. "To be honest, I could use the company." As she admits it, tears well up in her eyes. She blinks quickly, tightening her arms across her chest.

If Bea notices the tears, she doesn't let it show. "Sure," she says. "Sounds great. Let me just go change and I'll meet you out back in a jif."

Charlotte nods, keeping her lips pursed to conceal their quivering. It's not until she shuts the door that she feels the tears spill over. This is absurd, she thinks, brushing roughly at her eyes. Before she couldn't cry at anything, now she's crying at everything. She locks the door, double-locks it, yanks on the chain.

In the bathroom, Charlotte blows her nose and splashes her cheeks with cool water. Then she examines her face in the mirror, making sure it doesn't look too messy. She mimes conversation: raising her eyebrows, nodding, smiling. Good enough, she thinks, letting her face go soft. Her eyes are a little red, but it shouldn't be noticeable in the dark.

Leaning against the sink, she studies her reflection more closely. She thinks again of the way Joe looked at her this morning, and wonders what he saw. Up close, her face is no longer a whole face but an assemblage of details: pores and lines and freckles. Wrinkles that have gathered in the corners of her eyes, bunching when she squints, like fish gills, or feathers. Eyes that are not just blue but gold inside, near-orange, growing more intricate the longer she looks, like the insides of marbles. She notices a new sun spot emerging faintly on her cheekbone, then pulls back and cuts the light.

The moment Charlotte steps onto the patio, she feels herself relax. As she sinks into a chair, she takes comfort in the reliability of the outside world. It's always here. Always awake, always breathing. She used to think of the outdoors as an ominous silence, but she's come to realize it's made up of infinite sounds—not just the concrete noises, but pure tones. Listen hard enough at any given moment, and one will surface, disentangle itself, a tinny sound that wavers in and out according to the angle of your ear. It's always there, just takes patience to locate, like slowly turning a thermometer until the bar of mercury appears.

Charlotte hears the crunch of Bea's footsteps coming around the side of the house, each step punctuated by a smack of flesh. Absurdly, Charlotte's mind flies to Emily's speculations about whips and chains. As it turns out, naturally, Bea is wearing flip-flops. Faded black rubber with fake yellow-and-white daisies perched between the big toes. She has on black stretch pants and an oversized white sweatshirt that says HARD ROCK CAFE—LONDON, and holds two clear bottles in her hand.

"I figure I owe you a drink or two," Bea says, handing one to Charlotte.

Charlotte looks curiously at the label. Smirnoff Ice.

"It's not like beer," Bea assures her. "It's sweet. Here." She takes the bottle back and unscrews the cap on the hem of her shirt. "Try it."

Charlotte does. It tastes like sugary lemony water. And like the mimosa this morning, she likes it. After a drinking résumé that consisted mainly of wedding receptions spent sipping one glass of champagne over the course of five hours, this weekend has been a virtual education in alcohol.

Bea folds herself into the other chair, tucking one flip-flopped foot beneath her. She still has on her makeup and jewelry: pink eyelids, clumping mascara, large kinked gold hoop earrings. On her finger is a bulbous, purplish stone; it looks like the "mood rings" Emily was briefly obsessed with in junior high school. For a period of about six months, she consulted her mood ring constantly, using it to validate all her impulsive decisions. "Mom, I'm not going to gymnastics today," she would announce, then hold the ring up to Charlotte's face. "My body's just not up for it. See?" Or, after a boy called, she would frown at the ring for whole minutes, watching for the slightest change in shade. Eventually she would say, "It's just like I thought," and sigh deeply. "I just don't like Mike the way I used to."

Bea is uncapping her Smirnoff. "It's kind of a girl drink," she says, "but I like it. Whenever I get together with the other girls from work, this is what we have." She tips her bottle back and swallows. "Bill hates it."

Charlotte pauses. Is this her cue to ask what happened? Before she can decide, Bea continues. "So that guy last night. That was your ex-husband?"

"Yes," Charlotte says, then quickly adds, "and I want to apologize for his behavior."

"Don't worry about it."

"Really. He asked me to apologize to you. This morning. He said to tell you he was sorry. And out of line."

This news has seemingly no effect on her.

"He's not usually like that," Charlotte concludes.

Bea shrugs. "It was no big deal. I know his type."

She does? Charlotte has never thought of Joe as a "type." On the contrary, he's always seemed distinctive, unlike anyone else she's ever known.

"He didn't seem like a *bad* guy." Bea lets her flip-flop slip forward and dangle between her toes, held aloft by the plastic daisy. "Just a drunk one." The foot starts to swing, exposing the dusty imprint of her heel in the rubber. "Hot, though," she adds.

"Hot?" Charlotte pauses. "Joe?"

"Yeah. But that's no surprise. You're a good-looking woman."

She feels herself blush, but Bea doesn't seem to notice.

"So he's remarried now?"

"Joe? Oh yes."

"Do you like her?"

"I hardly know her, really. She seems very, I don't know. Stylish, I guess you could say."

"So you don't like her."

This is starting to feel familiar: first Walter, and now Bea, getting Charlotte to admit to not liking people.

"I guess you could say that," Charlotte says again, burying her response in her Smirnoff.

"What about you? Are you dating anybody?"

"Me?" She swallows. "I haven't dated in years."

"How many years?"

"Not since my divorce, actually."

"How long ago was that?"

"That was . . . let's see . . . fifteen years ago."

Bea's eyes bulge. Her foot stops swinging. She sets her bottle down and leans forward, speaking slowly. "Charlotte. You haven't dated anyone in fifteen years? You haven't had any action in a *decade and a half?*"

Charlotte just shrugs, but Bea seems genuinely distraught by this information. She must have orgasms, Charlotte concludes.

"Wait a minute." Bea raises one hand. From inside her sweatshirt, Charlotte hears her bangles go racing from wrist to elbow. "I have the perfect guy for you."

"Oh no, I'm really not in the market—"

In the market?

"Come on. He's great. Trust me. I wouldn't set you up with somebody awful. This guy's one of my regulars." Bea pauses, then picks up her bottle and starts swinging her foot again. "His name's Howie."

Charlotte knows, without question, she could never date a man named Howie.

Bea squints at her over the lip of the bottle. "He's older than you—fifty-five, maybe sixty. A sales rep. Pharmaceuticals. He's divorced too. I swear you two would hit it off."

Even though it's out of the question, Charlotte is curious. "How come?"

"Because." Bea swallows and rests the bottle on her thigh. "Howie comes in every Friday night. Same time. Same order. Same tip." She raises her eyebrows, as if to say she doesn't need to spell out the obvious reasons why Charlotte and Howie are meant to be. "He's like clockwork."

"What does he order?" Charlotte can't help herself.

"Bowl of clam chowder. Unsweetened iced tea. Turkey club SuperMelt, no mayo. He's watching his cholesterol."

"He told you that?"

Bea shrugs. "People tell me all kinds of things. Then for dessert he has a cup of coffee and a fudge brownie sundae. Tips me five bucks—that's twenty-five percent, by the way—and never leaves a drip or crumb on the table. He never calls me doll or sweetheart or any of that waitress crap. I'm telling you, Charlotte," she says, leaning back in her chair. "He's a catch." She takes a deep swallow, smacks her lips, then plunks her bottle on the table. It lands loudly, glass striking glass. Bea bites her lip and glances behind her. "Hope the cat lady didn't hear me."

"Ruth?" For some reason the possibility of Bea and Ruth knowing each other makes Charlotte feel surprised, yet oddly excited. "You know Ruth?"

"Not really," Bea says. "To be honest with you, I try and avoid her." She lowers her voice to a whisper. "She kind of freaks me out."

"Is it the—"

"The leash! Yes!" Bea yelps, then lowers her voice. "I don't know much about animals, but that seems very weird to me. Does it seem weird to you?"

"Oh yes," Charlotte says, nodding energetically. "Very weird. Very, very weird."

"Thank God," Bea says, flopping backward. "I thought I was the only one."

Charlotte lifts her bottle to drown the giggles bubbling up inside her. She wonders if this is what it feels like to have a college roommate: sitting around in sweats and pajamas and talking about cute boys and weird neighbors. "So," she says, feeling emboldened. "What happened with Bill?"

Bea seems to visibly deflate. Her shoulders sag, foot stops swinging. The heel of her flip-flop grazes the ground. "It's my fault, really," she says. "I started in on him last night. Not picking on him or anything—I just said I wanted to have a talk."

Charlotte nods. She is feeling sorry that she asked.

"Thinking back, it probably wasn't the best timing. It was late, he was tired, he just got done work. He was like, 'You're doing this to me *now?*' But I'm telling you, it wouldn't have mattered when I brought it up. It's never a good time for him. Bill just doesn't like having talks, period. He's a typical man."

Bea seems to possess a world of knowledge about the behaviors of men, Charlotte thinks. Maybe it's all her experience as a waitress.

"Anyway." Now that she's started talking, Bea doesn't seem to want to stop. "I got to thinking about what we're doing together, and where this is heading, and whether we'll ever really get married. Then I started thinking about never having kids and going through menopause and growing old alone. Once your brain gets stuck on one thing, it just runs wild, you know?"

If Bea only knew how well she knows.

"So basically, I did everything the magazines tell you not to. 'Don't pressure your man,'" Bea says, making her voice high-pitched and girlish. "'If you don't push him, he'll come around. If you do, you'll push him right out the door.'"

It sounds like she might actually have this advice memorized.

"But I'm thirty-eight, you know?" Bea says, voice returning to normal.

Charlotte nods.

"So screw it. If I take that advice, I could be sitting around unmarried when I'm forty-five." She glances at Charlotte. "No offense."

"Oh, none taken."

"It's just that I really want kids. And I love Bill, I do. I think he's the one. And I know he loves me. But the clock stops ticking sooner or later." She lifts her bottle, surveying Charlotte over the rim. "You were smart to have one so young. And now you're going to be a young grandmother." She shakes her head. "And Emily . . ." She lowers the bottle, looking at it wistfully. "I think that's actually what brought all this on last night, seeing them together and hearing about the baby. I was just sitting here, looking at them and thinking, they're so young and in love and they're just getting started. Then I went upstairs like, what am I doing? What if I'm wasting my time with Bill? What if I already let all my chances pass me by?"

"You haven't," Charlotte says. It's a meager gesture, and she berates herself for not saying more, but what? She doesn't trust her own advice. Then she reminds herself of Joe's words this morning: *You are comforting. You are.*

"I admire those two," Bea is saying. "They're doing it right. Jumping in with both feet. I wish I'd done that. But I wasted my twenties on an asshole." She smiles wryly. "That's how you get where I am, Charlotte. All us single women in our thirties, worried we're never going to have babies, we wasted our twenties on some asshole. Mine was named Jonah."

Charlotte cannot for the life of her picture Bea with any form of man named Jonah. Jonah is too conservative. Too white-collar. Jonah's not a man at all, but a boy at a prep school wearing khaki pants and a baseball cap turned backward. Unless—is *every* male name Charlotte pictures a conservative boy at a prep school wearing khaki pants and a baseball cap turned backward? Revise, she thinks.

"Why?" Charlotte asks. "What did Jonah do?"

"Oh, the usual. Cheated. Drank. Couldn't commit. I hung in there because I thought he'd change. And my mom loved him because his name came from the Bible."

"I'm sorry," Charlotte says, the words feeling strange on her lips.

"Thanks. I mean, I learned from it and all that. I paid my dues. I learned my lessons. What doesn't kill you. Blah blah blah blah blah." She takes a drink, bangles sliding up and down. "And Bill's a good guy. I mean, he drinks, yeah, but not like a problem. He'd never cheat. He wouldn't hurt a fly. And the sex is great."

Charlotte doesn't blink.

"His crime is, he's *lazy.* He could do more, he just doesn't apply himself. He never has. He's a youngest child, and you know what that means."

She nods. She has no idea.

"But he's a good, good guy. A good man. And that's what makes it so tricky—because it's easy to break up with someone when they're an asshole, right? You never have to look back and wonder if you did the right thing." Her voice is getting louder.

"He cheated on me. *Bam.*" She slaps a palm flat on the table, her maybe-mood ring hitting the glass. "He got so drunk he scraped up the car. *Bam.* He hit on my best friend. *Bam bam bam.*" At that, she slaps the table three times, apparently no longer worried about bothering Ruth O'Keefe. "But it's like my friend Meg at work is always telling me, they don't have to be assholes to break up with them. It's okay to break up with a good guy. It's even okay to break up with someone you love." She pauses then and looks at Charlotte, eyes glassy. "But how do you do that?"

Charlotte shakes her head.

Bea looks down at her toes, at the forlorn plastic daisy. Though the petals are fake, they actually appear more limp now than they did before. "How did you do it with Joe?"

"What do you mean?"

"I'm sorry." She looks up. "Too personal?"

"No, I just—I'm just not sure what you mean."

"Well." Bea considers her hand. Maybe she's gauging the mood ring too. "Why did you get divorced?"

Charlotte is deluged with familiar images, possible responses: Joe tapping his finger on her temple. Joe naked, splashed with moonlight, grabbing at his clothes. Joe romping with Emily in the backyard, flushed and laughing. For a moment, the progression actually seems that easy: from trying to get inside her to leaping out from inside her to being as far away from inside her as he could.

"Was there a big fight?" Bea asks.

"No." Of this she is sure. "We never fought."

"Never? Not even when you were breaking up?"

"Not really."

"Let me guess." Bea peers at her closely. "Not much sex either, right?"

"Not really," Charlotte admits, feeling her cheeks turn warm.

But Bea is unfazed. "Figures. The two usually go hand in hand. It's all passion—just thrown in different directions."

As embarrassing as it is, hearing her sex life described as in any way recognizable is such a relief to Charlotte that it inspires her to say more. "We almost never did it—" she confides. "After I had Emily."

"He got grossed out by the birth stuff?"

"Actually, no. Just the opposite. He was, kind of, fascinated." In fact, it was one of their happiest times. Joe treated Charlotte like a fragile new species, granting her privacy, acting as if she were surrounded by an invisible moat. They no longer had sex—it never occurred to her that they would—but Joe saw Charlotte as a mystery again. She contained one: literally. As her belly grew big, his eyes grew wider. "He was amazed by the process. The birth process."

"Academics." Bea reaches for her Smirnoff. "So, okay. You have a baby, you stop having sex basically. Then what happened?"

"Nothing, really."

"Come on."

"Really," Charlotte says, "it was just an ordinary night." In fact, she's tucked it so far out of reach, she wonders how much she'll even remember. But it's like an old injury: prod it once, and the pain comes flooding back. Haltingly, she says, "It was Emily's last day of first grade."

Bea sets her bottle down, listening.

"Her class trip to the Amish country. We were eating dinner—Joe and Emily and me. I remember Emily loved it, she was begging us to move somewhere where horses walked with cars on the streets." She looks at Bea. "She's always loved animals."

Bea smiles. "Cute."

"She was talking all about the Amish kids—how they rode in the backs of buggies and they weren't allowed to smile. And they didn't have TVs." She pauses. "The strange thing is, I hardly remember Joe being there."

"Maybe he wasn't?"

"No, no, he was. I remember because we had macaroni and cheese. And I made him a separate plate with ham in it."

Bea's eyebrows arch. "Because he had a thing for ham?"

"Because Emily was a vegetarian."

"In first grade? You weren't kidding about the animals." She leans back and fishes a crumpled pack of Marlboro Lights from her pocket. "Do you mind?"

"Go ahead," Charlotte says. At this point, it's the least of her worries.

Bea lights up, as if fortifying herself for the rest of the story. "Okay," she says. "Go on."

Charlotte's not sure if she can, or wants to. "Well—" She pauses. "After dinner I cleaned up. Joe and Emily watched *The Muppet Show.* Then Emily fell asleep on the couch, Joe carried her up and tucked her in." She looks at Bea, as if anticipating her skepticism. "Like I said, it was just an ordinary night."

Bea just exhales. "It always is."

Charlotte looks out into the backyard, feels a knot forming in her stomach. "Then I went to check on Emily—I did it every night, to make sure she was breathing." She glances at Bea. "Does that sound crazy?"

"I've heard crazier."

That was the comforting thing about Bea: there was never any surprise, never any judgment. Everything was absorbed as if it were a story she'd heard a thousand times.

"Then I came back down." Charlotte starts to feel queasy, her mouth dry. She can see the staircase stretching below her as she places one foot tentatively on the top. "The living room was dark, and Joe was sitting on the couch. He had his back facing me, so I couldn't see his face. And he couldn't see mine." The knot is tightening as she nears the bottom, hand gripping the cool metal rail. "When I stepped on the last step, he said: 'I'm not happy, Charlotte. There's nothing in this for me.'"

Bea skips a beat, as if giving the moment its due respect. Then she says, "What'd you do? Scream? Cry? Beat the shit out of him?"

Charlotte shakes her head. "I said, 'What about Emily?'"

"Of course you did." Bea sucks on her cigarette. "You're a good mom." Then she lets one flip-flop drop to the ground and tucks her bare foot beneath her, gazing thoughtfully through the smoke. "Sounds like you weren't all that surprised, Char."

"I guess not," Charlotte says, realizing it's true. "It didn't feel surprising as much as just . . . inevitable. It was sad, but it was also a relief. Like when someone's been sick for a long time and finally dies."

Bea gives this analogy a nod of approval, as if adding it to her arsenal. "So what did he say? When you asked about Em?"

"He started to cry." The images are rushing forward now, words coming back verbatim even after all these years. "He put his head in his hands, and his voice kept breaking, and he said, 'It's better, in the long run, for her not to live with parents who don't love each other.'" She turns to Bea, her eyes hard, glassy. "And the worst part was—I never knew."

"Never knew what?" Bea asks softly.

"That he didn't love me."

"Oh, Char." Bea reaches out and takes her hand. "What a prick."

"I mean—I knew we didn't say it, but I never imagined—" She takes a gulp of air. "I just assumed he loved me."

"Well, sure you did. Why wouldn't he?" She gives Charlotte's hand a squeeze. "But more importantly, did you love him?"

Charlotte thinks for a minute, then answers honestly, "I don't know." At the time, she had assumed what she felt for Joe was love. But was it? How did she know? How did he know he didn't love her? What did that feel like: to love, or not to love? "I guess I thought I did. But I'm not sure."

Bea sits back and takes a final drag. Then she crushes the cigarette out in her bottle cap and fixes Charlotte with a firm look. "I'm no Dr. Phil," she says, "but Char, if all you remember about the night is that the man ate ham, well." She raises her eyebrows. "In my experience, when you love someone, you know it. You can't help it. Like my friend at work, Patty. Ever since I've known her—that's six years—she's been looking for an Irish Catholic cop. Her father was an Irish Catholic cop, brothers, uncles. Textbook. Anyway, one night she's moaning as usual about her bad luck, and in walks Raul." She pauses for dramatic effect. "Hispanic bus driver, two kids from a previous marriage, blind in one eye." She shrugs, picking up her bottle. "Next thing you know she's madly in love. Some things are just out of our control." Then she raises the bottle high over her head, as if toasting the sky.

Book Three

chapter eight

Charlotte had thought the highway would be empty. She'd imagined anyone else would already be installed in front of football games or chilly parades or day-long dinners. It was part of the reason she'd chosen today to travel: to have the roads to herself. But the highway is crowded. They must all be people, people like Charlotte, trying to get to their families on Thanksgiving.

She glances at the cassette hanging from her dashboard. It's a Books on Tape recording called *Embracing the Now* that Emily sent her for the drive. Feeling guilty, Charlotte gives the tape a nudge until it's slurped into the car radio.

It is easy to let our minds be our enemies, to let our thoughts imprison us, like jail cells. On this journey, friends, we will work together not to worry, not to think . . . but simply be.

The voice on the tape—a man named Vu Khan—speaks with a soft lisp probably designed to be relaxing. Probably it's supposed to make his listeners trust him, to put them at ease with their own impediments and idiosyncrasies. But, like the Dream Machine, the lisp makes Charlotte more anxious. Which makes her distracted. When she was in southern Connecticut, Vu Khan lisping in her ears, she'd accidentally turned onto a local highway, then had to ask for help at Dunkin Donuts to get back on track. She'd turned Vu off then and has kept him off ever since. But now, the nearer she gets to New Hampshire, the more pressure she feels to keep him turned on. It's as if Emily, if in close enough range, might be able to sense she's not listening.

We must live every moment with our own minds, so why not get along? Why not be allies with our minds? Why not be friends?

From behind her Charlotte sees a long truck approaching, its silver grill filling her rearview mirror. It's the type of truck that's actually made of stacks of cars arranged on top of each other at precarious angles. The truck swerves into the left lane, the last third of its car pile swinging from side to side. Charlotte taps her brake. She has a vision of one of the shiny cars slipping from its foothold, crashing onto her hood, and flattening her inside. When a nut of gravel strikes her windshield, she flinches and slows down. She waits until the truck is well ahead of her, then reaches for the bag of Canada Mints on the passenger seat: Emily's recommendation for staying alert.

Be aware of the movement of your breath going in and out. Feel it moving through you like a tide. Imagine your breath as an ocean, constantly receding and replenishing, receding and replenishing. Imagine your body is the shore upon which it renews itself every day.

Charlotte pops a mint in her mouth. She is trying to remember the last time she took a road trip this long. There was Wesleyan, of course, though that drive is at least two hours shorter. Mini-vacations when Emily was little—Philadelphia, Ocean City, Hershey Park—but they were day trips only; Charlotte never liked being too far from home. There was the Virginia Beach honeymoon, but that drive was no more than four hours.

This is probably the longest road trip she's ever taken. Certainly the longest she's taken alone.

Without warning, she finds herself merging onto a narrow bridge. The car begins to shake and shiver. The rattle of her tires is deafening. The bridge is made of some sort of chain-link metal, like a fence, except supporting the weight of four lanes of traffic. Charlotte clenches her teeth and grips the wheel to keep the car from slipping. From behind her, she hears something shift in the trunk, thudding as it collides with the felt wall. She keeps her eyes fixed on the spot where the bridge ends, and when it does—metal yielding to smooth pavement—lets her breath escape. It seemed very New England, she thinks, that brief patch of roughness. As if providing a courtesy test run for the more difficult terrain ahead.

Her mint has disappeared. She must have swallowed it in the heat of the moment. It doesn't matter; the bridge was more than enough to keep her awake. As she nears the Massachusetts/New Hampshire border, Charlotte hears the contents of the trunk realigning. She hadn't known what Emily and Walter were cooking tonight but wanted to help out with the meal, at least a little. In truth, she enjoyed it. Thanksgiving was always "Joe's holiday," so Charlotte hadn't prepared a real meal in years. She was secretly thrilled when Emily decided to spend this Thanksgiving in New Hampshire, having seen Joe just weeks before. Charlotte was careful what she cooked, though, not wanting to make anything too traditional and risk doubling Emily's menu. She'd decided on two simple, mobile, meatless side dishes: candied yams and a cheese potato casserole. For Walter, she consulted the Internet (typed: *pie coconut chocolate,* clicked: *find)* and found a recipe for something called Amazing Choconut Pie. It was the closest thing to a pie-sized Needham she could come up with. And for Emily, strawberry pretzel salad. She hadn't unearthed that recipe in years—it was popular at barbecues and birthday parties, back when Charlotte was an elementary school mom—and was always Emily's favorite. Charlotte smiles to herself, imagining the gelatin wiggling behind her. She'd packed all the dishes in Tupperware, then cushioned them in a nest of pillows.

Remember to pause each day and thank the things that carry you on your journey. Your legs, for holding you up. Your lungs, for making a home for your breath. Your heart, for always beating, whether you notice it or not.

Charlotte tries to locate her heartbeat to say a quick thanks, though really, she can't be accused of neglecting it. She is all too aware of her heart's inner workings. Her mind wanders to one of her lesser road trips, one of the home-by-ten excursions when Emily was a child. Charlotte had taken her to the Franklin Institute, a science museum in Philadelphia filled with games and gadgets, wireless telephones, electricity that made your hair stand on end. But the main attraction was The Giant Heart: an enormous, pumping, walk-through replica. "You Are Now Entering the Inside of the Heart," said the rather benign sign at the entrance. But once she was inside it, the heart was a warm, low-ceilinged maze of dark hallways and cramped stairwells, valves and chambers. The walls looked smooth, damp to the touch, and the sound of *th-thump* was so loud it could have been coming from inside her own skin.

As she navigated the heart, Charlotte felt claustrophobic. She tried to keep an eye on Emily, but her little body was too fast, ducking around corners threaded with bright pink veins and bulging blue arteries, disappearing under signs like LEFT VENTRICLE, RIGHT ATRIUM, AORTIC ARCH. When Charlotte groped her way past the arrow pointing TO THE LUNG, the thumping was replaced by a breathy, sickening whoosh, like the inside of an enormous conch shell. As Charlotte fumbled her way out of the lung and back into the heart, the return of *th-thump* made her nauseated; the sound was coming from all around her, inside and out. The irony of this trip was not lost on her either: that she should be here, squeezing through an aorta made of plaster, not more than a year after her mother's heart attack. Stranger still, this fake heart pumping still seemed more plausible—more scientifically accurate—than her mother's coming to a stop. It wasn't high cholesterol, the doctors said, not blockage, but sixty-five years of silent worry capped off by a loss and a sorrow so deep that, in their medical opinion, it literally broke her heart.

When Charlotte emerged, she sagged on a bench beside a display of hearts in various states of disease. "Can I go again?" Emily had begged, and Charlotte nodded. For what seemed like hours she watched while Emily ran through the heart over and over, dutifully making eye contact each time, like she did at the swimming pool before and after going underwater. She waved to Charlotte when she entered the heart, then waved again when she popped out on the other side, unscathed.

Your goal is nothing more than to live the present moment. Do not think about the past or the future. Simply be here, acknowledging your thoughts and feelings right now.

Charlotte's feeling right now is that she wants badly to turn Vu Khan off. "Living the present moment" is completely at odds with her state of mind. At the moment, she can think of nothing but what will be happening *after* the moment, in the moment when she arrives at Emily's house and the moments after that. For the past five hours she's been trying to picture her arrival, scaring herself with images of a house exaggeratedly dilapidated and rambling. Loose shutters, cracked aluminum siding. No glass in the windows or screens on the doors. Skinny local animals pawing at the front porch, begging for handouts.

She passes a huge green billboard by the side of the highway: LIVE FREE OR DIE. Her official welcome to New Hampshire, and it couldn't be more fitting. It is exactly as she suspected: New Hampshire is a giant free-for-all. An ungoverned, untamed wilderness. A place with no rules, no grades, no shoes, no shaved legs, no report cards, no marriages. Quite literally: a state of chaos.

Charlotte reaches for the volume and turns up Vu Khan, as if making the words louder might make them more convincing. She is trying to be positive. Trying to reserve judgment. This trip will be a good one, regardless of what the house looks like. Tonight they'll have a nice dinner. Tomorrow Emily will take her on a tour of the town. And Saturday, they will arrive at the real reason for Charlotte's visit: Emily's twelve-week sonogram. Charlotte had insisted on being there for it—she told Emily she wanted to be involved in this process, and she does—but also, she wants to be sure this doctor is qualified. She needs to know for sure Emily is in good hands.

To be present is simply the experience of being awake and aware. Do not judge. Do not reflect on the past. Do not worry about the future. Simply rejoice in the—

Charlotte snaps the volume down. Does Vu Khan have children? She thinks not. She doesn't turn him completely off, so technically he is still talking, but his words are too low for her to make out. She can't handle this man's opinion on happiness right now; it's too blithe, too easy. As happy an event as this pregnancy is—as happy as Emily still seems—Charlotte knows it's not that simple. She remembers the glow on Emily's face when she announced they were keeping the baby. Charlotte's seen that glow countless times before: Emily recommending a great book, Emily adopting a new cause, Emily discovering an amazing new friend or painter or professor or rock band or organic peanut butter. Emily discovering Walter. It's the same look that was on her face at the Wesleyan graduation. That day, Charlotte had called it love.

And maybe it is. But already Charlotte senses Walter and Emily's dynamic changing. She can't help but feel he's more committed to the relationship than she is. In Emily's whole life, have any of her passions amounted to more than a bright flash? Has she ever made a decision and stuck with it?

Charlotte fishes in her purse for the directions Walter sent by e-mail. She smoothes them against the steering wheel with one hand, guiding the car with the other. Her eyes flick back, forth, from the notes to the road. *Go through toll ($1),* Walter instructed. *Follow signs for NH Lakes/White Mts. Take Exit 4, on left—*

She drops the directions in her lap. The toll is already approaching. Charlotte slows and rolls her window down, but when she stops, she sees a handmade sign in the empty window: HAPPY THANKSGIVING! She pauses, touched by the gesture. Like the metal bridge, it too strikes her as being very New England, softening the rough conditions with an unexpected kindness.

She follows Walter's instructions, turning off the highway, passing a few lights, making a few turns, and eventually finds herself on an abruptly rural road. She glances at the directions, puts her blinker on and pulls over. *Go straight on Song Lane—* she looks up, Song Lane it is—*about 8 miles.* Charlotte surveys the narrow road, bordered by topheavy trees. It doesn't look like it could stretch more than twenty feet. *Pass Mahar Pies & Real*

Estate on left. Cat hotel (no joke!) and produce market on right. After market, watch for Willow Rd. Turn left and . . . home sweet home! p.s. If you get lost, ask. People around here are nice. :)

Walter punctuated this last line with a smiley face made out of a colon and a single parentheses. "Emoticons," he explained, when Charlotte asked about them. He even e-mailed her a long list of facial expressions constructed of various combinations of punctuation. Semicolons for conspiratorial winks. An equals sign for a pair of eyes. Hyphens for noses. A mustache masquerading as the sign for greater-than.

She reads the directions once more, committing them to memory. Vu Khan is still murmuring vaguely from the dashboard. Tentatively, she starts driving down the dirt road until she spies Mahar Pies & Real Estate. She'd assumed it was two different stores, but no: real estate and baked goods in one establishment. On her right, she sees the cat hotel. *The purrfect place to board your pet!* The produce market is closed, but a very Thanksgiving-ish spray of corn cobs and gourds garnishes the entrance. Charlotte slows to a crawl—there's no traffic, after all—scanning the thick trees for Willow Road. If she hadn't been going nine miles an hour, she might have missed it, the sign so entangled with vines and leaves that it's actually become part of the landscape. Below the road sign, she spots a swath of manmade color: a homemade poster with an arrow pointing left and bubble letters that spell WELCOME MOM!

Her heart swells. She snaps her turn signal on, then off; it seems not only unnecessary here, but borderline offensive. As Charlotte turns into the driveway, her breath feels stuck in her chest. After so much worrying and conjuring, it is surreal to actually be here. In front of her stretches what looks less like a road than a long, rutted driveway, bordered on each side by deep trenches that look like they were gouged by a monster truck. In the middle, a hump of dirt is covered with sparse grass, like an old man's whiskers. Charlotte hears branches snapping under her tires, then something scraping the bottom of her car. She maneuvers to the right, planting one wheel in a trench and the other on the hump, and it is at this awkward angle that she approaches the alternative living arrangement.

The house looks like pieces of various houses patched together: a tall wooden middle section, a clapboard appendage jutting from one side, a porch poking from the other. In the yard sits an old-fashioned, slate-roofed red barn. The middle section of the house is painted magenta at the top, reverting to a dingy white about a third of the way down, as if the painter abruptly lost interest. Emily is waving from the porch, wearing what looks to be an apron. Walter is in the yard, beckoning Charlotte into a makeshift parking place. At the last second she remembers *Embracing the Moment,* and lunges for the volume so forcefully that Vu Khan's lisp is deafening when Walter opens the door. "Charlotte!"

She turns the car off, Vu disappearing. "Walter! Hello!" She is surprised by how happy she is to see him. Her legs are stiff as she stands and lets him enfold her in his customary hug.

"Mommy! Mommy!" Emily calls, skipping over the grass.

Charlotte feels Emily's strong arms around her neck, then steps back and takes her usual inventory. Nothing too surprising, except the apron, which comes as a mild shock; Emily always objected to her aprons, calling them "old-fashioned" and "demeaning." Underneath it she's wearing a bulky, oatmeal-colored sweater and scuffed blue jeans. Charlotte doesn't think she's showing yet, but under all those layers it's hard to tell.

"How was the drive?" Walter is saying. "Any traffic? Problems?"

They're the questions Charlotte has grown used to asking.

"None at all," she says, as he grabs her suitcase from the backseat. "Here, let me—"

"Mom, please. He's got it." Emily hooks Charlotte's elbow. "So how were the directions? Did you get lost?"

"Just once—"

"Where?"

"It was my fault," she says, glancing at Walter. "Somewhere in Connecticut, I think."

Emily frowns. "This is why you need a cell phone."

After twenty years of resisting an answering machine, she's not about to go catapulting into a cell phone. But rather than argue, she smiles.

"Come on," Emily says, tugging her hand. "Let me show you inside."

They step onto the porch, crowded with white wicker furniture and hanging plants. Up close, it's not as ramshackle as Charlotte had imagined. The screen door is a little crooked, the paint peeling in spots. She steps gingerly over a sagging porch step as Emily swings open the front door.

"Home sweet home!"

The first thing Charlotte notices is the smell: home cooking. Not a familiar cooking smell, though. Woodsy. Cinnamony. Had Charlotte ever gone camping, this might have been what it smelled like. The counters are dusted with fine brown silt and scattered with open spice jars, spoons, measuring cups. Pushed against the far wall is a wooden table (one of Walter's creations, Charlotte guesses) draped with a tapestry so long it pools like a curtain onto the floor. Table and floor are heaped with stacks of mail, books, candlesticks, potted plants, a pair of eyeglasses, set of keys, a plastic yellow timer that looks like it belongs to a board game. On top of the stove is something large, round, and wrapped ominously in tinfoil.

"Coming through!" Walter appears with Charlotte's suitcase in one hand and her purse draped over his opposite shoulder. "Mmmm," he murmurs, lifting the edge of the tinfoil. "Smells good, Em."

"Hey! No peeking!"

He drops it.

"It's supposed to be a surprise," she explains to Charlotte.

"You're the boss," Walter says, heading for the doorway. "Where's this stuff go, boss?"

"Mara's!" Emily calls, as his footsteps echo up unseen stairs. She shakes her head. "We've only talked about a million times about where you're sleeping."

"Where am I sleeping?"

"Mara's room. She's away for the weekend."

"Oh," Charlotte says. "Right." It had never occurred to her that the roommates might be there, but she's relieved to know they're not. "Of course," she says out loud. "They're with their families. For Thanksgiving." It's somehow reassuring that these roommates have families who observe Thanksgiving.

"Well, yeah, Mara is. But Anthony's still here."

Charlotte tenses. Does this mean Anthony is joining them for dinner? After her long drive, and this unfamiliar place, the last thing she needs is the social pressure of spending the evening with a stranger.

"His family's in Hawaii. He's leaving tomorrow to meet Mara down in D.C."

"So will he—"

"She just didn't want him dealing with all that holiday shit. Mara's family is completely fucking nuts." Seeing the worry on Charlotte's face, she adds, "Sorry, but they really are."

"So Anthony is—" Charlotte tries again.

"Going down tomorrow morning, just in time to deal with all the family fallout. Come on," Emily says. "Come see the rest of the place."

Charlotte tries to put this news aside and trails Emily into a large room awash with sunlight. The walls are filled with bright windows, each ledge crowded with plants of various shapes and sizes: thick reddish leaves, long spidery tendrils, tender leaf cuttings floating in empty yogurt containers and mason jars. The leaves are all tangled in one another, jostling for the light like a crowd of schoolchildren. On the floor are several large colored pillows substituting for a couch, a trunk doubling as a coffee table, a tiny rabbit-eared TV in a corner on the floor. In another corner squats a black potbellied stove and a stack of cut wood. The furnishings all feel somehow peripheral, as if the room has all the accents but none of the things they're supposed to be accenting. Taking up most of the floor is a multicolored, braided rug strewn with random magazines, socks, books, shoes, empty mugs, stray newspaper sections, half-melted candles, a game of Scrabble that looks like it was called off mid-play, words still frozen crisscrossed on the board: ASP, PLAN, FEELS.

"What do you think?"

There are many things about this house that would distress Charlotte. It's tangled. It's disorganized. It feels not particularly clean. And yet, there is something in the details and the disarray that makes her heart ache.

"It feels like a home," she says.

Emily smiles. "It does, doesn't it?"

Suddenly Charlotte hears footsteps thundering down the stairs. She looks up, expecting Walter, but finds herself facing an Asian boy with long silky hair.

"Ant!" Emily says.

The boy stops short. "Em!"

"Hey man, I want you to meet my mom."

The boy turns to Charlotte. "Hey, Em's mom!"

His ensemble is bizarre: thick rag socks with summer sandals and a bulky sweater with baggy shorts. He's dressed half in one season, half in another.

"Mom, Anthony," Emily says. "Anthony, Charlotte."

She steels herself for a possible hug, but Anthony just pumps her hand enthusiastically. He has an exotic look: olive skin, jet-black hair, dark eyes that shine like wet glass. Charlotte had assumed Emily meant his family was vacationing in Hawaii, but seeing his complexion, wonders now if they live there. Maybe that's why he's wearing shorts in November. His island disposition.

"So," he says, sweeping his hair away from his face with one hand. "You'll be joining us for the feast of the new millennium?"

Charlotte feels herself deflate.

"She's the guest of honor," Emily says.

"Ah." Anthony smiles. "Brave woman."

Emily punches his arm. "You can joke now, but you'll see. I'm multitasking in there."

"But it's all under wraps!" Walter's voice bellows from the top of the staircase, followed by a flurry of footfalls. "I don't know what the hell's going on in there," he says, emerging at the bottom. "But I got a bad feeling. I'm thinking it's all so healthy she doesn't want to admit what's in it. Good thing we're cooking too."

"Definitely." Anthony nods solemnly.

Emily rolls her eyes at Charlotte. "They're cooking *one* dish each," she explains. "That was the deal."

This too strikes Charlotte as oddly old-fashioned, but she keeps her mouth shut.

"Yeah, one *awesome* dish." Walter leaps from the bottom step to the floor. "That it for the car, Charlotte?"

"Actually, I brought some food too—"

Simultaneously, Walter and Anthony burst out in a laugh and slap five.

"Mom!" Emily wails. "I'm totally capable of making this—"

"Oh, no, I didn't think—"

"Charlotte's a great cook," Walter confides to Anthony.

Based on what? Charlotte wonders. A piece of toast? A cup of coffee he brewed himself?

"Good deal." Anthony nods. "So we got backup. Just in case."

"Maybe there's even meat in it," Walter says, rubbing his hands together. "Maybe we'll actually have *turkey* on Thanks*giving*."

"Quit it!" Emily says, swatting at them both. But she is laughing. Under other circumstances she might have taken offense, but today it seems like nothing can bring her down. "You're going to eat your words, boys. Along with some fabulous soy products. Come on, Mom. Let's go see your room."

"Nice to meet you!" Anthony calls up the stairs behind her. Charlotte gives him a quick smile before turning to follow Emily. The staircase takes a moment to adjust to: a steep, hazardous spiral lit by one dim bulb.

"Aren't these steps wild?" Emily is burbling from up ahead. "It's like a funhouse or something."

Charlotte trails her hands along the walls, watching Emily's bare heels to keep steady. When she emerges, Emily is heading down the hall. "La toilette," she quips. Charlotte doesn't have time for more than a glance before she's facing a doorway strung with sparkling, floor-to-ceiling, turquoise beads. "And this," Emily says, "is our room."

Intellectually, of course, Charlotte knew Emily and Walter shared a bedroom. Still, the physical reality of it takes a moment to sink in. Her first impression, stepping through the beaded doorway, is that the room is vastly out of proportion, like one of the wrong turns in *Alice in Wonderland.* Everything is much too close to the floor. The bed is no more than a flat, frameless mattress disguised under tiny pillows and bright blankets. Above it hangs some kind of purple-and-pink batiked sheet. A rickety-looking drying rack is propped by the window, crammed with wool socks, T-shirts, underwear. It occurs to Charlotte they probably don't have an electric dryer; as further proof, a pair of jeans and Walter's striped running pants are draped over the closet door. Lining the baseboard is a knee-length bookcase constructed of bricks and boards, sagging under the weight of a dense and random library. *Franny and Zooey. The Red Tent. The Women's Health Encyclopedia. 100 Love Poems by Pablo Neruda. Evening. Rule of the Bone.* Planks of raw wood lean against the wall beside it, probably the beginning or end of one of Walter's projects. The only thing standing at normal height is the loveliest: a dresser made of what looks like cherry wood with long, silky grains.

"What do you think?" Emily asks.

"That dresser is beautiful."

"Isn't it?" She runs her hand across the top edge, the only surface that isn't crowded with the accumulation of the everyday:

deodorants and hairbands and loose change and crumpled cash machine receipts and piles of tangled silver jewelry—hers? his? both?—a hammer and box of nails.

"I had no idea Walter was so talented," Charlotte says.

"Come on." Emily steps to the doorway, shoving the beads aside like a shank of hair. "Let's get you set up. And by the way, if you're wondering about these"—she gives the beads a shake—"the room had no door when we moved in. Walter was going to try to fit one, but we thought this was cooler anyway. Not totally private, but it has a nice flow, don't you think?" Not waiting for an answer, she points to the right. "That's Anthony's hell-hole."

Charlotte glances into a small room that looks like a cyclone hit it.

"Yes, he's a pig," she confirms, heading to the end of the hallway. "And this is your room. Otherwise known as Mara's."

"So Mara and Anthony don't—"

"Room together? No, they do. But they were sort of just friends when we moved in, now they're more than friends—I don't know. It's still ambiguous. It's like, they love each other, they're just trying to figure out what that means. Basically, they sleep in here and store stuff in there. We call Ant's room their walk-in closet."

In other words, Charlotte thinks, she's sleeping in the sex room.

"Don't worry, I put on clean sheets," Emily says, reading her mind. She turns to the door, draped with yet another aggressively multicolored sheet. "Mara makes these."

"Oh?"

"Yeah, she's great with fabrics. Listen, I need to go check on the food. And the boys are being suspiciously quiet. So just make yourself at home—wash up, rest, whatever, then come on down." She brushes her lips against Charlotte's cheek and smiles. "I'm glad you're here," she says, then skips off down the stairs.

Charlotte faces the door to Mara's. At least the room *has* a door. She nudges it open and, for a few seconds, thinks she's stumbled upon some kind of crazy tent. The entire room is swathed in sheets, rugs, pillowcases, wall hangings in an explosion of colors. The ceiling slants sharply in the middle, tapestries drooping to almost eye level. At first glance it looks chaotic, but as Charlotte ventures deeper inside, she realizes this may actually be the most organized spot in the house. On top of the dresser stands an orderly wooden earring ladder, each earring lined up next to its partner, butterfly backings intact. A moat of vials and bottles—sunscreens, hand lotions, flavored lip balms—surrounds the base, and two framed pictures oversee the tidy, scented village. In one, a tiny dark-haired figure stands on top of a snowy mountain—Charlotte vaguely remembers Emily once saying something about a roommate and Mount Kilimanjaro—could that be Anthony, that speck on top of the world? In the other, Anthony is hugging a young woman who must be Mara. She has a sweet face, fine blond hair, twin stripes of sunburn on her cheeks. The two of them are tangled in a canoe, laughing, wearing orange life preservers that engulf their chins.

It's a strange feeling, wandering the bedroom of someone Charlotte doesn't know. And yet, oddly endearing. There's something innocent, almost childlike, about Mara's belongings. In the far corner stands an old-fashioned school desk covered with more photos. Charlotte picks up one of a middle-aged couple, probably her parents, standing in front of a lake with arms around each other's waists. Both are wearing sunglasses and crewneck sweaters. The man has a fanny pack strapped around his middle, the woman a graying bob that's fluttering in the wind. Charlotte takes comfort in their ordinariness, then remembers what Emily said about Mara's family being "completely fucking nuts" and, gently, sets the picture back down.

She perches on the edge of the bed. To her right, the square of window could be a New England postcard: smoky blue sky, plush treeline bursting with color, old-fashioned red barn with a rake propped against the door. In the middle of the yard, two rainbow-striped beach chairs are angled toward each other, as if in conversation. So far, Charlotte thinks, the house is not at all what she expected. It isn't the physical details she finds surprising so much as the overall atmosphere of the place. She'd expected Emily's life here to feel younger, sillier, more like a college dorm, a group of kids playing grown-up. But there's a solidity about the place—the heavy wood furnishings, spicy cooking smells, handmade blankets, messy affectionate clutter—that feels legitimate. Lived in. The way houses should.

Charlotte suddenly realizes how exhausted she is. She could fall asleep right now, but forces herself to venture into the hallway. The bathroom, she discovers, is no bigger than a large closet, tiled in headachy black and white threaded with long thin cracks. Strewn on the sink ledge are three frayed toothbrushes and a misshapen brown lump that seems to have hardened permanently onto the porcelain. It resembles soap, but feels grainy, mealy. Charlotte shudders. Must be homemade. She splashes her face with cold water, skims two fingertips lightly over the soap cake, then dries her face on one of the mint green towels stacked on the hamper. Emily's old towel set from college. Charlotte can still make out EMILY WARREN in faded black marker along the edge.

She catches a whiff of something strange. She presses her face to the towel: detergent. Sniffs the soap, but though it looks repulsive, it smells only vaguely waxy. Then she turns and spots a box tucked in the corner next to an old claw-footed bathtub, filled with what looks like gray sand. She stares for a moment, then realizes: a litter box. Charlotte had no idea there was a cat in the house, and the realization (both the cat and the box) is mildly disconcerting. A young Hawaiian man is staying for dinner, a dirty cat is somewhere in their midst—what other surprises are in store?

Returning to the sink, Charlotte checks her reflection in the mirror on the medicine cabinet but is too distracted by the mirror itself to register what she looks like. The glass is marred with flecks of spit, toothpaste, God knows what else. The door is hanging slightly ajar. If she craned her neck at the right angle, she could probably see inside the cabinet without having to move it at all. She pauses, listens, and hearing nothing, leans her head against the tile and arches her eyebrows. She spies mint dental floss. Tom's All-Natural Toothpaste. Himalayan Herb Toner. Squinting, she tries to decipher the curly script on a jar the size and shape of her Noxzema: "Butter Dress." Butter Dress? She reaches out to nudge the door, just slightly—what if she needed toothpaste? if she'd forgotten to pack it?—until the full label is exposed: "Shea Butter Hair Dressing for Men." On the front is a drawing of a man with an Afro. It must be Walter's. Some kind of African-American hair pomade. Impulsively, Charlotte reaches into the cabinet, grabs it, unscrews the cap. True to its name, the stuff looks like congealed Blue Bonnet.

Now that she's so far in anyway, Charlotte can't stop herself from going further. She nudges the door a little more, and her eyes sweep over the clogged shelves, the numerous tiny bottles of essential oil: lavender, lemongrass, tea tree, jasmine, myrrh. Myrrh? She rewinds. Myrrh it is. Rubbing alcohol. Witch hazel. Band-Aids. Bug spray. A bottle of "Love Butter." Probably another hair product, she guesses, leaning closer to read the fine print. *Increase your sexual pleasure with* . . .

Charlotte pulls back, banging the back of her head on the cabinet door, her cheeks filling with heat. She's half expecting someone to leap out and yell: "A-*ha!*" She was accused of being a snoop once before. It was just after Emily's tenth birthday; she'd received her first diary from Charlotte's aunt Polly. The diary was old-fashioned—red leather with gilt-edged pages, oddly Bible-looking—and came with directions for safeguarding it from "snooping older brothers." It advised placing a strand of hair on the cover; if the hair disappeared, you knew the diary had been read. Emily had devoted herself to this experiment, despite the fact that she had no brothers, older or otherwise. Joe had moved out by then, so her only potential snoop was Charlotte. One day after school, Emily came racing into the kitchen, pointed a finger at Charlotte and yelled: "A-*ha!*" The hair was gone. Charlotte had sat Emily down at the kitchen table and explained the many ways it might have blown off: the rotating fan, a breeze from the window, even Charlotte's hip swishing by. But Emily looked so crestfallen that Charlotte actually began to feel badly for ruining the experiment. She told Emily maybe she'd snooped after all, and just forgot.

Gingerly, Charlotte repositions the cabinet door to its original angle, then takes a breath and peers into the hall. Coast clear. She picks her way down the funhouse staircase, listening to the medley of voices from below. In the kitchen, all three roommates are hard at work. Walter is chopping vegetables. Emily is checking a pot on the stove. Anthony is setting the table. The scene is comfortable, homey. Someone has lit a mismatched assortment of candles: squat, tapered, votives swimming like minnows in glass bowls. The windows are taped with brilliant autumn leaves, like an elementary school classroom.

"Hey Mom," Emily says, waving an oven-mitted hand. "You're just in time."

"What can I do?"

"You're not doing anything," Emily says, steering her to the table. "Have a seat. Try my artichoke dip." She plunks Charlotte in front of a bowl of something tinted an unnaturally bright green.

"Watch it," Walter says over his shoulder. "That's spicy."

"Mom's a spice eater now, Wal. We had Thai, remember?"

"What's in it?" Charlotte wants to know.

"Green chiles," Anthony says, sounding ominous. "And pimentos." He dunks a hunk of bread in the green, slurps it up, and raises both eyebrows. "Hot," he confirms, then takes a slug of the beer sitting on the table. "But good."

"He's exaggerating," Emily says.

"I'm not exaggerating. It's hot but good. What's wrong with hot but good?"

"Can I get you a drink, Mom?" Emily says, ignoring him. "Water? Wine?"

"Any other biblical liquid?" quips Walter.

"Water's fine," Charlotte says, as Emily opens the refrigerator. Unlike her own, Emily's refrigerator door is plastered with a mishmash of things: movie listings, cartoons, phone bills, invitations, scrawled Post-it notes. *Phone bill. Radishes? Good luck today—I love you!* In the center is a photo of a teenage girl in a red-and-white cheerleader's uniform, pompoms thrust in the air.

"Who's that?" Charlotte asks, pointing.

Anthony smiles. "That's Mar. She was captain of the cheerleading squad in high school, believe it or not."

Emily sets a glass of water on the table. "She hates that picture."

"But we love it," he adds. "Isn't it hilarious? It's so—*American.* We keep it up to remind her how far she's come."

Charlotte takes a sip of water. She'd thought the picture looked cute. As she's wondering what things from Emily's teenage years the roommates might find "hilarious" and "American," something slithers between her legs. "Oh!" she yelps, almost knocking over her water glass, and looks down to find a cat rubbing itself wholeheartedly against her shins.

Emily laughs, then runs over to scoop the cat up. "Ooh, look who came to say hi!" she says, nestling the animal against her chest. It's orange-striped, rail-thin. "Maggie Mae!"

"Her name's Magda," Walter adds.

"Don't bother Mom, Mags," Emily whispers into its fur. "She's not an animal person."

Anthony looks up from his utensils, all of them lined up on the same sides of the plates. "You don't like animals?"

"It's not that I don't *like* them," Charlotte says, hoping she hasn't offended him. "I just don't have that much animal experience, I guess."

"Magda's a sweetie-pie," Walter says, wiping his hands on a towel and coming over to scratch behind her ears. "Aren't you, kitty-cat?"

"I don't think I knew you had a cat," Charlotte says, knowing she didn't. "Did I?"

"She's Mara's," Walter explains. "She rescued her from the side of the road a few months ago. We put up signs, but nobody claimed her. Probably she was abandoned. Looks like she was attacked too. See?"

Charlotte realizes that the cat's left ear is mangled. What's left looks like a piece of bitten orange felt.

"Poor baby," Walter says, and the cat starts purring under his hand. He leans in, as if to gather the cat from Emily, and for a moment Charlotte has a flash of what they will look like as parents, passing a bundled infant from arms and arms.

Then Emily snaps: "I'm allowed to *hold* her, Walter."

He pauses. Magda, sensing tension, leaps to the floor. Emily returns to the stove, shoving the oven mitt back on her hand, and Walter turns to Charlotte. "She's not supposed to touch the cat."

"That's not true," Emily says, turning around. "It's not the cat. It's just the litter box. You're the only one freaking when I get near the cat."

"I'm not freaking—"

"Why can't you touch the litter box?" Charlotte asks.

"It's a pregnancy thing," Emily says, turning to the counter again.

Anthony is suddenly concentrating intently on napkins.

"But why?"

"Because of cat feces," Emily says. "Which can sometimes contain parasites, which can cause toxoplasmosis, which can infect a pregnant woman, which can then infect her baby." She recites this data almost mechanically, but Charlotte is in Walter's camp: alarmed.

"It's more serious than that," he adds, which doesn't help.

"It is *not* more serious than that."

"Em." Walter's voice is firm, almost parental. "You told me you're not even supposed to breathe near the stuff. That it can cause stillborns. Miscarriages. All kinds of mental—"

"I know what it can cause, Walter. I'm the one who told you about it in the first place."

"Then why aren't you more careful? You scared the hell out of me about it and now you act like it's no big deal."

It isn't the same way Walter argued with her back in New Jersey. There his jabs were playful, flirtatious. They don't sound playful now.

"A month ago you were on a goddamn crusade," he continues. "Then as soon as you had me convinced, you stopped caring. That's what you do, Em. You throw yourself into something, but soon as you convince everybody—soon as there's nothing to fight against—it's not worth believing in anymore."

He's right, Charlotte thinks, and is surprised at the simplicity of the explanation. But it's true. If Walter had remained unconvinced, Emily would be handling the cat with plastic gloves and surgical mask.

She looks at him evenly. "What do you want from me? You want me to live in a bubble? You can catch anything from everything." She heaves open the oven door, looks inside, and slams it shut. "I could get toxoplasmosis by touching raw meat, you know."

Walter leans against the counter, arms crossed loosely across his chest. "What's that supposed to mean?"

"It's not supposed to mean anything. I'm just stating a fact."

"No, you're not. You're implying because I eat meat, I get no say. Or because you *don't* eat meat, I should lay off when you're rubbing the cat all over your face."

Charlotte is losing patience. "Why can't you just get rid of it?"

All three of them look at her.

"Get rid of the cat. I mean, just until the baby's born."

"We're not getting rid of Magda," Emily says firmly. "She's

Mara's cat. What am I going to do, put her back on the street?"

"Hey," Anthony interjects. "Like Mara said, I can totally take her to D.C. until—"

"You're not taking her to D.C.," Emily cuts him off. "It's a totally negative environment down there. Mara doesn't want Magda near her mother. We all know that."

This is absurd, Charlotte thinks. It's a cat! Who cares about the environment! Just get it out of here!

"I'm just saying"—Anthony shrugs, placing the final napkin on the table—"it's an option."

Walter returns to his chopping. His back is rigid, knife moving in tense, measured strokes. Emily lifts the lid off a pot, her face obscured by a cloud of steam. Anthony picks up his beer and wanders toward her. Charlotte wonders how practiced he's become at deflating tension in this house.

"Table's officially set," Anthony announces, and peers over Emily's shoulder. "Smells good, little woman. What is it?"

"Gravy."

Charlotte watches, alarmed, as Anthony reaches around her and pours half his beer in the pot.

"With veggie sausage," she adds.

"Veggie sausage, huh?"

"I made it for Walter."

Walter pauses, mid-chop.

"Pseudo meat!" Anthony proclaims, flipping his hair away from his face. "Quite a concession, Em."

"That's right." She looks at Walter. "Fake sausage. If that isn't real love, I don't know what is."

Walter leans over and presses his lips to her shoulder. She smiles at him as he raises his head. "But if it was real love," he says, picking up the knife again, "it would be real sausage."

Emily's smile folds. Walter looks back at her, mouth open, but she turns away. He shakes his head and resumes chopping, loudly, muttering something under his breath.

"People, people," Anthony sighs. "Can't we all just get along?" He grabs a *New Yorker* from the floor, bops them each on the head with it, then heads outside into the cold, waning sun.

"Ta-da!"

The tinfoil is whipped away like a magician unveiling a flock of doves. The revelation is soft, pale brown, vaguely turkey-shaped.

"It's a tofurkey," Emily says proudly.

Anthony pokes it in the side. "More information, please."

"Tofu, shaped like a turkey, stuffed with bread and garlic and mushrooms." She is beaming. "With a mandarin mustard sesame seed glaze."

"It's very impressive, honey," Charlotte says.

"Not only can the kid cook," Walter adds, "she can sculpt." He pinches off a bite of fake drumstick with his forefinger and thumb.

It may be the oddest Thanksgiving feast ever assembled. In lieu of cranberry sauce, Emily has made chutney with raisins, apples, cranberries, cloves. There's steamed asparagus, sweet corn, artichoke hearts. Walter's contribution is a squash-and-green-apple bake. By contrast, Charlotte's dishes all look unnaturally dense, overly compact. It occurs to her how *real* the rest of the food is, how naturally occurring, all the ingredients existing in the earth. She, on the other hand, has forced gelatin and pretzels into the same Tupperware bowl. The only thing more awkward is an unceremonious six-pack of a beer called Red Hook and the vegetarian sausage gravy, which sits off to the side, as if taboo.

"Try my lau lau," Anthony says, holding out a plate to Charlotte. It's a Hawaiian food, apparently, resembling egg rolls wrapped in paper. "Rice, fish, and vegetables, rolled in banana leaves."

"How interesting." She perches two on the lip of her plate.

"She must really like you, Ant," Emily says, "because it's absolutely killing her to eat those."

"What's this?" Walter is peering through the side of the strawberry pretzel. "Are those pretzels in there?"

"Baked pretzels," Charlotte says quickly. "With Jell-O. And Cool Whip and cream cheese."

"Pretzels and strawberries," Anthony breathes, reverently. "That's genius."

Walter digs in, his plate already heaped with squash, yams, potatoes, a soft wedge of tofurkey, even the fake sausage gravy, his allegiances spread everywhere.

"It used to be one of Emily's favorites," Charlotte adds.

"Really!" Anthony props his chin on one hand. "What else used to be Emily's favorites? Did she love buffalo burgers? Please tell me she loved buffalo burgers."

"Yeah." Walter smiles and picks up his fork. "Give us some good Emily stories. This'll be fun."

"Wal." Emily holds his wrist. "Before we eat, we all have to say what we're thankful for."

He sets the fork down. Charlotte feels her heart start. Why wasn't she warned about this? Can't she just enjoy her meal without any impromptu public speaking?

"I'll go first," Emily says, sitting up. Walter folds his hands in his lap. "I am thankful for our warm and wonderful house. I'm thankful for this fabulous meal." She smiles at Charlotte. "And I'm thankful my mom is here to share it with us."

"Hear, hear," says Walter.

Emily twines her arm around Walter's, kisses his cheek. There's no accounting for the sudden affection, but Charlotte doesn't question it. "Okay, Wal," Emily says. "Your turn."

"Let's see. Things I'm thankful for . . ." He tilts his head back, musing to the ceiling. "The smell of cut wood. The colors of the fall leaves. A good dessert. My family. My faith in God. And"—he looks at Emily—"the incredible woman sitting right here."

"Awww," Anthony chimes in. "And *I'm* thankful I get a few days off from you two freaks this weekend."

All three of them laugh, then turn to Charlotte.

"Well." She racks her brain, feeling the pressure of their collective stare. "Well, let's see. I'm very thankful for my daughter." Then, not wanting to offend Walter: "And I'm thankful for you, Walter." And not wanting to be rude: "You too, Anthony."

They laugh again. Anthony reaches for his fork.

"And," she says quickly, "most of all, I wanted to say, I'm thankful for the new baby." Her eyes dart around the table. "That's it."

"Amen to that," Walter says, blessing himself.

Anthony raises a speared lau lau, and he and Walter clink forks. "This time next year, huh, guys?" he says, popping the entire lau in his mouth.

"Damn right."

"So that means—" Anthony calculates, chewing. "Taurus or Gemini?"

"The due date's May twenty-first," Emily pipes up. "So she'll probably be on the cusp."

"What's the cusp?" Charlotte asks.

"It means the baby will have some qualities of one sign and some of the other. Children born on the cusp are very complex."

"Taureans are stubborn," Anthony puts in, reaching behind him to fiddle with the stereo. "And Geminis are indecisive."

"Put them together, and it'll be the perfect kid," says Walter.

Anthony settles on some slow guitar and raises an eyebrow at Walter, who nods appreciatively, drumming the back of his spoon on the table. Charlotte takes advantage of the distraction to try a bite of tofurkey. The taste isn't too bad—it's even vaguely meatlike—but the texture is repulsive: a sudden softness not unlike warm, damp bread.

"So," Anthony says, "Charlotte. Are you into astrology?"

"Me?" She takes a desperate gulp of water, trying to be discreet. "Not really," she admits, swallowing, wondering again if she's offended him. Maybe astrology is common practice in Hawaii? Maybe it's considered sacred? She falls back on the animal excuse. "I just don't have much astrology experience, I guess."

"It's fascinating stuff," Anthony says. Charlotte wonders if "fascinating" is the official word of the alternative living arrangement. "I have a book you should borrow. I think you'd really dig it."

"Yeah, Mom. You really might."

Suddenly Walter is lunging across the table, both arms outstretched, headed for Charlotte. "Don't listen to them, Charlotte!" he cries out, and a moment later his palms are clamped over her ears. The sounds of music and voices are dampened, and all Charlotte can hear is the pumping of her blood, all she can feel is the warmth of Walter's hands. Then she is released and the world returns—"Save yourself while you still can!"

Emily and Anthony roll their eyes. Clearly they've heard these opinions before.

Walter plops back in his chair. "Stars are for gazing," he concludes, lifting a forkful of strawberry pretzel. "All a bunch of unsubstantiated, undocumented, unearthly crap."

"Yeah, but that Adam and Eve thing," Anthony smirks, flipping the cap off his Red Hook and onto the table, like a casino chip. "Apples, snakes, arks, walking on water. Man dying and rising up from the dead. All that's much more credible."

Charlotte tenses, sensing a debate, but they all go on eating and smiling. It's hard to know when differences of opinion are potential arguments and when they are just conversation.

"Ignore the dissenters," Anthony says, returning to Charlotte. "The study of astrology is totally fascinating. And valid. Take Emily—she's the quintessential Virgo."

"Really?" Charlotte feels a little guilty for not siding with Walter, but wants to know. "What's the quintessential Virgo?"

"Self-assured. Overly sensitive. Overly critical." He grins, knowing how apt a description it is, and takes a swig of beer. "Hungry for knowledge."

"Really?" Charlotte says again. It's strange to hear her complicated daughter summarized so neatly. "That does sound like you, Em," she says, before the warning look on Emily's face stops her from saying more.

But the boys are rabid for information. "So tell us what Emily was like as a kid," says Walter. "Was she a troublemaker?"

"Any bedwetting?" from Anthony.

"First words?"

"Really embarrassing outfits? Haircuts? Imaginary friends?"

"Start from the beginning," Walter says. "What was she like as a baby?"

It feels unusual for Charlotte to be in this position, the one telling the stories; usually, it's Emily who is revealing her.

"Well," she says, knowing she must tread lightly. Emily's face is vague: not pouting, not smiling, but almost deliberately blank. She's looking at the wall slightly to the left of Charlotte, as if not wanting to admit she's listening. "She was born early. By almost three weeks."

"Wow," Walter says, "a preemie," and squeezes Emily's knee. Charlotte can practically feel her daughter flinch.

"I guess she must have been eager to get going," Charlotte says. The boys laugh and she smiles, warming to her analogy. "She couldn't wait to get out, I guess. We hadn't even decided on a name yet. Joe—" She pauses. "That's Emily's father."

No one reacts. Of course they know who Joe is. God knows what they know.

"Yes, well. Joe always joked about naming her after himself. Jo. But the girl's name—with no *e*."

Anthony winces. "That's so *Facts of Life*."

"I thought he was kidding," Charlotte says, "but sure enough, after she was born, he tried to do it."

Walter tosses an artichoke heart in his mouth like popcorn. "Were you conscious?"

"Just barely. That was his plan, I think."

The boys laugh again, at her or with her or both she doesn't know, nor really care. She thinks of the son she's always imagined raising, the boy with the messy bedroom and untied shoelaces and voracious appetite. Anthony and Walter could be his older, slightly healthier counterparts. She suspects they are humoring her a little, doting on her a bit too kindly, but with boys it all seems so affectionate somehow. Maybe it comes from the natural distance sons put between themselves and their mothers, the intense way they guard their private lives, their awareness of all that would worry their mothers if only they knew. Sons feel guilty about their mothers not knowing, yet love them even more for not knowing, which translates into an apologetic kind of sweetness. With daughters, the relationship is more open, so the teasing is more literal, more personal, and can sting a little.

"So how did you decide on Emily?" Walter uncaps a beer.

"Well," Charlotte says, "as it turned out, we ended up staying in the hospital a few extra days. They wouldn't let Joe stay overnight—they had some kind of policy—but before he left he bought me some things. A book, a box of butter creams, and flowers. Daisies, I think."

Was it daisies? She hasn't thought of that gift in years.

"It might have been daisies," she qualifies, just in case. "I know he bought it all in the drugstore by the hospital. It came in a plastic bag like you get at drugstores. But Joe had this yellow necktie in his pocket. He'd been wearing it when he got the call at school—he was in the middle of teaching and wasn't expecting it, it was still so early—and he was so surprised he ran out of the classroom and left everything behind. His grade book, students' papers, everything." That he'd done this hadn't surprised her, but it had bothered her a little. She'd imagined his students tearing through his notes, erasing their grades and penciling in new ones. Now, though, the gesture has a certain charm, a spontaneity she finds, for maybe the first time, appealing.

"Anyway," Charlotte says. She's drifted far off track. "This yellow necktie, it had been stuffed in his pocket for two days."

Walter gives her a nod of encouragement.

"And when he walked in with my present, it had this huge silly bow on it." She can still picture that yellow necktie ribbon, limp and grinning. She can see Joe loping into the room with it, all loose limbs and kisses. He'd set the flowers on her bedside table, fed her chocolates from his fingertips.

"So where did the name come in?" asks Anthony. His expression is kindly, tolerant. Charlotte recognizes it as the look on the faces of younger generations when they indulge older generations in their stories, stories that promise to be dramatic and romantic but come across as mild, disjointed, rambling.

"Yes," she says, chastising herself for taking so long. "The name. It came from the book Joe bought—*Wuthering Heights.*"

"Emily Brontë."

She nods. "I never read it myself. It was Joe's idea."

Something flickers then across Emily's face. Not just disappointment, but something deeper: a lack of surprise. Of course she didn't read it, Emily is thinking, and Charlotte wishes suddenly, desperately, that she had. She can hear how she must sound to them, deferring to Joe, as she always has: *Joe* chose the book, *Joe* chose the name, *Joe* bears all the responsibility and takes all the credit. Joe, she is sure, has read *Wuthering Heights.*

"I was so tired," she explains, for the sake of her story and herself. "Exhausted. And then, with the baby at home, practically all I had time to read was the *TV Guide*—"

Anthony smiles. He forgives her. Charlotte doesn't dare look at Emily. She fixates on her food instead, the strawberry gelatin looking obscenely bright—*American,* she thinks—in the center of her plate.

"But wait," Walter says, sounding concerned. "Why did you have to stay in the hospital so long?"

Charlotte looks up, thankful for the change of subject. "Well, at first, because Emily was underweight."

"But that's not surprising, right?" he asks quickly. "Since she was early?"

"That's true. But when she was two days old, she got jaundice—"

Walter's hand moves back to Emily's knee. Her tongue ring clicks.

"—so they had to put her in a special kind of crib, like an incubator, except it shines a special kind of light."

"Was she really yellow?" asks Anthony.

"For a day or two. Then she was, well, you know. White."

"How about the delivery?" Walter wants to know. "Was it an easy delivery?"

"Wal—" Emily blurts, then expels a frustrated sigh.

"What? It's important, Em. It's probably a good indicator of how yours will go."

Charlotte pauses. Emily's face looks hard, and Charlotte realizes then that her daughter's annoyance isn't about the story. The impulse rises in Charlotte to warn Walter, tell him to stop crowding her, stop protecting her, that she's seen this look on Emily's face before.

"I wouldn't call it easy," Charlotte says, carefully. "It was long, about thirty-six hours. And my blood pressure was dropping on and off."

A look of genuine pain crosses Walter's face, and Charlotte summons what she hopes is a big, reassuring smile. "Don't worry," she says. "Emily's tougher than I am." She looks back to her daughter, but she is looking only at Walter, at his strong hand resting on her leg.

When Walter asks her to come out to the barn, Charlotte is finishing up the dishes. She'd insisted on doing them, and Emily hadn't fought her on it, retreating to the living room with a library book and a pair of furry bootlike slippers, curling up before the fire Walter had started in the wood stove. Anthony had gone upstairs to pack.

"I want to show you something," Walter whispers, beckoning Charlotte to the door. "Hey, Em!" he calls. "We're going to the barn. Gonna show your mom my stuff."

The evening sky has settled into a sleepy purplish black. The stars are beginning to pop, white, clear, unfiltered by artificial patio light. The stars look cold, the same raw cold that's pinching Charlotte's earlobes and nose. She hugs her sweater around her as she and Walter pick their way across the yard, comfortably silent. Past the vegetable garden, defunct for the winter. Past the pair of striped beach chairs. On the ground between the chairs, Charlotte notices a Chock Full O'Nuts coffee can filled with crushed cigarettes. She tenses instinctively, thinking of the smoke and the baby.

"Ant," Walter says.

"Hm?"

"Ant's the smoker. Mara, too, when she's in a mood." He nods at the ground. "In case you were wondering."

God bless him. Charlotte might actually love this boy. They walk on, feet shushing through the fallen leaves. Anthony was leaving the next morning, and throughout the evening Charlotte had increasingly found herself wishing he weren't.

"I guess he must be leaving early," she says. "That must be a long drive, to D.C."

"About eight hours, I think."

"It's such a pretty city," Charlotte says. She's drawing on a single day trip she and Emily took in 1990. "All those monuments," she adds, as if to prove she's been there.

"Impressive," agrees Walter. They've fallen into step now, wading through the leaf piles, Charlotte following the broad outline of his back against the sky. "I don't envy the guy, though."

"Oh?"

"He's got it rough down there. Mara's people are so old-school it's—"

Completely fucking nuts, Charlotte thinks.

Walter pauses. "Basically, they're not happy Ant's not white." He looks at her and raises his eyebrows, anticipating her incredulity. "They want her to end up with some frat kid with a corporate job and a good bloodline."

Charlotte flashes to the picture of the man and woman framed in Mara's bedroom. They had looked so kind, so wholesome. Then she winces, remembering her own initial impressions of Walter—her quick conclusions, knee-jerk reactions—and is thankful to the darkness for concealing the shame on her face.

As they near the barn, it gets a few degrees darker, the eaves blocking out the moonlight. "Watch your step," Walter says, pushing the door open. Inside it's pitch-black, windowless, smelling of raw wood and earth. It's cold too, like the inner sanctum of a church, pumped full of a cool air that seems otherworldly, without a source. She hears Walter fumbling by the wall, then a flashlight pierces the darkness. She follows the beam with her eyes as it alights on something in the corner: round, dark, chest-high.

"It's for Em," Walter says, "for the baby." The circle of light widens as they approach it, and after a moment, Charlotte realizes it's a cradle. Walter stops about a foot before it and caresses the wood with his flashlight. Charlotte can see the intricacy of detail: scalloped edges of the horizontal bars, detailed etching on the front and back panels, curves of the vertical rungs like lapping waves.

"I'll cushion the bottom," he says, maybe misinterpreting Charlotte's silence for concern, but it is just the opposite: she is awestruck.

"No, I—I think it's beautiful."

He reaches out and runs one palm along the top bar. His hand almost matches the wood. "Feel this," he says, and he places her hand on the cradle. The wood feels smooth, cool, like new loose-leaf paper—but something more than that. The texture is not just physical. It feels like labor, like love.

Then the light swerves, dousing the crib in blackness, and a pocketful of stars explodes before her face. "Check this out," Walter says. "This one's a Christmas gift." The flashlight is now buttering another set of wooden rungs: a rocking chair.

"It's lovely."

"Go ahead," he says. "Give it a try."

Charlotte grips both her elbows as she navigates her way across the barn floor, Walter training the flashlight on her feet.

"I made it for my mom," he says, as her spine connects with the solid wooden rungs. "She loves to just sit. But don't think she's lazy. Her sitting's a serious business. She spends hours every day out there on the porch, just sitting, talking to people, taking it in."

Charlotte attempts to picture this—Walter's mother, her porch, the passersby—and draws a blank. It occurs to her she knows almost nothing about Walter's background. She knows nothing of his family, not even where they live.

"Walter," she says suddenly. "Where do you come from?"

He laughs. "City of Brotherly Love. Isn't it obvious?"

"Philadelphia?" She pauses, letting this sink in.

"West Philly. Born and raised."

"And what about your family? Do you have siblings?"

Walter is wearing an amused smile. "Hold on," he says, then pulls up what looks like a stepladder and hunkers down. "Okay. Here we go. I've got two parents. Ambrocia and Walt Senior. Born in Philly, married in Philly, have their plots picked out in Philly. I grew up in the same house my dad grew up in and his dad grew up in and his dad grew up in. My aunt lives around the corner, two uncles live up the street. And I've got two little sisters."

This makes sense, somehow, Walter having sisters. "How old are they?"

"Not that little anymore, I guess. But I'll always think of them as little. Danita's sixteen, Tanisha's thirteen."

"And your parents?" Charlotte finds this fascinating: both the details themselves and the fact that she's never heard them. Has Emily already met these people? Hung out with Walter's teenage sisters on a porch in West Philadelphia? She wonders if he's ever traipsed through the thumping heart in the Franklin Institute. She imagines that he has. "What do your parents do?"

"They're really involved with their church, first off. Sounds strange, but that's primarily how they define themselves, more than any job. But, professionally, my dad sells water purifiers. You know, those tanks of spring water. To offices mostly. My mom's a receptionist for State Farm."

Charlotte tries to imagine this mother: Walter's mother. She pictures her strong, solid, with unabashedly wide swinging hips—then stops. Is that prejudiced? But she doesn't mean it in a bad way. It's a compliment. Unlike white women, who seem to contain their maternity to the bulges of their bellies, black women seem to carry their motherness in every part of themselves, every pore and limb.

Imagining this woman, Ambrocia Nelson, it dawns on Charlotte that the two of them will soon be inextricably linked. They will be the grandmothers: Nana and Grandma, or Nana and Gran (will she have to clear "Nana" with Ambrocia first?). Charlotte will potentially know this woman for the rest of her life: christenings, birthdays, graduations, band concerts, school plays. Maybe they'll coordinate recipes, trade grandparenting stories on the phone.

"My parents," Walter says suddenly, and his voice makes Charlotte pay attention. It's striking in its earnestness, as if speaking under oath. "Are two of the greatest people on this earth. I mean that. They're great parents, but they're also just great people. They've been an amazing example—of love, marriage, family. Everything."

Charlotte wants to ask what Ambrocia and Walt, Sr., think about the new baby, but before she gets it out, Walter stands. "I have something else to show you," he says, "but it's a secret. You have to promise not to tell."

When he seems to wait, she confirms, "I promise."

Then he disappears, and Charlotte hears the sounds of sliding, thumping, uncrumpling. A few moments later he is standing beside her. She can feel the warmth of his skin near her shoulder, hear his measured breaths. A pool of light appears before her eyes, in the middle of which floats a diamond ring that takes her breath away.

"You can't tell Em."

She is speechless. The ring is suspended on a magic carpet of light.

"What do you think?"

"Oh—" is all she can manage. "It's beautiful."

"I made this part," he says, running his thumb along the outer edge of the box. "But the diamond, that's God's work."

His breathing is heavier than usual, as if winded by his reverence. "Think she'll like it?"

Charlotte nods, imperceptibly. She can't bring herself to look at his face.

Walter snaps the box shut, gently, and retracts the flashlight. The space the ring occupied is swallowed by blackness, like a rock flung in a pond. As he returns the box to its hiding place, Charlotte feels an ache inside her, a combination of sweetness and sorrow so sharp it's almost too much to bear. She remembers the afternoon Walter first confided in her about the baby—it seems like years ago—how she'd thought he was asking her permission to propose. How fearful she had been, how opposed to the idea. Never for a second had she wondered what Emily's answer would be.

"Listen." Walter has returned to his makeshift seat. He holds the flashlight under his chin, like a child by a campfire. "I know this all probably worries you a little. You're probably thinking we're too young, and we *are* young, I know it. But I don't want this kid born to parents who aren't married. Or at least not planning on getting married. There's no reason we shouldn't."

Charlotte looks into his face, splintered with light and shadow. His expression is hard to find. It's broken into shards, and each looks like it contains a different emotion: a worried slice of left eyebrow, a hopeful right eye, a slash of upper lip that looks firm, resolute.

"I know we have our problems, just like everybody. You probably sensed some stuff this weekend. I know you pick up on things. But we'll deal with it, you know? We argue, yeah, but it all comes from love. It comes from the right place." The shadowed slice of mouth curves into a smile. "Em's headstrong, and some days she just about kills me, but I wouldn't love her any other way."

"Yes." Charlotte smiles back. She thinks of the young man she always predicted Emily would end up with: steady, traditional, a rational match for her daughter's tough will. She had thought, meeting Walter, that he was completely wrong for her. But listening to him now, she realizes the opposite is true: the physical details aren't what she imagined, but Walter is everything she expected, and wanted, Emily's husband to be.

"I know you know what I mean," he says, then the flashlight beam is wriggling on the ground. Walter aims it at her face. "Charlotte?"

She squints. "Yes?"

"You know what's going on."

"I do?"

"You pick up more than you let on. I can tell." He lowers the flashlight, shines it on the wall. "But sometimes you sell yourself short, and I hate to see it happen. Like today, talking about Em being tougher having a baby—" The beam slides to the floor, as if exhausted. "I bet you were plenty tough."

"I really wasn't."

"I can't see you complaining, though."

"Well, that's true," she admits. "I didn't complain."

Walter's gaze drifts toward the wall, following the flashlight, which wanders lazily, touching on a sack of mulch, a stack of wood, a glassless window, then comes to rest where it began: the cradle.

"It's a damn fine crib," Walter pronounces, "if I do say so myself." He laughs, then instantly sobers. "I love this kid so much already."

"Me too."

They are silent then, and the silence is loud with many things: night creatures and whispering leaves and fear and memory and promise.

"A good night's sleep—" Walter starts, then stops. "You just can't underestimate the importance of that, you know?"

"Yes." She nods. He is just about breaking her heart. "I do."

Two-twenty-seven A.M. and the ceiling is too close. The outdoors is too loud, the bed too cold. All the warmth this house contained during the day feels as though it's been sucked out by the nightfall, replaced by an uneasy chill. The tapestries on the ceiling droop too close to Charlotte's face; the patchwork blanket is rough to the touch. Her fingertips and nose are freezing, the only heat in the place coming from the wood stove still burning in the living room—a fire hazard for sure—its thin heat rising through haphazard ceiling vents. All the flaws of the house feel more pronounced in the dark: the spiral staircase, dirty litter box, weak water pressure, dribbling heat. It's not a place fit for adults, much less a new baby.

Charlotte turns on her side, pressing her face to the pillow. But it isn't physical discomfort that's keeping her awake. It's something internal. Invisible. Her skin itches, as if struggling to contain what's inside. At precisely 2:30, she swings her feet to the floor and slides into her slippers. With eyes averted, she creeps into the hallway, past Walter and Emily's beaded bedroom door, past the Love Butter, down the winding staircase, and into the living room—where she sidesteps a coffee mug, a crumby pie plate, the still-untouched Scrabble board—then grabs her coat, unlocks the door, and steps outside.

Charlotte has never seen so many stars. They are so clear, and so many—it feels like she's in a planetarium. She wanders into the driveway and tilts her head back. It must be hard to lose perspective, living in a place like this. The size of the world is unavoidable, it's everywhere. It's impossible to escape your own smallness. As she drinks in the enormity of the sky, she has a flash of herself at age ten, riding in the back of Becky Freeman's car after that fateful day at the movies. How for the first time she realized her own insignificance. Back then, it was alarming; now it feels like a relief.

Charlotte starts to cross the yard. The air is freezing, the coldest she's ever felt November. The wind is so crisp, it feels as if it could give you paper cuts. Dry leaves swirl around her ankles, the nightgown hugs her legs. When she reaches the rainbow beach chairs, she sits in one and stretches her legs out, long grass tickling the bare backs of her shins. She closes her eyes and listens to the silence. Here in the woods, sounds are impossible to distinguish. It's as if the place has its own pulse: fleshy, primal, thrumming with the energy of a million unseen wings.

Charlotte looks at the house in the distance, a paper cutout against the night sky. She imagines Emily and Walter tucked somewhere inside it, skin pressed against skin, breathing in the starry darkness. No wonder Emily got pregnant within weeks of living here: you can practically taste the sexual energy in the air. A hint of danger, too—but the danger doesn't feel sexual. It comes from the immediacy of the place, from everything being so close to the surface: all the things that you fear, that you know, that you want to feel and avoid feeling. There's an ominous quality here that doesn't come from the crowded trees or the saturated sky. It comes from within: the threat of your own truth, the knowledge that you couldn't avoid yourself if you tried.

Charlotte feels a pang in her gut, like the kick of a baby. And suddenly she feels deeply, desperately, alone. She's not unaccustomed to aloneness—she's spent most of her adult life that way—but it's never really bothered her. In fact, it's distinctly *not* bothered her. After her divorce, when people sympathized that she was single, Charlotte would tell them she didn't mind, she was fine, and she meant it. Losing Joe, though initially hard (and slightly humiliating), was more than anything a kind of long exhale. Deep down, she felt she knew a secret the rest of the world didn't: that you don't *need* a partner to be happy. That without one, you could actually be happier: free of tumult and tension and the threat of being left.

And since then, she's never really seen that "other half" as something she wanted—certainly not needed. She's resisted the importance of not being alone. But sitting here, feeling the pulse of the woods, the restless wind, something is stirring inside her. It's not overtly sexual, but simply *alive.* She's aware of human closeness in a way that's unfamiliar, and a little unsettling; the awareness smacks of need. That kick she felt, it wasn't homesickness for Dunleavy Street, or her condo, or New Jersey. Charlotte isn't just alone. She is lonely.

Charlotte lets her eyes fall shut. She presses her fingers to her eyelids. The reflex is automatic, though she hasn't done it in many years; it was a game she used to play as a child. She'd press on her lids, wait until the darkness settled, then watch the patterns start emerging. It was like a secret slideshow, a magic inner life of swirling colors, spinning squares, exploding stars that merged and folded like a helix tumbling in space. When she opened her eyes it would take several moments to readjust, sparks appearing here and there like a firework's dull final pops. She would wonder if all eyelids had hidden kaleidoscopes inside, and if so, why weren't people raving about them? She decided most people probably had them, just hadn't taken the time to figure it out.

Now, though, Charlotte can't access the kaleidoscope. She

presses harder, but her inner life will not oblige. Opening her eyes, she feels suddenly aware of her body. She recalls the way Emily pressed her face into Joe's neck. The way Walter kissed Emily's shoulder. The way Joe's voice softened on the phone the afternoon she stood alone in her kitchen, telling him about Emily: *Don't worry,* he said, *this will all be okay.* What would life feel like with such things to lean into? The pressure of lips on her arm, whisper of comfort in her ear, warm hollow between another person's chin and shoulder? What kind of difference would that make?

chapter nine

The Feminist Health Collective looks less like a doctor's office than some kind of secondhand clothing store. It's another large, rambling house at the end of another woodsy, winding road. Apparently these are the qualifications for every house in New Hampshire, whether psychic, gynecologist, or alternative living arrangement. Were there no cinderblock office buildings at all in this state?

As Walter steers the station wagon down the gravel driveway, Charlotte registers the small circle of parked cars. Most look old and probably deliberately beleagured, their dented bumpers swaddled with brightly colored decals. MEAN CORPORATIONS SUCK. MY OTHER CAR IS A BICYCLE. FIGHT TERRORISM—GO SOLAR!

He turns the car off and touches the back of Emily's neck. "Ready?" he says. Emily murmurs in reply. When he leans toward her, Charlotte turns to face the window, fixing her eyes on the back window of a rusty van that says EVE WAS FRAMED.

"Come on, Mom," Charlotte hears, and suddenly her door swings open. She grabs her purse—she hasn't managed to adopt the policy of wholehearted trust in New Hampshire—and as she steps out, Emily hooks her arm. They crunch across the gravel toward the entrance, Walter following behind them. When Charlotte steps inside, she's expecting some approximation of a waiting room, but instead comes face to face with a policeman.

"Hey, Dan," Emily greets him, unhooking Charlotte's arm.

Charlotte is frozen. The man looks nice enough, heavy-jowled, pink-faced. He could be a mailman or crossing guard if it weren't for the gun strapped to his waist.

"Feels like snow, huh?" says Walter, as he steps through what Charlotte realizes is a metal detector.

"A little early yet."

"Soon enough. Be here before you know it."

When it's Charlotte's turn, the machine doesn't make a chirp. But on the other side Policeman Dan extends a hand. Charlotte stares.

"Your bag, Mom," Emily says. "He needs to check it." There is no mistaking the apology in her voice.

Charlotte hands the policeman her purse, face burning. Why didn't Emily just tell her to leave it in the car? She didn't need it. She could have left it, and *would* have, if they all weren't so damned trusting. Policeman Dan is whistling as he nudges a thin flashlight around inside, searching for—what? guns? explosives? Which is worse, she wonders, the thought of what he's looking for or the prospect of what he'll find? An unraveling roll of peach-flavored Tums, wadded squares of used Kleenex, a plastic bag containing the last of the Canada mints.

"Looks suspicious, doesn't she?" Walter jokes.

Dan smiles, but mildly, as if to say, *You'd be surprised.* He clicks the clasp shut and hands the purse back to Charlotte.

"Thanks, man," says Walter, heading toward a staircase. "See you on the flip side."

Emily pokes him in the back. "Dork."

As Charlotte follows, the implications of what she just saw register slowly. They must have incidents of protest here. Which means they must perform abortions here. She wants to ask Emily but figures now is exactly the wrong time. They're here for the sonogram: a *happy* thing. They're here for the *new baby.* She focuses on this as they reach the waiting room at the top of the stairs. It resembles, unnervingly, an unkempt den. Sagging couches, fish tank, mismatched lamps, rug with threadbare patches exposing the wood floor. It could be an extension of Walter and Emily's. Charlotte looks at the two other girls waiting and wonders what they're here for. Both look awfully young. But then, so must Emily. One is alone, scribbling in a notebook. She has the tousled bun and sloppy, baggy look of a college student on a Saturday. The other is wearing a sweatshirt that's much too big, as if trying to dilute what's underneath. She's sitting with what is probably her boyfriend. His face is long, blank, drained of color; in a city he might look dangerous, but here his edges are softened by a fuzzy winter hat with stripes. It must be hard to maintain a sense of "coolness" in New England, Charlotte thinks, the elements so harsh your basic human needs are helplessly exposed.

"Emily Warren?"

Emily steps toward the desk. "Yeah. Sorry we're late."

Charlotte realizes she has no idea what time it is, and checks her watch: 11:45 A.M. They hadn't mentioned running late. She wonders if the appointment was for 11:00 or 11:30.

"Just note any changes," the receptionist is saying, handing Emily a clipboard with a sheaf of forms attached. She can't be more than eighteen, Charlotte thinks. Her hair is pulled back in a scrunchy.

"Hey, Charlotte," Walter says. "Have a seat."

Reluctantly, she looks to where Walter is sitting, a sagging sofa with claw marks at the corners. She perches on one end, leaving an empty cushion between them. On the end table beside her is some kind of book, felt-covered with a pen attached by purple yarn. "A Journal for Sharing," says the cover, in friendly block letters. "Treat this book as you would a friend! It's a place to talk freely about your thoughts and feelings, to share your own experiences and read about the experiences of others . . ."

As if on cue, Emily drops down in the middle of the couch. She smells like a blend of warmth and winter, the cinnamon coffee Walter made that morning mingling with the frosty air that lingers in her scarf. As the scarf is unwound, static crackling, Charlotte spots the forms on Emily's lap. Contact Information. Confidentiality Agreement. Medical History. A long list of illnesses and symptoms and afflictions.

"Did you remember to put down Grandpa's cancer?" Charlotte whispers.

Emily points her pen cap at the tiny blue checkmark on the line next to *Cancer.*

"And Grandma's heart?"

She slides the pen to the bottom of the page. Next to *Heart Disease,* she's crossed out *Disease* and written *ATTACK.*

"Emily?" A woman appears from behind a wood-paneled door beside the reception desk. She's wearing a nametag and white lab coat, which is reassuring. Underneath it she has on a fisherman's sweater and jeans.

The woman crosses the room, holding out a hand. "You must be Emily's mom."

"Charlotte Warren," Emily supplies, as they all stand.

"Joyce," the doctor says. No last name. Not even a "Dr." She grasps Charlotte's hand, smiles, then turns toward Emily and Walter. "All set, you two?"

"Yeah," Emily says. "Be back soon, Mom." She flashes Charlotte a smile. Then the three of them vanish behind the softly clicking den door, Joyce's hand guiding the small of Emily's back.

Charlotte glances around the room. She feels suddenly self-conscious. The fish tank is burbling. The college girl still has her head down, scribbling. When her gaze snags on that of the blank-faced boy, she looks away. He's probably wondering what she's doing here. *That young woman was my daughter,* she wants to tell him. *She's having a baby.* As if in response, the boy's sneakers shift, one toe rising like a skeptical eyebrow. *Believe me,* Charlotte asserts, *she wants me to be here.* The toe stays put.

Charlotte looks down at her lap. She wishes she could tell someone how, though today she might seem peripheral, she used to be integral at doctor's appointments. *Those wisdom teeth are going to need to come out,* said the dentist. *Looks like she'll need braces,* said the orthodontist. *It's not necessarily dangerous,* said the pediatric nutritionist, when Emily began refusing to eat meat, *just be sure she's getting enough protein.* He'd handed Charlotte a brochure with a peanut tap-dancing on the cover. She wants to tell someone how, for the longest time, Emily couldn't swallow pills and Charlotte disguised them in blueberry yogurt, her favorite kind. How every time Emily got her braces tightened, Charlotte treated her to a cherry-mixed-with-rootbeer-flavored Slurpee from 7-Eleven on the way home.

Now, the doctor is a woman in blue jeans. What kind of experience does this "Joyce" really have? Charlotte suspects that Emily chose this place for its liberal leanings, not for the quality of the care. She looks up, suddenly distracted by a faint humming sound coming from the direction of the desk. There on the floor is a Dream Machine, looking exactly like the one in her bedroom. But why would they need one here? To conceal screams? Cries? The churning of machines?

Blinking hard, she scans the magazines on the coffee table, hunting for something fluffy, friendly. But everything has an edge. *Vanity Fair. Jane. Self. Spin.* At her gynecologist, Dr. Barr's, the waiting room is stocked with things like *Parenting* and *Reader's Digest.* The entire office has a positive, life-affirming quality; even if you're only there for an annual checkup, you feel included in the happiness of the pregnant couples who sit waiting for their names to be called. The cover of *Oprah Magazine* beams mantras like "Believe in Yourself!" and "Love Your Life!" The walls are peppered with Anne Geddes babies in frames.

In this office, Charlotte realizes, there is no trace of pregnancy. Instead of babies nestled in walnut shells and flower petals, the walls emphasize women. Naked women, mostly. Abstract and painterly, random swirls of feminine curves. A few are photographs: one a woman peering backward over her bare shoulder, another stretched out on a kitchen counter like some kind of odalisque. Even the coffee table looks vaguely erotic, its wooden legs curved like a woman's calves. Charlotte's gaze alights on the bottom rungs of the table—where, in a different kind of house, one might find a glossy picture book on *Lighthouses of New England* or *Country Kitchens*—and finds herself confronted with a haggard copy of *The Joy of Sex.*

Charlotte glances quickly at the boy. Girl. Receptionist. All are conveniently unaware of her existence. Her eyes crawl back to the book; it's the original edition, from the 1970s. Charlotte recognizes it because she, in fact, owns a copy. Joe brought it home during their month-long bout of a sex life. When he first drew it from his briefcase she'd thought it was a cookbook (thanks to the deceptively innocent cover), then saw the explicit drawings of a hairy, hippie-looking couple inside. Joe all but followed her around the house with it, gleeful as a child with a new toy: leaving it splayed open on the kitchen table, laughing when the pictures made her squirm, lying with his feet up on the couch and paging through with excruciating nonchalance.

Then, once Charlotte got pregnant, the book—like their sex life in general—was something she felt unburdened of, relieved of dealing with. She'd pushed the negligees to the back of her dresser drawer and pushed the book to the back of the bookcase: out of sight, out of mind. It wasn't until more than two decades later, packing up Dunleavy Street, that she found it again. At first glance, like the first time, she thought it was a cookbook. And then she remembered. Holding that book was like coming face to face with a ghost, someone who knew you in a different life: a reminder of all your uncomfortable memories, insinuation of all your personal failings, evidence in the present of all you tried to leave in the past.

But sitting there in Charlotte's hands, twenty-odd years later, the problem the book posed was less emotional than logistical: she didn't know, practically speaking, what to do with it. She considered throwing it away, but was afraid of it being discovered in her garbage. (This was illogical, but no more illogical than her nighttime break-in scenarios. It was too easy to picture the lean, muscled men who clung to the back of the trash truck flinging her bag onto the pile, watching it rip as it landed, pointing at *The Joy of Sex* exposed among the wet tea bags and onion skins, then braying to each other every time they passed her house on Monday mornings.) She knew she'd only feel comfortable if she knew exactly where the book was. Which raised the issue of where to pack it. It seemed wrong to include it in the box labeled BOOKS—EMILY or, worse, BOOKS—DAD, these being her father's old philosophy texts that she'd never opened but would linger on, guilt-heavy, in the basement storage area of Sunset Heights. She'd finally decided to create a new box called BOOKS—OTHER and placed *The Joy of Sex* in the bottom, along with *Easy East Coast Day Trips, Big Book of Crosswords,* and *Where Babies Come From,* then topped it off with a few vases (she never used) and two pillows (she'd never liked) and surrounded it all with a moat of newspaper so the movers wouldn't find it.

Charlotte glances again at the young couple, convinced they can somehow read her thoughts. But they are whispering quietly, heads bent, their four hands clutched in an awkward bouquet. Charlotte's heart goes out to them. She wonders if their parents know they're here, if they ever talked to them about sex, if it might have avoided whatever predicament they're in now—not that it worked for Emily. Charlotte has a flash of the pink-covered *Where Babies Come From* still stashed in the bottom of BOOKS—OTHER, the version of sex she'd presented when they had "the talk."

Emily was ten at the time, which seemed the right age to Charlotte: old enough to at least grasp the concept, not so old that she was picking up misinformation from other places. Charlotte felt some urgency about getting to her before others did—"others" being Gretchen Myers (Emily's best friend and cohort in palm-reading) and Valerie (whose existence in Joe's life Charlotte had just begun to pick up on). Charlotte had planned her approach carefully, spending nearly twenty minutes weighing her options in B. Dalton. *Where Babies Come From* did the job best, she felt, relaying the necessary information without being overly explicit. The pictures combined medical renderings of the reproductive systems with drawings of a couple engaging in the act. Unlike the hairy hippies in *The Joy of Sex,* this couple was rendered pink-tinged and slightly fuzzy, as if behind a gauze curtain, which suggested a subtlety and privacy Charlotte could appreciate.

That night, when Emily climbed into bed, Charlotte came armed with *Where Babies Come From.* She introduced the book with the necessary parental confidence, keeping her tone clear and firm as she read phrases like "the man's penis fits into the woman's vagina" and "this liquid contains what is called sperm" and, worst of all, "because the testes are shaped like balls, they are often referred to as simply *balls.*" Assured as she sounded, Charlotte was dying to get it over with. She wanted to hurry downstairs where she would reward herself with a little TV; she'd purposefully chosen that day (a Monday) and time (9:00 P.M.) so Emily would go right to sleep after and Charlotte could watch *Northern Exposure.* It was about charming people in a small town in Alaska, and was one of her favorite shows.

The plan didn't work, of course. It shouldn't have surprised her. For a child whose curiosity was piqued by where grapes and raisins come from, *Where Babies Come From* was a windfall. Though another child might have felt awkward and wanted the sex lesson to end, Emily was bursting with questions.

But what happens to the eggs the sperms don't get to?

What about the sperms that don't get to the egg?

What happens to the eggs if a baby's in there?

Charlotte spent nearly an hour trying to address her concerns—many of them concerns in the literal sense, as Emily seemed genuinely worried about the fate of the various sperms and eggs that didn't succeed in becoming a baby. Finally, close to eleven (she missed all but the final credits of *Northern Exposure*), Charlotte surrendered *Where Babies Come From* to Emily's bookcase, where it mingled unabashedly with *Tales of a Fourth Grade Nothing, A Wrinkle in Time,* all the Ramonas and Anastasia Krupniks. Emily kept it there all through high school—for its "kitsch value," she said.

"Excuse me?"

Charlotte looks up, blinks at the teenage receptionist.

"Are you Charlotte?"

"Yes?"

"Okay, Charlotte," the girl says. "Want to follow me?"

Fear floods her heart. It's bad news. It must be. Something is wrong with the baby. Emily has asked her to be brought back, have Dr. Joyce explain what's happening, let the Dream Machine muffle what they're saying. In a haze, Charlotte stands and follows the girl across the waiting room, past the humming Dream Machine and down a long hallway, wood floors creaking and slanting under their feet. Charlotte focuses on the scrunchy nestled in the girl's ponytail. Thick, purple, sprinkled with yellow stars and slivered moons. It looks homemade, as if fashioned from an old bedsheet. When the girl pushes open a door, Charlotte prepares for the worst. Emily is lying on a table, feet up, belly exposed. Walter is sitting on the edge of the bed holding her hand.

"Mom," Emily says. She is smiling. "Look."

Charlotte turns toward Joyce, who is standing beside a TV screen.

"Isn't it incredible?" Emily breathes.

On the screen is a blur no bigger than a thumbprint: white, fuzzy, with a pulsing dot in the middle.

"That's the heart," Emily says, as Charlotte steps toward the bed. "That white spot. Do you see it?"

Charlotte's eyes swim with tears. It's unmistakable: bright white and beating, the only thing moving on the screen. How fitting that the heart is the first part of the body that's recognizable, the first detail of any new life to be defined.

"Do you see it, Mom?"

"I see it," Charlotte says. She blinks through her tears until the tiny heart regains its focus. "I see."

Joyce turns a series of tiny silver knobs. "Listen," she says, smiling, and a moment later the room is filled with beating. Emily reaches out to grasp Charlotte's hand. With the other, she touches Walter's cheek. The three of them sit there in silence, listening to the sound of this new heart beating, so tiny yet so fearsome, a sound that drowns out Charlotte's own completely.

Charlotte and Emily sit on the porch. It's getting cold out, but Emily thought the air would be "refreshing." They're nestled into wicker chairs, armed with heavy blankets, jackets, mugs of chamomile tea. Emily is wearing her fuzzy orange scarf and a light blue wool hat with flaps over the ears. She pulled a ski cap over Charlotte's head—"How could you come to New England without a *hat,* Mom?"—brown and snug and smelling of stale snow. Charlotte obliged her, though normally she avoids hats; she feels self-conscious in clothing she can't see.

Charlotte holds the mug under her chin, letting the steam warm her face. Inside, Walter is poking at the wood stove, and the sound of snapping logs drifts through the window. She watches smoke rise from the chimneys of neighbors' houses, houses in which sensible people are no doubt propped in front of space heaters and fireplaces. She looks at her car, sitting patient in the driveway. From this distance, Sunset Heights feels like another world—unreal, almost cartoonish. And yet, come tomorrow she'll be heading back there. She knows she has to say this now, before she goes.

"I want you to let me pay for a real doctor."

After mounting in her for the past eight hours, the sentence comes out oddly flat, as if numbed by the cold. When Emily doesn't respond right away, Charlotte wonders if she said it out loud.

Then: "Joyce is a real doctor, Mom."

"She certainly seems like a nice person, honey." Charlotte has anticipated this. "But you have to put the baby first. The baby needs to have the best care."

"Mom—" Emily shifts in her chair, yanking the blanket up around her shoulders. It's one of Mara's creations: a patchwork of salvaged bridesmaids' dresses, squares of gaudy pink and peach and periwinkle blue.

"It's not even an office."

"What do you mean?" Emily sighs. "It's an office."

"It's a house. It's probably no more sanitary than *this* house."

"What's wrong with this house?"

"Well, nothing. Now." Charlotte sets her mug down. "But it'll be different once you have a baby."

"Why?"

She pauses, and something clicks in her brain. "You're not raising the baby *here,* are you?"

"Why wouldn't we?"

Cold sidles under Charlotte's blanket, tightening her spine notch by notch. She hasn't rehearsed this part. The explanation seems so obvious, she doesn't know where to begin. "Well." From inside she hears logs pop and sputter, like a cue from off-stage. "There's not enough heat, for one thing. It's much too cold for a baby."

Emily's mittened hands appear at the top of the blanket, two small red fish.

"And there's that staircase—it's so steep and curvy. It's not well lit. A baby could just go tumbling right down it." At the click of Emily's tongue ring, she decides to skip over the controversial litter box and cigarette-filled coffee can. "You just can't live here after the baby's born."

"Mom." Emily draws her feet onto the chair, knees to her chin. "This place is fine."

"Fine for young people. Fine for living on your own for the first time. But you're not going to live with—with Mara and Anthony once you have a baby."

"Why not? They're good people. Our house feels like a home. You said so yourself."

"Yes, but—" Charlotte closes her eyes, then bursts. "A newborn can't have *roommates!*"

"It's fine."

"It's *not* fine." Despite her freezing nose, her numb earlobes, anger is making Charlotte warm, reckless. "You just—you have no idea what you're getting into."

Charlotte looks out at the sky, a thick salting of stars. Against the dark mass of pines, the birch trees look stark, stripped of their leaves, bleached by the cold. It seems to have gone from fall to winter in the three days she's been here.

"The thing is, Mom," Emily says, "this isn't a situation we're stuck in, you know? We chose it. I just wouldn't be comfortable raising my child in the suburbs. I *want* a doctor who's untraditional. I *want* wood stoves. I *want* fresh air."

In essence, Charlotte thinks, she doesn't want to raise her

child the way she was raised. She wants to be a different kind of mother. In other words: she doesn't want to be like Charlotte.

"It's not a criticism," Emily says, reading her mind. "It's just that we have different opinions. We don't have to agree on everything, do we?"

"No." Charlotte feels tears start to thicken in her throat. "But do we always have to disagree?"

"What do you mean?"

Charlotte swallows. Her eyes are blurring. She feels numb on the outside, but the cold seems to be having the inverse effect on her insides, making them unfreeze. From the kitchen, she hears the sound of Walter's footsteps and prays he stays inside.

"Mom?"

"I mean . . ." She keeps one ear trained on Walter. "I mean," she says again as, thankfully, his feet clomp faintly up the stairs. She lowers her voice. "I mean, it is possible to make a life choice I'd actually agree with."

Emily's face twists in confusion. "I didn't know we weren't."

"Weren't what?"

"*Agreeing.* I feel like we're always agreeing. About everything. My entire life has been like one big happy handshake. At least on the surface. Deep down you were probably always freaking out about everything, but you never came out and said it."

"I told you what I thought about the—"

"About the baby. I know. But that was like the first time ever. The first time I heard my mother express an opinion, and I'm twenty-two years old."

Charlotte wants to disagree with her, but like a microcosm of the accusation itself, can't bring herself to say the words.

"And now you're speaking up, but I'm starting to think it's

only because—" Emily draws the blanket tight to her chin. "I think it's because I don't live with you anymore."

"What does that have to do with it?"

"I don't live with you," she says, carefully, "so there's not so much at stake."

"Oh, that's ridiculous."

Emily sucks in her cheeks and closes her eyes, something Charlotte used to do when she was a young mother losing patience. *Inhale. Close. Count to ten.* But around four Emily opens and exhales, breath billowing into the air like a lungful of smoke. "You always, always say that when you hear something you don't want to hear, Mom. 'It's ridiculous.' Maybe it's not ridiculous! Maybe you just don't want to believe it. I'm trying to *tell* you something here. I'm trying to tell you—" She falters, choking on the words, then her voice drops to a whisper. "God, you can be so hard to talk to."

"What do you mean?"

"I mean—that. There. You just did it. You get defensive. You don't stop to listen to what I'm saying. It's like you—you *refract* it. You don't want to *hear* anything."

"Yes, I do," Charlotte snaps. But she doesn't. This conversation is making her tremble. She looks at Emily and is surprised to see her top lip quivering too, the telltale pink splotches rising on her skin. In this cold, it is hard to tell what's affecting the face—the elements on the surface, or the emotion underneath—but this, she is sure, is coming from inside. "Tell me," Charlotte says.

Emily lets out an unsteady breath, leaking into the air like thin clouds. "Okay. Here's what I think. I feel like things have changed between us since I moved out. I feel like, when I was little, you were really lonely. So you wanted to keep me happy.

So you always agreed with me. But now that I'm older and I'm out of the house and not coming back—"

—Charlotte feels a stab in her gut, though she knew this, of course she did, of course she's never coming back—

"—you can think what you want, and say what you want, and you can admit that you don't agree with me. Or maybe don't even like me." In the faint starlight, tears cling to her lashes. "I don't even know."

Charlotte's mouth feels like cotton. Her temples pound. She feels as though she's moving into uncharted territory, stepping inside the rooms of the heart, its thick, wet, swelling, pumping chambers, unsure of how or when she will ever find her way back out. "Don't like you?" she says, eyes swimming. "Of course I like you."

Emily shrugs, trying to affect nonchalance, but her shoulders are a quick, miserable spasm.

"I love you," Charlotte adds, but the words sound too mild for their meaning.

Emily looks out at the sky. "I know you do. I didn't mean that. I mean, I don't really think that. It's just that lately it seems like there are so many things you don't like about my life, it makes me wonder what was going on all those years I was in high school and college, if you were just pretending to back me up, or if you were kind of—I don't know, faking it. Because you were afraid I'd leave."

"Leave?" Charlotte asks, but her heart jumps in recognition.

"Leave you." Emily turns to her. "Go live with Joe, in Seattle."

Charlotte wants to deny this, to disagree, but the truth of Emily's words is confirmed by the very precision of fear they recall. A fear of conflict with her daughter. A fear that her daughter would stop wanting to live with her. A fear that her daughter would leave her. Because, unlike other daughters, Emily could have. Though Charlotte had legal custody, it was an unspoken fact that if ever Emily decided she wanted to live in Seattle, Charlotte wouldn't have stopped her, and the reality of that alternative life—a life on the West Coast with her father and his stylish wife/girlfriend and coffee shops and grunge music and ocean views—hovered always on the brink of their life on Dunleavy Street. Not that Emily ever actually threatened leaving. But she asserted the option in subtle ways: calling Joe when she was bored with New Jersey, or fed up with the stores at the mall, or frustrated with the kids in her high school—"provincial," she called them—who only listened to Top 40 and hated the taste of coffee and had never traveled farther from home than the Jersey shore.

It's true: Charlotte was always painfully aware that her life with her daughter was not a given. That her situation was fragile, precious. She didn't have the luxury of other mothers, mothers whose children were stuck with them, so to speak. How she envied these women who had their daughters in their houses year-round, who knew for sure they'd be there until they left for college, slumped over bowls of cereal in the mornings, sprawled in front of the TV at night, fruit shampoos crowding the tub ledge and shoes piled on the landing and phone cords straining around bedroom walls and under closet doors. These women could afford to get angry with their daughters without fear they might pack their bags and leave. Ultimately, it was probably why Emily's personality grew so forceful: it had the room to grow, the space to fill, her mother too afraid that if she boxed her daughter in, she'd fly away.

"I wasn't being dishonest," Charlotte says. "At least I wasn't trying to be. But maybe you're right, about the other—being afraid you would leave me." It hurts to even say it. "I knew how much you loved Seattle. It was definitely hipper than New Jersey."

The word sounds so wrong coming out of her mouth—is it even a word, "hipper"?—that both of them smile.

"So I guess it did worry me," Charlotte concedes, laughing a little. "There I go again, huh? Agreeing with you again?"

Emily sniffles, but laughs too. Charlotte feels her lungs expand, her heart relax. She knows she could end this conversation now, duck out a side exit, and some part of her deeply wants to, but another part of her can't. She's always known Emily was strong, but she's realizing now just how much bravery it requires to simply be honest. Charlotte wants to be that strong too. She hears last night's conversation in the barn with Walter unspooling in her frozen ears: *Sometimes you sell yourself short. You know what's going on.*

"But sometimes—"

Emily looks at her.

Charlotte chooses her words carefully. "Sometimes, I feel like you do things I won't agree with, just *because* I won't agree with them."

"Like what?"

"Like—" She thinks for a minute. "In ninth grade, when you painted your bedroom black."

Emily laughs. "Okay."

"Or in college, when you pierced your belly button. Or when you dated that boy who was a Communist. Or going on that no-eggs diet, or ordering Thai food when you came to visit." She hesitates. "I hate Thai food."

"Why did you eat it then?"

"Because you made me."

"I didn't *make* you," Emily says. "I'm just trying to open you up to new things."

"New things I don't like!"

"How do you know you don't like them? You don't even try them!"

Charlotte falls silent, chastised. "I guess I feel sometimes like you choose things I won't like. Just like you do things I won't like. Because you know they'll make me feel—" She pauses, then yields to herself. "Scared."

Once released, the word feels heavy in the atmosphere, not floating but hunkered down, solid as a coin in a fountain. Maybe it's the cold, Charlotte thinks. Unlike the wind or the waves, this cold air doesn't whisk conversations away; it makes the words feel permanent, every breath and sigh frozen into place.

Emily tucks her chin in her mittened hands. "Mayyybe." She draws out the word as if reluctant to commit to it. "Maybe when I was younger, like with the belly button. But not now. I don't make decisions to freak you out, we just have different tastes. We have different opinions. Besides, that's not even true anymore," she says, looking up. "Because you like Walter."

It's true. She *has* grown to like Walter. Simultaneously, she realizes, Emily seems to be having doubts about him. It occurs to her that this—she, Charlotte—might be part of the reason Emily is losing interest. Maybe the fact that she likes Walter is making Emily shy away. *That's what you do, Em,* Walter had said. *You throw yourself into something, but soon as you convince everybody else, soon as there's nothing to fight against, it's not worth believing in anymore.* Was *she* the thing Emily was fighting? Was Walter more attractive when he was controversial? Because initially, they were a radical idea: an interracial couple, unmarried, pregnant. But now that the world was accepting them—even *supporting* them—Emily was pulling away.

"Yes, but—" Charlotte lowers her voice to a murmur. "But now you're having doubts."

Emily says nothing. Charlotte wonders if she heard. Cold has coiled under her blanket, swollen her toes, lodged in her jaws like two aching copper pennies. "Aren't you?" she asks, a note louder.

"I guess," Emily says. "Yeah."

As much as Charlotte sensed this, it hurts to hear. She tucks her hands between her thighs. "Honey," she says, "do you like Walter less because I like him?"

"Mom, seriously."

"Do you?"

"It's not that simple."

"Maybe it is."

Emily shakes her head. "It isn't."

Charlotte waits for an explanation, but Emily doesn't offer one. She starts picking at her bridesmaid blanket, a pink taffeta patch coming loose at one corner.

"Walter's a good man," Charlotte says, keeping her voice low. "And he's the father of your child."

Emily frowns. "So that means . . ."

"I just don't want you to make a mistake. Walter loves you." She recalls the conversation around the dinner table on Thanksgiving, about pregnancy and Emily being in labor. She remembers the genuine concern that filled Walter's voice that night, the wave of pain that rippled across his face, and suddenly she feels angry. "I sometimes wonder if you know how lucky you are."

"I know I'm lucky."

"Do you?" Charlotte snaps. She feels her eyes water and widens them defiantly, letting the cold air touch her eyeballs, drying them on contact. "Do you really? Do you know how lucky it is to have someone who cares about you that much? Someone who winces at the thought of your pain? Do you know how *rare* it is to have that?"

Emily stops picking at the blanket and looks up. And at the same moment, Charlotte feels herself disengage. She is exiting the conversation, buoyed by alarm at her own outburst, focusing on Emily's chunky, mittened hands. Her mind spirals back to the mittens Emily loved as a child. Freezy Freakies. She can picture them in the hall closet on Dunleavy Street, blank puffs of white except for the body of a peacock: featherless, just a stem with head and feet. Once the mittens hit the cold, its plume would surface, the feathers made of brightly colored hearts. Once Charlotte had felt a draft in the living room and found Emily kneeling on the kitchen counter, window yanked open, dangling the mittens outside to watch the hearts rise.

But now Emily is looking at her closely. "It's not that rare."

Charlotte looks up and is surprised to see her eyes are teary. "What isn't?"

"Having someone care about you. People have that all the time."

People. Charlotte widens her eyes until they burn. *People who aren't Charlotte.*

"And they *should.*" Emily sits up straighter, brushing at her eyes. "This is why you should get out more, Mom. Because it kills me to hear you say that. This is why you shouldn't be alone." Her voice is getting louder, hands fluttering like wings in Charlotte's peripheral vision. "Because it's not enough."

"What?" Charlotte blinks, eyes filling the moment their guard is down. "What's not enough?"

"Me."

Charlotte looks out at the stars. As if from a distance, she hears Emily's voice drifting toward her. "I've actually been thinking about this a lot lately," she says. "You being alone. And what happened after Dad left."

It's the first time Charlotte's heard her call Joe "Dad" since she was in high school, but it's not nearly as jarring as the statement itself. *What happened,* she said. But nothing *happened.* If anything, life after the divorce went on more smoothly than it did before. There were no glitches, no ruptures, no conflicts. Charlotte had made sure of it.

"What do you mean?"

Emily pauses. "We're being honest, right?"

Charlotte nods.

"Well." Emily crosses her arms across her chest, mittened hands hugging her shoulders. "I think after he left, and it was just the two of us, you kind of stopped living for yourself. You started, kind of, substituting my life for yours." She sighs, and the sigh takes shape, a cloud hovering for a moment before dissolving into the darkness. "Walter and I have been talking about this, and—"

A horrible picture enters Charlotte's mind, shattering the calm: the two of them—worse, four of them—sitting around the kitchen table, smoking cigarettes and comparing childhoods, laughing at Mara's pompom picture, using words like *dysfunctional* and *codependent* and *completely fucking nuts.* And Walter, hand clasped over his heart, saying: *My parents are two of the greatest people on this earth.*

"I think it's helped me see some of this stuff more clearly,"

Emily is saying. "You were really lonely—I mean, understandably. But then, because you were unhappy in your own life, you started living through mine." She concludes in a rush. "I mean, I don't know, maybe this is all completely off, but it's possible the reason you never wanted to disagree with me was that if you're that involved in somebody else's life, then they do something you don't agree with, then where do you . . ."

Where do you turn? Charlotte closes her eyes and completes the question. *Where do you go without a life that is your own?* It isn't crazy, she thinks, and squeezes her eyes shut, jaws singing with cold. She's wandering deep in the heart now, squeezing through its narrow stairwells, groping its smooth velvety walls. Her only option is to move forward and trust she'll emerge safely on the other side.

"I know it was all because you care, Mom." Emily's voice is gentle. "It all comes from love."

It all comes from love. Walter had said this, hadn't he? Last night, in the barn, reassuring Charlotte about him and Emily. *It all comes from love,* he'd said. *It all comes from the right place.* Emily is quoting him directly. Or else, she realizes, Walter was quoting her.

Emily is sitting forward now, face bright and urgent. "I mean," she says, "can you imagine it? Us sharing a life?" Her tone is more animated, cheeks flushed with the cold and the effort. "It would never work. I'd drive you crazy. I sleep until the middle of the afternoon. I drink soy milk. I'm constantly piercing things."

She smiles, hopefully and through swelling tears, and Charlotte feels a rush of love. Love for her daughter, love for her trying to make her smile at the same time she's telling her something she so needs to hear.

"Not to mention," Charlotte adds, "you have a treacherous staircase."

Emily's expression hovers for a moment, unsure whether Charlotte is criticizing her or playing along, then melts with relief. "And a school with no report cards," she smiles, joining in.

"An obstetrician who wears blue jeans."

"Exotic spices."

"Tofu turkeys."

"A litter box."

"Love Butter."

"Mom!" Emily shrieks, and her face freezes, mouth open. "You were spying!"

"I wasn't *spying*. I just—saw it."

"How?"

"I don't know. I needed something in the cabinet."

"Oh, my God." Emily starts to giggle, the sound loose and uncontrolled, like a rolling marble. "You must have died. I would have paid money to see your face."

She laughs harder, and the sound is contagious. Soon Charlotte finds herself laughing too, both of their faces turning pink, the sight of the other making each laugh harder. It occurs to Charlotte how close the mechanics of laughing are to crying: the same watering of the eyes, expunging of the insides, aching in the chest.

"This," Emily says, as they calm down, "is why you need to get out there."

"Out where?"

"The dating game."

Charlotte wipes her eyes. "And why is that?"

"Because you need some Love Butter of your own."

Though usually her instinct would be to snap, "Don't be silly," something about the cold and the laughter and New Hampshire make Charlotte feel reckless, fancy-free. "Actually," she says, "Bea's trying to set me up with someone."

"What?" Emily's eyes bulge, and she stops laughing. "Who? Wait—forget that. It doesn't matter. You're so going. Bea wouldn't set you up with a loser. So wait—who?"

"One of her regulars. At the—" She considers saying Friendly's, but sidesteps it. "The restaurant."

"Age?"

"Mid-fifties."

"Job?"

"A sales rep. Pharmaceuticals."

Emily taps her top lip. "Maybe he can score you some sleeping pills."

"Emily."

"I'm kidding. Name?"

Charlotte pauses, then bites the bullet. "Howie."

She can see Emily trying to suppress a smile, then they both burst out laughing again. It's not very nice, Charlotte thinks. She'll do it just this once, to get it out of her system. The laugh feels good, and necessary, like a final purge, the last firm shove out of the labyrinth of the heart and back into the world.

"Who cares." Emily shakes her head. "Names can be misleading, right? Look at Walter. He's nothing like a *Walter.*"

Charlotte nods, remembering their long-ago conversation on graduation day. Now she can't imagine Walter being named anything else.

"You said so yourself once. Remember?"

"I do."

"At graduation."

"Yes."

They are quiet for a minute, sniffling, as the cold reasserts itself.

"Are you cold?" Charlotte asks. "Want to go in?"

"In a minute," Emily says. "I'm sorry if I hurt your feelings, Mom. Some of those things I—"

"Don't be," Charlotte stops her. "You didn't."

And she means it. Their conversation has left her hollow, wrung dry, but the feeling is a good one: exhausted and depleted but lighter, somehow. She looks around at the world, noting that it appears unchanged. The moon hasn't tilted, the stars haven't gone out, the house behind her is still standing. You can have an honest conversation, and the world doesn't flinch. There's something almost addictive about such honesty. To get a thing off your chest, out of yourself—it's like cleaning out the rooms of a house, paring down the old stuff to make room for the new.

Charlotte looks out at the stars, really looks at them for probably the last time before she leaves New Hampshire. Tomorrow, she'll return to the paler lights of New Jersey: the dim glow of the patio bulb at 7:00 P.M., the streetlamps that diffuse like ink stains into foggy nights. She looks up and feels the vastness of the universe, and the smallness of herself; but tonight, the connection feels different. The universe is no longer something to recede comfortably into, but a landscape in which she has to move forward, strike out, carve a tiny place. A line pops into her head, one Emily used to have pinned to her bulletin board in high school, spiked pink letters chopped out of a magazine: *Get A Life!* Charlotte used to think it sounded harsh, and was glad when it was eventually smothered by more relevant clippings and cartoons and corsages. Tonight, though, she is beginning to see its value.

"But how?" she hears herself ask.

"How what?"

Charlotte's voice sounds thin, faraway. "How do I get my own life?"

Emily stands. For a second Charlotte thinks she might be frustrated, heading back inside, but she drops to her knees beside her. "Just think about what you want out of life."

The night hums around Charlotte, swelling in her ears. "What if I don't know?"

"Then you figure it out," Emily whispers. She leans toward her mother, resting her head in the empty space between her chin and shoulder. Charlotte flinches, surprised by the contact, then cradles the back of Emily's head with one hand. She closes her eyes for a moment, breathing in her daughter, then gazes out into the night beyond her.

chapter ten

Charlotte picks through the small pile of mail on her kitchen table. Electric bill. Visa offer. Coupon ValuPak. She'd asked Bea to collect the mail while she was gone, leave it hidden under one of the chair cushions on her patio. She wonders, briefly, if Bea shuffled through the envelopes, examining the return addresses, then feels a flash of guilt remembering the time Emily stole her then-anonymous upstairs neighbor's Victoria's Secret catalog.

She should feel more tired, Charlotte thinks. She left New Hampshire at dawn to avoid traffic, but the drive had been endless anyway, clogged with chugging mufflers, steaming windows, weary travelers crawling back toward home. Yet now, she feels oddly alert. Disjointed. She looks out the window at the night sky, but the stars are bleached by the safety lights perched at even intervals around the parking lot. If she closes her eyes, she hears a hum, but it's unnatural, a choir of appliances and heat. She looks at her blank, orderly kitchen and wishes there were more disarray. She's come back, physically, but feels none of the sense of home that should accompany her return. Even though she went through the motions of settling in—easing out of shoes, watering plants, sorting mail—she felt herself being extra careful. She walked softly, tore envelope flaps tenderly, made sure the dried New Hampshire mud on her shoes didn't touch the foyer tiles—as if reentering the house of a stranger.

When she hears a knock, Charlotte glances at the time: 8:35 P.M., though it feels much later. She peeks through the window and sees Bea's profile: dressed in Friendly's uniform, face frozen in a cringe.

"I didn't wake you up, did I?" She winces as Charlotte opens the door.

"Oh, no. I was just—"

"Writing? Am I bothering you?"

"No, no, not at all."

"You're sure?"

"No. I mean—" In fact, Charlotte is surprisingly glad to see her. She is wearing a gold nametag that says:

Friendly
You Bet We Are!
BEA

"Yes," she says. "I'm sure."

Bea's wince relaxes. "Okay, then. Good. I probably sound like a worrywart, but I just saw your car out there and thought I'd check in, make sure you got the mail, you got back okay . . ."

Charlotte has no trouble understanding this impulse. When Emily was growing up, she used to make her call home whenever she arrived anywhere: a friend's house to sleep over, Joe's house after her plane landed in Seattle, her dorm room after driving back to Wesleyan after a vacation. Charlotte would worry until she heard Emily's voice on the line. *I'm here,* she would report. *Made it. 10-4.* On the road trip Emily took during college, Charlotte had had her checking in from phone booths all across the United States, her voice altered by any variety of poor connections: staticky, whiny, faint, underwater, on the moon.

But never had Charlotte been on the receiving end of such concern. Looking at Bea, listening to her ramble on apologetically, her disjointed feeling is suddenly lifted and replaced by a different feeling: home.

"You okay?"

"Oh yes," Charlotte says, returning to the moment. "Fine."

"You must be wiped out. I should let you get to bed."

"No, that's okay. Really. In fact—I was just going to make tea."

Sitting in Charlotte's kitchen, the two women fill each other in on their Thanksgivings. "Tell me everything," Bea instructs, and Charlotte believes she really means it. So, as she boils water and opens up a Pepperidge Farm Sampler, she does. She tells Bea about the tofurkey, about the Hawaiian roommate, the litter box controversy. Bea snorts at the Feminist Health Collective and shakes her head at the unlocked cars. She howls at the discovery of the Love Butter (adding, "Wal seemed kind of kinky").

By the time Charlotte runs out of stories, Bea is staring over the rim of her teacup. "Well, your weekend was a lot more exciting than mine was." She lifts the cup and takes too big a swig, as if not used to handling drinks so delicate. "I served cranberry sauce out of a can, and Bill fell asleep in front of the TV at seven-thirty."

"It was just the two of you?"

"Oh God, no." Bea puts her cup down and runs two fingers

along the creases at the corners of her mouth. "I'm exaggerating. It wasn't really that boring. My sister dropped by with her husband and their two kids, and a couple of the girls from work came for dessert. And Bill's mom, of course." She rolls her eyes and reaches for a Chocolate Chunk. "Mrs. Dunne. That's what she makes me call her, if you can believe it. Mrs. Dunne." She bites into her cookie. "She's a piece of work."

"Why's that?"

"Oh, typical overbearing mom stuff," Bea says, chewing. "It's her way or no way. Or actually, Bill's way. Like Thursday—here's a classic example—she insisted on putting mini marshmallows in my sweet potatoes because that's how Bill likes them. The man's forty-two years old, mind you. Not that the mini marshmallows are the problem, I don't care if he likes mini marshmallows, I think it's *cute* he likes mini marshmallows. Believe me, that's nothing compared to some of the things customers at work ask for." She takes another bite, crumbs sprinkling down the front of her uniform. "Men in three-piece suits asking for their ice cream with extra gummy bears. Men begging for a cone hat on their sundaes. Men ordering their pancakes tie-dyed."

"Tie-dyed?"

"With the M&Ms baked in. Some even whisper, can they have the whipped cream hair and the bacon ears put on too? Let me tell you something. Kids?" Bea leans in, as if imparting top-secret information. "Friendly's isn't for the kids. Kids can have ice cream any time they want. Friendly's is for grown-ups who have to feed their childhood cravings. Bottom line, Char, it's for men with mother issues."

She leans back again and pops the final chocolate nub in her mouth. For some reason, the nickname doesn't bother Charlotte when Bea uses it. With Joe it always sounded ultra-chic, and therefore patronizing, as if he used it to emphasize just how much it didn't fit. With Bea, it sounds like a different name entirely. Its shortness isn't blunt and breezy, but intimate, familiar, the mark of a good friend.

"So anyway," Bea says, brushing crumbs from her lap. "Mrs. Dunne shows up with this bag of marshmallows in her purse. Her *purse.* Unsanitary, if you ask me. But she whipped them right out as soon as she saw I didn't have any. She was probably thrilled I forgot." She crosses one leg over the other, nylon scraping nylon. "I mean, God love the woman, she's just being protective. She's a mom, through and through."

Charlotte feels a pinch of self-recognition.

"It's understandable. I feel bad for her, really. Bill's dad died young, and she just doesn't have a whole lot else going on." She exhales a stream of air, as if from an imaginary cigarette. "But spend five minutes with her and you'll know just why Bill turned out the way he did."

"What way is that?" Charlotte reaches nervously for a cookie.

"Thinking everything will be done for him. Not taking initiative. And I'm not just talking about his dinner cooked and his laundry washed—although believe me, Mrs. Dunne would wash the socks on his feet if he let her. I mean the big stuff. The *life* stuff. Making decisions."

Bea pauses then, and the pause feels heavy, freighted with the memory of another conversation. Charlotte remembers Bea's tears on her patio, her worries about Bill's laziness and fears of growing old alone.

"So," Charlotte ventures. "How have things been?"

"Since the fight, you mean?" Bea sighs, blowing the air upward, making her bangs puff out. Charlotte can tell it's not true exasperation: it's affectionate. "Pretty good, believe it or not. Sometimes you just need to have it out, you know? Sucks when you're in the middle of it, but when it's over, you can put it behind you and move on."

Though at one time Charlotte might have accepted it as one of those dynamics other people understood and she didn't, this time she nods. "I think I know what you mean."

"Yeah," Bea says, but Charlotte wonders if she heard. She seems suddenly preoccupied, a faint smile pushing its way onto her lips. "We're doing a lot better. Matter of fact," she says, "we're getting engaged."

"What?" With that, Charlotte's assurance goes down the drain. "You are?"

"I know it must sound like a one-eighty, Char, but this is the way it goes with men. I'm telling you. Same thing happened with my friend at work, Lily." Bea's speaking with her waitressy assurance, but her mouth is pinched, as if trying to squelch an enormous smile. "Her boyfriend John, he kept saying they'd get married someday, and what was the rush, and what would it change anyway, blah blah blah. Same old, same old. Then one day Lil packed up her stuff and was like, that's it. I'm done wasting time unless we're getting married. She moved out, and he proposed the next day. Kind of unromantic, but believe me, that's the way it goes ninety-eight percent of the time. Men need to be pushed to the edge. You got to have one foot out the door before they make their move."

Not all men, Charlotte thinks, remembering Walter. She recalls their conversation in the barn, the diamond ring that appeared from the darkness. It was the one part of her weekend she couldn't bring herself to share.

"Well, congratulations." She's not sure it's the right response—congratulating the *prospect* of an engagement?—but

Bea is glowing as she reaches for a Mint Milano. "So do you know when he'll . . . pop the question?"

"Oh, who knows," Bea says. She dunks the cookie in her tea and starts nibbling on the damp end. "Could be a month, a year . . . I'll have to hold his hand through the whole thing, I'm sure. Probably remind him on a Post-it note. Probably drive him to Zales myself." On the surface her words are bitter, but she is smiling as she's complaining, as if part of her enjoys Bill's typical-male cluelessness and her role in it.

"Will he move in upstairs then?"

"Where? Here?" Bea laughs. "God, no. We'll get our own place. Probably try to buy out closer to the main street. My place wasn't meant for a man, Char. There's not enough room up there for Bill's DVDs alone. And he cranks his music so loud, that cat lady would have a stroke."

Charlotte smiles, happy to see her friend so happy, though the prospect of Bea moving makes a heavy feeling settle in her chest.

"Speaking of men." Bea leans forward, eyes suddenly mischievous. "Guess who I saw Friday."

"Who?"

"Howie."

Charlotte feels as if she has been plunged into a tub of nerves, ice-cold and electric. She wraps her hands around the edge of the table and raises her eyebrows, going for vaguely inquisitive. "Oh?"

"Yes, *oh*. And I told him about you, *oh*. And—" Bea pauses dramatically. "He said he wants to meet you."

Charlotte's heart begins to gallop.

"I said I had to double-check first it was okay to give him your number. It is, right?"

Charlotte remembers how brazen she sounded the night before, telling Emily about her pending date, but the reality of it shakes her to the core. "I don't know."

Bea holds her half-eaten Milano aloft in one hand. She places the other over the red Friendly's insignia on her left breast. "Charlotte," she proclaims, gold nails glowing against the faded blue of her shirt. "I swear to you on my mother's head. Howie is a great great guy. I would not stick you with somebody who wasn't. Besides," she says, dropping the hand and taking a bite, "what's the worst that can happen?"

Charlotte pauses. The worst that can happen is: Howie and she have nothing to talk about. The worst that can happen is: Howie makes an excuse to leave early. The worst that can happen is: Howie thinks she's bland. Boring. Not spontaneous. Not mysterious.

"I don't know," Charlotte says.

"Well, I do. Nothing. If the sparks don't fly, the sparks don't fly."

Charlotte doesn't want to admit how far removed she feels from the concept of "sparks flying," but an image pops in her head of two rocks rubbed together, grinding for hours for a hint of a reaction.

"I know it must be weird," Bea says, and Charlotte cringes, watching her dunk the crumby, bitten end of her cookie in her teacup. "With Joe, and how that all ended. I know it's been a while since you did the dating game thing."

This is more than an understatement. Charlotte's experience with Joe hardly counts as the "dating game thing." He saw her, was intrigued by her, and proposed to her; she barely had to say a word.

"But I can't think of a better guy to ease back in with than

Howie." Bea extracts the dripping cookie. "He won't curse. He won't get trashed. He won't grill you with questions, then pass out on your porch."

She cocks an eyebrow, and Charlotte feels a prickle of guilt, remembering the night Bea is referring to. She pictures Joe's long leg stretched across this very kitchen, loafer dangling from his toe, wineglass tipping in his hand.

"He was asking all kinds of questions about you."

Joe's foot disappears. "He was?"

"Yup."

"Like what?"

Bea shrugs. "What you're like, what you like to do, what your status is."

"What's my status?"

"I told him you're divorced. But not recently."

"Is that a good thing?"

"Not a deal-breaker," Bea says, chewing. "But the less fresh the baggage, the better."

Charlotte stares at the wet crumbs floating on the surface of Bea's tea.

"I told him you have a daughter who's very cool. I said she's a teacher, and she was having a baby with a great guy. And let's see . . ." She taps one fingernail on the table. "I said you do some writing on the side."

Charlotte winces.

"And you're the only person in this whole building cool enough to hang out with."

The distinction makes Charlotte feel oddly touched. Privileged, even.

Bea picks up her cup and takes a swig, crumbs and all, then plunks it down with finality. "Worse comes to worst, Char, you have a nice conversation with a nice man." Her shoulders and eyebrows rise and fall in one synchronized shrug. "What do you have to lose?"

Charlotte glances around at her new house. The drawn curtains in the living room. The spotless kitchen counters. The rubber place mats carefully positioned to conceal three red drops of spilled wine. The moving announcements still stifled in their tight cellophane. "Nothing."

"Atta girl." Bea starts rooting in the pocket of her money belt. "So I'll give him the number when I see him Friday night. In the meantime—" She pushes a small, slightly crumpled business card across the table. "Here."

Howard Janson
Sales Representative
Pharmaceuticals

"This doesn't mean you have to call him," Bea clarifies before Charlotte can articulate her alarm. In the top left corner of the card is a blue ribbon and the words "25 Years of Service." "He'll call you. He just gave me it to give you. As a, you know, gesture." She presses both palms flat on the table and scrapes her chair back. "Well, I better get going." Then her voice rises in an endearingly awful British accent. "Thanks for the spot of tea!"

Charlotte can't help but smile. "Anytime."

Bea talks over her shoulder as she walks toward the door. "I'm glad you're taking a chance on Howie. I really think you two might hit it off. I mean, no pressure if you don't, but"—with one hand on the knob, she smiles her lopsided smile—"I hope you do."

Charlotte returns the smile, faintly.

"And I'm glad you had a good weekend," Bea says, then adds, "You deserved one," before shutting the door.

Alone again, Charlotte washes the teacups. She repackages the uneaten cookies. Unpacks her suitcase, puts her dirty clothes in the hamper. Gets into her nightgown, brushes, flosses, washes her face. Still, she isn't close to being tired. Standing in the middle of the bathroom, she considers the tub. She yanks back the curtain and looks down at the square of Ivory perched on the soap ledge, the sandpapery blue footsteps welded to the porcelain to prevent slipping. Tentatively, she reaches for the diamond-shaped knob and cranks it toward H. The pipes sing out, as if in surprise. As the tub begins filling, she locates the lavender bubbles she bought for Emily. "L'essence de Lavande," the label says. "Pour le bain." On the back, the dramatic text promises in both French and English: "Prepare for the powers of lavender to relax your mind, body and spirit in this soothing, blissful, harmonic bathing experience."

Charlotte empties some potion under the spigot, watching it turn to foam, then keeps pouring much more than is necessary. As she lowers herself into the water, the suds shift to accommodate her body. Bubbles rise up around her in great celebratory gulps, lavender slopes, an extravagant coat of icing. She closes her eyes and tries to focus on nothing but the sensation of her face warming. Her skin softening. She listens to the whisper of the bubbles, a gentle sound, like the rustling of crinolines. Later, when the tub is drained and her eyelids heavy, the hallway cloudy with scented steam, Charlotte pads out to the kitchen. She turns on the tiny light above the stove. From the table, she retrieves the business card of "Howard Janson, Sales Representative," and secures it under a magnet on the refrigerator door.

Four-fifteen on Friday afternoon, towel-bound, hair wet, Charlotte consults her bedroom mirror. Despite the countless times she's paced this floor, stared into this mirror, pulse thumping, mind racing, she doesn't think she's ever looked or felt more terrified. She picks up the cordless. Luckily, Emily answers on the third ring.

"Everything okay?"

"No." Charlotte stares at her ghost-white reflection. "I have a date."

Emily promises to guide her through every step of the predate preparations. Howie isn't picking her up until seven, but Bea had advised leaving a solid three hours to get ready—what she will do for the next two hours and forty-five minutes, Charlotte has no idea. After a quick but thorough inventory of her mother, however, Emily concludes that the only thing not requiring attention are her fingernails (thanks to the Friday-afternoon manicure). She instructs Charlotte to start by moisturizing her face. Waits while she runs a blow-dryer through her damp hair. Agrees, reluctantly, to the outfit she'd planned on wearing: khakis, gray sweater. ("The color of pantyhose," Emily groans. "But you're nervous, so you should wear what makes you comfortable. Just throw a *little* color on—a scarf or a necklace or something. That blue silk scarf. That looks pretty. Go get it. Got it? Good.") Emily's makeup regimen is minimal: light dusting of powder, one coat mascara, subtle lipstick. She okays Charlotte's gold drop earrings but forbids her flat brown shoes ("They scream librarian") and advises forgoing the control-top pantyhose ("Better to have a little gut than be so uncomfortable you're not any fun, right?"). Charlotte imagines Bea's advice would have been along slightly different lines.

"What's the weather like?"

"Raining." Of course.

Emily prescribes a little olive oil to keep the hair from frizzing, and reverses her decision on the mascara when Charlotte reports it isn't waterproof.

"And last but not least," Emily says, "the underwear situation."

"What situation?"

"You should decide now how far you want to let things go, then plan your underwear accordingly. Just in case."

Charlotte lowers herself to the bed, phone pinched between chin and shoulder.

"If you don't want him under your shirt, wear an old scummy bra. But if you want to fool around, wear nice underwear. And shave your legs."

"I don't think I have to worry about that."

"You never know," Emily sings. Her smile is audibly bursting. "Personally, I'm hoping you get a little action. But"—and here her voice turns serious—"don't feel obligated to do anything you don't want to do. Just because he pays doesn't mean you owe him anything."

Now it is Charlotte's turn to smile, at her daughter's protectiveness. She might just be ready for motherhood after all.

"And listen," Emily goes on, "later, if you're feeling stressed, just go in the ladies' room and take some deep breaths. And if you start to feel nauseous, try massaging the skin between your thumb and forefinger."

"Okay," Charlotte says dubiously.

"And when the check comes, offer to pay for half."

"Really?" This is news to Charlotte.

"But you won't have to. He'll pay. Or he should, anyway. Not because he's the man, just because he's the one who initiated."

"Right."

"Where's he taking you to eat, anyway? Someplace romantic?"

"He hadn't decided."

"A surprise. Cool." Emily hesitates. "As long as it's not—"

"Oh, no," Charlotte leaps in. "Not Friendly's. At least, I don't think . . . I can't imagine he would. Would he?"

"Let's hope not." Emily's tongue ring clicks. "If he does, let him pay."

By 6:55 P.M., Charlotte thinks she may have legitimately come down with something. Flu, maybe. Self-induced flu, but flu nonetheless. She is perched on the edge of the living room couch, listening to the smattering of rain, prodding madly at the web of skin between her thumb and forefinger. She feels acutely uncomfortable. She imagines her body in layers, a series of onion skins, one fragile tissue unpeeling to reveal the next. On the top layer: the pressure of a scarf around her neck, twin weights of earrings in her lobes, waxy taste of lipstick on her mouth. Next: belly soft and spreading under non-control-top pantyhose, neutral white bra, noncommittal cotton underwear. And beneath that: stomach gurgling, mind reeling, heart flipping like a deranged jack-in-the-box.

Charlotte has spoken to Howie just once—Saturday, the day after Bea gave him the number—and they had a brief, polite conversation. She had worried it was a bad sign, too forward, too desperate, his calling less than twenty-four hours after he got her number, but when she intercepted Bea on her way to work, she disagreed.

"It isn't needy," Bea diagnosed. "It's mature. Real men don't screw around waiting the correct number of days to call, Char. He wanted to call, he called. That's what mature men do." She fished a pack of cigarettes from her pocket. "So what's the plan?"

"He's taking me to dinner. On Friday."

Bea's eyebrows shot up. "That's his Friendly's night."

"I know." Charlotte had already invested considerable time realizing this and worrying about its implications. "Do you think *that's* a bad sign?"

"Not at all." Bea lit a cigarette. "It's about time he stopped spending Friday nights doing crosswords. As a matter of fact, I think it's kind of—" She inhaled, and a beam spread across her face. "Gallant."

Now, Charlotte feels a strange fluttering in the deepest layer of herself. She had liked that word: *gallant.* It reminded her of old-fashioned courting, an era of modesty and ponies. As the hour hand grazes the hook of the seven, she prods her hand harder, wondering at what point she's allowed to call the date off due to illness. It wouldn't be a lie. She didn't sleep the night before, she's been nauseous all day. On top of which, she's hosting the book group the next afternoon. It had seemed like a good idea earlier in the week when she suggested it—a step in the direction of "getting a life," and a way to show everyone the condo. But since triggering the phone chain, she hadn't done a thing to prepare. She hadn't bought snacks. She hadn't even read the book! Really, she should cancel the date and spend tonight cleaning. Besides, what are the chances this will really go anywhere? Why put herself through it? Deep breathing, leg shaving, anxiety so acute it makes her sick. It isn't worth it. When it comes down to it, the only real reason she's still going is to avoid the fallout from Bea and Emily if she backs out.

Howie's knock sounds at 7:00 P.M. exactly, coinciding with the flare of the patio light and the TV announcer bellowing:

"This! Is! Jeopardy!" Reluctantly, Charlotte turns her show off. She tugs at her sweater, touches her scarf, refrains from sneaking a peek at her date out the kitchen window for fear he might catch her. She unlocks the door more slowly than usual, not wanting to appear eager, wondering if the sound of multiple rattling locks betrays how paranoid she is.

"Charlotte?"

And there he is: a strange man standing on her front porch. He is wearing a red turtleneck, tan pants, a puffy green L. L. Bean jacket. His head is bald in the middle, pink, gleaming, with a moat of fluffy white hair around the sides. Eyeglasses hang from a plaid cord around his neck. Rain droplets sprinkle the toes of his brown shoes, the shoulders of his jacket, the crown of his hair. He is smiling thinly, arms arrow-straight at his sides. He looks, Charlotte thinks, as nervous as she's feeling.

"Yes?" she says, which sounds absurd, as if he's a traveling salesman she wasn't expecting.

"I'm Howie." He extends one stiff arm. "Nice to meet you."

As they shake, Charlotte realizes his other hand is gripping a bunch of flowers, held slightly behind him and pointed toward the ground. When he lifts the bouquet of daisies, they are embarrassingly large.

"These are for you."

"Oh." Charlotte senses she should do something feminine here: bury her face in the petals to inhale them, gush that they are "beautiful" or "lovely." But for some reason, she can't bring herself to say the words. "Excuse me," she says instead. "I'll go put them in some water."

Leaving Howie in the foyer, Charlotte hurries into the kitchen and confronts the flowers' complicated wrapping: crunchy plastic, reams of tissue paper, thick wet rubber bands.

The stems are gathered at the bottom in a chubby green plastic syringe that squeaks as she pops it off. She isn't used to such floral extravagance. But daisies: she does like daisies. She chops the ends off the stems, fingers slippery, a few pulpy chunks falling to the floor. As she scoops them up, she catches sight of her reflection in the oven door: nervous, but not her usual late-night nervous. This nervous is disarrayed, expectant, the flush on her cheeks visible even in the dark glass. She leans in closer and straightens the scarf, replaces an errant strand of hair. Then, realizing all her vases are still in the basement storage area, she pours out the last of a carton of orange juice and pops in the bouquet, where it sprawls wildly, effusively, defiant.

When she reemerges empty-handed, Charlotte detects a flicker of disappointment on Howie's face. "They look nice," she assures him.

"Oh, good."

"I put them on the kitchen table."

"That's good." There is an awkward pause. He looks toward the closed door, as if gazing out a window. "I think it's stopped raining."

"Oh." She follows his gaze. "Good."

Howie helps Charlotte into her coat (her left elbow wedging, briefly, in one of the armholes), then holds the door for her as they step outside. She opts to wrestle with just one lock, in the interest of diverting attention from her shaky hands and cramming them inside a pair of gloves as quickly as possible.

"All set?"

She nods. The rain has stopped, but the sky is an uninviting steel gray, the walkway dotted with puddles.

"After you," Howie says. Charlotte feels uncomfortable being the object of such chivalry, but remembers the approving smile that spread across Bea's face as she pronounced her new favorite word: *gallant.*

As they head toward the parking lot, Charlotte keeps her hands in her pockets lest Howie try to take her arm. At least now that the rain's stopped, there's no chance of them sharing an umbrella.

"So," he says, "you and Bea. You're neighbors?"

"She lives above me," Charlotte replies. "Right upstairs." She stops and points, and Howie stops too, both of them gazing up at Bea's kitchen windowsill. Unlike Charlotte's, it is crammed with candles, flowers, picture frames, a cookie jar in the shape of a potbellied pig. Had she not been working, Charlotte is sure Bea herself would have been up there waving. As she was leaving, she stopped by Charlotte's to wish her luck, which involved whipping a bottle of Elizabeth Taylor's White Diamonds from her money belt, instructing Charlotte to flip her hair forward, then liberally spritzing the base of her neck.

"She's a wonderful neighbor," Charlotte says, taking comfort in the thought of her. "She takes in my mail when I'm out of town," she adds, though Bea has done this exactly once.

"Oh? Do you travel often?"

"Well, no, not really."

Both pause for a moment, then turn and keep on walking. "So, Charlotte, how long have you lived here?"

"Only since August."

"It's very nice," Howie says. "A nice—complex." His lips part as if to say more, then close. "I really don't care for that word, complex, but that's what my children call the building I live in. I prefer community. Complex just sounds, I don't know, industrial. It reminds me of an office complex. Do you mind it? Complex?"

She glances at him sideways. He is talking quickly. His face is rather red. She wonders if she should ask for specifics about his children, then guesses that might be getting too personal too soon. "I don't mind it that much," she says.

Silence widens around them, drawing them in like quicksand, spared only by the sounds of their shoes navigating the puddles: her low square heels, his soft brown loafers. Click, squelch. Click, squelch. As if from a great distance, Charlotte hears the tinkle of Ruth O'Keefe's seashell wind chimes.

"I moved a few years ago too," Howie continues, "into a smaller place. I assume this place is smaller. Than your last place, I mean."

"Oh, yes. It was a house. It wasn't in a—complex."

"Did you live there a long time?"

"Twenty-four years."

Howie lets out a low whistle, then stops walking. For a moment she thinks the statistic froze him in his tracks, then she realizes they are standing next to what must be his nondescript, mustard-brown car. She checks the bumper: Ford Taurus. She couldn't know less about cars, nor care, but imagines Bea or Emily might want this detail later.

"Not much to look at," he apologizes. "But she runs well."

Charlotte manages a faint smile, heart banging against her breastbone. Howie unlocks the passenger door. As she slides inside, she is wishing he hadn't whistled, wishing he hadn't referred to his car as "she," wishing his face weren't so red. And, now, wishing he weren't hustling quite so quickly to the driver's side. She is having trouble swallowing. It occurs to her she's about to be alone in a car with a man who could be anyone. What does she—or even Bea—really know about Howard Janson? That he's worked the same job for twenty-five years? That he goes to Friendly's every Friday? Who works the same job for twenty-five years? And who goes to Friendly's every Friday? She remembers Bea's assessment: *Friendly's is for men with mother issues.* Why did neither of them do the math? If Howie is a weekly customer, his mother issues must be through the roof!

She hears him fumbling with the lock and wonders if she should unlock it for him (Emily would, she thinks; Bea wouldn't), but he's in the car before she can decide. They buckle their seat belts, elbows banging. Charlotte clutches her purse to her lap, unnerved by the proximity of Howie's hands, the sudden size of his knees.

"I was thinking," he says, fumbling with something in his lap. Charlotte feels a moment's alarm, then realizes that his car key has gotten somehow stuck in his key chain, a blue lanyard that looks like it was made at a summer camp. "We could go to McFadden's Shoreside. Have you ever been there?"

"No," Charlotte says, politely trying to ignore the key-chain struggle. She takes advantage of his distractedness to canvas the front seat for suspicious details. Tire gauge. Orange Tic Tacs. Change compartment that is, she must admit, impressively organized. "I don't think I have."

"There's a huge tank of lobsters swimming by the entrance. It's all lit up like a lobster village. You would remember it, I guarantee." She wonders if Howie takes all his first dates to McFadden's Shoreside, using the huge lobster tank to lure them in. Then he says, "I've only been there once myself," making her feel a pinch of guilt. "With my daughter," he adds. Another pinch. "She said the seafood was very good. Are you a seafood eater?"

"No. Not really." She resorts to her new standby line: "I just don't have much seafood experience, I guess."

"I'm not either." He is still wrestling with the key chain, face turning redder. Are his breaths sounding shallow? Charlotte thinks nervously of his high cholesterol. "But I'm trying to be," he says, managing a glance in her direction. "I'll probably order seafood tonight. There are other options, though. Chicken. Steak. Or pork, if you don't eat red meat. I know a lot of people don't these days. Pasta, for vegetarians. Are you a vegetarian?"

"No," Charlotte says. Then she offers, "But my daughter is."

"Is she?" At last, the key comes free. Howie turns to her with his face a wash of relief: that he can finally start the car and, presumably, that Charlotte has finally volunteered personal information. "My daughter tried to be once," he says. "But it only lasted about two months. How long has your—"

"Seventeen years," she blurts, feeling suddenly proud of Emily's tenaciousness. "Ever since she was five years old."

"Really?" Howie marvels, sliding the key in the ignition. "Five years old?" He starts the car, and they're off.

The menu at McFadden's Shoreside Restaurant isn't as intimidating as Charlotte had feared. In retrospect, it couldn't have been too exotic, coming from a regular at Friendly's. She orders the chicken piccata, though just the thought of food makes her queasy. Howie orders salmon. When he asks if she'd like to get a bottle of wine, she agrees, but defers to him for the choosing. Now the bottle stands awkwardly between them, like an odd lamp that doesn't go with the rest of the decor.

As Howie fills their glasses, Charlotte takes in the dining room. As far as she can tell, there's no actual "shoreside" at McFadden's Shoreside. But it's New Jersey; maybe the entire state is considered fair game. The decor does, however, have a pronounced seashore theme: seashell ashtrays at the bar, thick nautical ropes wound around ceiling beams, candles flickering in mini-lighthouses on each table. When they arrived, a four-foot fisherman statue stood snarling by the entrance, right beside the famous lobster tank. (It *was* impressive—an intricate village with signs like LOBSTER CROSSING and PARK YOUR CLAWS HERE—though from a business perspective, Charlotte didn't see how imagining the lobsters as villagers would be any enticement to eat one.)

"So," Howie says. She watches a pearl of merlot slide down the side of her glass. He flashes her a nervous smile.

Despite the playful details, there's a formality about the restaurant that feels much more awkward than the car ride. They'd managed to talk the entire way, about innocuous things: vegetarians (Howie likes meat too much to give it up), the rain stopping (how lucky for them), the forecast for tomorrow (cold but sunny), and any establishment they could latch onto as they drove past it (Charlotte offered that she likes Bed, Bath and Beyond; Howie finds Chiles too brusque and too spicy). At one point he offered her an orange Tic Tac, and twice, fiddling with the dashboard, he asked if she was too warm or too cold.

But now Charlotte is starting to wish they'd gone to Friendly's after all. There they would be surrounded by bright lights, screaming children, gummy bears on sundaes. Bea would be checking in on them every once in a while to jump-start the conversation and put them at ease. *What do you have to lose?* she can hear Bea saying. *Worse comes to worst, you have a nice conversation with a nice man.* But they hadn't speculated what would happen if there *was* no conversation. She sips her wine, feels her non-control-top pantyhose beginning to unravel.

"How is it?"

She looks up.

"The wine."

"Oh, very good."

"That's good," Howie says, and tugs at his turtleneck. "I didn't really know what kind to order. But as long as you like it."

Charlotte feels the silence stretch again, forming a moat around them. She longs for her living room. Alex Trebek must have read the answer to Final Jeopardy by now. She wonders if yesterday's winner—Jean, a four-day champion who breeds Alaskan huskies—became a rare five-day champ.

"I've heard white wine is good with chicken." Howie is still staring at the label on the bottle, as if second-guessing himself. "Seafood, too."

"Yes." Charlotte takes another sip, trying to help reinforce his selection.

"I've never been much of a fish eater, but seafood is supposed to be good for reducing cholesterol. I'm working on getting mine down."

She nods with extra interest, to suggest this is new information.

"I just had it tested in September, and it was up to two-seventy. Two-fifty is the upper limit of what's considered high. They say it's possible the results can be affected by what you ate the night before—for instance, if you have Chinese food, your test could be unnaturally high the next day—so they retested me a week later, but it still came back two-seventy. Must be right, I guess." He swallows. "Ever since my kids found out about it they've been after me to eat more healthy."

Again she thinks she should ask about these children, but the prospect makes her feel paralyzed. It's the same feeling that stopped her from gushing over the flowers. *These flowers are just beautiful, Howie. So tell me about your children, Howie.* The words seem harmless, she knows she should say them, it's rude *not* to say them, but just the shape of them in her mouth makes her feel vulnerable. Unsafe. Those are the words of a woman willing to forge intimacies, to take risks, inch toward a commitment. To say them would be saying that, after fifteen years of being on her own, Charlotte is ready to be that woman. And she's not sure she is. She's already been left once.

Howie's hand moves back to his turtleneck, prompting her to touch her scarf. She wonders if he's unused to turtlenecks. Wouldn't it be a coincidence if both things clutching at their necks were unfamiliar? Both worn, perhaps, on the advice of their children?

"You know," Howie lurches, as Charlotte reaches for her glass again. The nerves on his face are a mirror of her own, but thankfully, it seems their responses to awkward silence balance each other out: she can't talk, he can't stop talking. "They say wine is supposed to be good for cholesterol too. I never would have thought it, but recent studies show. My son just sent me an article. He's in med school, so he's always sending me articles about eating right, living longer. You'd think I was on my deathbed."

Charlotte smiles, apologetically. The waiter appears with a basket of dark rolls and a silver dish with seashell-shaped pats of butter.

"The last one he sent," Howie says, "was about the magic of garlic." He shakes his head. "I don't know where they come up with this stuff."

Charlotte, perhaps buoyed by twenty-four hours without food and four sips of wine, finally finds her tongue. "My daughter is the same way."

"Oh?" Howie brightens. "The vegetarian?"

"Yes. Well, she's been a vegetarian since—well, you know, since she was five. But her phases don't usually last that long. She's always full of some new idea or—or new project." Funny, Charlotte thinks, how things that have historically frustrated her, even intimidated her, about Emily now feel like a source of pride.

"Like what?"

"Let's see . . ." Nylon is sliding rapidly down her belly: non-control-top pantyhose out of control. "There was reflexology. Palm reading. Mindfulness."

"Mindfulness?" Howie tears a roll in half. "That's a new one."

"It's all about being in the moment," Charlotte recites. "Being in the body and not the mind. For instance, when you butter that roll, you would want to really experience the moment of buttering the roll. Make it the best buttered roll it can be." She stops and bursts into an awkward laugh.

"It does sound kind of funny," Howie says.

"Oh, no. It isn't. Or it is, but only because—I've never explained it before, to anyone. I'm always the one having it explained to me."

"Ah." He picks up his knife and slices into a butter shell. "Sounds like me and the cholesterol. I have to tell you, Charlotte, I might work with pharmaceuticals, but I really don't know the first thing about medicine. All that stuff before, that was my son talking."

His words make something awaken inside her, like a stirred ember: her conversation on the porch in New Hampshire with Emily. She feels a cool ripple in her chest, as if the air from that night is still trapped inside her. "Maybe," she says, "the longer we're parents, the more we speak through our children."

The moment the words leave her she is surprised. And quickly, embarrassed. She wants to run to the ladies' room and hide in a stall. Maybe try taking some deep breaths.

But Howie is looking at her with interest. "I think that might be true," he says, nodding. "I find it much easier to talk about my children than myself." Then he reddens, and they both look at their plates, until he clears his throat. "How's this?"

Charlotte looks up. He is holding up his roll.

"My buttering job," he says. "Is it mindful?"

She laughs. "Oh, very. Very mindful."

Howie laughs too. Her chest blooms with relief. It is, in fact, as Bea had promised: a nice conversation with a nice man. Whether sparks are flying, Charlotte couldn't say for sure. All she knows, for now, is that she wants to keep on talking. "So," she says. "Tell me about your children."

As Howie talks about his kids, he's transformed before her eyes. His face simultaneously drains and brightens, the dark red of embarrassment fading and replaced by an inner glow. He has two children, he tells her, one boy and one girl. Meg is twenty-six, Doug twenty-eight.

"You probably thought they were younger, judging from the key chain." He smiles sheepishly. "Meg made it when she was seven and won't let me get rid of it because she says it's the first project she started and actually finished. I even tell her how my keys get stuck in it all the time, but she won't budge."

Charlotte smiles. This attitude sounds familiar. "Do they live near you?"

"Meg does. Which gives her all the access she wants to dear old Dad. She's always stopping by with vitamin supplements and leftover suppers and . . . oh, who knows. I think she's afraid I forgot how to cook. And she doesn't like it that I go to Friendly's." He pauses. "That must seem strange to you too."

"I wouldn't say strange—"

"I'm a creature of habit." He shrugs. "What can I say. And

going there feels homey. It's, well, it's friendly. And it's the same thing every week. It's nice to have a ritual like that."

Charlotte nods, thinking of Pretty Nails. "I think I know just what you mean."

Howie pauses, and his look lingers on her face an extra moment, recognizing that she isn't just being polite: she means it.

"Well." He clears his throat again. "I don't think Meg gets it like we do. She's been trying to monitor my diet ever since the cholesterol test. She's the one who made the appointment in the first place."

Typical man, Charlotte thinks. The response is automatic, and takes her by surprise. *Needs a woman to make his appointments. Otherwise, except for being born, men could go their whole lives without seeing the inside of a doctor's office.* It's as if Bea's voice has crept into her own head. She takes a gulp of wine to conceal her smile.

"Then after the results came back, my son stuck his nose in, calling the doctor and asking all kinds of questions. So it goes." He sighs, but Charlotte can tell their meddling pleases him. "I used to be the one embarrassing my kids, now my kids are embarrassing me."

"Your son—he's a doctor?"

"Not yet. Med school. He's in his third year, in St. Louis." Howie leans forward, and the candle heightens his glow to a beam. "He got married last summer. A wonderful girl. Very—unique. They got married on the top of a hill in Arizona—that's where she comes from—and I was never much for outdoor weddings, Charlotte, but I'll tell you, it was really very nice. There's less worry about rain in a place like that, I guess. She's studying to be a doctor too. Between the two of them I'll live to be a hundred and ten. I'll get my birthday read on the *Today Show*."

He stops, and Charlotte smiles, appreciating the reference.

"I'm talking too much," Howie says.

"You're not, really."

"Sometimes I have the tendency to ramble." He sits back in his chair. "But I want to hear about you. Tell me about your children. You have just the one daughter?"

"Emily. Yes." Now it's Charlotte's turn to glow. "She graduated from Wesleyan this spring. Now she lives in New Hampshire. She teaches elementary school at, well, it's called an alternative learning environment."

Howie's eyebrows rise.

"No grades, no report cards. That sort of thing."

"Huh." He bites into his roll. "Wish they had schools like that when I was going. And is she—did Bea say—having a baby? Or am I—do I have my facts straight?"

"Yes," Charlotte says. "You do."

Although she wishes the facts were different. She wishes that, when Howie asks about the father, she could tell him her daughter was having a wedding too. But he doesn't ask. Instead he stammers, rather endearingly, "When is it—the baby—arriving?"

And like a reflex, Charlotte feels that knowing instinct kick in again. *Typical.* The voice is waitressy, worldly. *Men never know how to talk about pregnancy. They don't want to say "deliver," don't want to say "expecting." "Arriving"—as if the baby shows up in a FedEx truck.*

"May," she tells him. "May twenty-first. She—well, they think it's a she, they don't really know—she'll be right between a Taurus and a Gemini. On the cusp."

"Cusp?" Howie's eyebrows rise again, and it occurs to Charlotte that he might be getting a very wrong impression of who she is. "Do you know a lot about astrology?"

"Oh, no. Almost nothing, really. That's my daughter again. She knows all about these things—astrology, mindfulness, all kinds of spiritual things. I'm much more, I guess you would say, traditional. But Emily . . ." Charlotte trails off. She feels her spirits dip, gazes at her empty glass. "We're just very different," she says. "She's not like me. Not at all." Her mind feels fuzzy, swimmy, sad.

"Charlotte?" she hears Howie asking. "Are you all right?"

She looks up. Blinks and sees his face. She feels a tremor inside her, somewhere deep beneath the knotted scarf and unrolling nylons and hammering heart, at a layer of herself she hadn't known existed. Something about the gentle lilt of Howie's voice, the use of her name, the concern on his face, makes her want to tell him everything.

"She lives with her boyfriend." The first admittance: like dipping a test toe into water. "Walter. He's the baby's father, and they live together. But they're not getting married. At least right now."

Howie waits, listening. *You can have an honest conversation,* Charlotte remembers, *and the world won't flinch.* "Actually," she admits, submerging to the thigh, "I don't think they ever will."

"And you wish they would?"

"Walter wants to." Then she confesses what she hasn't confessed to anyone. "He showed me the ring. He has it hiding in their barn." Suddenly she is back there again: a night she had reduced to a kind of hallucination, afraid that if she acknowledged what happened, she would have to acknowledge what might happen next. "And I knew when he showed me that she didn't love him the same way he loves her, and I think when he asks her, she'll say no, but I couldn't bear to tell him. But if she does, they'll have to break up." Her eyes sting. "Won't they?"

"I wouldn't know," Howie says tenderly. "I'm no authority on these things."

Charlotte smiles. She thinks: He is kind. Like all the "essential qualities in a man" she's heard Emily assert over the years, "kindness" may well be Charlotte's number one. Who would have thought kindness could provoke a fluttering of butterflies in a rib cage? Who knew kindness could, just maybe, coax a spark?

Then the waiter appears. The moment dissolves. Charlotte's fuzzy cocoon is punctured by the reality of sizzling chicken. Her memory of the barn, shadowy, smudged like an old slide, is replaced by the artificial green of parsley, the alarming flesh-pink of Howie's salmon, the dark hairs on the waiter's wrist as he refills their glasses. She clutches at her napkin and dabs quickly at her eyes, realizing how much she's just confided. Whereas two hours ago she just wanted to get this date over with, now she worries she might have ruined everything.

But when she looks up, trying to formulate some comment on the food—*Everything looks delicious, Howie*—he isn't looking at the table. He's looking at Charlotte, his mouth twisting as if searching for the right words.

"Who was it," he says, "who wrote, the older I get the less I know?"

Or, maybe he's mulling over a nagging crossword clue. "I'm not sure," she says.

"Me either." He shakes his head. "And it's not important. It could have been me, is what I'm saying, because most of the time that's how I feel." She realizes that he is indeed trying to comfort her, and the fact of his effort is a comfort in itself. "Except when it comes to marriage. There I think I've learned a thing or two."

It's the first allusion either has made to their divorces, and Charlotte tenses, sensing the sudden presence of former lives, marriages, ex-spouses lurking in the room.

"I learned you can't take it too seriously," Howie says. When Charlotte looks confused, he amends: "Not, I mean, not that you *shouldn't* take it seriously. That it's not possible to take it seriously *enough*." He looks down at his salmon. "This is why I should never give advice."

"It's good advice."

"It probably sounds obvious, take marriage seriously, but I learned it the hard way. So I'd much rather see my own kids being cautious than jumping in if they're not as sure as they can be." He adds, "I hope that didn't sound preachy."

"It didn't."

"Because like I said, what do I know." He picks up his fork, then just looks at it. "My kids"—a blush fills his face again—"they think I'm an old fuddy-duddy. That's my daughter's nickname for me." He looks up. "Fuddy-Daddy."

Charlotte giggles. Howie's face is visibly deepening, one shade of red to the next, like swatches of house paint. But this time the blush doesn't bother her. She is grateful for it. Grateful to Howie for not being suave, for not claiming to know everything, for offering his own vulnerability in exchange for hers.

"Even though these kids really have no business talking," he goes on. "I may be an old fuddy-duddy, but some of the things they do are out of left field." His mouth pinches into a small, reluctant smile. "Jennifer, my new daughter-in-law, she started spelling her name differently right before the wedding. She never said a word, it just showed up that way on the invitations."

"Jennifer?" Charlotte pauses. "But how else would you—"

"You'll love this." Howie leans toward her, the candlelight dancing on his face. "J-e-n-a"—he lingers on each letter, smile stretching wider—"p-h-y-r."

Charlotte's laugh is an explosion of delight.

By the time Howie walks her to the door, it's started to rain again. On the way home he turned the defroster way up, then drove hunched way down, squinting to see through the single unfogged patch at the bottom of the windshield. They hadn't talked much, which was fine by Charlotte. She was preoccupied with their pending good night.

Now, standing on her porch, her face is damp with the rain. They'd hurried across the parking lot, not bothering with umbrellas. Under the porchlight, she can see a few droplets clinging to Howie's hair. She fumbles for her keys, then pauses, not knowing what to do with them. She wants him to kiss her. She doesn't want him to kiss her. She wants to thank him, run inside, and jump under the covers. She wants to kiss him, stay up until Bea gets home, crack open a few Smirnoffs, and recount every detail.

"I had a really nice time, Charlotte."

They are facing each other but not touching, all four arms at their sides. Charlotte looks at the ground, at the door, over his shoulder at the night sky. The sky looks strangely bright, she thinks, as if cleansed by the rain. Howie puts his hand on her arm.

Then his other hand is under her chin, lifting her face upward. She has only seconds to register that his eyes are closed before she meets the warm pressure of his lips. She feels a surge in her gut, a sudden splash, alive and flipping. She closes her eyes, aware of the presence of flesh on flesh, the space their mouths occupy, tiny yet overwhelming. As she kisses him, all the vastness of the sky and moon and rain are winnowed down to just this: miracle of miracles, the meeting of two people's lips, absolute proof of being awake.

chapter eleven

Funny how a thing so small—no bigger than a quarter, no longer than a minute—can alter everything. Despite the enormous list of things she has to do in preparation for the book group (shopping, cleaning, choreographing condo to be seen in best possible light), it is there, just there, tucked in the back of her mind like a secret: a man and a woman, the weight of a hand on an arm, slight rise of a chin, smell of fresh rain on a jacket. Small details on the surface—almost negligible—and yet, everything else is dwarfed by their magnitude.

Charlotte manages to funnel her giddiness into preparing for the group's arrival. She scours the kitchen. Swiffers the hardwood. Vacuums the beige rug. Yanks open the curtains to show off her patio, dappled in the promised rays of Saturday sunshine. Even gets uncharacteristically cute with her snack choices, running to the 7-Eleven for honey-flavored candies to tie in thematically with *The Secret Life of Bees.* She leaves her laptop open on the kitchen table—which gives the misleading impression she's been writing, though to have it on isn't unusual. Not since

Walter called last week, explaining how to convert Emily's sonogram picture into a screensaver.

With the rest of the house ready, Charlotte considers the centerpiece: Howie's daisies. They're still on the kitchen table, looking ridiculous in their juice carton. Charlotte pulls on her coat, pockets her key ring. Then, armed with a pair of scissors, she ventures into the bright cold to the basement storage area. It's about five condos down, past the K–H doors, some of them already hung with pine-cone Christmas wreaths and red velvet bows. She steps carefully, last night's rain having congealed into slippery patches, until she finds the door marked STORAGE and descends.

This is the underworld of Sunset Heights: cool, cavelike, a maze of alphabetical eight-by-eight wooden crates hidden away below the rows of identical foyers and garden patios. The crates are huge, slatted; they could contain circus tigers. Instead they are crammed full of people's belongings: detritus of memories, evidence of past lives. Peering through the slats in the dim light, Charlotte can make out shoe bags, steamer trunks, grills, lampshades. The ornate edge of a picture frame, rubber handle of an exercise bike. She pauses to admire the fabulously precarious tower of boxes inside L2. Unlike Charlotte's generic cardboard, Bea's boxes proclaim their contents loudly: an electronic foot massager, set of tequila glasses, chip-and-dip set, George Foreman grill in hot pink.

Charlotte digs out her tiny key to unlock L1. There are at least ten boxes in there, all unopened since her move. About half are her father's old textbooks, labeled BOOKS—DAD. She picks her way around these and punctures the top of a box marked DECOR, expecting to find random furnishings. Instead it's a pile of holiday decorations she'd forgotten that she had. Reindeer cookie cutters, pastel Easter baskets, a gluey rubber skeleton, an ancient tree stand. She lifts them out gently, each a subtle sharpening of breath. She untangles strings of colored lights, fuzzy Christmas stockings, rolls of red-white-and-blue crepe paper Emily once used to decorate her bike for the Fourth of July parade. Digging into the next box—SCHOOL—she uncovers stacks of Emily's old three-ring binders, Velcro-flapped Trapper Keepers, tests with stickers at the top that say "Terrific!" and "Great Job!" STUFF yields a compact history of Emily's collections: owls, pennies, stickers, erasers in the shapes of lightbulbs and Hershey bars. When Charlotte pries open MISC. and finds, draped across the top, the sign for EMILY'S OFFICE, she sinks to her knees.

The red yarn ribbon is still intact, but the colors are looking faded. The edges of the cardboard are starting to curl. Her eyes well up as she traces the letters with her fingertip, remembering so clearly the afternoon she found Emily drawing them, the kitchen table an avalanche of Magic Markers. She remembers how Emily would dispense advice from inside the kitchen closet, walls thrumming, phone cord like a tensile tail, how Charlotte couldn't see her but could sense her, and how that had been enough.

Now, it's almost too much. Charlotte is overcome with a feeling of emptiness that almost knocks her out. She gazes around at her memory vault, just one in a maze of memory vaults, and feels exhausted. Indifferent. She could curl into a ball right here on the basement floor. Then she thinks about the book group. She thinks of Howie's neglected flowers. She picks up her scissors and places the sign back in its box.

It's in the misleadingly labeled BOOKS—OTHER that Charlotte finally finds what she came for. She removes the vases from their inky wrappings, varying in size and shape and color, most of them acquired through some long-ago boyfriend of Emily's. Charlotte burrows deeper, through a layer of *Jersey Tribunes,* a soft sediment of pillows, more *Tribunes,* and finally, like a bed of rock, books. She pulls one to the surface. *The Joy of Sex.* She surveys the crate for any trace of a hidden camera. Then, without pausing to think, she stuffs the book inside a cobalt blue vase, repacks BOOKS—OTHER, hurries out of the storage area and across the slippery walkway and into her warm condo, where she shoves *Joy* to the back of a living room shelf.

When the book group arrives, they are twenty minutes late and minus one member. From her kitchen window, Charlotte watches the remaining five of them pull up in Cathy's Hyundai, emerging one after another like a clown car.

"Apologies," Rita Curran says as Charlotte opens the door. Rita is wearing sunglasses, despite the fact it's about thirty degrees outside. "We know we're more than fashionably late. But it's not our fault."

"We were waiting for Linda—"

"—she never showed—"

"—we finally called—"

"—turns out they picked up Rachel from the clinic this morning."

"Did they?" Charlotte is genuinely elated. "That's wonderful!"

"She said she just forgot to call us," Kit explains. "Which is understandable. Considering."

"Of course it is," Charlotte says, then awkwardly flings her arms apart. "Well—welcome!" The group doesn't need any encouragement. They crowd into the foyer like a swarm of real estate agents, heels clicking, eyes digesting and probably mentally pricing every detail. Charlotte leads them through the condo en masse.

"This hardwood's just gorgeous."

"Is that patio all yours?"

"Oh, the bathroom's adorable! I've always liked fish prints."

"Aren't these rugs plush? It's like they've never seen feet!"

They conclude in the kitchen, where they all begin unwrapping snacks. They comment on the honey candy, the hippo soap. Someone claims to have always wanted an icemaker.

"You know, Char," Rita says, apropos of nothing. "I've been meaning to ask you. I could have sworn I saw Joe in town a few weeks ago."

The group collectively skips a beat, necks stiffening.

"You probably did," Charlotte replies evenly. "He flew in when Emily and her boyfriend came to visit." She feels a wave of recollection ripple through the room: *The daughter! The one with the black boyfriend!*

"And how is she doing?" Rita asks. "Your daughter?"

"Very well."

"Things with the boyfriend still going strong?"

"Oh, yes. Very strong."

"Well, please tell her I wish them all the best. Joe too. I can't imagine the last time I saw him—it must be seven years ago. More! I knew it was him the minute I saw him, though. I came home and said to Ed, I could swear I just saw Joe Warren downtown. I think I told you too, didn't I, Marion?"

"You might have," Marion says, with a glance at Charlotte.

"He was jogging," Rita continues. "That's the reason I noticed him in the first place. Must be a West Coast thing. I don't know many men in this neighborhood who jog!"

The group laughs, a touch uncomfortably.

"He *is* on the West Coast, isn't that right, Charlotte?"

"Seattle."

"That's right. I thought so. Seattle." Rita sighs. "Well, good to know I'm not losing my mind—or my eyesight. Not yet, at least. With the calcium and the estrogen, I've got enough on my hands. Speaking of which—" She pauses, and Charlotte looks over to find her peering at the refrigerator door. "Who's this?"

Charlotte's stomach does a flip.

"Howard Janson, pharmaceuticals," Rita reads, frowning. "Do you recommend him? I can always use some new meds."

"Actually," Charlotte says, her face growing warm. "I don't know him like that. I mean, not professionally." Her body is a series of small explosions. "I had a date with him last night."

The room falls silent. All snacks are abandoned, all eyes turned to Charlotte. "In that case," Rita says, pushing a stack of books aside and dropping into a chair. "You're dealing with a roomful of married ladies here. Take it from the top."

So, holding court in the middle of her kitchen, Charlotte describes her date with Howie. It's not that she feels obligated; she just can't resist an opportunity to talk about it. She explains to the group how she has a neighbor upstairs, Bea, and how they've become friends. How Bea is a waitress at Friendly's (a flickering of glances), and Howie is one of her Friday-night regulars (more glances). How he took Charlotte to McFadden's Shoreside Restaurant (a few nods of approval), and how there was a lobster village in the tank by the door and the butter was shaped like seashells. She giggles as she recounts Howie's key chain, his cholesterol. The buttered roll story is hilarious in the retelling, at least to her; the group looks bewildered. She omits the good-night kiss, though there had been no avoiding it with

Bea and Emily, who had collectively kept her up until 1:30 A.M. the night before (Emily immediately asking "Did he kiss you?" and, when Charlotte hesitated, cheering, "Go Howie!").

By the time she concludes that, yes, they're going to see each other again, her giddiness is bordering on hysteria. But unlike when she told the group about Walter, this time the shock effect isn't engineered: it's real.

"So you like him?" the group confirms, but hesitantly, as if unsure how to interpret what they've heard.

"Yes. He's—" Charlotte takes a breath. "He's kind."

"Hot?" from Rita.

"I'd say there were sparks."

But Charlotte doesn't elaborate any more than this. Her reasons for liking Howie are things she isn't sure the group would understand. Like the fact that he's tentative about expressing his opinions. That he sees the humor in a ridiculous spelling. That he says her name often. That he glows when he talks about his children. That he uses the word "supper," and that she could picture him a grandfather, and that, when he kissed her, he guided her chin with his hand.

"These must be from him," Cathy says, gesturing to the daisies.

"Oh, I love flowers." Kit sighs. "They're so romantic."

"Romantic?" Sandy reaches for a blondie and takes a bite. "What's that mean again? It's been so long, I think I forgot."

"Hear hear," from Marion.

"I'll tell you what's *not* romantic," Cathy confides, plucking a truffle from a Tupperware bowl. "The Howard Stern TV show. It's bad enough Dan listens to him on the radio, but when it comes on at night and I'm going to bed, it's like he's downstairs watching porn."

And from there, the book group begins to officially unravel: from comparing notes on literary themes and symbols to comparing notes on marriages and husbands. One by one, their shiny veneers come down as they admit to the fissures, the conflicts, the daily trials, all while devouring lemon squares and toffee bark and (for the more traumatic confessions) bear claws and Rocky Road fudge. Charlotte just listens, sneaking occasional glances at her daisies, exuberant in the sun.

When Sandy slaps a palm against the table (emphasizing her disdain for her husband's mayonnaise sandwiches), the sleeping laptop springs to life. The dark screen fills with the photo from Emily's sonogram.

Rita squints. "What's this?" she says. "Is that a sono?"

"Yes." Charlotte's voice trembles with pride. "My daughter is having a baby."

The group freezes mid-snack: mouths half-filled with chocolate, hands cradling crumb-covered napkins, unlicked fingertips coated with powdered sugar. Their eyes widen and dart from one to the other, as if trying to silently reach consensus on how best to respond. At last Sandy ventures, "The daughter with the—boyfriend?"

"Only daughter I have," Charlotte quips.

"And he's the—father?" from Kit.

"That's right."

The group exchanges another glance, all of them no doubt wanting to ask the same thing. Rita does it. "So are they getting married?"

"No," Charlotte says. "At least—not now."

"But he's sticking around?"

"What do you mean?"

"The boyfriend. He's taking responsibility? For the baby?"

"Of course." Charlotte feels the heat rise in her cheeks. "He would never not—he's very responsible. He's *thrilled* about it. He wanted it more than she did!"

Rita's eyebrows float upward, two punctuation marks in a sea of liquid base. "Okay," she says. "Sorry I asked. You just never know. A lot of times they're not so committed. Especially, and I hate to say it, but males of—African-American descent."

The group registers another look of surprise; this time, it's tinged with discomfort.

"Well, I'm sorry, ladies, but it's true. I'm not making this stuff up. They're more likely to leave, because that's how they were raised. They learn it from their fathers."

The women look toward Charlotte, as if she—newly experienced in race relations—will be able to steer their response.

Charlotte's voice is hard. "Walter's father didn't leave," she says. "And Walter isn't going anywhere."

She clenches her jaw. She wishes Linda were here. Someone she considers a friend, someone who would, if not stick up for her, at least send her a reassuring smile across the room. But when she looks around at the women crowding her kitchen, it isn't unease staring back. There is apology on their faces, and gratitude, and even—could it be?—admiration.

Marion sets down a half-eaten bear claw and brushes off her palms. She bends toward the laptop and asks, "So how far along is she?"

Charlotte is equal parts surprised and unspeakably relieved. "About four months," she says.

"Do they know if it's a boy or girl?"

"Not yet. They're convinced it's a girl, though."

"Well," Marion says, straightening. There's a note of defiance in her voice. "I think it's wonderful news." Then she steps out of the way to make room for the others, who start buzzing around the screen. "Oh, look," they murmur. "So tiny!" "I just adore babies." "I'm dying for a grandchild, but at the rate my sons are going, I'll be dead before their weddings." "You're so lucky, Charlotte."

Listening to them, Charlotte feels an unfamiliar sense of pride. Their comments are more than just polite; they are wistful, wishful. Never before has she found herself in a position to be envied. Her pride swells as she watches the group cluster around her vase of sprawling daisies, her thumbprint of a grandchild, the gallery of her heart.

"Well, I give her credit," Rita pipes up. "It'll be quite the challenge."

Charlotte shrugs. Confident, Bea-style. "She can handle it." She speaks to the sunglasses perched on top of Rita's head. They are, she decides, ridiculous. "She's no younger than we were."

"No, of course not. I was nineteen. I could barely drive a car much less raise a baby. I just meant—" Rita lowers her voice. "Raising a child who's half black."

The group stiffens again, eyes shifting from Rita to Charlotte.

"I think they'll do fine," she says.

"I'm sure." Rita brushes imaginary lint from her lap. "I'm sure they will. It just won't be easy. You know how people can be."

"Yes," Charlotte says. "I do."

An awkward silence drapes the kitchen. Charlotte feels no pressure to alleviate it. In fact, she enjoys it. She takes advantage of the moment to inform the group that their next book will be Emily Brontë's *Wuthering Heights.* For once, no one objects.

That night, Charlotte settles on the couch in front of the crackling fire. In her lap sit her address book, letter opener, and the long-sealed packages of moving announcements from her kitchen windowsill. There are two packs, twelve cards in each. She slices into the first, the tight plastic yielding with a snap. Opening up the top card, she poises her pen over the inside, where it announces, in elegant purple letters: *I've Moved.*

chapter twelve

December is the month for giving and receiving. December is the woodsy smells of cedar and pine. December is the *Today Show* festooned with boughs of holly, heartwarming human interest stories, crowded malls, colorful commercials, a spirit of hope and optimism that doesn't feel quite as genuine any other time of year.

In 1976, December was the month Charlotte Rainer wore an unintentionally bold red dress to a Christmas party and caught Joe Warren's eye. In 1979, it was the month Charlotte Warren insisted she and her new husband get a full-size Christmas tree and he got pine needles in his hair. December was the month she faked orgasms, that she unwrapped a silk negligee, that her only child was conceived. It was the month, when Joe lived with them, her little family was the happiest; and the month, after he left, when things felt worst. When Emily was in middle school December meant Joe picking her up on Christmas Eve afternoon, waiting on the front porch with his hands balled in his pockets. When he brought her back, it meant Charlotte trying to drown her daughter's sadness in fresh-baked ginger snaps, thick hot chocolate, extra presents Rudolph "dropped off early." Until the December Emily was eleven, when she looked at the presents and shook her head. The romance was gone; she no longer even pretended to believe.

When Emily was in high school and college, December meant the arrival of a huge package from Seattle. The return address was "V. Warren" and the box was filled with presents, the gift tags covered in effusive Xs and Os. Charlotte displayed them good-naturedly, even playing along when Emily rattled them and sniffed them (some had the distinct scent of potpourri). But this year, when the box arrived, she shoved it in a closet. She'd bring it out when Emily arrived.

Because this December, Charlotte's life felt different. This was the December she would get a full-size tree instead of the half-tree she used to prop on her hall table. This was the December Bea and Bill would drive her to a tree lot off Route 9—where they knew a guy who would give her a deal—and Bill would set the tree up in Charlotte's living room, even stringing the lights for her and affixing the star to the top. And this was the December Charlotte would go Christmas shopping with three new people on her list: Walter, Bea, and Howard.

"Howard, is it?" asked Emily, when they were on the phone one night making Christmas plans.

"He said he prefers it," Charlotte said.

"Before or after you started using it?"

"Fine," she admitted. "After. And I'm hoping if I use it enough it will stick."

"I better meet this guy," Emily laughed. "Actually, you might as well know, I'm not leaving Jersey until I do."

The plan was for Emily and Walter to arrive late on Christmas Eve. They were making a "roommates brunch" that morning, then dropping Mara and Anthony at Logan Airport, continuing on to New Jersey to spend Christmas Day with Charlotte, and visiting Walter's family in Philadelphia the next morning. "Wal went totally overboard for his mom," Emily said on the phone. "You should see what he made."

"Oh, I saw," Charlotte said, remembering the rocking chair. "He showed me. It's lovely. Isn't it lovely?" She paused, biting her bottom lip. Every time Emily mentioned Walter, Charlotte felt herself becoming overly enthusiastic, as if to drown out any misgivings Emily may have.

"Yeah, it's lovely," Emily said. "It's perfect. It's so totally perfect it's almost enough to make you puke." Charlotte tensed. "And believe me, I've done enough of that to last me a while."

For December was also the month Emily's morning sickness abated. It was, however, the month her clothes started feeling tight. The month she resigned herself to taking out her belly ring. All of these things—the mutterings about pregnancy, mutterings about Walter—made Charlotte all the more determined to make this the best Christmas she could. From the storage area, she dislodged some old things from the box marked DECOR: the reindeer-shaped cookie cutters, a styrofoam snowman, the stockings with EMILY and MOM written in gluey glitter across the furry tops. She even had a stocking glittered WALTER at a mall kiosk, the afternoon she went shopping with Linda Hill.

It was five days before Christmas, later than Charlotte ever liked to shop—much less at the Millville Mall, on a Saturday, with snow in the forecast—but what with bringing Rachel home from the clinic, Linda had barely started shopping. She hadn't wanted to leave her home alone, Linda said. Charlotte was glad she'd asked her along, thinking Linda might be frazzled. But despite the mob scene at the mall, she seemed unfazed. As they threaded in and out of stores, Linda checking things off her list, Charlotte filled her in on what she'd missed at the book group: the uncharacteristic husband-bashing, the sonogram photo, *Wuthering Heights.* When Linda added, "And I heard there's a new man in your life?" Charlotte gladly relayed the details.

Charlotte wanted to ask about Rachel, though it seemed too serious a topic to broach among the piles of sweaters in the Gap or the throbbing music in Sam Goody (Linda had detailed instructions on CDs to buy her younger daughter, none of which either of them had ever heard of, some of which they skipped when they saw the PARENTAL ADVISORY decal). It was when they took a snack break, sitting in the food court with their shopping bags, fountain Cokes, and cinnamon-covered soft pretzels, that Charlotte finally asked.

"So how is Rachel doing?" she said, suddenly unsure how to phrase it. "Is she—better?"

Linda straightened her back and crossed her legs, as if arranging her body in the proper position before replying. "Yes," she said, every muscle alert, composed. "Well, yes and no. She's better, but not cured. Her doctors say it's something she'll struggle with for years, probably. Maybe all her life." She delivered all of this very matter-of-factly, her face remarkably calm. "For now, I'm just glad she's home. I don't think I could have handled knowing she was there, for Christmas."

Charlotte watched as Linda rubbed two fingertips together, cinnamon dust falling to the table.

"I can't tell you how scary it was, Charlotte," Linda said, "how terrifying—to see something happening to your child and know there's nothing you can do to stop it. To feel like you can't protect them—when all you've ever tried to do, ever since they were born—" She looked up and her face was suddenly weary, as if exhausted by the effort of holding itself together. "Well, it was the most scared I've ever been."

Charlotte nodded. "I can imagine."

Linda smiled, a tired smile. Then she picked up her soda and was raising it to her mouth when her cell phone rang. It was a neutral ring—a ring for practical use only, no frills, no rock-n-roll songs—but somehow its neutrality made it all the more urgent. A look of alarm flashed across Linda's face and she began rooting through her handbag, tossing aside wallet, keys, lipstick, grabbing at the phone. "Honey?" she answered. She listened for a moment, then her face relaxed. Charlotte relaxed too. "Tell Allison's mother it's fine. Dad can drop her off tomorrow morning . . ."

Though her voice remained sprightly, Linda's body seemed to collapse inward, one elbow leaning on the table, forehead sinking against the heel of her hand. Charlotte, out of a kind of maternal respect, looked away. She gazed around at the food court, marveling at its obliviousness. Yet even a place as carefree as this one was scattered with minefields: cell phones in handbags, security guards at doorways, red Clubs pinching steering wheels. Charlotte looked at the harried young mothers pushing strollers or clasping children by the hands and remembered a recent story on the news about a baby stolen from a mall parking lot. She saw a pregnant woman stepping on an escalator and her mind flew to Emily: to the kind of mother she would be. Her fearlessness would be an asset, Charlotte thought, though in the end it didn't really matter who you were: how loving, how devoted, how strong. Bringing a child into this world was an act of faith and danger, heart and nerve.

Linda placed her phone back inside her purse. Calmly she began retrieving her things from the table, tightening her lipstick cap, brushing cinnamon from her wallet. "It's just—my cell phone never rings," she explained, and snapped her purse shut. Charlotte nodded, wanting her friend to know that she knew, that she understood panic, but Linda's gaze had shifted to the unwieldy line forming beside their table: irritable shoppers and jostling teenagers inching toward the register at Chick-fil-A.

"You know," Linda said, seemingly to herself, "I was in line at a fast-food place the first time I really stood up for myself. It was a Wendy's, and I had Rachel with me, she couldn't have been more than four or five. We were waiting in line and this man shoved in front of us." She turned back to Charlotte and smiled faintly. "The thing is, if I had been alone, I probably wouldn't have had the guts to say anything, but he shoved in front of Rachel, so I did. I had to. That was my job." A glimmer of pain stole across her face, so quick it might not have been there at all. "It was my job to keep her safe."

That night, Charlotte hung the three Christmas stockings in a row across her mantel. She liked the way they caught the faint glow of the moonlight, the names glittering like the surface of new snow. She walked over to the sliding glass door and looked outside. The cold was visible, the whole world bleached and bald: the grass patchy, branches stark, even the glass-topped table looked frosted. Charlotte nudged the door open and hugged her shoulders. The air was so cold it burned her throat. It hurt to breathe. And when she paused to listen, the world was strangely silent, as if even sound had frozen, bracing itself for what was to come.

By Christmas Eve the snow has started falling. By noon there is a dusting; by late afternoon, an inch or two. Charlotte keeps the news on, the weather reporters giving continuous updates from beneath their fur hats and coats. Thankfully, despite their dramatic graphics, the snow doesn't appear to be falling too hard. It doesn't have the single-mindedness of a serious storm; the flakes take their time finding the ground, swirling and eddying like the inside of a snow globe. Charlotte had called Emily and Walter the day before to be sure they knew the forecast, and Emily assured her everyone in New Jersey was a wimp and living in New England had made them winter weather professionals.

Meanwhile, Charlotte has kept herself busy making Unit L1 the most tastefully festive in all of Sunset Heights. While some of her neighbors propped gaudy blinking ornaments on their front lawns, she placed a simple white light in each window. She bought poinsettias for the foyer, a green pillar candle for her coffee table (yuletide scent). Her refrigerator is chock-full of ingredients for tomorrow's Christmas breakfast: eggnog, cheese-broccoli bake, cranberry walnut muffins. The bottom drawers clank when opened, packed with cans of rootbeer and bottles of Sam Adams (she took the liberty of upgrading the Summer Ale to Winter Lager). There's even new coffee for Walter, a Christmas Blend Charlotte picked up at the mall.

Under the tree she's piled the gifts from Joe and Valerie, wrapped in shimmery, iridescent paper or pulpy gift bags made of pressed flowers. Charlotte's presents are wrapped in grinning reindeer, the stockings above the fireplace filled to bursting. On Dunleavy Street, even after Emily was in college, Charlotte had gone through the motions of bringing out the gifts after she was asleep. But since Emily and Walter would be sleeping practically under the tree tonight, this ritual seemed, at last, impractical.

Charlotte's present from Bea is displayed under the tree too; they'd exchanged gifts the night before, as Bea was leaving for the dreaded three-day Christmas extravaganza at Mrs. Dunne's. "This is what you get," she groused, but happily. "Decide to marry a man and you're stuck with his mother on Christmas Day."

Charlotte gave Bea a set of jangly bracelets, which she immediately shoved halfway up her arm. Bea gave Charlotte a new bathrobe: silky purplish-pink with a V-neck that plunged much deeper than she was used to. "No offense, Char," Bea said, "but that old orange thing you wear could be in a museum for the single woman. You need to upgrade. Howie'll be sleeping over before you know it."

Charlotte and Howard hadn't yet had a "sleepover," but they were spending more and more time together. Sometimes they went out, to dinner or a movie. Weeknights they often stayed in and Charlotte cooked; it was nice having someone to cook for. She even liked having someone else's needs to be aware of as she browsed the supermarket or searched the Internet for recipes with low cholesterol. Howard began to enjoy watching *Jeopardy!* or at least pretend he did. He was good at the history and geography; Charlotte was good at 10-Letter Words and Potent Potables. Last week, Howard made lunch for Charlotte and his daughter Meg—an attempt to prove to them both he wasn't hopeless in the kitchen. Unfortunately, the experience wasn't too reassuring. He made tacos from a kit, consulting the back of the box an inconceivable number of times, and broke most of the shells as he stuffed them. "Fuddy Daddy," Megan sighed, as she and Charlotte exchanged cringes. Ultimately, though, Howard served the meal wearing a sombrero, which was so uncharacteristically absurd they gave him an A+ for effort. Tonight, Charlotte is invited to Midnight Mass at Howard's church. Emily and Walter are scheduled to arrive around nine, which will give her just enough time to fix them something to eat before he picks her up.

For now, Charlotte watches the snow. The low urgency of the weather reporters leaks in from the living room, but the flakes floating past the kitchen window look nonchalant, unfocused. She lets her gaze slide to the dried flowers hanging on the wall, and smiles: Howard's daisies. She hadn't wanted to throw them out, even after they began to shrivel, so Emily had explained how to dry flowers by stringing them upside down. The bouquet rebelled at first, and for two days Charlotte was sweeping up leathery white petals and bright yellow dust from her kitchen floor. But now, the flowers seem to have adjusted to their role in the decor, like something in a magazine spread on rustic country kitchens.

Her eyes are drawn back to the window. This snowfall has the same casual, seemingly oblivious quality as the one she watched out the window of her doctor's office, more than twenty years ago, the winter day she found out she was pregnant. Charlotte had sat staring at it long after the nurse left the room, amazed that these two things could be happening simultaneously: a baby growing inside her and, outside, this light, almost whimsical flurry. She'd been alone that afternoon, and somehow the quality of the snow made her feel more so. But, Charlotte thinks now, she hadn't needed to be alone. She had suspected what was wrong when she made the appointment, could have asked Joe to cancel class, but she hadn't told him anything. Not that she had an appointment, not even that she was late. And despite this, she'd felt angry at him for not being there. Which was unfair, of course. The fact was—that day, and many days since then—Charlotte's aloneness was something she had chosen.

The whiteness before her eyes begins to blur. Charlotte feels suspended between two snowfalls, two windows, two young pregnant women, two bouquets of daisies. For it was daisies Joe brought her the day Emily was born—at least, she thinks they were. If she closes her eyes she can almost see them poking from the top of their plastic bag, white with a red drugstore logo, cinched at the top with Joe's yellow necktie in a makeshift bow. But the flowers themselves are vague; those she can't quite remember. She should, she thinks—and yet, how young she was. A wife for almost two years, but only slightly older than Emily is now. Whenever Charlotte remembers her marriage, she pictures herself an awkward adult, but in reality, she wasn't much more than a child.

She looks at the oven clock. Not even six. No point sitting here making herself more worried. She could be getting out the sheets and towels. Slicing fruit for tomorrow. Ironing the new dress she bought for tonight. She heads to her bedroom closet and is unsheathing the dress from its clingy plastic when she hears a knock. Pauses. It's too early for Emily and Walter. She wonders if it's Bea—maybe she and Bill had a fight over his mother. Or Howard—would he have come early to surprise her? More likely it was one of her neighbors coming to wish her a Merry Christmas. She'd spotted Ruth O'Keefe earlier, trotting across the lawn with Ernie strapped into what looked like antlers. The knock sounds again. With a pinch of annoyance, Charlotte hooks the dress to her closet, marches into the foyer, unlocks the door, and Emily bursts into tears.

Charlotte opens her arms as her daughter falls into them. "Ssshhh," she says, a pure reflex: no questions, just comfort. Emily's body goes limp as she cries into Charlotte's shoulder, deep, shuddering sobs. "Ssshhh," Charlotte repeats, "ssshhh," over and over. She strokes Emily's hair, damp with snow. She gazes over the top of her head at the station wagon silhouetted against the pearl-white sky. The car flashes an unnatural green, red, green, red, reflecting the blinking reindeer on a neighbor's front lawn. But other than that, there is no movement. No Walter opening up the trunk. No Walter walking toward them with gifts in his arms. Emily is alone.

Gradually, Charlotte feels her daughter's body taking shape again: muscles firming, breaths growing even, sobs reduced to sniffles and the occasional ragged breath. When Emily disentangles herself, her face is a mess of tears, runny nose, melted snowflakes dripping down her forehead from her hairline, but she doesn't seem to notice.

"He proposed."

Charlotte nods. She holds her daughter's face in both hands.

"Last night. He—he wanted to do it before we came. He wanted us to tell everybody on Christmas. He—he got down on one knee—"

She starts to cry again. "Oh honey," Charlotte says, pulling her in, murmuring into her hair. "I'm so sorry." From behind them, the weather reporters continue droning. A spasm of music eases into a commercial. Through the open front door, a sharp gust scatters the foyer with snow.

Charlotte draws back to look into Emily's face. "Why don't you get out of those wet clothes," she says, tracing a thumb under each wet eye. "And we'll talk. Okay?"

"Okay," Emily hesitates, sniffling. "But my stuff's in the—"

"I'll go get it. It's freezing." Charlotte reaches behind them to shut the door. "You stay inside."

As Emily sloughs off her coat and boots, Charlotte sets the water on to boil. She pockets Emily's thick, clotted keyring—wondering, briefly, what all these keys could possibly unlock—and heads outside. The snow is up to her ankles. It must be cold, but she doesn't feel it. The station wagon is parked at an odd angle, slicing across the spot. Charlotte can't help but picture how Emily must have flown down the highway, wipers flapping, tears mixing with snow, then swung into the parking lot, barreled over the speed bumps and jerked to a stop.

Charlotte shrugs off the image, opens up the trunk. Inside are a lumpy duffel bag, spiral notebooks, Nalgene bottles, reams of pastel construction paper, a scattering of gifts. Each gift is covered in Emily's trademark homemade wrapping: pages from magazines, theater playbills, construction paper decorated with stickers or stars. In a far corner, Charlotte spots one that looks different: a square box, neatly wrapped in red paper. *To: Charlotte,* the tag says. *From: Walter.* A pressure lands on her heart. Tears squeeze from her eyes, but she blinks them back. Now isn't the time. She shoulders the duffel and scoops up Emily's presents, but leaves the one from Walter where she found it.

In the kitchen, Emily is looking slightly better. Her eyes are red, but her face is rubbed dry. She's wearing a gray wool sweater that hangs almost to her knees. Charlotte wonders if it's Walter's.

"I turned off the TV," Emily says. "The weather people were driving me crazy."

"Oh, I know." Charlotte deposits the duffel on the couch. "So overdramatic, aren't they?"

"Plus, I'm here." Emily smiles wanly. "So you can stop worrying."

Charlotte manages a smile back but the truth is, she feels

nothing but worry. This, she thinks, is her daughter. *Her* daughter. Not another mother's story, but her own. This is her daughter who once seemed so invincible, now huddled in a chair, drowning in a shapeless sweater, tear-streaked, pregnant, and most of all, alone.

Charlotte places two mugs on the table. Steam rises. She sits. Then, in fits and starts, Emily tells the story of what happened. Walter's proposal was exactly as Charlotte would have predicted: early morning light, a gentle snow, Walter down on one knee in the backyard. The perfect diamond glinting in its perfect wooden box. Emily pauses on certain details, her eyes filling. Charlotte just keeps nodding, much as the story breaks her heart.

"The ring, he—he said—" She stops, draws a breath. "He said it wasn't just for me. It was for me and the baby. And that's the part I keep going back to, you know? The whole way down here I just kept hearing those words over and over, and thinking of the baby, and how maybe it's selfish to not say yes. I kept thinking, did I do the right thing? Did I make a huge mistake? Why did I even say no anyway? It's like I didn't even think—all of a sudden I was shaking my head and I don't even know *why*." She blinks and tears pool in her eyes. "Maybe it was just fear stopping me. Fear of, you know, leaping into a big decision. Maybe it was just the magnitude of the moment."

There's a note of hope in her voice, and Charlotte is tempted to agree. To get her on the phone with Walter, encourage him to come down here. Amazing how two months ago his coming here bothered Charlotte so deeply. Now she wants nothing more than for Walter to walk through the door.

But she knows she must be honest. "I've known you a long time, honey," Charlotte says. "And I would never describe you as a person who's fearful."

Emily's face crumples a little. "True."

"In fact, I'd say you *like* leaping into big decisions. Wouldn't you?"

"I guess." Emily looks miserable. Her eyes are round, her voice genuinely bewildered. "But then why didn't I leap at this?"

Charlotte looks at her. For one of the first times in her life, her daughter is turning to her for insight. Not Joe, not Valerie, not one of her friends or roommates or books or brochures. She's looking to her mother as someone who knows more than she does, someone who can illuminate what she doesn't understand.

"Well," Charlotte says tentatively, "I know you had your reasons. You never seemed—sure."

"Do you think I did the wrong thing?"

"No." Charlotte pauses. "I think you listened to your gut."

"But that's just it." Emily's eyes are glistening. "I *did* listen to my gut, so it's impossible to break it down into real reasons. Because it's like there *aren't* any. There's no reason I shouldn't marry Walter—I mean, we're different. I know we're different. But everybody's different. And when I look at the big picture, it just seems silly. I mean, we're having a baby together, so if we *can* be together, maybe we should be."

Charlotte feels the pressure of words from her past. She hears Howard that first night in the restaurant: *I'd rather see my kids being cautious than jumping in if they're not as sure as they can be.* She sees Bea on the patio, her face soft, baffled, talking about men, about love. *It's okay to break up with a good guy. It's even okay to break up with someone you love.* But the last voice is unexpected.

"You know what your dad said to me the night he left?"

Emily looks as surprised to hear it as Charlotte. She shakes her head.

"He said—" Suddenly Charlotte is standing on those stairs again, facing Joe's slumped back, hearing his voice crack. "He had just told me that he was unhappy. In our marriage. And I said—well, I asked him about you. And he said, it's better that she's not raised by parents who don't love each other."

For a moment, Emily seems to forget her own sadness. "Oh Mom."

"Please," Charlotte says, reaching for her teacup. "It was years ago."

"But still—"

"Really. It's okay."

Charlotte takes a sip of tea. Emily fingers the edge of her placemat, rolling it like a scroll. "But even if that's true," she says, "why *don't* I love Walter? I mean, he's amazing. You think so, Joe thinks so. I mean, he *is.* And he loves me. After I said no, he started—" Her voice catches and she lets the placemat unfurl. "I'm telling you, Walter literally never cries. And it made *me* so sad to see *him* so sad, I thought—maybe I *do* really love him. Maybe that's what love means. Because, honestly—I can't imagine feeling worse for anyone in the world." Her face is broken into a million desperate pieces. "He's just so good."

Charlotte nods.

"There's no one in the world with a better heart," Emily says.

Charlotte fixes on those spilled drops of red wine. She chooses her words carefully, much as it pains her to say them. "But that doesn't mean you have to be with him," she says. "And it doesn't mean you have to be in love with him."

Emily looks up at her with eyes wide, incredulous. "But how can that be?"

For a long moment they stare across the table, each watching the other, waiting for an answer. But neither of them knows. Neither can claim to understand the heart's inner workings, its urges and impulses, flutters and leaps. It might be the most alike they've ever been.

When the phone rings, Charlotte jumps. "It isn't him," Emily assures her. "I promise."

Still, her pulse is thumping as she answers. "Hello?"

"Hello, um, Charlotte?"

The surge of comfort she feels hearing his voice almost takes her breath away.

"Oh—hello. Howard." The name is for Emily's benefit. "Hi."

"Are you in the middle of something? You sound a little—like you're in the middle of something."

"No, not really. Just sitting here with Emily. Having a cup of tea."

"Wow. They made good time, huh?"

"Well—yes. She did. Yes."

Howard is silent for a beat. Then, "Oh Charlotte."

She turns slightly so Emily can't see her face.

"They broke up?"

"Yes," she says again, and the definitiveness makes her feel her face might break.

"I'm sorry."

She nods into the phone, knowing that he means it. And as sad as she feels, it is tinged with consolation: with the knowledge that she has someone to sympathize with her, someone who realizes she's lost something too. Even though with Emily she must remain steady, later, with Howard, she can be as sad as she's feeling. What a comfort that is: having someone to share your sadness.

"Maybe you should stay home tonight," he says.

Charlotte had been thinking the same thing, but doesn't want Emily to feel guilty. She chooses her words vaguely. "It might not be a bad idea . . ."

"Mom," Emily snaps. "What are you doing?"

"Hold on," Charlotte says, tucking the phone to her shoulder. "Honey, did you say something?"

"I said, what are you doing?"

"What do you mean?"

"You're not canceling your plans because of me, are you?"

"No. Well, yes. But not *because* of you. It's just that, well, it's getting late."

"It's called Midnight Mass, Mom."

"Right, I know. But the snow's getting bad. It really is. It's not a big deal."

"Mom," Emily says, "I saw your new dress. It *is* a big deal."

Charlotte pauses for a moment, then stops pretending. "Fine," she sighs. "Yes. It is a big deal. And yes I am staying home because of you. Of *course* I'm staying home. Do you really think I would leave you here alone tonight?"

"I'm not letting you stay."

"But I want to—"

"No way." Emily tosses her head from side to side. "I've worked too long and hard to get you out of this house to watch you pass up a hot date on my account."

"But it's Christmas Eve!"

"All the more reason." Then Emily smiles, her first real smile since she arrived. "I know you'd stay in a heartbeat if I asked you to, but I'm okay. Really. It might do me good to be alone. Maybe I'll take a bath or something . . . plus I want to call Joe to—you know." She falters a little. "To tell him what happened.

So you have to go. At this point, it's the only thing that might redeem my Christmas Eve."

"Charlotte?" Howard is saying.

"Yes." Charlotte presses the receiver to her ear. "I'm here."

"I was thinking." He clears his throat. "Why don't I just stop by tomorrow sometime. I don't want to create problems. You should be at home tonight."

"Well, actually," Charlotte says, "I'm not allowed."

"Oh?" He pauses. "Are you sure? Because to be honest with you, it's not even that great a Mass."

"Em," Charlotte whispers, lowering the phone. "He says it's not even that great a Mass."

"It's kind of boring, actually," he adds.

"He says it's kind of boring—"

But Emily is on her feet, marching across the kitchen, and snatches the phone from Charlotte's hand. "Hello, Howard? It's Emily. Listen. I've had a really shitty day, and I'm sick of thinking about my shitty day, and bottom line, we're running kind of low on men tonight." She pauses, says, "Good," and hangs up. "He'll be right over."

Sliding into the unlocked position, the deadbolt is silent. The knob unfastens with only the faintest click. The key is eased out, the door inched open, the shoes slipped off and placed on the floor. Then the deadbolt is reset, the knob relocked, and the chain guided tenderly across its brass groove so the loose links don't touch the wall. Stocking feet mince across the tiles, are swallowed by the rug. They pause beside the couch and the sleeping form under a nest of blankets.

Emily is lying on her back, just as she always used to, bathed in the white lights of the Christmas tree. Behind the drapes, the snow is silhouetted in the porch light, and the falling flakes comb the blankets with shadow. Charlotte leans down toward Emily's face. She can see the almost imperceptible rise and fall of the blanket, proof that she is breathing. Beneath it is her strong frame, and beneath that, a baby breathing her breath.

Charlotte straightens. From the distance, she hears Howard brushing off his car and has to smile. They'd stood whispering on her porch for so long fresh snow must have accumulated on his windows. As she turns from the couch, she notices the silk bathrobe has been dislodged from its box. Emily must have examined it—approvingly, she is sure. Then, tucked behind the tree stand, Charlotte spots the red box from the trunk. She feels her heart catch. In part because Walter sent it, and in part because Emily, seeing it was missing and despite her sadness, went and brought it inside.

Maybe it would be wise to open it now, alone. Charlotte steps quietly to the tree, reaches for the box and takes it to the kitchen. It is silent except for the dim buzz of the stove light, the refrigerator's electric hum. The ice shifts, once, as if rolling over in its sleep. Charlotte unwraps the gift almost soundlessly, not tearing the paper, gently peeling up the tongues of tape. What she finds inside isn't a box after all, but a plaque made of wood. Carved across the front are the words *Home Sweet Home.*

Charlotte says a silent thank-you, then tucks her gift under her arm. She turns the lights off in the kitchen, the foyer. As she approaches her bedroom she can just make out, in the silvery overspill of light from the tree, something hanging from the doorknob. Squinting, she leans down to read it: an index card, attached by a glinting length of tinsel. *Howard is nice.* Charlotte smiles. She leaves the note hooked to the door, shuts it behind her, and within minutes is fast asleep.

Book Four

chapter thirteen

She awakes to bright sunlight pouring through the window and a knot of excitement tingling in her chest. There's a vague feeling of importance about the morning, but it takes a few seconds to remember why. Then it clicks: April 12th. Emily's baby shower.

Slipping into her purple bathrobe, Charlotte gets the coffee started, opens up the kitchen blinds and tugs the windows up. The spring air is warm, sweet, tinged with the smell of cut grass. In the bathroom, she extracts her Noxzema from its spot in the medicine cabinet, next to Howard's silver razor. She'd told him he could have a whole shelf if he wanted, but he didn't want to "invade her space." So he stored essentials only, all bought in the travel-size section of the drugstore: miniature bottles of Barbasol, aftershave, mouthwash.

These were minor invasions, relatively speaking. Because for the past month the world had been bombarding Charlotte from all sides. Phone ringing, Internet zapping, shower guests RSVPing with questions about what to bring, what to buy, was it a boy or a girl? "Girl," Charlotte told them, then added, "but no pink." Dr. Joyce had confirmed the sex of the baby a few months ago; Emily's instincts had been right. Of course it was a girl, thought Charlotte, another girl in a lineage of girls, another girl to cause her mother worry and wonder.

As Charlotte puts the kettle on, Emily appears in the kitchen doorway. Her hair is mussed, belly round under a XL men's T-shirt that says LIVE FREE OR DIE.

"My God," she says, squinting. "Is today really happening?"

"It sure is," Charlotte sings. "Sit. Eat."

As Emily shuffles toward the table, Charlotte grabs her vitamins from the cabinet (the folic acid Dr. Joyce recommended) and pours a glass of water (tap, Emily informed her, because Brita can filter the minerals out). Even though Emily is just here for the weekend, Charlotte's kitchen has become a veritable pregnant woman's grocery store: seeds, nuts, calcium, iron, essential fats, whole grains. She abolished every egg from the refrigerator, even tossed her mayonnaise.

"Just promise me," Emily says, lowering herself to a chair. "No frills. The minute your book group starts oohing and aahing you have to make it stop."

"I promise."

Emily pops the vitamin in her mouth. "Thank God this thing is coed," she says. "What time's Joe getting here?"

"Soon." Charlotte plucks the whistling teapot from the burner. "About an hour and a half. At nine Bea's stopping by with desserts and extra chairs from upstairs. Ruth's giving us some chairs too." She sets a steaming teacup on the table. "And Howard's stopping by at nine-thirty with a card table, and Meg loaned him an extra serving tray. I'm so excited for you to meet Meg. I think you'll really like her." She pauses, overwhelmed at the thought of all these people converging in the same house. *This* house.

"Mom," Emily says. "Chill. It's going to be great." She raises her cup in a toast and they clink, coffee to decaffeinated organic raspberry-leaf tea.

Bea arrives at 9:00 on the dot. "I have ice cream cakes!" she announces, hefting four Friendly's boxes from a shopping bag. "Vanilla, chocolate, and two tiramisus. Where do you want these, Char?"

"I made room in the—"

"Bea!" Emily calls, making her way in from the couch.

"Hey you!" Bea squeals, swiveling around to hug her. "You look great!"

"I'm a cow," Emily says. "See? This is why people shouldn't eat cows. Because they might turn into one someday."

"Oh please." Bea brushes her off with one French-tipped hand. She's been taking extra care with her nails ever since Bill popped the question. "You look gorgeous. How are you doing? How are you feeling? Is this all so exciting?"

"Um, hold everything," Emily says, grabbing at her finger. "Check out this *rock.*"

Bea grins, more than happy for Emily to examine her engagement ring. Bill proposed on Valentine's Day, hiding the ring in a box of chocolates. ("Predictable," she said, "but what can you expect?")

"I can't take any credit for it," she explains now to Emily. "He picked it out all on his own."

As if on cue Bill trudges into the foyer, thick forearms draped with folding chairs. "Again with the ring, Bea?"

"But she hasn't seen it yet! I was just telling her how you picked it out all by yourself."

Bill rolls his eyes. "She makes it sound like I can't tie my own shoes," he says, as Bea plants a kiss on his cheek. "Where to, Charlotte?"

"Living room's fine," she says. As Bill crosses the kitchen, she notices what looks like a giant pink inner tube propped by the front door. "What's that?"

Bea glances over her shoulder. "Oh, isn't that cool? It's our bubble chair." Charlotte realizes it is indeed shaped like a miniature armchair, but made of inflatable pink plastic. "I know it's not your style, but the kids might like it."

Charlotte winces as all her tasteful intentions go flying out the window. She glances at Emily, remembering the ban on pinkness, but she gives a firm nod. "Very cool," Emily confirms. "It stays."

When Joe's taxi pulls up, he and Charlotte hug.

"Well," he grins, taking a step back. He's wearing black sunglasses, tiny square ones like celebrities wear on the red carpet. "If it isn't Charlotte Rainer-Warren."

Charlotte flushes. He's referring to the return address on the invitations, where she'd neatly written *C. Rainer-Warren* above the address. "I just thought—I don't know. It seemed like the right time."

"Hell," he says, pushing the glasses to the top of his head. "I don't blame you. I wouldn't want to be associated with me either."

"Hey Joe," Emily says, appearing in the foyer behind them. She's changed into her party dress, soft blue cotton batik. Her hair is clipped back loosely in a silver barrette, eyelids coated in pale shimmery shadow. Long beaded earrings swing from her ears.

"Well if it isn't the radiant mother-to-be," Joe says, lifting her off the ground. "Eight months pregnant and still light as a feather."

"Yeah right," Emily says, but she is smiling as her feet touch down. She's wearing what look like ballet slippers. "Thanks for coming."

"Are you kidding? It's my first baby shower. I wouldn't miss it for the world." He slides his leather duffel off his shoulder and it slumps on the floor. "Val wishes she could be here. She was really bummed."

Valerie was originally scheduled to come, then Joe sent Charlotte an e-mail in late March saying it would be him only. "A work thing," he typed, in his slapdash lowercase, but Charlotte had wondered if there was more to the story, if the trouble he alluded to back in October had gotten worse.

"A work thing," he says now to Emily, flashing her a smile. But it's overly bright, unconvincing. He offers his elbow, as if in consolation, and Emily takes it. As they head toward the kitchen, she pats his arm. Charlotte wonders who's consoling who.

"So," Joe says, as Charlotte quickly shoves his duffel bag in the hall closet. "Who else is coming to this shindig? Tell me I'm not the only guy."

"Not that kind of shower," Emily assures him, as he deposits her in a kitchen chair. "It's untraditional. Men included."

"Like?" Joe pulls open the refrigerator, scanning the contents. Charlotte starts to offer something, a drink at least, then thinks better of it.

"My old roommate," Emily says. "Anthony. And his girlfriend Mara. They're the ones Walter lives with." She fingers one long earring, pulling it away from her face. "And Walter, of course."

Joe closes the refrigerator and gives her a long look. "Things peaceful between you two?"

"Relatively." She twirls the earring like a lock of hair. "I mean, it still feels sad, and I still wonder sometimes if I did the right thing, but—my apartment's only about twenty minutes from him, so he'll be around a lot. And Mom's coming up for part of the summer." She drops the earring. "We're doing the best we can."

Joe presses a kiss to the top of her head. "Good girl."

"The Nelsons are coming too."

"Which Nelsons?" Joe says, peering into the freezer. "Bad metal band? Long-haired twin brothers?"

"No." Emily rolls her eyes. "Walter's family."

"Walter's family's coming where? To New Hampshire?"

She giggles. "To the shower. Plus you get to meet Howard. Mom's boyfriend."

"So I've heard." Joe shuts the freezer and raises his eyebrows at Charlotte. "Boyfriend, huh?"

"Kind of," Charlotte says, taking a seat across from Emily. *Boyfriend.* It's such a silly word. "If that's what you call it."

"It *is* what you call it," Emily says emphatically.

"In that case," Charlotte says, then blurts—"yes." The thrill of affirmation is accompanied by a twinge of awkwardness. But why should she feel awkward? They've been divorced for fifteen years, for God's sake!

"Howard," Joe muses, leaning against the counter. "That's a solid name. What's this Howard do?"

Charlotte pauses, flashing to the night Joe grilled Bea on the patio. She doesn't want to subject Howard to that kind of scrutiny.

"Oh come on," he says. "It's been fifteen years and my own

life's annoying the hell out of me. Throw me a little something."

"Well," Charlotte says, hesitating. "He's a sales representative. For a pharmaceutical company."

"Divorced? Widowed? Career bachelor?"

"Divorced. He has two children, a son and a daughter."

"And he adores her," Emily adds.

"As he should," says Joe.

Charlotte listens for a smirk in his voice, but there isn't one. Joe isn't teasing her; he means it. She feels her cheeks grow warm under their two pairs of eyes, and hurries to change the subject. "His daughter's coming today too," she says. "And a few neighbors."

"None of them male, I take it?"

"One male cat," offers Emily. "He talks, too. He's a medical miracle."

Suddenly Bea bursts through the door shouting: "Ribbon! We need ribbon! Char, do you have any—" When she sees Joe, she pauses. She's changed into her party outfit: black leather skirt, bright blue blouse, black boots, and a silver linked belt that jingles when she cocks her hip to one side. "Oh. Hello."

Joe clasps his hands together, repentant. "Bea." He drops his chin to his chest, the black sunglasses still clinging tenuously to the top of his head. "I owe you a very sincere—and very overdue—apology."

She shifts to the other foot, rattling faintly. "Don't worry about it."

"No. Please. Usually I don't have the opportunity to say I'm sorry—" The sunglasses fall and go skidding across the tile. Joe keeps his head bent. No one makes a move to pick them up. "But I am. Really."

"Okay," Bea says, then runs her left hand deliberately through her hair.

Knowing Joe may not notice, Charlotte helps out. "Joe, I don't think you heard," she says, as he dips down for the glasses. "Bea got engaged."

"Is that right!" he says, swiping the glasses up and righting himself in one motion, like a sloppy matador. "That's fantastic," he says, a touch overzealous. "Congratulations. I would hug you but your fiancé might clock me in the jaw." As if in defense, he pops the sunglasses not on his head but on his face. "Where's the lucky guy? Is he coming?"

"He's right behind me," Bea says, "tracking down more chairs. Come to think of it—" She hands Joe a bag of limp balloons. "You can get to work too."

In the basement storage area, Emily treads carefully behind Charlotte. She insisted on coming, even though Charlotte explained the staircase was steep, the basement poorly lit. This only piqued Emily's interest. "It's good for the baby," she insisted. "It'll give her a thirst for adventure."

Now, as they navigate the maze of wooden crates, Emily is even more excited. "Look at this stuff! It's like the Smithsonian down here. Check that out—it's an old-fashioned beauty salon chair. And look, that guy has like fifty shoehorns. This stuff is fascinating."

Charlotte stops before the door to L1, extracting her key.

"What are we looking for again?"

"Ribbon," Charlotte says. "I'm sure I saw some down here last time."

"It wasn't pink, was it?"

"I think it was red, white, and blue."

"Perfect," Emily groans. "Let's at least spread the colors out. Try to keep the patriotism at a minimum."

Charlotte swings the slatted door open. "Careful," she says, glancing at the ballet slippers. "Watch your step."

As Charlotte crouches down beside DECOR, Emily scans the stacks of boxes. "I can't believe you kept all this stuff," she says, peering into the top of SCHOOL. "Oh my God. Check this out." She pulls out an old three-ring binder, its cover almost entirely graffitied in dark blue ink. "This was my notebook in eighth grade. Look—*EW plus RG.* Ross Gratner. Remember Ross Gratner? I was obsessed with him. We dated for like two weeks before he became a pothead."

Charlotte pauses, holding a box of plastic Easter eggs. "Ross Gratner? The one who wore the—"

"Sunglasses all the time. Exactly. They were those ugly silver ones too. They looked like rearview mirrors." Emily rests the binder on her belly, leafing through it as Charlotte returns to digging. "Algebra. Seriously, did algebra ever serve me in the real world?"

"Here they are," Charlotte says, surfacing with three rolls of patriotic crepe paper.

Emily wrinkles her nose. "What did we even have those for?"

"Fourth of July. At the house on Dunleavy Street. Remember you wanted to decorate your purple bike? You put crepe paper in the wheels, and you made stars for the spokes—"

Charlotte could go on and on. She remembers every detail. But Emily is watching her with a funny look, mouth twisted in a smile.

"I know, I know," Charlotte says, pushing off the ground. "I remember the littlest things."

Emily shakes her head. "That's not it."

"What is it then?"

"It's just—" She slides the blue binder back into its box and knots her hands loosely on her belly, like a podium. "Why do you always call it 'the house on Dunleavy Street'?"

Charlotte brushes off her knees. "What do you mean?"

"Ever since you moved, you call it that."

"Well, what am I supposed to call it?"

"Just call it, I don't know, 'the house.' 'The old house.' Everyone knows which one you mean. The House on Dunleavy Street—it makes it sound like some magical cottage from a fairytale or something. Like it was this idyllic place where nothing bad ever happened."

Charlotte straightens up. "Well," she says, "what bad *did* happen?"

"Um, I don't know . . . Joe leaving?"

"Well—sure. But it was still a happy house."

"Mom, come on," Emily says, with a thin laugh. "It wasn't all *that* happy."

Charlotte pauses, flustered. "Yes it was."

"*You* weren't happy."

"Emily, that's not true—" she protests, then stops.

Emily drops her arms to her sides. "Maybe you felt happy," she concedes. "You just never really seemed it."

"But how can that be?" Charlotte is genuinely stunned. "I was always happy around you. I was *happiest* around you. Remember that night you came home from Seattle—"

A look of apology flashes across Emily's face, and Charlotte knows then, for sure: she doesn't remember. She and her daughter have very different versions of those years on Dunleavy Street. And not only do they remember different things, they remember the same things differently.

Charlotte sets down the rolls of ribbon. "How did I seem?" she says, voice soft. "I hope I wasn't miserable."

"You weren't miserable. Just—worried."

"You mean fussy?"

"No. It was more than that. You were kind of—a spaz. I mean, a subtle spaz, but still. Checking the locks a thousand times, tiptoeing into my room when I was sleeping . . ."

She remembers the palm reading Emily gave her at age ten, clutching Charlotte's hand in her sturdy little fingers, pronouncing her future with such earnestness: *You shall not be sad. You shall smile every day.*

"You knew I came and checked on you?"

"Of course I did. You were a subtle spaz, but not that subtle," Emily laughs, then her voice grows gentle. "I mean, it's not a bad thing. I always felt—safe." She smoothes her dress down over her stomach, then looks up and meets Charlotte's eye. "I just don't want you to think you were happy in the old house so you can't be happy in this one."

Walter's family arrives first, in a van from Crystal Springs Water Cooling Systems. They honk as they pull into the driveway, and greet Emily with kisses and hugs. Walt Senior is toting a jug of spring water on his right shoulder. Ambrocia is wearing a bright orange dress and hauling a duffel bag that says *I'm Too Blessed to be Stressed.* Walter's sisters hang back, wearing identical dark blue skirts with silver studs arcing across the back pockets.

"Come on," Walter says, poking them forward. "At least pretend to be friendly. This is Charlotte. Charlotte, these are my sisters, Danita and Tanisha."

"Very nice to meet you," Charlotte says.

They smile shyly, but Walter steps around them and wraps her in a hug. "Good to see you, Charlotte."

"You too." They've exchanged a few e-mails over the last few months, but this is the first time Charlotte's seen him since Thanksgiving. Everything about him looks thinner, she thinks, less vivid somehow. His frame is narrower, his hair razored close to his head. Even his energy seems depleted. She follows his gaze across the room, to where Ambrocia is standing in the corner, talking to Emily.

"I'm glad you came," Charlotte says.

Walter turns back to her. He musters his old jovial smile. "Better get used to it," he says. "Once the baby gets here, you won't be able to get rid of me if you tried."

His smile stretches wider, as if straining to be positive. Charlotte reaches out and, lightly, touches his shoulder.

"Coming through!" Walt Senior calls out. He strides past them and dumps the water jug on the kitchen floor, where it lolls like a beached animal. "For you," he says to Charlotte. "Best stainless steel cold water reservoir on the market."

"Oh, you didn't have to—"

"Uh uh," he says, wagging a long finger. "It's a gift. For having our son as your guest." He bypasses the handshake and kisses her on the cheek. "Walt Nelson."

"Charlotte," she says. "Rainer-Warren."

"Nice icemaker," he says, tapping the finger on her refrigerator door.

"Charlotte!" Ambrocia is heading her way with arms flung wide. "Finally!" she says, smothering her in a hug. "The other grandmother."

"Finally," Charlotte agrees. Funny to think how rattled she was the first time Walter hugged her; now it's clear where he gets it.

"Can you believe it?" Ambrocia steps back, fingering the cross around her neck. Her fingernails are painted gold, each one at least two inches long. "*Grandmother?* I still feel like I'm eighteen."

"Oh, I know."

Ambrocia's daughters wander by wearing identical bored expressions. She hisses their names, then jabs two long nails at the corners of her mouth. The girls oblige her with begrudging smiles.

Then all at once the other guests start arriving. The book group. Howard and Meg. Mara and Anthony. Ruth O'Keefe, dragging Ernie. Introductions are made, greetings exchanged, presents piled in the foyer. Mara and Anthony say hi to Joe. Meg shakes hands with Emily. The book group clusters instantly around Walter. Bea hops from group to group, gathering purses and coats. Six months ago Charlotte had lamented the fact that the condo had no presence of memory. Now the place was cracking open, filling up.

"Excuse me," Charlotte says to Ambrocia, and threads her way across the foyer. On the far side of the living room, she can see Joe and Howard shaking hands. She finds Bea unveiling an enormous pinwheel of cold cuts, and leans close to her ear. "Can I leave you in charge for about twenty minutes?"

Charlotte starts off quickly, fueled by a combination of giddiness and disbelief. She's just left a houseful of guests, most of whom have never met, and is zipping down Route 9. She won't be gone long, she tells herself, she'll slip back in before they even know she's missing. Still, sitting at a red light outside the Super Fresh, guilt almost makes her turn the car around. Then the light changes, her foot falls onto the gas pedal. The minute she's in motion her worries start fading, receding like the speck-sized buildings in the rearview mirror.

As she nears her destination, Charlotte takes the drive more slowly. She knows it like the palm of her hand: the intersection where Emily ran her bike into a stop sign, the corner where she waited for the middle school bus, the parameters of her trick-or-treating. As she turns onto Dunleavy Street, she recognizes the slight dip in the pavement outside the Fullers', the Carmichaels' invisible fence that Emily always called inhumane. She pulls up next to the curb in front of the Watsons'—they've repainted their garage, she notes—then, feeling vaguely criminal, cuts the engine and gazes at the house across the street.

Even after almost nine months, it feels instantly familiar. She enters with her eyes. Meandering up the front walk, she sees the grass starting to sprout from the cracks; they look nicer if you keep them tweezed, she thinks. She wonders how many times she walked up and down that path—thousands? millions?—dragging groceries, pushing Emily's stroller, following Joe's long loping strides. She remembers when they came to tour the house, a few months before their wedding. Their footsteps had echoed on the bare floors, bouncing off the walls of the vacant rooms, and Charlotte had been daunted by the strangeness—both the empty house and the man guiding her through it, squeezing her shoulders when the Realtor's back was turned. Now Charlotte's eyes mount the three steps to the front door, the tiny porch bordered by forsythia just starting to sprout yellow flowers. The bushes are starting to encroach, she thinks, and is mentally trimming them back when the screen door bangs open and a boy pops out.

Charlotte knew, of course, that new people were living here. Still she is shocked by the sight of him. The boy looks about twelve or thirteen, dressed in the baggy jeans that are the fashion these days, covered in pockets, crotch hanging to the knees. He hunkers down on the bottom step, shrugging off the yellow backpack hooked to his shoulders. As he starts rummaging inside it, Charlotte's eyes float above his head. She notices a new brass knocker on the front door. The curtains in the upstairs windows are pale green. The orange tot finder decal from Emily's window isn't there anymore.

The boy has retrieved a video game from his backpack, oblivious to Charlotte. Even from a distance, she can see his concentration as he hunches over it, shoulders jerking, thumbs jabbing buttons. Had she still been living on Dunleavy Street, the sight of a strange woman watching the house would have had her hovering around the windows. Given enough time she would have concocted all kinds of sinister scenarios about kidnappers and spies, when the reality was only this: a harmless middle-aged mother tearing up in her front seat, a woman who had moved out almost a year ago but never left.

A car slides up in front of the house, honks once. In the front seat are a blond woman and another boy about the same age. Probably going to the movies, Charlotte thinks. Maybe the mall. The boy on the step lingers a few seconds, probably resolving whatever car chase or explosion is happening on his tiny screen, then scoops up his backpack, trudges down the walkway, climbs in the backseat and slams the door. As the car pulls away, Charlotte wipes at her eyes. She takes one last look at the house on Dunleavy Street, then starts the car and heads home.

Unnoticed, Charlotte slips in the front door. Sounds of voices and laughter spill from the living room. Pausing in the foyer, she holds very still and listens—at last, she thinks, maybe this is what a foyer is for. She can distinguish the high pitch of Bea's voice, the low pitch of Walt Senior's. Joe's quick, sarcastic staccato, countered by the new water cooler's slow, steady glug. She hears Walter laugh heartily, Ambrocia exclaim, "Really?" Their voices tumble over each other, rising and falling in an unfinished chorus, the collective sound at once strange and familiar. At first Charlotte can't define it, then she realizes what it is: the sound of a house settling into itself.

Charlotte moves into the kitchen and scans her guests, tangled in unlikely combinations. There's Linda, Meg, and Ambrocia clustered appreciatively around Bea's left hand. Walt Senior explaining to Kit and Marion the virtues of Crystal Springs Water Cooling Systems. Ruth talking energetically to Bill, who wears a look of pained politeness. Ernie rubbing against Bill's leg, while Mara tries to pet him from where she and Anthony sit squashed in the pink bubble chair. Walter's sisters huddling on the hearth, whispering, clutching cans of rootbeer. Joe holding court with Sandy, Cathy, and Rita, who is laughing too loudly at something he just said. Howard and Walter talking in the corner, next to the wooden crib.

Seated in the middle of the room, surrounded by gifts, Emily is the only one to notice Charlotte. Their eyes meet and Emily smiles. Charlotte smiles back. Then the scene shifts, the tableau moves, and Ambrocia is leaning down to talk to Mara and Anthony. Linda turns to admire the crib. Howard and Bea share a laugh, Bill touches the back of Bea's neck. Emily looks up as Walter bends down to whisper in her ear. Standing in the doorway, Charlotte watches for just a moment longer, then she joins the party.

up close and personal with the author

YOUR FIRST BOOK, *GETTING OVER JACK WAGNER,* WAS A FUNNY NOVEL WITH A TWENTY-SOMETHING, POP CULTURE–SAVVY PROTAGONIST. IN *THE HAZARDS OF SLEEPING ALONE,* THE TONE IS MORE SERIOUS AND THE MAIN CHARACTER IS A FORTY-SEVEN-YEAR-OLD MOM WHO THINKS M.C. HAMMER IS PRONOUNCED "MCHAMMER." WHERE DID THE IDEA FOR THIS BOOK COME FROM?

Actually, from sleeping alone. Or more accurately, *not* sleeping. About three years ago I was having an impossible time sleeping through the night. I finally became so annoyed at all the time I was wasting tossing and turning that I decided to do something useful with those wasted hours: I would write about a woman who couldn't sleep. I planned on it being a short story, all taking place within the parameters of one sleepless night, but suddenly there was a boyfriend, and an ex-husband, and an upstairs neighbor. I kept trying to shove them out of the way because I wanted to keep the scope tighter, just about a mother and her daughter, but the "story" took on a life of its own.

YOU'RE ORIGINALLY A SHORT STORY WRITER, ISN'T THAT RIGHT?

I wrote primarily short stories when I was working on my Master's [at the University of New Hampshire], published several of them in various magazines, and and now I teach a short story workshop at the University of the Arts in Philadelphia and at the New School in New York. I love the form—I think in many ways it's much more difficult than the novel. You're trying to do so much is so little space. The length of a novel used to intimidate me, but now I find it rather luxurious. With stories, there's this continual process of reinvention, creating new people and figuring out their problems, their histories, their states of mind. There's something comforting about just sinking in with the same characters for years on end, feeling your knowledge of them deepen.

THIS CHARACTER MUST HAVE BEEN SOMETHING OF A STRETCH. YOU'RE OBVIOUSLY NOT FORTY-SEVEN.

For whatever reason, I think I've always felt older than I am. I'm told when I was little I preferred to hang around with adults. So getting inside the skin of a person older than me felt comfortable. Despite the difference in our ages and experiences, there are fundamental parts of Charlotte I understand. We're both observers, with rampant imaginations. In general, I don't think emotion—worry, fear, loneliness—is age-exclusive.

STILL, IT WOULD SEEM EMILY, HER TWENTY-TWO-YEAR-OLD DAUGHTER, MIGHT HAVE BEEN A MORE NATURAL CHOICE FOR POINT OF VIEW. WHY DID YOU CHOOSE TO WRITE THE BOOK FROM CHARLOTTE'S PERSPECTIVE?

I suppose I wanted the challenge of looking at the mother/daughter relationship from the mother's vantage—to try walking around in different shoes. But ultimately this is Charlotte's story, and Charlotte's journey. She's the character with the most at stake and the most potential for change. Though Emily changes by the end of the book, she's more open from the outset, more adventurous. Emily's realizations remind me of the kind of maturation my friends and I went through in our early and mid-twenties, being faced with adult decisions and starting to see our parents as human beings. But for Charlotte, so set in her ways, so fearful of trying new things, growth would be much harder to achieve—both for her as a character and for me as the author, trying to make that growth feel earned.

THERE'S A LOT OF HEART IMAGERY IN THE BOOK–BOTH LITERALLY AND METAPHORICALLY. WHY DID YOU CHOOSE TO INTEGRATE THAT IDEA?

I think it's interesting how the pounding of the heart is a symptom of both fear and excitement. When you're waiting for a date to pick you up, or you're at the peak of the roller coaster, or you hear a strange sound in the middle of the night—the physical responses are so similar. You heart thuds when you're falling in love, and it thuds when you're scared to death. For Charlotte, the things that ultimately bring her comfort—connecting with people—are the things that always scared her most.

WHAT ARE YOU WRITING NOW?

I'm working on a short story for an anthology to be published in Summer 2005, a collection of stories evoking summer.

ONE MORE QUESTION: WHY THE TITLE *THE HAZARDS OF SLEEPING ALONE?*

A couple of reasons. On the one hand, the hazards of being alone with yourself in the middle of the night are very literal. Your mind might start to run wild, you might find yourself wandering the house checking the locks on the windows, you might mistake your own heartbeat for someone pounding on your door. But the hazards of being alone go deeper than that too, as Charlotte comes to realize. They're about being lonely, about not having someone to share your life with.

AND THESE DAYS, ARE YOU SLEEPING THROUGH THE NIGHT?

Not every night. But more than I used to.

Then don't miss these other great books from Downtown Press!

Great storytelling just got a new address.

PUBLISHED BY POCKET BOOKS

10403